To Know the Road

For Diane

Annie Coyle Martin

Annie Coyle Martin.

PNEUMA SPRINGS PUBLISHING UK

First Published in 2011 by:
Pneuma Springs Publishing

To Know the Road
Copyright © 2011   Annie Coyle Martin
ISBN: 978-1-907728-08-2

Pneuma Springs Publishing
A Subsidiary of Pneuma Springs Ltd.
7 Groveherst Road, Dartford Kent, DA1 5JD.
E: admin@pneumasprings.co.uk
W: www.pneumasprings.co.uk

A catalogue record for this book is available from the British Library.

To Know the Road

It's never the leaving; it's only that you know the road.

- Old Irish maxim

Dympna Power 1929 - 2003
Ita Corrigan 1927 - 2006
In memoriam

Flights of angels sing ye to thy rest.

ACKNOWLEDGEMENTS

Thanks to my family for their support, especially to Sean Monaghan for technical expertise and help with research.

Ann Decter of McGilligan Books provided invaluable advice and editing. Marty Popoff was helpful on a variety of matters to do with publishing. Ciara O'Shea provided good editing advice. Dr Barry Martin corrected a number of errors in an early draft. Thanks to Jerry Villa for a conversation on wireless receivers and to Eilish Lennon for sharing her stories. Mary Yalfani was, as always, a friend to me and to writing. Thanks to Ken Adcock for sharing his knowledge and invaluable help with the paragraph on tennis. I'm grateful to Tony Monaghan for a discussion about country funerals in the 1940s and to John D. O' Neill for sharing his memories of Dublin trams.

Viv Darcy, who sadly is no longer with us, was a wonderful source of stories about all things Dublin. May he rest in peace.

TO KNOW THE ROAD

1

1937 The Party

*U*nobtrusive and pleased, Margaret Mulholland made her way from her front sitting room through the open glass doors into the dining room. The drinks table with white lemonade and mineral waters in the centre of the sitting room, and a punch bowl on the buffet in the dining room, encouraged her guests to move about, rather than congregate at one end or the other. The narrow house was difficult for parties but, with the connecting doors open, the July evening light poured through from the back garden and the rooms seemed larger. The round dining room table was draped in white cloths, her Waterford bowl with roses in the centre. A rose stand held up the flowers, the guests circumnavigated the table rather than reaching across it. Margaret believed circulation was the life of a party. She'd given Kathleen her instructions, "Keep to the kitchen until I need you to bring in the tea and coffee."

She suspected Kathleen of listening at doors. All maids gossiped! Margaret smiled sweetly at her son-in-law Richard, Georgina's husband, dutifully talking to old Mrs. Butler, "I'm so glad Peter persuaded you to come, Mrs. Butler."

"Oh, I came for his sake you know. He thinks I'm too much at home. Not many boys are so considerate of their mother."

Margaret avoided Richard's knowing look. Peter was not exactly a boy, fifty if he was a day. But he was single! Her youngest daughter Victoria was perched in the window seat talking to Jim Stewart, one of the few eligible men around. Their neighbour from across the street was entertaining them, pontificating, waving his glass about for emphasis. A bore, but one had to invite one's neighbours. When Margaret and her sister Nicola were young there were scores of boys at tennis and musical evenings. But they had been swept away like paper boats in a fast river. On her dressing table, Nicola kept a picture of her lad in leather puttees. He'd left in December 1914 and never came back. Nicola nursed a broken heart and she drank too much: disgraceful for a Protestant girl. And she flirted at parties, fancied herself still one of the New Girls of her youth. Fortunately the house was large enough to provide room for her. A lost love could unhinge a woman. It could also, Margaret mused, make her tiresome. Nicola was no longer young; it was twenty-three years since her young soldier left. Margaret and Henry had offered her a home. Otherwise, with only her meagre war widow's allowance, Nicola would be marooned in some tiny room in the city. Margaret walked back to the drinks table.

"What can I get you?" her husband Henry wanted to know. She moved closer, he bent his head to hear. "Nothing just now. Keep an eye on Nicola. She's drinking."

She went to speak to their minister the Reverend Arthur Gordon and his wife Celia, who were helping themselves to food.

"Such a lovely party!" Celia gushed.

"So glad you both could come."

"Victoria is looking so well this evening, Margaret."

"Thank you. I think she is enjoying herself."

She moved on toward Victoria and Jim. What had the Reverend's wife meant? Had she heard something? Then she decided it was the new hairstyle she had insisted Victoria adopt, precise Marcel waves flowing neatly from the flat centre parting. She'd been right to insist on her getting rid of her untidy curls, unkempt, unsophisticated. Her youngest child, her favourite. She frequently thought longingly of Victoria as a bride, although she could never fully imagine the man she might marry. Looking at photographs in *The Tatler*, she'd plan Victoria's wedding dress. No wide flounces. Since the American woman had scooped up the King, narrow silhouettes and padded shoulders were the rage. But Victoria's escapade was a setback. The less said about it the better. And Victoria's quarrel with Margaret's brother William and Helen. Awful! Margaret had long ago decided that her childless brother would leave part of his wealth to Victoria. Ever since she was a child, she had spent her summers with him and Helen in Obanbeg. Helen, enthralled by Victoria's sweet nature and blonde blue-eyed prettiness, often said she was like their own child. Victoria, under Margaret's direction, had written a suitably humble note asking forgiveness for the embarrassment the affair had caused. Margaret herself wrote asking that the matter be forgotten, never mentioned again in the family and received Helen's assurance that the subject was closed. Consequently, Margaret had kept the entire matter from her husband. He was a Northern Presbyterian from Enniskillen, born between the bridges of Lough Erne, a true North of Ireland man. He bitterly resented what he saw as the triumphant bigotry of the Catholics in the South. His bank had plenty of Catholic clients but she felt her husband would never accept the new order of things, never resign himself to the departure of the British from Ireland. Margaret herself had been brought up in the Church of Ireland, which maintained civil but aloof relations with Catholics. She met Henry in the summer of 1905 at her elder sister's house in Enniskillen. She was twenty-four. Her mother had been worried, before Henry appeared on the scene, that Margaret would be an old maid. Two years later, when Henry's work took him to Dublin, Margaret returned to Blackrock, County Dublin, the village of her childhood. She sent her two older daughters to Mercer's School in Dublin to be prepared as Church of Ireland wives who lived at a cool distance, but not necessarily in enmity, with the Catholic majority.

Victoria had attended Alexandra School and was the success of the girls, a university graduate, so her flirtation with a Catholic was certainly not in keeping with her mother's plans, but Margaret thought William and Helen could have been more reasonable. They had exaggerated the whole episode. Wasn't it a bit pre-war to be so aghast at what was just a fling? Of course, the boy was completely unsuitable and Henry, if he had known about it, would have been furious. But it wasn't as if Victoria had been serious. She had probably been bored, and the boy was a diversion.

Margaret decided she would rescue Victoria and Jim from what was surely a boring conversation with their neighbour Jack Byrne who appeared to be finishing up a speech as she approached. "Of course the papers have to write about something. This fight in Spain will blow over. Makes it blasted hard to get a decent bottle of sherry."

This neighbour was the silliest man Margaret knew. "How is your garden coming along?" she asked, taking his arm and leading him away. "I've never had such roses as this year."

"He's a bit of a talker, isn't he?" Jim said mildly, when they had left.

"To say the least."

"Who drinks sherry any more, anyway?"

"He does, apparently."

"How was your trip to the country, Victoria?"

"Oh the country is always wonderful in the summer."

"Now that you're back, we should make up a set for tennis. Nicola is always game for a match and so is Peter. If I set it up for Saturday at two will you come?"

"I'd like that."

It would get her out of the house, away from her mother's nagging advice. Jim was nice and anticipating tennis would distract her from thoughts of Donny Maguire. She had assured her mother the affair was over. Her mother was terrified her father or someone of their circle in Blackrock would hear of it, or that Victoria might become like Aunt Nicola, marooned in the past, poring over old letters.

They watched Nicola get up a little unsteadily from her seat at the fireplace and wander over to talk to their minister's wife. Her friend Mary Frazer followed her. The minister moved on to talk about the church repairs with Henry. Georgina was still listening to Peter Butler. Peter was tiresome but listening to him was better than talking to the boring neighbours or to no one. She couldn't very well talk to her husband, who, having noted that his host was in a serious discussion with the minister, took the opportunity to help himself to a whiskey. Georgina decided to ignore that. Richard was so discontented in Ireland that, although she had not yet told her parents, she and Richard were planning to join the wave of Protestant emigrants and head for England where Richard's uncle was arranging a job for him.

The July night cooled. It was dark and the curtains had not been closed. The electric lamps glowed in the black mirror of the windows; the clusters of guests, forming and reforming, reflected like actors on a stage. Margaret, noticing a lull in the talk, had Kathleen bring in the tea and coffee. Victoria got up to help Kathleen pour and pass the cream and sugar. She offered Mrs. Butler another blackcurrant tart.

"That's lovely dear."

Jim was at her elbow. "Now let me get you some tea or coffee."

"Actually Jim, I'm hungry all of a sudden."

Together they walked over to the table and filled a plate with smoked fish, cucumber, beets and a slice of bread.

"I've talked with Peter and he's okay for the club next Saturday. Two o'clock."

"I'm sure I can get Nicola to play so we're all set."

Victoria picked up a fork, walked over and perched on the window seat as perfectly at home as a bird on a branch, so confident among her own set one could see that she had always been cherished and beautiful. She ate a mouthful of salmon and concluded that her mother, who usually gave one or two parties a year, had given this one for her, to close the door on the episode in the country. A Friday evening gathering of neighbours and friends, the women in summer dresses, some of the men in shirtsleeves, and only her best friend Clemmie was absent. She was on holiday in England.

By eleven the party was winding down. Nicola and Mary stood a while talking in the hall, before Nicola drifted upstairs to her room at the top of the house. Mary approached Margaret. "Thank you Margaret. Lovely party. I enjoyed myself. I'll just slip away. Good night, now."

Then everyone was leaving. Victoria, suddenly tired, couldn't wait to go to bed. She stood in the hall beside her mother and father, dutifully saying her goodbyes. Kathleen was very quietly clearing glasses and dishes. Margaret knew she was listening.

"I think I'll go to bed now, Mother. I'm exhausted."

"All right, dear."

"Good night, Father."

Victoria felt her mother's eyes following her up the stairs. Her legs were heavy as if she slogged through deep water. When she reached her room she switched on the electric light and sat at her dressing table gazing at her reflection, wondering why she was so weary. She looked at the flat precise waves that ended in curls above her ears, at her plucked and pencilled eyebrows, and at the tears overflowing her eyes and rolling down her face, her makeup running, a clownish parody of her beauty.

Downstairs her father, having checked the levels in the whiskey, sherry and gin bottles, locked them in the liquor cabinet and put the key in the pocket of his waistcoat. He ran an abstemious household, and his sister-in-law Nicola was a tippler.

2

At the Carnegie Library

Victoria dreamed of a firelit room and Donny Maguire kissing her. Almost awake, she dreamt his hand caressed her breast. A shudder of desire coursed through her, and then she was awake, soaked in sweat, shaken to her very core with longing. Donny Maguire, she was helpless with love for him. The room was so hot. She stared at the July morning sun that streamed in the window and remembered the party her mother had given and for a moment was grieved for the worry she'd caused her. Her next thought was how marvellous Donny's love making had been, she would never forget that night of passionate sex. So new. So wonderful. She was profoundly saddened to know she could never see him again.

But she couldn't stop thinking about him. Always daydreaming, and longing to see him and at the same time telling herself that the root of her desire was that he was forbidden fruit. She'd get over it. She knew she would. She had to.

Duffy, the librarian, was on holiday. Victoria had been savouring the freedom of his absence, sitting and reading at the desk behind the low sign-out counter with the light streaming around her from the cupola above. He'd be back on Monday. She mused on Donny Maguire as she shelved books, her body softening with the thought of being in his arms. She had her mid-morning break in the staff room, tea and Marietta biscuits, and allowed herself to think about him and how they had walked by the river under the May moon. She vowed not to think about him again, washed her cup and saucer and returned them to the cupboard.

Victoria pushed the creaky wooden cart between the shelves replacing returned books, shelving them precisely, occasionally opening one, reading the fly leaf, examining the binding or the table of contents and then replacing it. The library was Saturday summer quiet and unusually warm,

11

no breeze from the open windows. Two pensioners sat at the big oak table across from the sign-out counter. They came at ten each morning to read the newspapers. Apart from them and a tall woman perusing the detective story section, there were no other customers. Victoria shelved the last book, and as she manoeuvred the cart into its storage place, she was almost overwhelmed by a wave of nausea. Instinctively she clapped her hand over her mouth. Bile scorching her throat, she ran between the shelves, round behind the office to the staff lavatory. She knelt on the tiled floor, her hands around the bowl and vomited the tea and biscuits. She sat back on her heels, mopped her face with a folded square of toilet paper. Her empty stomach heaved again. What had come over her? The milk she had put in her tea must have been sour. Well, she felt better now. She just hoped no one had noticed. She washed her hands and face went back out through the library and stood outside on the crescent steps and breathed the fresh air. That felt better. Mahaffy, the wiry little library porter, came from the storeroom and took up his position at the glass doors. It was ten to twelve. At twelve they would close for the weekend. A small bald middle-aged man who had obviously been drinking came up the round stone steps.

"Is this the Carnegie Library?" he asked Mahaffy.

"You know bloody well it is. Can't you see it written above there?" He pointed to lettering above the door. *The Carnegie Library 1912.*

"Ah right enough. I wanted to get that new book about Casement. Do you have it?"

"The bloody pervert," said Mahaffy.

"Well, he died for Ireland, so he did."

"Anyway, we're closing now," Mahaffy said, importantly.

"You could check back in a few weeks," Victoria told him. "We don't have it now, sir. But we may acquire it."

Mahaffy's lips turned down in disgust. Two girls in flowery summer dresses walked up the steps. Mahaffy's wizened face assumed a sorrowful expression. "We're closing, ladies."

The tipsy fellow glared at Mahaffy and walked unsteadily down the steps. The girls whispered, heads together, giggling, and followed him.

Victoria went back inside thinking of Roger Casement, such a divisive figure. So despised for his homosexuality! His name could never be mentioned in her father's house, but sometimes she wanted to challenge her father, to remind him that Casement's reports, from the Congo and Brazil, had forced an end to the murderous conditions imposed on rubber plantation workers in those countries. If the library acquired Maloney's book about him she would read it, but secretly; her father would not have such a book in his house. "Sir Roger, the nancy boy," he'd said, his voice dripping with contempt.

She was curious to read what the book would say about Casement's infamous Black Diaries, which were said to detail his homosexual encounters, and the White Diaries, which reported the slavery of native workers. Of course, the Irish maintained the Black Diaries were fakes, concocted by the British authorities to build their case against him for treason.

The men who had been reading the newspapers were leaving. "Grand day," said Mahaffy as they passed him.

"'Tis indeed."

The tall woman went to the sign-out station and put two books on the counter. Victoria followed her, and raised the counter flap to let herself in. She took the title cards from the slot under the back covers of each book, wrote the date on the cards and put them together with the library card in the long narrow drawer behind the red sign, *Due August 2nd*. She handed over the books. "Back in two weeks please."

The woman thanked her and left. Mahaffy pushed up the button to secure the Yale lock.

Victoria walked back behind the stacks of shelves into the bathroom, and splashed water on her hot face, pulled on the roller towel on the back of the door to free a fresh section to dry it. She checked the staff room: all was in order, took her purse from the cupboard under the window and walked out through the silent empty library. Mahaffy was closing the windows, pushing them up with a long wooden pole. He laid it against the wall and came to open the door for her.

In the street busy with Saturday shoppers the warm summer breeze was pleasant. When the tram came, she gave her money to the clippie, took her ticket and climbed the stairs. The upper deck was empty. She sat level with the top floors of the houses and watched the sun glinting on the windows and the polished door knockers as the bus swung along. She felt fine now, it was definitely something she'd eaten, maybe the egg she had at breakfast. Suddenly, she was thinking about making love with Donny Maguire again. She had to stop this. She deliberately switched her mind to Monday. The library would be back to its usual ways, Duffy overbearing, lecturing her on how things should be done. She alighted at the stop by the corner of the Terrace, walked up the footpath and let herself in with her key.

Victoria played the worst tennis match of her life. The July heat left her sweltering. In the final crucial game of the three set match, with Peter and Nicola dominating the play, she and Jim managed a few good rallies, but when the game climaxed at deuce, Victoria desperately tried for an ace, but the ball smacked the top of the net tape and it was out. She faulted her second serve, the ball landing out of the receiving area. They'd lost: game, set, match!

She was furious with herself. "Better next time," Jim said, as they headed to the clubhouse.

Sunday morning as she fastening the hooks on her brassiere, her throat filled with bile and she ran to the bathroom, her hand holding her mouth closed, the same sudden hurt in her belly, the same helpless heaves. She knelt on the floor thinking. She pulled the chain to flush the bowl and sat up on the side of the bathtub. There was definitely something wrong with her. She had a sudden memory of her sister Beatrice sick like this when she had been expecting Stella. But it couldn't be that. She couldn't be. Never! Her mind scanned back over the previous weeks trying to remember. When had she last had her period? Did she miss her period in June?

She tiptoed back to her bedroom and stood looking at herself in the glass. I'm pregnant, she said silently and terror emptied her of all other feeling. She felt her heart stop, then beat very fast.

"Victoria, dear, breakfast is ready," her mother called.

She fumbled into her dressing gown and half opened her door. Her mother was at the top of the stairs. "I've a headache, Mother, I'll go back to bed for an hour."

"Oh dear. Will Kathleen bring you up some tea?"

"Yes, please. Thank you Mother."

Victoria closed the door. In bed she pulled the bedclothes up to her chin and stared up at the ceiling. She pulled back the clothes and felt her stomach. It seemed as flat as it had ever been. A sudden dread hit her, panic, the realization of a shocking error like the seconds before a motor crash. When she heard Kathleen's step outside with the tea tray, she sprung out of bed and sat on the chair frantically trying to compose herself.

"Rain today, Miss." The maid placed the tray on the dressing table and left. Victoria sat with her face in her hands, weak with fear. After a few minutes, she opened her eyes and looked at the four triangles in the toast rack, the pot of marmalade and the flowered china. She was ravenous. How could she be hungry when she'd just been so sick? Maybe she wasn't pregnant. Her mind scanned back through the weeks. That Friday in May when they had spent the night together! The night before she left Obanbeg. An icy wallop at her heart and she pushed the tray aside and went to check the calendar on her writing table. The twenty-first of May. A Friday. When she had that horrible row with her uncle and aunt. When her uncle came in from his day at his sawmill, they had both confronted her with what they had heard about her and Donny Maguire.

"What's this I hear about you walking out with an RC?" Her uncle's face flushed scarlet and he roared at her.

She stared at him, shocked.

"Victoria, is this true?" her aunt demanded.

"He's perfectly respectable and very nice, Aunt Helen."

"Nice?" her uncle mocked. "Listen to her. Nice? He's not your class or religion. I'm ringing your mother in the morning about this."

"You needn't bother, Uncle William, I'm going home anyway."

"It's well you do. I won't be responsible for having you in my house when you are acting the whore."

"I'm not a whore. You've no right to call me that, Uncle William."

"What else are you? A proper slut."

She'd run from the house then. They hadn't tried to stop her. Remembering her uncle's outburst, a torrent of misery broke over her. How could she have been so utterly foolish, so dense? She should have known before now she was pregnant. Imagining her morning sickness was something she'd eaten. Now there was no doubt. Her parents? Her father would kill her. She wouldn't tell them. She couldn't. She the youngest, the favourite! Her mother had been kind when she had returned from the country subdued and miserable.

"It will all be forgotten," her mother had comforted her. "Your aunt and uncle didn't really mean what they said. Of course, you know Victoria, it was very wrong of you to involve yourself with that boy. I'd like you to write to your aunt and apologize. You have been very silly, very stupid. "

She did write but her aunt had not answered. Her mother felt this deeply. Although she wanted the matter forgotten, she thought her brother's wife should have written to Victoria on whom, before her indiscretion, Helen had doted. She could hardly believe that her brother had never even enquired about Victoria when he telephoned in the last week of June, to tell her their eighty year old mother had suffered a stroke and was quite ill. Of course,

Margaret had reasoned, William was no doubt wary of the telephone exchange staff listening in. But Victoria had lost her favoured place with her brother and sister-in-law.

Victoria lay in bed remembering. There had been an opening for a librarian in the county library in Obanbeg and when Victoria arrived for her holiday her aunt persuaded her to apply for the position. She had been walking up toward the County Council offices to hand in her letter of application when Donny Maguire had carelessly stepped on the brake of his old Morris, neglected to declutch and stalled the motor. She stopped to help. She had steered the car while he pushed it and they had succeeded in restarting it on the hill. He was so angry with himself for stalling the car, and so obviously impressed by her ability to help get it restarted that she could not be anything but amused. And of course, her amusement further infuriated him. She thought him very handsome but never expected to see him again. But the following Friday she ran into him in the dining room of the local hotel. And this second meeting led to their first date, that wonderful, romantic walk along the river under a May moon. Now she was lying in bed in utter misery, listening to the sounds of the house, her mother talking to Kathleen in the hall, then her steps on the stairs going to her room to dress for church, then Nicola coming back up from the dining room. She thought with unexpected sympathy of her aunt, whom she usually dismissed as a silly irrelevance. Then, with a sudden shocking insight she realized that the previously contemplated successful arc of her own life was now also interrupted, ruined, by so ordinary, unsophisticated an event as to make her aunt's lifelong mourning for a dead soldier seem noble by comparison. But what could she do? There had to be a solution. She had to talk to someone. She jumped up suddenly, went up the six steps to Nicola's room at the top of the house, and knocked.

"Who is it?"

"It's Victoria. Can I come in?"

"Of course! Do come in."

Queenie, the Pekinese, sat up, staring, black eyes like pansies. But seeing that this visitor was not offering treats, turned round once, curled up and lay inert in her basket like a heap of dirty yellow feathers. Victoria's aunt was sitting on the chaise under the round attic window, a cork-tipped Craven A dangling from her scarlet-nailed fingers. Her pink robe matched the swans down puffs on the toes of her heelless slippers. She patted the seat beside her.

"Come and sit down."

Shrinking from such cosiness, Victoria sat on the bed. "I tossed and turned all night."

"Oh. What's the matter? Thinking of your country lad?" Nicola sucked hard on her cigarette and looked calculatingly at Victoria through the smoke. "Want to tell me about it?"

"I'm pregnant," admitted Victoria in a dull despairing voice.

Nicola's eyes widened. She was quiet for a minute. "How inconvenient!" Then, seeing Victoria's wounded face, she asked more gently, "Are you sure?"

"I'm sure."

"Really sure?"

Victoria nodded miserably.

"What are you going to do?"

"I don't know." She was weeping now "I'll have to tell Mother soon."

"Oh, I don't think you can do that. There would be the most frightful row, and she's in no humour to deal with that with your grandmother ill."

"Then what am I to do Nicola? I'm going out of my mind. It's worse every day. Soon people will notice."

"Keep quiet about it 'til we decide what to do. There are ways to get rid of it you know. These things can be arranged. Mary Frazer will know. She's Assistant Matron now."

"Do you think she can help me?"

"Of course! But now, my dear," said her aunt, getting up and going to the corner cupboard, "first we'll have a little gin-gin."

It seemed that, as her aunt had put it, things could be arranged, everything sorted out. Mary Frazer would know what to do.

While her parents were at church they rang Mary. Nicola asked to see her immediately for advice about a problem.

"Are you ill, Nicola?"

"No. It's Victoria. I can't talk about it on the telephone."

"Tell Mother I'm feeling better and we went for a walk to get some fresh air," Victoria instructed Kathleen. Nicola stood before the hall looking glass and crimped the waves in her hennaed hair between her red-nailed fingers.

"It's me half day Miss, I'll be gone out," Kathleen said.

"That's alright, Kathleen. I'll leave her a note."

They left a note on the hall table and took the tram into the city. The rain stopped, the sun shone, and as they walked along the river and north to Brunswick Street, Victoria's spirits lifted. A solution was forthcoming. They went up the broad steps of The Richmond Hospital and the front hall porter directed them to the nurses' residence. As they climbed the stairs, three student nurses came down talking excitedly. Victoria envied them their carefree chatter as she had never before envied anyone.

Mary Frazer had been Assistant Matron at the Richmond Hospital for two years. She ordered tea and scones from the kitchen. They sat in her sitting room and Nicola sipped her tea and smoked and explained Victoria's predicament with the air of someone discussing some minor domestic difficulty. She was convinced Mary could help. "All we need is a name, Mary. I know there are places in Dublin where these things can be fixed."

Mary was horrified! Had they any idea of the seriousness of what they were proposing? She knew of no place. And if she had she would not have told them. Abortion was a crime. It was a crime under the new constitution to even advise someone to have an abortion. She could land in jail. Most of the maternity hospitals were run by orders of Catholic nuns. By now Victoria was almost nine weeks pregnant. There was a huge risk. The Richmond had no obstetrical service, but its emergency department saw girls who had gone to some unscrupulous untrained operator and had had a botched abortion. They invariably died.

Nicola's hand shook and she crushed out her cigarette in the ashtray. Victoria covered her face with her hands, then she fumbled for her handkerchief and dabbed at the tears spilling from her eyes.

"No sense in crying," Mary said briskly, and she touched her nursing sister's badge pinned in one corner of her spotless apron. "The only sensible thing, the only safe thing, is to have it. I assume the man won't marry her." Mary directed this last question to Nicola.

"There is no question of that," Nicola told her. "They're Catholics."

"Oh dear," sighed Mary. "Well there's adoption. Holles Street Hospital or the Rotunda can arrange things."

"But Mary, the scandal!" cried Nicola.

"It's a little late to think of that now. In these cases the girl usually hides away in the country, or in England. Would her sister in England not take her?"

"That would be a last resort. Beatrice's husband would have to be considered."

They were talking about Victoria as if she weren't present.

"If the man is a Catholic, Catholic girls go to the nuns, work in the Magdalene Laundries for the duration, or longer if their families don't take them back. The children go to the orphanages." She put down her cup. "Do your parents know?"

"No. I don't want to tell them."

"It may not be possible to keep it from them."

In the end it seemed that there was nothing to do but go home. Mary Frazer couldn't help. She strongly advised that Victoria tell her parents and they would between them decide what was best. Victoria sensed Mary couldn't wait to get rid of them. So they said goodbye and plodded dejectedly in the sunshine back along the river, Victoria dabbing at her streaming eyes. Passersby stared.

"Do stop snivelling Victoria," said Nicola. "What we both need is a stiff drink."

They crossed over O'Connell Bridge and Nicola led the way into the Westmoreland Hotel. They sat in the snug and when the barman pulled back the little sliding panel, Nicola ordered gin and tonic for them both. He pushed the drinks through and Nicola shoved the door back quickly. Victoria took one sip of her drink and pushed it away. She was so alone. Already her corset felt tighter. Nicola sipped her gin. Victoria sat looking at her glass. Her whole being rejected the thing growing inside her. She simply did not want to be alive if she had to go through with this, the unspeakable shame, the gossip, the scandal! And yet she did not want to die. She remembered Nicola's answer when Mary suggested that the man might marry her. "There's no question of that."

But why? Donny loved her, she knew that. She had been determined to forget him because a romance between a Catholic and a Protestant was doomed. But it was different now. And there were mixed marriages. Nicola assumed she couldn't marry Donny. Why couldn't she? Was she at twenty-four not capable of deciding for herself? It was the obvious solution, no matter that he was a different religion. Somewhere quietly, they would marry. She had promised him she would write. She hadn't really intended to because she had been trying to forget him. She would write now.

Nicola's voice broke into her thoughts. "Maybe Mary is right. You should go to Beatrice in England, have the baby and have it adopted."

Go to her sister in England? But how would she go to her sister without telling her mother and father? And what about Edward, Beatrice's cold, moralistic husband? There was the possibility that Edward wouldn't have her. "I can't go there."

"Why not?"

"Mother and Father would have to know."

"I'm afraid they will. But it's your only choice. We'll tell Margaret tomorrow when your father's at work. We may be able to persuade her not to tell him for a while."

"I can't face her Nicola. And she tells him everything."

"No she doesn't. She never told him why you came back in such a rush from the country. She kept your little affair from him."

"I'm terrified of Father. I can't face him. He'll kill me. You know what he's like."

"Yes I do know. But they're your parents, dear. I'll never forget how kind they were to me when Mathew was killed."

"But that was different."

"Still, they are your parents."

"Please Nicola, can we wait a week?"

"Well a week makes no difference now. It seems that, like it or not, you're going to have that baby."

That night Victoria stood naked before the looking glass of her dressing table. Her reflection was cut off at her thighs but she thought she could see a slight rising bulge that pushed her belly upward, so that her waist seemed thicker. With shaking fingers, she lifted her discarded underclothes from the chair and pulled the stays from her corset, tears overflowing her eyes. She flung the bent steel rods of the corset in the wastebasket, then sat at her table and wrote to Donagh Maguire to tell him that by February 1938 he would be a father. She calculated three months back from the night they had spent together, May the twenty-first. As she wrote she sobbed, tears fell on to the letter, the black ink ran in blobs and she had to begin again. Putting words on the paper calmed her, eased the anxiety that had begun to spread like a paralysing rot through her and she allowed herself to think fondly of Donny, and to ease the raw emptiness of her spirit, she imagined herself once again in the circle of his arms.

Monday at her lunch hour she walked to the post office and posted the letter. It would be in Ballynamon on Wednesday. She would have his letter by return post Friday, Saturday at the latest. And they would meet and their love for each other would be as it was on that fateful night in May.

After the horrible row, she had run from her uncle's house and they had spent the night together. She'd bicycled away from her uncle's place pedalling furiously, her skirt looped on the crossbar of the heavy Rudge bike, rain pelting down, moving so fast on the country road that men driving carts stared after her. It was nightfall when, drenched and cold, she arrived at his digs. His car was not there. She'd sheltered from the rain in the shed, crouching there, determined she wasn't going back to her uncle's. She couldn't, unless Donny drove her there. The bicycle had no light and it was now dark.

After what seemed an age, she had heard his car and saw the lights as he drove into the laneway. Then its lights quenched and she heard him talking to the dog, a match was struck, there was a door opening and closing and the light shining in the window above. She had hesitated for a few minutes, then ran through the rain and knocked on his door. She remembered now how they had fallen asleep, their limbs entwined, wakened in the night and made love again and then returned to sleep. When they woke, the lamplight was weak in the dawn and robins were chirruping in the hedges. Now sitting in her bedroom in Blackrock, waiting for his reply to her letter, she asked herself how did it happen? How could she have been such an utter fool? Looking into the future she knew they would make a go of it.

What would she do when his answer came? She would tell her parents she was marrying him, and she and Donny would brave the opposition of her family and his. She couldn't marry him just to save herself from scandal. She wasn't sure about the details, but she knew the new Constitution forbade divorce. It even forbade people who divorced in England or America from remarrying in Ireland. She didn't know what it said about mixed marriages, but if she had to become a Catholic she would. What did it matter now which church she went to? To her social circle it meant everything, and she didn't know any Catholics except Donny. And she loved him, or did she? She had tried so hard to forget him and now she could think only of her misery and the disgrace if her secret was known. Whatever was required, she would do it.

Her father would never forgive her. He felt betrayed by the Constitution and the prominence it gave to the Catholic church. "I'm a hostage in my own country," he declared and raged at De Valera. "That blackguard. Courting the extremists when it suited him and now he's outlawed the IRA and he's kowtowing to Rome."

21

But why tell her parents? She would just leave. Obviously, Nicola would tell them, but by then, she'd be gone. She felt a lifting of her spirits. The morning sickness seemed to be over. Donny was sweet. She believed she loved him, knew he was crazy about her and when he heard the news he would be full of affection and concern. She knew that, knew he loved her, she was longing for any word of sympathy, hungry for tenderness, for someone just to listen to her story. And he would provide all that. And she'd get away from home, from the sickening prospect of her condition becoming apparent, from the terror of her father knowing, from the shameful confession she would have to make, the unspeakable row. She could imagine the probing questions. She supposed she should go to a doctor. Certainly not to Quinn, the gruff white-haired old fellow that vaccinated her against smallpox and stuck a cold instrument like the handle of a spoon half way down her throat when she had tonsillitis. She'd wait 'til she got to the country. As soon as she heard from Donny she would send him a telegram to meet her train and she would slip out of the house in the early morning before anyone was awake. She'd just leave a note. They wouldn't follow her or try to get her back, not now; her disgraceful secret precluded that. They'd concoct a story to cover her absence, some lie about her having gone to England to visit Beatrice.

That night she started a list of the clothes she would take. Since she would be taking the tram to the railway station, she could only take one bag. That didn't matter. Soon none of her clothes would fit.

3

In The Country

*M*asie O'Shea had been reading the *Irish Press*. Nothing in it worth reading, she decided, nothing but De Valera's Constitution. She didn't see what difference it made, although people said Protestants were mad about it. They'd all voted against it, or refused to vote at all. What odds about them. If they all packed up and left for the North, wouldn't it be good riddance? The country would be well shot of them. There was a crowd of them from Obanbeg that nearly killed her lodger, Donny Maguire. Beat him within an inch of his life, and the Gardai hadn't done one blessed thing about it. They said they had no evidence, couldn't discover who had done it, still investigating. But even the dogs in the streets knew who the guilty party was. And all over a slip of a girl! A Protestant one at that. She looked at the clock above the range. Time for her mid-morning tea. She filled the black kettle from the tap over the porcelain sink, lifted the smallest of the three plates off the range and put the kettle to boil. Then she folded the newspaper and went round to the front of the house. In the hall, she almost fell over a fishing rod. She tidied it away and proceeded into the office.

It had been the front parlour when Masie's husband was alive, but now it held a desk, a glass fronted cupboard full of jars and bottles, a sink in the far corner by the window and rows of bookshelves either side of the cold fireplace. The man was snug enough here. Calculating whether she might raise the rent a shilling, she put the newspaper on the desk, walked outside and stood on the step in the warm smell of wild woodbine, the sun softening her stiff old muscles, and waited for the postman who was making his way along the street.

"Grand day, Ned."

"Great day, thank God," he agreed, handing her the post.

"Thanks, Ned."

He passed on and she looked at the letters. All three were for Donny. The two buff envelopes were, she guessed, bills. The third letter was addressed *Donagh Maguire, Veterinary Surgeon, Main Street, Ballynamon.* Now who was that from? No one included Main Street in the address. All you needed was *Ballynamon* and the county. She turned back into the dispensary, left the two buff envelopes on the desk. She took the white envelope with the neat rounded hand writing back to her kitchen. She stood looking at the writing. Was it from the girl? As if she hadn't caused Donny enough trouble. He'd been nearly three weeks on his back, and now the poor lad was just getting on his feet.

The kettle was boiling now, steam slapping the lid up and down. She moved the kettle to the side, covered the opening in the range with its plate and moved the kettle back. Steam poured more gently from the spout. Masie set her mouth in a determined line. She'd see what this was about. She held the letter by its edges and passed the sealed opening back and forth over the steam, a musty smell of melting paste curled her nose. She sat at the table and with the edge of her yellow ridged thumbnail eased up the softened mushy back flap. The envelope began to dry. She stood up and again passed it over the steam and at the second attempt succeeded in curling back the flap halfway. She inserted a knife at one end between the flap and the envelope and gently opened it. Donny would never notice and if he did see it had been tampered with, he would blame the postmistress. She unfolded the sheet of white bond writing paper, read Victoria's letter, then read it again. God between us and all harm, thought Masie, the girl was going to have a baby! And they not married, nor ever could be. What did that brazen strap of a Protestant one think they all were? Did she take them for fools? First she got herself in the family way, up the pole, and now she was trying to trap a decent Catholic boy into marrying her. After her relations had almost killed him! The affair had gone further than Masie had realized and she was quite affronted that she had been deceived in the matter. She knew they had been walking out, that Donny was making a proper fool of himself over her. The whole county knew that. But that it had come to this? She had been completely blindsided. Or maybe it hadn't. The girl could have another man in Dublin or somewhere and just looking for some fool of a boy to give the child his name. The oldest trick in the book! She clenched her mouth decidedly, stood up, moved the kettle aside, took the plate off the range and threw the letter on the coals. It flamed for a second. Masie slapped the lid back on the range. No need to bother Donny with that. She reached up on the chimney piece for the canister of Lyon's tea. Donny would never know a thing about it. What he didn't know wouldn't sicken him.

At a quarter to one, she heard his car. She went out and stood watching as he parked in the laneway. His dog was sitting up on the front seat staring ahead. When he stepped out of the car, the dog jumped out, ambled across and lay down on the step of the dispensary.

"Hello, Masie. Any post?"

"Oh, a couple of letters. I left them in there on the table."

Stepping over his dog he went into the dispensary. The dog turned her head and looked after him.

"Your dinner will be ready shortly," she called over her shoulder.

"Thanks Masie, I'm coming."

When he came round to the kitchen and sat at her deal table she noticed his face leached pale with exhaustion and for a fleeting instant had a prick of remorse for her deceit. Then she decided he was a young fool and what she had just done was saving him from being an even greater fool. She couldn't know that the same man, despairing of receiving a letter from Victoria, was trudging through his days trying to forget her and avoided the river where they had walked. Sometimes when he went into Obanbeg to buy supplies he found himself looking for her in the streets and finding that the idea of her, her walk, her easy walk, sauntered ahead of him while the details of her face became daily more difficult to recall.

Waiting for his response Victoria daydreamed of her escape as she shelved books. She felt sick in the mornings but did not vomit, and spent her evenings reading. But by Saturday there had been no reply. Monday she left work early, unable to contain her impatience. But there was no letter on the hall table. Her mother was out and Kathleen was backing down the stairs adjusting the brass stair rods and polishing them as she went.

"Did a letter come for me, Kathleen?"

"No, Miss. The only post was for your father."

Victoria pushed past her up the stairs to her room and lay face down on her bed. Was it possible the letter was lost? Perhaps it was mislaid.

She wrote again and waited all of the next week, preoccupied, alternatively hoping and despairing, sometimes standing looking at the spine of a book, not seeing it. She knew he wasn't going to answer her letter and she knew why. He was dumping her because she was a Protestant. All his protestations of love were lies, and she'd been a fool. She began to see her father's point of view. Catholics were, before anything else, loyal to

Rome. She remembered when she was a child the hurtful chant of girls skipping rope near the sea wall.

Proddy woddy on the wall,

half a loaf would feed yo' all.

Her mother had said, "Pay no heed to that, Victoria. They're very common girls."

But the Catholic influence was everywhere, nuns in their long black habits shepherding lines of schoolgirls, the Franciscan brothers in their medieval robes and sandaled feet, and streams of worshippers walking to their chapel on the saints' feast days, while Protestants went about their work.

Thursday after tea, Nicola whispered, "Come upstairs, Victoria."

Nicola sat with her legs curled under her on the chaise. Victoria sat on the bed. "Victoria we have to tell them. You must come clean with it."

"I'm terrified, Aunt Nicola."

Nicola got up and took a cigarette from the box on the table.

"Soon they'll know anyway. They'll notice. Anyone can see there is something wrong with you. You're so pale."

"I dread it, Nicola."

Nicola flashed her cigarette lighter and looked intensely at her niece. "You have to face the music, old girl. We'll tell Margaret and let her tell your father."

"Could we wait a little?"

"Victoria the longer you wait the more upset they'll be."

"Can we wait a week?"

"And then what? I'll get blamed for deceiving them. Saturday, okay?"

Nicola was more forceful than Victoria had ever seen her and she finally saw that she had to agree. But she lay awake all Friday night and Saturday she asked to leave work early saying she was not well. Duffy looked at her over his spectacles. "You look pale, Miss Mulholland. I'll expect you on Monday."

She trudged home exhausted. She just wanted the scene with her parents to be over. Her father was still at work and Nicola asked Margaret to come to her room. When they told her, Margaret blanched white as paper.

"My God," she whispered, "are you sure, Victoria?"

"Yes Mother. I'm sure." Victoria thought she could have borne anything easier than her mother's suddenly aged face.

"And the man's a Catholic? How could you Victoria?"

"I'm sorry Mother," and Victoria began to weep.

"I've noticed there was something the matter with you. But I never dreamt of this. I wish you'd told us earlier. I don't know what your father will do when I tell him. I can't imagine telling him. But I must. And you Nicola! You should have told me."

"We had thought if we went to talk to Mary Frazer she might know of a doctor or someone." Nicola's voice trailed off.

They heard the sound of the front door opening.

"I think that's your father now. You stay here. I'll go down." She stood up quickly, dabbed at her eyes smoothed her skirt over her hips, leaned into Nicola's dressing table and plumped up her cheeks between her fingers. She left closing the door so quietly it never made a sound.

Margaret Mulholland waited till Sunday to tell her husband. It was Kathleen's half day and she had gone to the pictures. After tea Margaret said, "Henry I must talk to you."

They went into the sitting room and closed the doors. Victoria waited, tense, sick at heart, straining to hear. The murmur of voices seemed to go on and on. If only they would come out. Then the door opened and her father said, "Victoria! Come here!"

She walked into the room. Her father was standing staring into the cold fireplace, her mother sat on the sofa under the window, her head bowed in her hands. Her father spun round. "What's this your mother tells me? Is this true?" he began. Then his round face reddened and he shouted, "Are you carrying that bastard's child? Are you?"

"Yes. Father," Victoria admitted miserably.

He rushed forward and slapped her face hard twice, on both sides.

"Henry!"

Victoria shrank back, her face burning. A devastating rage filled the room, a shocking permissiveness, as if this were not the sitting room but some place where a vicious fight might break out, her father might kill her. Then he took a deep breath and turned away. He appeared to be trying to control himself. "A papist! I'd sooner see you a street walker! Get out of my sight!"

Victoria looked at her mother but her face was turned away. She burst out the door, her face burning, ran up to her bedroom and threw herself on her bed. Her fate was in her father's hands now. She had nowhere to run. So great was society's abhorrence of an unmarried pregnant woman that she could think of nowhere to go apart from walking into the sea. But they would run after her, or someone on the beach would pull her to safety.

Victoria now entered a strange looking glass world, peopled, as it had always been, by her parents and her aunt. But she lived isolated in the shell of their disapproval. She wrote a letter of resignation to the library saying she had been offered a position in England. She spent all day in her room, coming downstairs only for her noon meal. She never saw Nicola or her parents, and ate her breakfast and supper in her room. Kathleen put the tray on the dressing table. "Now eat up miss. No sense in making yourself sick." She stared at Kathleen. What did she think was wrong that Victoria was confined to her room?

Her father had said, "I'll decide what's to be done and I'll tell you when I've decided."

She hated him, astounded by the depth of her loathing. Her mother seemed to have formed a united front with her father in rejecting Victoria. Watching from her window, she saw them leave the house to go for a walk, her mother leaning on her father's arm. Never had they seemed so close. And Nicola aligned herself with them.

"Don't upset him further, Victoria," she whispered, coming into the dining room when Victoria was eating her lunch. "It will do no good. Just go along with whatever he decides."

Her father's solution was to take the Reverend Arthur Gordon into his confidence and the Reverend's idea was, as was usual in such a case, to find someone within the parish who would agree to marry her. Victoria had been summoned to the sitting room to hear this. She was appalled.

"Father, I can't just marry anyone who'll agree to marry me." Her mother sat near the fireplace, her head turned away as if she read something in the crepe paper fan that filled the cold grate.

"You'll do what I say, madam," her father shouted and walked out to the hall. Her mother rose and went after him, but he'd left the house, slamming the door behind him. Her mother turned back. "Go to your room, Victoria, and stay there."

A prisoner in her room, Victoria imagined the clergyman visiting one man after another with his proposition. Would he ask Peter Butler, who was such a bore, and lived with his mother four doors away? She definitely would not marry him. She stood before the looking glass in her bedroom, the sight of her thin face and her hair lying in streaks around her forehead saddened her, but she had no tears left. A cold despair settled on her, an overwhelming sense of shame. They were wearing down her resistance.

The third Wednesday in August, she sat wretched, trying to read. Nicola knocked at her bedroom door, came in sat on the edge of Victoria's bed holding her dog Queenie against her shoulder.

"We've had a telegram from Enniskillen, Victoria. Mother died last night." And she turned her face into the little dog's side.

"Oh Nicola, I'm so sorry."

Nicola turned back toward her and Victoria saw that there were tears in her eyes. "For your mother it's the last straw!"

"I know Nicola. But what can I do?"

"If only you could have gotten rid of it before we had to tell her."

"Nicola, do you think I want to be like this?"

Nicola lifted her thin shoulders in a hopeless gesture, walked slowly toward the door, then turned back. "We're going up to Enniskillen for the funeral. We leave early tomorrow morning."

"Am I going?" Even to herself Victoria sounded like a small child.

"I hardly think you are. That's the last thing your father would allow."

All afternoon and evening Victoria waited for her mother: surely she wouldn't leave without speaking to her. In the morning her mother came. She stood inside the door of Victoria's bedroom. "Nicola has told you about your grandmother?"

"I'm sorry, Mother."

"She was an old woman. And if she had recovered, how would we have kept your disgrace from her? It would have killed her."

She came closer to the bed. "I must go," she said and stooped to kiss Victoria, then changed her mind and turned away. At the door she said. "We will be back on Saturday."

Victoria looked at the closed door. She was so angry with her mother she had barely restrained herself from turning away when she had approached her. She heard her giving instructions to Kathleen, heard Nicola reminding her to feed Queenie, and felt the air pressure in the house change when the door opened and closed. They were gone.

Her mother! She had never asked how she felt, made no attempt to defend her when her father slapped her. She sat on her bed bitterly remembering shopping in Grafton Street with her mother for summer clothes before she left for Obanbeg. Watching her try on dresses her mother had said, "Victoria you're the prettiest of the girls. You must make the most of your chances."

And another time, "Victoria, I know you're my brother's favourite. He and Helen will invite young men for you to meet."

Before the party four weeks earlier, Margaret had insisted on Victoria having her hair cut and waved, setting her up for the marriage auction.

"You have to look a little smarter Victoria, less the schoolgirl. You don't want to be on the shelf. You want men to notice you."

Victoria had shattered her mother's dream. Now, heaven forbid anyone should notice her. From her school days her mother had set her up for the marriage market. Victoria hated them all, her mother, her father, Nicola. When they came back from the funeral she would confront them. How unfair they were, concerned only about their own sensibilities. She'd come down at breakfast on Sunday and face them. She rehearsed telling them that they were hypocrites worried only about what neighbours might think. But eventually she decided it was hopeless. There was nothing she could do to alter things. Then, it dawned on her that they were gone and she could get out of the house.

Even before she opened the front door she felt the warmth of the sun. She saw their neighbour Mrs. McFadden was leaving her house two doors away. Victoria slunk back into the doorway until she passed. Then she walked quickly in the opposite direction, dizzy with the expanse of bright sky after so long indoors, crossed the road and walked down a long narrow lane to the beach.

The tide was out. On the sea front were families, children digging in the wet sand, building sandcastles, a boy unwinding the string of a red kite that fluttered high in the blue summer air. A young lad, chasing another, fell against her almost knocking her over. Clemmie was long back from her holidays, but she hadn't called. Or had she? Had her mother made some excuse, some tale that she had gone back to the country to stay with her aunt? The carefree air of the beach was admonitory. Victoria should be at work; she was an intruder. No single young women on the beach, just mothers with children. It was awkward to walk alone and she was self-conscious; the privilege of going every day to work was lost. What if she met someone she knew? Someone who would inquire why she was not at work? She turned back for home and trudged up to the house. Kathleen was singing in the kitchen. *"I'll sing a hymn to Mary, the mother of my God ..."*

Victoria went in and Kathleen stopped singing. Victoria sat at the table under the window. "Like a cup of tea, Miss?"

"I would Kathleen."

Kathleen filled the kettle from the tap, put it on the stove and lit the gas under it. "Just be a few minutes."

She put a cup and saucer, butter and jam and a turnover loaf on the table. She looked sharply at Victoria. "Miss, are you all right?"

"I'm fine," said Victoria, her eyes overflowing with tears.

Kathleen sat down on the chair opposite her. Her sharp brown eyes had a knowing look. "You're in the family way, aren't you Miss?"

Victoria nodded.

"Well sometimes that happens." The maid's voice was gentle, almost conspiratorial.

"I wish I knew what to do. What can I do Kathleen?"

"Get rid of it!"

"How can I do that Kathleen? Do you know anyone?"

"Well me pal Theresa that works up on Vico Road knows. I'll ask her."

"But when can you do that? I should do it now while my mother is away."

"The business will cost something."

"How much money, Kathleen?"

"A few pounds, maybe six."

"I have that."

"And cab fare home. You won't be fit for the tram, Miss."

"I have that too. I was going to go away and I took all the money out of my bank account."

"No time to lose by the looks of you, Miss. I'll go now and ask her. I'll get the tram. Can you make your own tea? I won't be long."

It was as if this was for Kathleen an adventure, a break in monotony of her life. She took off her apron, smoothed down the faded print dress over her hips, and went down the three steps and through the back hall to her bedroom. She was back in a minute decisively belting a blue summer coat around her. She took her rosary from the shelf in the cupboard, kissed the cross and put it in her pocket and stood in front of the small glass inside the kitchen door. With a licked finger she smoothed her eyebrows and patted down her black unruly frizzy hair. "I'm a sight! Make your tea now. There's scones as well from yesterday for your elevenses. I won't be long."

Victoria watched her pass the kitchen window. The kettle began to boil. Her thoughts raced forward to when it would be over and she would be back in the stream of living again. She took the brown teapot from the cupboard and made her mid morning tea. Her elevenses, Kathleen had said. Margaret would have called that a common expression. Well common or not, Kathleen was helping her. Kathleen had been with them for years, ten years at least. Sometimes Margaret declared she didn't know what they would do without Kathleen, it was so difficult to get a good maid any more: all the good girls were gone to England. Victoria now suspected that Kathleen had known about her pregnancy for some time. How strange that she knew where one could procure an abortion: a Catholic maid who went to mass every Sunday and sometimes performed such additional rituals as the Nine First Fridays, who prayed to Saint Anthony to find her purse if she mislaid it and had never tasted meat on a Friday in her life.

Victoria now thought herself a fool. Exasperatingly silly or even pathetic like Tess on Salisbury Plain. Well this would soon be over. And when it was she'd get another job and move out. She'd be an independent woman, a different woman than the one abandoned with such highhanded distain by a lover who had never even answered her letters. How humiliating.

4

In Dublin's Fair City

"**H**ave you the money Miss?"

"Yes, I have."

Late afternoon and they were walking up toward the tram stop.

"And we need to stop and get sanitary towels. At Boylan's Miss."

Victoria stared at her. "What?"

"You're going to bleed Miss."

She hadn't thought of that.

In the gloomy shop, the assistant wrapped the package in brown paper, took the ten shilling note, wrapped the bill in it, and sent it in the cash cup on the overhead trolley to the cashier in the glassed-in box in the middle of the shop. They waited impatiently for the change. Kathleen carried the parcel and in silence they rode the tram into Dublin among chattering women going to the city to shop, the conductor calling out the stops, *Williamstown, Bootherstown, Ballsbridge.* Victoria handed Kathleen the money in an envelope, "You take care of that."

They left the tram at Nelson's Pillar and Kathleen led her towards Mary's Street, then through a short web of winding streets, down a narrow lane and up the back steps of a shabby shuttered house. An obscene geometry of black pipes descended the dirty brick wall. No brass nameplate announced this doctor's office. Victoria told herself to be brave; it would be over soon. Kathleen rang and they were admitted by a hard faced woman in a green flowered wrap-round apron. There were four wooden chairs, an old-fashioned hallstand and patches of dampness on the yellow wallpaper in the dark hallway.

"Are you to see the doctor?"

"Yes Ma'am. This lady." Kathleen handed over the package of towels. "Wait here." The woman motioned them to the chairs, and went up a flight of stairs. In a few minutes she called from the top, "Send her up."

Victoria's knees trembled as she mounted into the gloom. A passage led to a room at the back of the house. The room was dark, a tall goose neck lamp at the foot of a high narrow table shone a bright light on the red rubber sheet that covered it. An enamel pail on the floor, steel instruments, one like a huge duckbill, gleamed on a trolley. Something steamed over a blue flame. A blind obscured the window. She had an impression of horrid torture, of secret wounding. She heard the door close behind her, felt the thump of her heart lurch and then slither in her chest. From the shadows at the back a small bald man came towards her, a green rubber apron almost to his feet. "Now dear, come right in," he said softly.

Instinctively Victoria turned, struggled blindly with the door handle, then she was out of the room. She ran stumbling down the stairs. "Kathleen," she shouted, rushing out, around to the front of the house, through the lane into the street. She stood terrified, not sure of her way, her heart slowing, unnaturally quiescent. She was astounded to see two men pass carrying a ladder between them, a woman with a child by the hand, a group of laughing girls, an ordinary summer's evening in a Dublin street with the sky above the city smoky purple in its evening light. My God, what was she doing here? That doctor had made her skin crawl. Kathleen came round the side of the building, red faced, flustered.

"Kathleen, I couldn't go through with it, I couldn't. I'm too frightened. I'm sorry I brought you all this trouble." She was shaking. Kathleen took her arm.

"That's alright Miss. It's only that old one stuck me for a quid," and she handed Victoria the envelope with the rest of the money. They began walking toward the tram stop.

"What'll you do now, Miss?"

"The Minister, Reverend Gordon, is trying to help."

"When I worked in Waterford the daughter in that house got in the family way too, and she went and lived in England with a couple that couldn't have children, and when she had the baby they kept it. A girl it was and she came back home. It was never mentioned. Their minister, it was, that arranged it."

They walked on slowly. "Was that a real doctor, Kathleen?"

"Theresa said he was qualified and all, but one time he blotted his copy book, and they took him off the list. He's what they call struck off the register."

She gave Victoria a sidelong look. "Easy enough to blot your copybook sometimes, Miss."

Despite her nervous state, Victoria smiled back. She was no longer trembling. "I just want it all to be over."

"Good job it doesn't last long."

"Would you believe I'm hungry? I'd like some tea."

A little further on they turned into a teashop and sat in silence at a small corner table. A waitress brought them tea and cheese and ham sandwiches.

"Whatever you do, Miss, don't let them put you in the Laundries. You might as well be in jail at hard labour."

"I think they'll marry me off to someone."

Kathleen stared at her. "So you'd have the little baby to keep then?"

Victoria had never considered that.

"That girl in Waterford, that's what they tried first but there's a scarcity of fathers."

That was what Victoria's mother might have said. A shortage of suitable men, ever since the awful war, but who would they find willing to marry her in her disgrace?

"You know, Miss, there's that place *The Birds' Nest,* up Temple Hill way, where the Protestant girls go."

"I never knew that, Kathleen."

"Oh, it's for girls from other places, from the country. You probably couldn't go there. It's too near, people would get to know."

So there was a home for unwed Protestant girls in Blackrock! Of course they wouldn't send her there. But it was strangely comforting to know that other girls had fallen from grace. She opened the envelope with what was left of the money.

"I'd like to give you something for all the trouble you've taken."

"Indeed, Miss, I wouldn't take it."

When they had finished Kathleen said, "I'm going now to the old hook and eye."

Victoria stared at her. "To the lavatory, Miss. Best you come too."

It was dark when they left. The streets and shops lit, the Bovril sign flashing in the sky above O'Connell Street. They sat on the top deck of the tram. The sea in the distance and the lights of the mail boat headed for England shone on the water.

"If only you had a plan, you could take that boat to England Miss."

"I don't know where I'll be going but hardly to England."

"You know Miss, I was brought up in the orphanage in Kilkenny."

"Were you Kathleen? I didn't know."

"I was one of the lucky ones. I had a family. It's just that my mother and father died and my relations put me in there. They kept my brother because he could work on the farm, but they put me in the orphanage."

"How old were you, Kathleen, when that happened?"

"Eight at the time."

"Was it awful?"

"Well, they taught us to read and write, but they were hard on us. Bad food, bread and lard, never butter. We were hungry all the time. And cold! I'm sure of heaven for all the masses I went to. Whenever they needed an audience in the cathedral, a priest's funeral or ordination, they paraded us to mass. I kept out of trouble. But we had our times together. Theresa was my friend and when we were fifteen they got us jobs. They sent our photographs out and I got a job in Waterford and she got one here. The mistress she has thinks the world of her. They're rich that family. The house so high you can see out over the sea. Must have cost a bomb! We wrote to each other and then I got the job with your mother."

"How did you know about that doctor?"

"Theresa knew. He got rid of a baby for her once. She didn't want to go to the Laundries or send a child to the orphanage. She had a bad time in the orphanage. The nuns beat her and one time they thought she was telling lies and they put Epsom salts on her tongue."

"My God! You did well to get out of there, Kathleen."

"I did Miss."

"How old are you Kathleen?"

"Thirty-two next October."

Victoria had thought she was older. How strong Kathleen was, shouldering all the work of the house for a pound a month and a bare room with a narrow bed. She'd never known her to have a man friend. Not that she had ever taken any interest in Kathleen. She was just the tall thin plain woman who worked ten hours a day for their comfort. "Are you ever lonely?" she asked now.

"Well no, but at night in bed I am sometimes. What I'd wish beside me is my pal Theresa, just for the company, the comfort of it."

How extraordinary, Victoria thought, how touching.

They alighted from the tram and walked in silence. Between the street lamps their shadows alternatively proceeded and followed them and Victoria was perturbed by the strangeness of the journey and the day that had been. As they neared home she felt a growing distance between herself and Kathleen. "Kathleen, you won't tell anyone about today will you?"

"I never would Miss."

"Goodnight, Kathleen."

"Goodnight, Miss."

Resigned to whatever was to happen Victoria mounted the stairs. In bed she lay curled on her side sleepless, tortured with self reproach. She wished she had not run out on to the beach in the morning, what if a neighbour had seen her? And she shouldn't have confided in Kathleen or undertaken the journey to see the abortionist. She had acted so impulsively, without forethought. And this same thoughtlessness had led her to Donny Maguire's bed. My God how impulsive she was. She despised herself.

The next afternoon when her parents and her aunt returned from the funeral, Victoria stayed in her room enduring the lonely monotony of the hours, sometimes leaning her elbows on the sash of the window looking at people passing the house.

5

Wireless Dreams

*T*he quarrelling crows in the poplars disturbed Saucebottle Moran's dreams. He awoke slowly. The bakelite and rubber cup over his right ear was pressed painfully into the side of his head, and the thick rubber band that held the cups in place was tight on his scalp. He inserted his finger under the band, eased it off his head and opened his eyes. His darling Crystal, his beautiful wireless Galena was balanced on a safety pin in the sauce bottle. He touched the lever and heard a spurt of crackling. Nothing but noise! Always better at night. He lay back, his hands joined under his head, and thought about all he knew that no one else knew. Other people might know it in a few days, or they might never know, but Saucebottle knew.

In Hourigan's pub they turned on the wireless when Athlone came on the air at half past one. That wouldn't be for another six hours. Sometimes the wet battery failed and they had to wait to get it recharged in the town. A fine waste of money.

The daylight came through the potato sack nailed over the window and cast a netted shadow on the earth floor. By the slant of the morning light, Saucebottle estimated it was almost seven o'clock. In this first week of September the sun rose at half six and when its dusty rays threw the netted shadow on the hob of the hearth, it was time to get up. Saucebottle's neck was stiff. He delayed rising, closed his eyes and thought of last night's news, the rally in Nuremberg. The voice coming from somewhere out in the darkness, fading in and out, now loud and clear, now weak and distant, told of women fainting with the heat. He had never seen a women faint. The very idea of it conjured up visions of languid willowy creatures with melting eyes, sensuous, exotic. The first week of September, was it as hot as all that? Or was it something else? Some madness? When he heard the sound of cheering in waves over the voice of the announcer, he pictured an immense herd of humans roaring, each outburst louder than the one that preceded it, or church bells pealing and the Master standing in an open car, one arm stiffly outstretched.

Hard men, tough men was what was wanted. The strong men of Ireland were gone soft as women. But Saucebottle knew what was buried beyond the far end of the long field, under the high rock behind the lone whitethorn bush on Crew Rock: buried for seventeen years.

He threw his legs over the side of the bed and stood up, a thin wiry bald man of thirty-one with a pale sickly face and wide open red-rimmed grey eyes. He crouched down and lovingly fingered the ground wires attached to the leg of his iron bed then stood to examine the lead wire that ran along to the window, out and up to the roof and the antenna. He ran his palm over his chin. No need to shave today. Weekdays he worked at the creamery, mopping up between the big churns and shifting the flat capped steel milk cans on the loading dock. Two quid a week. If Callaghan needed help on a Saturday, he was their man for the hay, or the harvest. He had his reasons. From Callaghan's fields he could keep an eye on Beechwood. Watch the lay of the land as he worked the fields, could see Dominic cutting the grass or rolling the lawn and Matt driving the cows to pasture. He had a fine view of the big house. Big houses? Middlebrook, now that had been a big house. No tennis parties now at Middlebrook. It was a rat-infested ruin. He remembered a little nostalgically the old mistress at Middlebrook pinching his cheek and giving him a three penny bit for fielding tennis balls that flew astray into the shrubbery. There would be apple cake and tea in the kitchen for him, and sometimes the officers that came from the barracks in Killcore to play tennis and sip whiskey on the terrace would give him a few pennies. There had been peacocks on the terrace then and ivy and azaleas in big stone urns. All gone now, and good riddance. Good riddance to bad rubbish!

He pulled on his trousers and his grubby grey shirt and navy blue jacket. He raked the embers of last night's fire, added a few sticks for kindling, then two sods of turf, crouched down and blew on it and the kindling caught and flared weakly. He filled the black kettle from the bucket of spring water and hung it over the fire to boil, then opened the door and stepped outside. Crows rose from the poplars in a black fluttering cloud. The ripe September sun glinted on the metal of his antenna. Magnificent! Saucebottle sat in the doorway and had his first cigarette of the day. He blew a mouthful of smoke, watched it rise and decided this morning he'd go by Beechwood. When he heard the kettle singing he ground out the cigarette in the earth and went to brew his morning tea. He cut himself a thick slice off of a loaf he kept in a biscuit tin, smeared it with butter and ate it with the black hot tea laced with sugar. When he had finished, he rinsed the mug with the water in the kettle, walked to the door and emptied it out. The water puddled in the dust. He replaced the mug on the shelf, retrieved his leather drawstring purse from behind the loose stone in the chimney, counted out enough money to buy a few drinks at the pub in the evening, and hid the purse again. He dipped his finger in the holy water font by the door and went out into the bright morning. Saucebottle mounted his push bike, pedalled into the road and turned up toward Beechwood. He cycled up the avenue then veered left. The white gate was open, so he took the fork where the lane led off the avenue and ran round by the orchard wall and the north wing of the house, to the archway that led into the yard. He could see that the tops of the windows were open to the September air. He dismounted and pushed the bike into the thick hedge and crouched low beside it. Stone buildings enclosed three sides of the cobble stoned yard: old stables, only one in use now; empty pig sties; a row of cow byres with a steaming heap of manure beside them and, opposite the house, the milking parlour and the old dairy with the hen house behind it. The green Morris motor car, the milk trailer attached, was parked beside the dairy. He stood looking at the house. In his imagination smoke billowed from the windows, the glass cracked and flames jumped in the interior. He saw Josie cross the yard to the dairy and snuck back the way he had come.

6

The Road North

Victoria's thoughts raced. What would happen? Would she be called down one day and told a husband had been found for her? Would she ever get out of this bedroom, where the walls leaned in over her? From her window she could see three houses opposite and the short lane down to the sea. The house faced east and on one side she could see a lime tree in the neighbour's garden, on the other side, the street. The late summer had wound wearily away and finally it was September. Every day she checked the calendar, heard the bells of the Catholic Church ring at eight, at midday, and at six; on Sundays she heard the Protestant bell. She listened always for the sounds of the house, but saw no one but Kathleen who brought her meals. She read and reread the same books from her shelf, Jane Austen, Stevenson, Dickens. She was appalled at how accustomed she had become to her prison. Sunny afternoons she watched for a black cat with a white spot on its breast to step delicately round the corner of the house opposite and settle in the sun. She looked at the larch tree in the garden on the other side of the street and saw the edges of its leaves had become dried and crinkled. When the sun moved round to the back of the house and dusk shadowed her room, another day was ending. When rain washed down the window, obscuring the view, she was unbearably sad. At night, she awoke drowned in sweat and with a strange metal taste in her mouth, as if she sucked a copper coin; and she thought they were trying to poison her. When Kathleen brought her breakfast she refused it. "Kathleen, I just want toast. Just dry toast."

"Are you sick Miss?"

"I just have no appetite."

Kathleen nodded her expression full of pity. "All right Miss."

Surely Kathleen wished her well. Victoria stood up to walk to the window and a wave of dizziness swept over her and her knees gave way.

41

Kathleen caught her and eased her back in the chair. "Take it easy, Miss. You'll be alright. I'll get your mother."

"No, Kathleen. No!"

"Alright, Miss. But get into bed."

She helped Victoria into bed, left and shortly returned with the toast. Victoria devoured it. Poisoning her? She must be mad to think that. She closed her eyes and saw her father's face, his mouth opening and closing, berating her. When she opened her eyes the window and the wardrobe were blurred. She picked up her book to read but her attention wandered, the lines on the page ran together. She stood up, walked round her room, then lay on her bed and wept.

One evening at the window, Victoria saw the Minister approach the house, heard her mother greet him in the hall, and the sitting room door close. She knew they were talking about her. Then she heard the Minister leave. What had he told her parents? What solution had he brought? Had he found some man willing to marry her? She was so helpless. Then her mother called her from the top of the stairs. "Come down, Victoria. We need to talk."

Her father stood with his back to the fireplace. Her mother walked over and stood beside him. "Reverend Gordon has found a place in the country for you. I hope you're grateful," her father announced.

"Where am I going?"

"A Mr. Andrew Wynne north of here, near the Meath Cavan border, needs a companion for his mother. He's agreed to have you. I want to hear no objections."

"I'm not objecting, Father. When do I go?"

"The sooner the better."

"Your father is right," her mother said. Her parents, whose relationship had always seemed somewhat formal and distant, were now united in an intimacy she had not seen previously, as if they had drawn together in their haste to be rid of her.

In reality, since their trip to Enniskillen, Margaret Mulholland sometimes detested Henry. She had stood beside him in the grey church on Bridge Street at the funeral service for her mother, dabbing her streaming eyes, knowing he was embarrassed by her weeping. And afterwards, in the old red brick terraced house, he had ignored her, talking to the other men in the back garden. Now, having informed his daughter of her fate, he walked through the hall and out of the house.

"Victoria, you will be going by train on Saturday. Reverend Gordon said you will be met at the other end. This is the best that can be done. Think of what you need to pack."

Margaret felt there was more she should say but didn't know how to begin. After her mother's funeral, her brother's wife had told her there had been a fire at their lumber yard and they had decided when the insurance money came through they would sell and move to the North. Margaret felt that would further distance her from her brother. She did not tell Victoria this. What she wished for was Victoria to have this pregnancy over, forgotten, and life, as it had been before, restored. Now Victoria turned back to go upstairs and Margaret could think of no parting word.

Friday Victoria spent another sleepless night tossing and turning, waiting for dawn. At seven her mother brought her breakfast tray and sat watching while Victoria ate. "The Reverend told us Mrs. Wynne is not an invalid, just elderly. Mr. Wynne is a farmer, a bachelor. And you'll get paid a monthly wage, which is a good thing, Victoria." Her mother smoothed her skirt nervously. "Of course the local maternity hospital will look after everything else."

"Like what, Mother?"

"Please Victoria! This is the usual thing. Reverend Gordon said they will arrange an adoption or The Department of Education Industrial Schools and Orphanages will take the child. Then you can come home and forget about it all."

Her mother stood up quickly. At the door she turned, "You had better get dressed now."

Getting dressed Victoria vowed never to return to her family, or have anything to do with them. But the thought that all this would be over by spring lifted her spirits a little.

When she was ready to leave her mother stood in the hall, stern faced. She handed Victoria a tiny cardboard box with gold lettering, *Mac Dowells The Happy Ring House*.

"You have to wear a ring, Victoria. You have to look respectable."

Meekly, like the desperate child she had become, Victoria put the ring on her finger and turned away. Her mother gently touched her arm, "Goodbye, Victoria."

Impatiently, her father jingled change in his pocket. From the top of the stairs Nicola called, "Tour-a loo kid. See you in the spring." Kathleen was nowhere to be seen.

Outside, the brilliant sky reeled above her. At the station her father put her suitcase in the baggage compartment and came back to where she was standing on the platform.

"Behave yourself with these people," he said sternly. He handed her the rail ticket, then held out his hand to say goodbye. Victoria turned away.

It was a slow journey in a stuffy railway carriage. She watched the moving shadow of the train, its plume of smoke thrown on the fields, then disappearing temporarily when the hedges were high. A young man seated beside her had his head and upper body hidden by the *Irish Press*. Across from her a sallow skinned middle-aged couple appeared to be praying, beads moving through their fingers. He wore black worsted trousers and a worn tweed jacket. The woman had black eyes and a hooked nose, wore a black dress and coat and sat with her thin feet on her suitcase. The sinews stood out in her sunburnt neck when she turned her head. He led and she answered turning toward him as she muttered the prayers. They each crossed themselves, put both rosaries in a small brown paper bag, which he then put in his pocket. They appeared so comfortable together, and Victoria watched, fascinated. It seemed barbaric, but also artless and simple and in some way it completed them as a pair. The ritual seemed primitive but look how nonchalantly they had performed it in public. She knew Kathleen had beads and said the rosary. Did Donny Maguire? That bastard never answered her letters. What use was praying? She had prayed as a child and read her bible but now she saw no purpose in it. She didn't believe it would help her who had lost everything: work, friends, home. And for what? Because she was pregnant and unmarried, and had not fulfilled her mother's dream of a brilliant marriage. She sat listening to the clack of the wheels and remembered the scene in Anna Karenina when Tolstoy's tragic heroine heard that same ominous rhythm. But it *was* 1937 and women didn't jump in front of trains because they were pregnant. She leaned her head back and looked at the black framed photographs above the cracked green leather seat, scenes of Bundoran and Tramore. The people in the carriage were going about their regular lives and she was hurtling to heaven knew what. What a fool she was. Suddenly she began to weep, tears overflowing her eyes, her shoulders shaking. The woman who had been praying stared at her for a minute then moved over and squeezed in beside her. "Are you alright, Missus?"

Victoria stared at her. Missus? Then she remembered her wedding ring. 'I'm fine, really I am," she protested, mopping her tears.

"Are you sure?"

"Yes, I'm sure."

The woman patted her shoulder and moved back. The man reading the paper gave her a surreptitious look. Victoria straightened up and pulled herself together. There had been no mention of an arranged marriage with this Mr. Wynne. It was a better solution than she had anticipated. By the end of February, it would be all over. She would return on this train, her figure normal again, this awful interval past and done with. She'd get her own flat, and never live in her father's house again. Everything to come in her life, all her future, would be an aftermath to this frightening trip into the unknown.

The train's whistle startled Victoria. She had fallen asleep. They were lurching through a level crossing then the train swung on between high banks and began to slacken speed until it crawled to a grinding halt at the platform across from a line of trees. The guard shouted, "This halt, *Killcore*"

Victoria stepped down and looked about her: one other traveller on the platform and a porter sweeping, and in the station yard, a horse and trap and a green sloped-backed Morris, a trailer behind. A man in an oilskin jacket over a rough collarless blue and white striped shirt and blue serge trousers stood in the light misty rain beside the car. Was this Andrew Wynne? He didn't look like a landowner. When he saw her, he dropped the cigarette from his hand and stepped on it. "Miss Mulholland?"

"Yes," said Victoria.

"I'm the servant boy, Miss. Dominic's the name."

He looked to be a little older than she was. Red hair and blue eyes in a freckled face and a faint red stubble on his cheeks caught the sun. When he smiled, his front teeth were slightly crossed over one another.

"I'm sorry you had to wait in the rain."

"That's all right. It rains often here, seldom lasts though. I had to come in to Killcore anyways. Do you have a suitcase or anything, Miss?"

"Yes. A trunk in the baggage car."

Dominic opened the back door for her and went to see about her trunk. The station was a low grey stone building with a green roof and doors. Beyond the station yard she could see the white globe of a petrol pump. Dominic and the porter came back carrying her trunk between them and lifted it on to the trailer. They drove slowly out of the station yard through the town, farm carts drawn up to the footpath, a few young lads standing at the corner, past a line of terrace houses then out into the country, by cottages and a grey stone church its graveyard neglected with long uncut grass and old yew trees. The road bent left beyond the graveyard and a hundred yards further Dominic halted at the closed gates of a level crossing. A train thundered past. The gatekeeper opened the gates and waved them on. The car veered west, into a narrow white winding road that curved around the side of a low hill. Dominic drove sitting forward in the seat, swaying from side to side as the car took the turns in the road. From the back seat, thick hedges formed a green tunnel and hid the landscape from her as the car gained on the slope. They emerged into the light of a high cloud littered sky having driven out of the rain. To the left the flank of the hill, and in the sloping fields cattle moved through the daisy-dotted grass grazing or lay together in great contented blobs in the shade at the hedges. Below them was a black slate roof and chimneys in a nest of trees.

"There's it now below Miss. Beechwood. Still standing!"

She leaned forward as the car began a slow descent past the cow pastures. As they came down the hill the hedges again obscured the house, the road curved down past a large white stone house, then thatched white washed cottages, and a little further they turned in through open gates hung on two crumbling piers, past a derelict gatehouse. The car proceeded up the beech lined drive and swung round in a curve before the house, the wheels scoring furrows in the gravel. She could see that the hill rose gently behind the house and from its grey limestone heap twelve windows faced south over a terrace and gardens.

7

Jim Jams

A heavy oak door opened onto an inner glass door which gave onto a dark hall. Antlers above an old fashioned mirror looked across at a table and a grandfather clock. They passed closed doors on either side and into the brightness of a big room.

"If you wouldn't mind waiting here in the Square Room, I'll tell Josie, and I'll leave your trunk above in your room, Miss," Dominic said departing.

Josie must be the housekeeper, Victoria thought, sitting in her loose yellow dress. She looked at her feet, puffed over the straps of her shoes. She hoped Josie would not notice. Tight shoes showed some neglect on her part and she desperately wanted to make a good impression. Victoria hardly noticed the dilapidated white cane furniture, animal skins on the worn dark floorboards, tiger's eyes glittering. There was an ancient gold tasselled fringe over the top of two narrow windows and glass doors led to a domed conservatory, which opened to a side garden. The garden had tall grass, a six foot stone wall, and a garden bench in front of the wall with its green paint peeling. Laurel and rhododendron showed above the wall from the other side, and beyond tree top apples shining in the sun. Victoria started at the click of dog nails on the hall tiles. Two red setters trotted in and sniffed her skirt and then a tall, stooped man came toward her. The elbows of his baggy knitted jumper, which he wore over threadbare twill trousers, were worn through. He came forward holding out his hand. The dogs retreated and sat up in the doorway of the conservatory. "Andrew Wynne, Miss Mulholland. How was the journey?"

"It was fine." Her mouth was dry, her voice hoarse.

"Well, we're glad you're here. Mother will be happy to have you. May I call you Victoria?"

"Please do," she said, recovering her voice, which seemed to her own ears too eager.

"Sit Sally," he said sharply to one of the dogs that had run forward, tail wagging. The dog went back and sat beside the other. The man looked at her closely. "You will not find your duties too onerous. Mother is quite reasonable most of the time. Just sometimes in the late evenings she has a fit of the jim-jams and needs someone to stay with her. Think you can manage that?"

"I'm sure I can."

Jim-jams? Was the woman a dipsomaniac? She hoped not. Her Aunt Nicola sometimes drank too much gin, but she was never difficult, just stayed in her room and slept. What had she gotten into? What awaited her here? She watched his melancholy hound-like face, to see if he glanced at her figure, if her thickened waistline registered on his countenance as she had thought she had seen it do with others. But the grave grey eyes held hers for a minute. His lank grey hair needed cutting. Then he said, "She's in her sitting room. I'll take you up."

He led her back into the hall and the dogs pushed at each other to get ahead. "Stay!" he told them and they went back and turned their heads to watch him and Victoria mount a staircase that turned onto a wide landing. She saw a bow window, old prints of hunting scenes on the walls, doors either side and a passage leading back to the rest of the house.

"This is your room on the right and here is Mother's sitting room."

He knocked once and opened the door. A white haired woman sat at a table spread with playing cards. She was tiny, her loose blue dress reached almost to her ankles, the blue cardigan to below her hips. The same grey eyes as her son, hers cloudy and vague.

"Mother, this is Victoria."

"How do you do?" The old woman held out her hand.

"Victoria is going to stay with us for awhile, and keep you company."

"Do you like cards?"

"I've played a little whist."

"Victoria might like to wash up after her journey, Mother."

"Of course."

"I'll leave you to it," he said and left.

The old woman said, "The bathroom is just back along the passage way. It's the second door. Do you think you can find it?"

"Oh I'm sure I can."

Anxious to get away from the woman's solemn stare, Victoria retraced her steps, her handbag clutched in her hand. She opened the first door, holding the doorknob tight so as not to make any noise. Her trunk was under the window. There was a wardrobe with a long mirror set in the door, an iron bed with brass knobs on the headpiece, and a chair at the fireplace. She closed the door gently and tried the next one. An enormous deep copper bathtub, a porcelain sink, a high lavatory.

When she returned Mrs. Wynne was standing at the front window clutching the curtain. "It's a beautiful afternoon," she said and from a writing desk under the west window, she took a pack of playing cards from a drawer and handed them to Victoria. "I'm amusing myself with Patience," she said as she sat down, and with her small arthritic hand swiped the cards from the table, shuffled them and began to lay down the first row. Not knowing what else was expected, Victoria put her handbag on the floor, sat opposite her and began to lay down her own cards.

The front window faced south and late afternoon light flooded the room. The fireplace grate was filled with green branches, on the mantelpiece two reared horses held aloft an ormolu clock. Two shabby armchairs and a book trough sat beside the writing desk under the west window. Victoria noted the jumble: George Elliot, Trollope, Dickens, and almost wept at the thought of her lost job. But she told herself she would get all this over and rebuild her life. That thought left her feeling so raw and uprooted. But this had to be better than the jail of her bedroom in Blackrock.

The house was at the head of a shallow valley. Through the south window she could see over the terrace and the sundial, two willows and a monkey puzzle tree, a lawn marked with roller lines, clumps of pampas grass, pale, exotic, rising from their green base, waving in the breeze. West of the lawn the tree lined drive, and beyond that was the long slope of the fields she had seen on her way in. Victoria was hungry. When would they have tea? Mrs. Wynne was completely absorbed in her cards. She wore old fashioned jet earrings, the pierced holes of her ears encrusted. This seemed pathetic to Victoria. "How did you get here?" Mrs. Wynne asked, her eyes still on the cards.

"I came on the train."

"And did you have a good journey?"

"Yes, I did"

Mrs. Wynne put down another card. "Doubtless you would like some tea."

49

"Yes please. I would, very much."

"It's almost tea time. Let's go down and see Josie."

She rose and led the way out of the room. She pointed to a door opposite. "That's my bedroom, Victoria"

They went along the landing and down the stairs by the Square Room now flooded with early evening light, and back along the narrow passage past two closed doors and through a baize door to the kitchen.

Josie Mulligan sat at the kitchen table, her greying hair drawn back in a bun from her long plain red face. She was shelling peas, slitting the curved pods with her thumbnail and turning them inside out to squeeze the peas into a bowl she held on her lap. She put the bowl on the big deal table and stood up, wiping her hands in her white apron.

"Josie, this is Victoria."

"Yes Ma'am."

She avoided Victoria's eyes but glanced at her belly and then at the ring on her finger. Victoria felt a hot flush suffuse her face and neck.

"We'd like some tea now." Mrs. Wynne said.

"Yes Ma'am."

"Can I help you with it?" Victoria asked.

"No! I'll bring it up." Josie turned and filled a copper kettle at the sink and slammed it on the big black Stanley range. A clothes drying rack draped with tea towels and two white aprons hung on pulleys from the ceiling over the range. Mrs. Wynne walked over and looked out at the eastern sky through the bank of low windows over the sink. Then she turned back. "Alright Josie. And we'd like some sandwiches too, egg and parsley, and if we have any, cucumber." She walked back the way she had come and Victoria followed, feeling dismissed by the housekeeper.

They sat again at the table and Mrs. Wynne said, "Josie can be headstrong but she has a good heart."

She gathered up the cards, held her hand out for Victoria's and put both packs back in the drawer of the writing table. Mrs. Wynne turned toward the side window. "We have a fine crop this year," she said.

Behind the high stone wall, men were working. Andrew Wynne, in a battered lacquered straw hat, was standing on a ladder picking apples. Dominic was picking on another tree just beyond him. They were handing the bags of apples down to a heavyset lad who packed them in boxes stacked on a cart. Mrs. Wynne sat gazing out at the men. Soon they heard stout steps on the landing and Josie entered with a tea tray and placed it on the table.

"Thank you Josie."

"No bother at all, Ma'am."

The rectangular wooden tray had a raised edge and dull metal handles. There were sandwiches and scones and damson jam. Victoria was so ravenous she had to restrain herself from falling on the food.

"You have the sandwiches my dear. I just want a scone."

After tea they sat in the lovely September evening light, the old woman nodding off from time to time, awaking with a start to sit staring ahead and then dozing again. Victoria stood up and looked out the window. In the orchard the men went on picking apples. She wondered where they sold them. Their destination could be Lenehan's greengrocer where Kathleen shopped for the family, or Findlaters. Blackrock seemed so far away and remembering the days as prisoner in her bedroom she was glad to be gone from there.

When the light began to fade Mrs. Wynne got up and put a match to a small lamp on the dressing table and Victoria said, "I should take the tray down."

"Thank you, dear."

The kitchen was cosy now, filled with the smell of roasting meat, the two wall lamps lighted and glowing on the worn red tiles.

"Josie, I could help you with the dinner preparations," Victoria offered.

"I'll manage," Josie declared, slamming pot lids about. "Dominic helps me. You see to your own business, see to Mrs. Wynne."

Victoria was stunned. What kind of a servant spoke like this? Why had she done that? She should have asked Mrs. Wynne before offering to help the maid. She went back upstairs and sat again opposite her charge.

When they went down to dinner just before eight, Mrs. Wynne appeared perfectly well able to see to herself. Andrew Wynne had changed into tan trousers, a green tweed jacket and a pale green shirt, a dark tie. He seemed a different person, more sophisticated. To Victoria he looked like a Trinity professor. They sat at a long old mahogany table in the dining room, Mrs. Wynne at one end, her son at the other and Victoria facing the huge sideboard with its smoky mirror. There was salad of lettuce, beets and tomatoes arranged on three plates. Victoria hesitated, unsure, not wanting to lead. Then Josie appeared with a loaded tray and, in spiteful triumph, arranged serving plates and a gravy boat on the sideboard.

"Thank you, Josie," said the old woman.

"The gravy's thin, like you'd like it, Ma'am."

Andrew rose and served his mother beef, peas and roast potatoes.

"Victoria, would you like to serve yourself?"

She put a slice of beef and some potatoes on her plate and sat down. Andrew filled his own plate.

"The blessing, Andy."

"For what we are about to receive may the Lord make us truly thankful. Amen."

Mrs. Wynne lifted her knife and fork and then the others began too. Salad was eaten after the main course in this household.

Two darkened cracked portraits stared down on them from one end of the long room: Wynne forebears, Victoria thought. The window at the other end looked out on the garden where the wind stirred the fronds of the willows that hung down like the hair of a tragedienne in an old tale. The late evening sky was the darkest blue above the trees. A host of crows swooped like a black cloud and pecked on the grass. A pair of low candles on the table and four tall ones on the sideboard gave a light so frail that Victoria felt they should whisper. Andrew Wynne's voice boomed from his end of the table reporting to his mother. "The herd is doing well, excellent milk yield."

"And the creamery cheque Andy?"

"Satisfactory, Mother. Never as much as we'd like, but satisfactory."

"And the hay, Andrew?"

"Saved, Mother. In weeks ago now."

The old woman ate slowly, like a well brought up child, putting her knife and fork down between each bite. To Victoria, the meal seemed endless, the food heavy, the vegetables thick with butter and cream. No refreshment was offered except water. Then Josie arrived with a coffee pot and dessert.

"You're better without coffee, Mother. Josie will bring you some tea."

"I prefer coffee, Andy."

Josie came back with the teapot. Andrew poured her tea. "It's too weak."

"Now, Mother!"

Mrs. Wynne took a sip of her tea, put the cup back on the saucer and looked up reproachfully at her son.

"Victoria's from Blackrock, Mother."

"Isn't that where James Gordon's son is?"

"It's his grandson, Mother."

Victoria felt a hot blush of shame on her face and in the low light met Andrew Wynne's eyes. Her own slid away. Had the minister begun by suggesting marriage between herself and this man? The man was old enough to be her father. Had the man rejected the idea but offered her a home instead for the duration? She read nothing in his unconcerned gaze. Mortified, she sat looking at her plate and then heard him say, "The pudding is not half bad. May I serve you a little?"

She nodded quickly, knew she seemed too eager to please, and watched him carefully put a serving of blackberry and apple crisp on a plate and put it before her. It seemed to her that there was the agitation and tension of things unspoken and unexplained between them. Her position felt very vulnerable, her claim to be there flimsy. She was in a situation of almost total dependence, with nowhere else to go. But, she reassured herself, quickly, in February, barely five months, she would be gone.

Then Andrew said, "I haven't been to Dublin for a long time. But I loved to go there years ago. I used to go often, in the Twenties. I knew the city like the back of my hand."

He seemed a little wistful when he said this. Dressed as he was tonight Victoria could see him in Dublin.

When dinner was finished Andrew poured three small glasses of port and they went across the hall into the drawing room, each carrying a candle from the dining room. Mrs. Wynne sat in a fireside chair and motioned Victoria to sit in another. Andrew put a match to the paper and kindling in the fireplace. Then he sat behind them and patiently turned the stubby knobs of the wireless set searching through the repeating frequencies for the BBC. Josie and Dominic could be heard talking as they cleared the dining room table. There was faint light from the candles on the mantelpiece and the firelight cast melancholy shadows. In the far dusk of the room Andrew's cigarette glowed intermittently, and in the quiet, the uneven pitch of the radio announcer's voice filled the room. When the nine o'clock news was over Andrew switched off the wireless and came over to leave his empty glass on a table. "I'm going to turn in. Mother, you do the same. Victoria will help you. Good night now."

Mrs. Wynne continued sitting looking at the fire. "Perhaps you should think of getting ready for bed," Victoria ventured.

The woman looked at her with a frank almost childlike expression. "No."

"It's getting a little late. It's almost ten."

"No."

They sat on by the dying fire. Victoria felt some tension in the woman. She wished she would retire to bed but did not know how to broach the subject. "Are you not tired?" she asked.

"I'm always tired."

"Then you should rest. Come upstairs and I'll help you get undressed."

Mrs. Wynne stood up from the chair and turned and took a candle from the mantelpiece, Victoria took the other and they went out to the hall together. A small oil lamp burned on the hall table. They went up the stairs and when they reached the turn Mrs. Wynne said, "Who'll keep watch?"

"Keep watch for what?"

"Keep watch on the house."

"There's no need for anyone to watch. We're all here."

"We must check for fire."

Their candle flames leaned toward each other in the gloom. Mrs. Wynne's face was the grimace of a child about to cry. She looked as if she might run. Victoria took her elbow to guide her on to the landing and to her bedroom but she broke away and ran back down the stairs, one hand clutching the railing the candle wavering dangerously in the other. Victoria ran after her. The old woman put her candle on the hall table. Victoria put hers beside it. She considered calling Andrew, or Josie. It was early, hardly ten, but the house was silent. Then Mrs. Wynne was through the glass door and pulling back the bolts on the front door.

"It's dark, Mrs. Wynne. Don't go out."

She had the heavy door open and was outside. A high full moon lit the old woman hurrying down the steps, over the gravel and into the maw of darkness that was the avenue, Victoria following the pale blur of her dress. At the gates Mrs. Wynne halted, then walked round the derelict gatehouse. The dew that lay like hoarfrost on the grass soaked their shoes; Victoria felt brambles scratch her legs. "Let's go back Mrs. Wynne. Please," and she took her arm. The woman pulled away, ran quickly to the right through the orchard, then turned back again and up the avenue. Victoria felt she was going back, and that the ordeal was over but when they neared the house she veered off into the lane that ran round to the yard and slowed looking up at the house, its chimneys huge against the sky. "I'll look through the yard, Victoria."

Victoria was startled that the woman remembered her name, so strange and mad her actions seemed. They walked almost leisurely together through the black shadows into the outbuildings. Long daubs of moonlight entered through open doors. Victoria heard the jangling cow chains and smelt the rich, bovine breath. In the stable a horse snorted. She smelt the manure heap and heard, in the hen house at the back, the stirring and cluck of disturbed fowl. Anthracite gleamed in the moonlight when they shoved open the coal shed door. In the milking parlour, the machine hoses dangled sinisterly and the tiled floor glittered. A black cat crept out and startled Victoria but Mrs. Wynne stooped and carried the animal. They walked back to the house seeing the predatory shadow of an owl on the cobbles and Victoria looked up and thought madly, "The Owl and The Pussycat."

Mrs. Wynne took the path on the east of the house round the greenhouse and in by the front door. She gently set the cat on the floor. "There you go, Mog."

Their candles still burned on the hall table. "You must go to bed now Mrs. Wynne."

"I'll sleep now."

She trailed up the stairs. Her wet shoes left footprints on the worn stair carpet; the cat crawled behind her. Victoria took the two candles from the hall table and followed. There was a lighted candle in the bedroom and the coal fire had burned down to a red clump. Mrs. Wynne collapsed in a low chair. "I want to wash my feet."

Victoria crossed to the washstand, poured water from the big heavy blue jug into the basin and put the basin on the floor in front of her charge. "The water is cool, I'm afraid. Would you like me to go downstairs and boil a kettle?"

"It's fine. The room is warm."

She removed her stockings, put her feet in the basin and instinctively Victoria knelt on the floor and sponged the woman's blue corded feet. Then she dried them.

"I put a little ointment on them," Mrs. Wynne said pointing at a tin of Zam Buk herbal balm on the shelf of the washstand. Victoria rubbed a little ointment on her feet and Mrs. Wynne walked over and climbed on her bed, put on bed socks that had been left on her pillow, slipped under the clothes, put her head down and closed her eyes. "Oh, the comfort of a hot water jar."

"Aren't you going to undress?"

"No. I'm too tired tonight."

The cat blinked her green eyes from the hearth rug. Mrs. Wynne patted the eiderdown and the cat jumped on the bed and settled beside her. "Bedtime Mog," she said and stroked the cat, neck to tail; Mog purred like a motor. Victoria pulled the eiderdown up over Mrs. Wynne's shoulders. "Quench my candle, Victoria. Thank you. Good night."

Victoria took her own candle, shut the door, went across to her assigned room, kicked off her shoes and lay on her bed. Her feet touched the hard hot porcelain through its quilted cover. So she had a hot water bottle too. No fire, just a fan of red crepe paper in the fireplace, but the room was not cold. She sat up and peeled off her wet stockings, took her candle and her wash bag and tiptoed along the passage to the bathroom, furious with Andrew. What a nerve to leave her like that without warning or explanation. And her parents? How could they have dumped her here? My God, a mad woman. And an ogress in the kitchen! All that was missing was Mr. Rochester.

In the bathroom she splashed cold water on her face, brushed her teeth and went back to her room. Tomorrow she would speak to Andrew Wynne, demand to be driven to the railway station and the train. Even at the risk of disgrace her parents would have to accept her. One thing was clear she wasn't staying here. There had to be somewhere else she could go, some boarding house in a country town, or a charity hostel or those RC Laundries, if they would take her. The baby would be adopted and she would begin a new life, shed this madhouse like a dress she had inadvertently put on. She closed her tired eyes and slipped into sleep, with her last thought of her bedroom at home in Blackrock.

In Blackrock, her mother lay sleepless thinking of Victoria, her youngest, her prettiest. What did they know about the Wynnes? Only what Arthur Gordon, their minister, had told them that they were highly respectable people, Church of Ireland. Henry had acquiesced at once, eager to be rid of his daughter before her disgrace was known. Past the worry that someone would discover the truth, Margaret now admitted to herself that she too was relieved to be rid of Victoria. She wept quietly, remembering when she could not imagine a solution and had almost wished her daughter dead. How glibly the lies came out of her mouth when she told friends Victoria was gone to England to take up a position. Now, she wished she could go and see Victoria. But it was out of the question. Henry would never permit it. He had no patience with sentiment. He was still very angry and he had never mentioned Victoria's name since he'd taken her to the train. Margaret remembered Victoria as a little girl. How precocious she had been, how early she had talked and walked. How helpless a mother was and how she loathed her husband now.

As light began to creep up over the houses from the sea, she slipped out of bed and went downstairs. She sat at the sitting room window and watched the street. She saw the light come on in the house opposite, and the neighbour emerge to walk his dog. Kathleen left her bedroom beyond the kitchen and as she tiptoed through the hall to go upstairs to the bathroom she saw Margaret. "Is everything alright, Ma'am?"

"Everything's fine, I just woke early."

"Will I make you a cup of tea, Ma'am?"

"No thanks. Just go on with what you are doing."

Kathleen turned and went up the stairs, knowing a lot more than Margaret suspected. Apart from Nicola, who kept a taciturn silence, there was not a person in the world Margaret could confide in, except Kathleen. And it was unthinkable for her to speak intimately to a servant.

Victoria woke from the soundest sleep she had had in months, immediately aware of the strange bed, still in her daytime clothes. She ignored the awful hollow of anxiety within her and considered the day ahead. She was leaving! She had not unpacked her trunk so there was nothing to pack. Grey light edged the window blind; she sat up, struck a match from the box on the table and lit the candle. A quarter to seven by her watch. The mirror in the huge old wardrobe reflected the wavering candle, Victoria in the bed and the window beyond. The fireplace and the dressing table loomed in the darkness. The big house Sunday silent. It's an hour, at least, before she can decently get up and speak to Andrew. She quenched the candle and turned on her side, her limbs soft, relaxed. She had a long day ahead and she tried to sleep, picturing herself talking to Andrew, Dominic driving her to the train.

Almost asleep she felt a ripple in her side, a flutter, as if a tiny fish, a minnow, flashed in still water, under the arch of her ribs. What was that? She held her breath, lay very still, waiting. No sensation at all. She had imagined it. Then, as if a bird had fluttered its wing, had touched her swiftly, gently, a feather stroke just beneath her heart. The child. How marvellous. The child alive! She tried to picture her internal landscape. Where is it? What does it look like? Did that miniscule being have a heart, the blood flowing in and out beating, as hers was now, fast, excited? She waited for the child to move again and as it did she realized she had ceased wishing to be rid of it. She thought of it as something rare, precious, unique to that moment, and was grateful to be alone to contemplate the idea of it. Outside, a dawn bird gave a wistful warble, just once, and then again more urgently. A robin. Territorial even now, in autumn. Victoria began to weep, softly, not in sorrow, but overwhelmed by sheer astonishment, the wonder of it. Kathleen's words came back to her. "You'd have the baby to keep."

Her trunk was underneath the window and when she opened it for an instant it seemed the contents belonged to someone else. When was it she had packed that plaid dressing gown and slippers, the loose green dress? Just yesterday? She undressed, put on the dressing gown and slippers, and took her soap bag. Outside Mrs. Wynne's door she listened. No sound at all. Cautiously she opened it. A drift of eau de Cologne, Mrs. Wynne turned away from her, asleep. She closed the door and made her way along the landing to the bathroom. When she ran the water it was warm, the boiler already going. Victoria bathed and brushed her teeth. In the wavy mirror over the basin she saw her hair was growing out, its stiff Marcel wave obliterated by the heedless curls clustering untidily around her head. She had hated that artificial wave. She had to think, to sort things out. Back in her room she removed her dressing gown. She looked at her naked reflection in the dressing table mirror. Just under her waist a high bulge, faint blue markings. How interesting! She had not gained weight, but she had a different shape. Why is it shameful? The weeks in her parent's house, forced to hide and masquerade as something she was not, made her something she did not want to be: something less than herself, turned her into a punished child. Here in this bizarre household no one knows her, nor cares about her. She's free. And she is going to have this child. She is not giving it up. She put on her slip and the loose green dress and, checking herself in the glass, saw that the deep green of the dress had transformed her. Her blonde hair had grown and was running riotous around her flushed freckled face. Excitement rushed through her. She ran a brush through her hair and put on some lipstick, ready to face the household. In a sudden rush of curiosity on her way downstairs, she turned to explore the back of the house. She tiptoed past the bathroom. Up three steps, the corridor was quite wide and on the east side were three low windows. Two doors led off the corridor on the west and at the end another door. The house was L shaped, one wing stretching back. There were two wooden armchairs with worn needlepoint cushions in front of the windows. She sat and looked out through the soft cover of mist drifting off the hill. How strange it seemed, deserted except for ghostly blobs of grazing sheep. How far away from home she was. A jumble of emotions raced through her, one jostling another. She wanted to go home, to turn the clock back, to be working in the library again. She didn't want to be pregnant and afraid and at the same time, she was speculating about having the baby. She sensed the beginning of something new. Somehow she felt she was on the other side of some obstacle. The second door opened and Andrew Wynne came towards her. She stood, a little embarrassed to be there.

"Good morning, Victoria. Sleep well?"

"Very well."

"Sit a minute, it's a lovely morning."

She sat back down and he took the other chair, and they looked out at the morning. "It rained in the night. But the fog is lifting fast."

His long face was tired, a blue bruised look around his grey eyes, his hair falling carelessly over his forehead. He was dressed in last night's jacket and trousers. "Are those your sheep?" she asked, feeling the need to say something.

"They belong to my neighbour, George Mac Adam. He has the farm just beyond us." Then a smile transformed his face, "But that's my heaven kissing hill. It's grand when the sun shines on it."

She wanted to say something about last night, about his mother's behaviour, but the remark about the hill has disarmed her. Already last night felt a long time ago, elapsed time and the fresh morning diminishing the strangeness of the night. Maybe it was less mad than it seemed. The woman was, after all, only checking her property.   Andrew broke the silence. "I should have warned you about mother, about how she sometimes goes strange at night. But I thought I would leave it to you and Josie."

"Josie? She never showed her face."

He seemed taken aback, "I suppose she expects you to shoulder it all." His grey eyes held hers. There were yellow flecks in the pupils.

"Why did you not tell me?'

"I hardly knew how. I suppose you're leaving now."

His long hand rested limp on his thighs, the hangdog expression on his face implied her leaving was his fault.

"It would have been better if you had explained things to me, if you had stayed up a little longer, not left me alone."

"I'm sorry Victoria, but I just can't deal with my mother, I just can't. I can't bear to see her like that. I expected Josie would help get her to bed."

"How long has she been like that?"

"About four months. Pat Curran, our medical man, comes every few weeks. He doesn't know what to do with her. He'd put her in the asylum like a shot if I consented to that, but I won't. Most of the time my mother is fine. Just sometimes at night she behaves very strangely."

"How do you mean very strangely?"

"She has an idea someone is going to burn the house down and she goes running round the outbuildings like a crazy woman. It's impossible to persuade her that those days are over, she lives so much in the past."

"That's what she did last night. I had no idea what to do and I just went along with her. It was awful."

"And now you're giving up on us."

"I didn't know what to expect, what my responsibilities are."

"I'm sorry about that, Victoria."

Victoria realised they needed her to watch the old woman and she had five months to make her plans. "Andrew, I'm willing to stay. I have little choice. You know my situation."

He shifted in his chair, a little uncomfortable when she said this.

"I haven't had an easy time, Andrew."

Now he looked penitent. "I know that."

"I just need to know what is expected of me."

"I just need you to be a companion to my mother. Read to her sometimes; she likes that. Most of the time she's a very sweet lady and often she goes quietly to bed, especially if she has gone for a walk in the evening. And for some reason she is less frantic if it happens to be raining."

"I'll stay, Andrew."

He stood up quickly. "That's just great. Mother won't wake for several hours. Come down and we'll see what Josie has for breakfast."

She went with him down the stairs and back through the passage and the baize door to the big kitchen. It was warm and morning light came through the windows over the sink. A pan was sizzling on the range and Josie was slicing soda bread at the table.

"Good morning, Josie."

"Good morning sir."

"I'm going to show Victoria around before breakfast. Come along now Victoria."

He led her out the side door and through the scullery and the back porch into the cobblestone yard. Victoria now saw more clearly than the previous night the layout of the property. The house had been built in two parts, a main building which she had seen when she arrived and a wing leading back toward the farm buildings.

"The house is over a hundred years old but the wing was added about thirty years ago. I think my father intended to extend it further but never got around to it."

The farm buildings looked smaller and less sinister than the previous night. He pushed open a door in a long low building. "This is the old dairy. We no longer churn. The milk goes straight to the creamery."

Cobwebs netted over the old cream separator and the big tumble churn, and wooden butter paddles lay jumbled together on a table.

"We no longer use this place. Of course before the war we had lots of help here. Now we just have Dominic and Matt Fitzsimons, a local lad. He helps on weekdays. The milk herd is our big earner. It takes almost all of Dominic's time, and quite a lot of mine too."

He showed her the milking parlour and the machines. A generator fed by four huge batteries ran the milking machine and provided power for two light bulbs hanging from a beam in the roof.

"Of course," he said, "I would like to have electric light in the other buildings and in the house, but we don't have enough power. We scarcely have enough battery power to run the milking machines."

In spite of herself Victoria was interested. Then Andrew said, "We should see if breakfast is ready. Then I have to give Dominic a hand before we go to church. Do you wish to go to church, Victoria?"

"Will your mother go?"

"Not if she was as late settling to bed as you told me. But if you wish to go to church Josie can stay with her and Dominic will drive her to twelve o'clock mass."

She had no wish to meet new people, to be introduced to neighbours. She imagined their curiosity, the gossip. "I don't think I want to go to church."

"That's fine then. Dominic and Josie go to half ten mass and drop me at church on the way and afterwards wait for me till service is over. "

In the kitchen, Josie put a tea cosy on the teapot and placed it on the tray with a plate of sliced soda bread. Andrew carried the tray into the dining room and put the bread and the teapot in the centre of the table. He lifted the lid of a dish on the sideboard and they helped themselves to bacon sausages and black puddings.

"Let's eat," Andrew said, pulling his chair out. Victoria sat down opposite him and held out her cup and saucer when he offered to pour.

"You'll find it quiet here after Blackrock."

"I'm glad to be here, glad to be away from home."

"I'm sure you are," he said, his expression so frank and open it stopped her cold. This was the first time anyone has accepted her and her pregnancy at face value. The relief was so great she almost wept. To cover her emotions she got up from the table and stood biting her lower lip and put another rasher of bacon on her plate but when she looked in the mirror on the sideboard she saw he was still looking at her with the same expression.

"My mother won't wake 'til near noon so you have some time to yourself."

"I haven't unpacked yet so I'll do that."

He ate quickly, then said, "I'd better be getting along," and left the table.

Victoria sat there feeling anxious and tense, and completely on her own in this house. She looked at the men in the two cracked portraits. One was a young man in the uniform of an Indian cavalry regiment; his straight hair, large eyes, and long face resembled Andrew. The other was a thin older man with a short white beard. The room was less intimidating than it had seemed the previous night, for the furniture was old, and the tablecloth mended at one corner. What should she be doing? After a few minutes she got up, took the tray Andrew had left leaning against the sideboard, piled the dishes on it and took it to the kitchen. She filled the sink with hot water, swirled the soap cage round in the water and put the dishes in to soak. Josie was nowhere to be seen. Leaving the dishes she went upstairs and from the landing window saw Dominic and Andrew sitting in the car in the drive. Josie emerged from the shadow of the house and sat in the back seat and they drove off. Suddenly, she felt free and wanted to explore this house. She quietly opened Mrs. Wynne's bedroom door. She was still sleeping. Then she tiptoed back along the corridor and opened the first door beyond the bathroom. A linen cupboard, its shelves built around the copper hot water cistern. She opened the next door. It was almost a replica of her room: big old brass bed, a huge wardrobe, a washstand, and a wooden chair. Here with the addition of a tallboy, it was clearly Andrew's room. She closed the door quietly and then tried the one at the end of the corridor. It opened inward onto stairs, the steps leading up and down. She followed the steps up to the next floor. Up here the ceilings were lower, with a small round window at the end of the landing and two doors leading off it. She looked in the first room, saw it was obviously Josie's, with a holy water font fastened to the wall inside the door just as in Kathleen's room in Blackrock, and Josie's apron and dress on a chair. The slanted attic ceiling leaned over the black iron bed. The candlewick bedspread neatly tucked in, a small wardrobe and a mirror on the wall, a servant's room. She expected the next room would be Dominic's but when she opened the door she discovered it was not in use. Where did Dominic sleep? The room was dark, the tasselled cretonne curtains closed. The angles of the attic walls threw deep shadows on a bed frame covered with a yellowed dustsheet, a book trough beside the bed with the books jammed tightly into it, Dickens, Trollope, Conrad and, to her astonishment, Flaubert and Zola. What about the Censorship Board? Where had they come from?

A case of butterflies sat under the window, the glass almost opaque with dust and on the wall over the mantelpiece, framed tinted photographs. A group of boys in tennis flannels, Andrew among them. A snap of men and girls on a terrace: the girls in mid-calf length dresses with dropped waists and wide white hairbands of the pre-war fashion. A photograph of two boys in school uniform, clearly Andrew and a boy who resembled him. A later photograph of one in army uniform. The room had obviously not been used for a very long time but brushes still sat in the dust on the old dressing chest. Worried that the old woman might wake she closed the door gently and crept down the stairs. All quiet on the second floor. She opened the door of Mrs. Wynne's room again. She could hear her heavy breathing; she was still sleeping. She slipped downstairs to the main floor and opened the first door in the kitchen passage way. It appeared to be Andrew's study: a narrow room with a roll top desk and chair, and a gramophone, a stack of records and a bible on a table under the widow. The bible was open at The First Book of Samuel, Chapter 16 and a verse was underlined - *for the Lord seeth not as men seeth; for man looketh on the outward appearance, but the Lord looketh on the heart.* Well she certainly hoped so, she with her belly getting bigger by the day! Two shabby armchairs upholstered in worn blue striped material stood before the fireplace and above the mantelpiece a large framed photograph. The curtains were drawn and it was difficult to see. She went closer, a young bearded man in an old fashioned high collar and striped coat. Had she seen that photograph before? On the mantelpiece were three books, FS Hartnell's *All About Railways*, Aymer Maxwell's *Pheasants and Covert Shooting*, and another bible. A door opposite the fireplace was ajar and she walked through into the next room and saw that it was Dominic's bedroom: an iron bed the ornamental markings on the head picked out in flaking yellow paint, no wardrobe; Dominic's oilskin coat and his work clothes hung on hooks behind the door. His Wellington boots under a chair. Was the adjoining study Dominic's? Couldn't be, had to be Andrew's. Last night when Mrs. Wynne was running round the grounds was Dominic here? Was Josie in her room on the third floor? Was she watching them from the window? Victoria went back into the passage and on to the kitchen pondering the silence and the strangeness of this house. How little she knew about these people. Whose was that neglected room on the third floor? Had Andrew been in the army? Had one of those girls in the photographs been his sweetheart? Where were they all now? From the clothes the photographs seemed to be more than twenty years old. She went back upstairs to unpack. In her bedroom, she thought, if Mrs. Wynne had got up and found her prowling about, what explanation could she have given? Why was she always acting without thinking? She promised herself never to do that again.

8

The Confession of Sins

Saucebottle knelt in the pew before the confessional waiting his turn. He heard the slot inside slide over, the curtain moved and he stood aside to let the young woman who emerged pass. He took her place on the kneeler behind the curtain. He heard the murmur of prayers and the wicket door on the far side close, then the one on his side open. He raced through the ritual, "Bless me Father for I have sinned. It's four weeks since my last confession."

He watched the silhouette of Father Hanrahan's face, the long nose, the jutting forehead and began the recitation of his sins. The priest sat motionless.

"I missed mass Sunday. I stole a shilling."

"Anything else?"

"No Father."

"No impure thoughts about girls?"

"No Father."

"Or about boys, about men?"

For some reason, the question left Saucebottle a little sad. "No Father."

"And no touching yourself impiously?

"No Father."

"When you get your wages, make restitution for the shilling, and don't miss mass again. For your penance say three Our Fathers and three Hail Marys."

Father Hanrahan made the sign of the cross, muttered the absolution and Saucebottle begins his Act of Contrition. "*Oh my God I am heartily sorry for all my sins*"... and he's out of there kneeling in the pew saying his penance. A clean slate. Though for a minute when the priest said "Anything else?" he had wanted to confess the horror, the long held secret of killing. But he was afraid. Confession might be the tip off. Maybe the secrecy of confession was all a cod, or the priest was an eejit. Asking him if he had impious thoughts about boys, about men. Rubbish! The priest didn't know the half of it. What about the fifth commandment? *Thou shalt not kill?* But the Catechism also said killing was okay *in a just war, in self defense...*

A just war, that's what it is. The fight for Ireland. And he, Saucebottle Moran, is the man. And Beechwood is cursed. They'll never have a day's luck, that Andrew Wynne, the strange old Protestant bachelor. Saucebottle himself had no luck with girls. Not yet. He had been mad about Attracta Benson, beautiful she was, and she liked him. Late one evening he stood behind the wall of Benson's back garden watching the clothes blowing on the line, knickers and slips, wondering which of those mysterious garments were Attracta's, so intent on his study of the clothes he heard nothing till he was grabbed by the coat and swung round to face her father. "What the hell are you doing here?" Her Da. Big, pig ignorant!

"I was just passing, Mr. Benson," he stammered.

"Well make damn sure you don't pass this way again. If I catch you here again I'll cut the head off ya," and he shoved Saucebottle roughly aside.

Still, Attracta had come out with him one early spring evening. They cycled to the Meagharduff crossroads, then walked the back way along the river through Wynne's land. She let him kiss her. Then she drew back and he said "Let's go for a walk," and with his arm round her they walked along in the fading light. "Where are you taking me, Sauce?"

"Oh a special place. You know I was with the IRA," he boasted, "and I'm going to show you something."

"What Sauce? What will you show me?"

"Where we hid the guns, the arms' dump."

She stopped dead cold, and pushed his arm away. "You get away from me now." She took off running back to get on her bicycle, and next thing he heard she was gone to England.

But Saucebottle yearned to tell, to cleanse himself of the pictures in his head. They tormented him and yet some of them he loved. They were more exciting than Sunday night at the Magnet Picture House, as riveting as when the masked horsemen wait in the shadow of the rock listening, the stage coach getting closer and closer, rounding the turn and they're there waving long barrelled guns, the driver holding the reins taut to his chest, his eyes rolling in his head. The music loud, then quiet for a second, then faster and faster.

Saucebottle has never owned a gun. He'd heard you could buy one from a soldier for a pound. The soldier would say he was held up. When he told Slasher, Slasher said, "Aye lad, if you had the pound. But you don't want to be getting too fond of them things, sonny. You're too young. The knife's a better man. Quieter! You know where you are with a knife."

What he had loved was that they had been comrades, the soaring of his spirit when Slasher said he was a soldier. He tried to remember that but sometimes other memories tormented him. And he was mostly afraid. Afraid the IRA were watching him. What was the IRA now? The ragtag men reduced to attacking pubs for selling English beer, or holding useless demonstrations, or chaining strike breakers to railings in the night? Or was there another IRA, more secret, more deadly?

In '19 he'd gone to Dunsagart to join up to fight for the cause. He'd got a lift in a lorry delivering Bass Ale. His mother, God rest her, had asked, "Where are you off to?" and Saucebottle lied and said he was going up to Middlebrook to help in the stables. The driver dropped him at the town pump and he'd gone round the corner to McKiernan's News Agents, waited till the shop was empty and then told the girl behind the counter he wanted to see Mr. McKiernan. She went in the back behind a curtain and he heard the murmur of voices, then a red faced man with a handlebar moustache came out and Saucebottle told him he wanted to join the IRA.

"Come back when you start shaving, when you're out of short trousers," the man said and went back behind the curtain. Humiliated, Saucebottle wandered the town looking in shop windows seeing his reflection darkly, a small fourteen year old boy, his trousers high above his knees. In the late afternoon he got a lift home in a cart with a man returning from selling a load of turf.

A year later the Slasher Mulligan whispered to him at the creamery gate, "Tonight, nine o'clock in the bottom field behind the school."

There were four of them. The moonlight was bright as day, the peaks of their caps shadowed their faces. Moore's thin mouth appeared momentarily and then faded out as he drew on his cigarette.

"Now lads," said Tom McConnell, "like I told you, Middlebrook is first. Then Clover House. Middlebrook this Saturday!"

A sudden stab of terror passed through Saucebottle, as if he'd lost his footing on a height; constriction in his throat, his mouth dry. First it had been a wild notion, setting fire to the big houses. But over in the west of the county two had gone up in September and another in November. And all over Ireland the gentry were leaving, leaving for England.

"We should go ahead and poison the two watchdogs," said Moore.

"Bloody brilliant," McConnell growled. "And have the whole barracks there ahead of us, waiting for us."

"Them dogs would rise the dead, we won't get near the place," Moore insisted.

"That's where the lad comes in. He knows them dogs. Don't you sonny? And the dogs know him," said Slasher, stroking Saucebottle's cheeks gently with the back of his hand, first one side and then the other. The hair on the back of Saucebottle's neck bristled. "Sure no one knows them dogs like you."

He knew then why Slasher had come up to him after mass two weeks earlier and chatted him up, talked to him about the great cause, the fight to rid Ireland of the 'Tans. The seven hundred year struggle! They needed him. He might be only just gone fourteen but they wanted him. He helped out in the stables in Middlebrook and worked with the two dogs.

"And when is Wynne's going up?" Moore challenged.

"We're not touching Wynne's."

"And why not? Tell me that. Why? Why do they get off?"

Saucebottle saw Slasher reach inside his coat and when he withdrew his hand metal glinted. He rested the revolver nonchalantly on his knees.

"You shut the hell up Moore," McConnell warned, "or I'll break your neck."

It became very quiet. The December frost lay in long white ridges on the empty field that stretched away from them into nothing. The cold seeped up through Saucebottle, his feet and hands froze. He became conscious of a fearful lump in his throat. If Slasher would only say something, make some declaration. Moore wouldn't let it go. "So, just because Slasher's sister works there, they get off."

The sneer just hung there in the silence.

At last Slasher spoke very quietly, "Mike, you can walk away from here this very minute," he taunted. "Just walk away."

"Aw, I'm with you, Slasher. You're safe with me. I'm with you. You know that."

"You better be! Or I'll cut your throat."

The threat lay there for a while, then McConnell said, "Now here's the plan. We'll meet behind the Protestant church, in the graveyard, at half eleven. Slasher and me, we'll have the petrol and muzzles for the dogs."

Saucebottle felt rather than saw Slasher put the gun away.

Saturday night they walked the last mile from where they had hid their bicycles to Middlebrook, the men carrying petrol cans and boxes of Friendly Matches, Saucebottle with heavy gloves he'd stolen from the harness room at Middlebrook, muzzles for the dogs and a string of McCarne's sausages in his pocket. Another moonlit night. Their boots crunched on the frosty fields. When they were within a few yards of the house, McConnell gave Saucebottle a little shove, "Go on sonny, and settle them dogs. I'm here behind you."

Saucebottle and McConnell crept ahead. McConnell threw the grapple over the wall and cupped his hands for Saucebottle to stand on and hoist himself on the rope. Saucebottle almost cried out as the broken glass imbedded in the top of the wall pierced his hands through the heavy leather gloves. McConnell gave him a hard shove and he was able to stand and save his knees, then he jumped down into the yard. The dogs had started up barking over near the stables. He hunkered down in the shadows. "Rufus, Rufus, Snipe," he called softly and they came to him. He fed them each a little sausage and put his arms round Rufus, held him tight. Snipe snuffled at his pocket whimpering, smelling the sausage. "Good boy, Rufus, good dog," and he fastened the muzzle on, and then the other one on Snipe. Dead easy! He slid back the bolts and opened the door in the wall for the others.

"Are we right?" whispered Slasher, behind him.

Before he could answer the other three were running toward the house, emptying the cans along the window sashes. The stink of petrol, then a soft smash as newspaper wrapped stones broke glass. A flash of petrol soaked rags lighted and pitched into the interior. The hot wind started up when the curtains and rugs caught fire, air from the broken windows fanned the flames. The dogs ran round them whimpering. Slasher turned, Saucebottle winced at the hollow mushy sound of Slasher kicking Rufus in the belly. He heard the wretched muffled whimper as the dog slunk away.

"The job's a good one," whispered McConnell. Then as the others raced away Moore doubled across the yard and lopped a Mills grenade over the half door of the stable. First a flash, then the loud bang and the ear splitting slamming and screaming of the trapped horses. They stopped once, to look back at the flames. Slasher slapped Saucebottle on the back. "Couldn't have done it without you sonny."

Then they ran like scalded cats to where they had left the bikes, Saucebottle's heart thumping with a wild joy as his feet pounded the earth. They'd done it and got clean away. They'd struck the blow.

Captain Waterson had escaped the fire, helped out the window onto the roof of the porch by the housekeeper and the kitchen maid. His son, daughter-in-law, and the groom arrived home at three in the morning from a Christmas party in Dublin to find the house still burning, the smell of roast horseflesh drifting through the smoke. The weeping old man and the housekeeper were shivering in the summer house, the gardener from the gatehouse had been sent for help, and his wife stood helplessly watching the fire.

If Slasher had just quit then. If only they'd been satisfied with that much. Now Saucebottle took off his bicycle clips and put them in his pocket and leaned his bike against the back wall of Hourigans. The pub was full: Higgins the schoolmaster, Keating the creamery manager and Mrs. Byrne the postmistress were sitting over by the wall when Saucebottle pushed open the door. He nodded at Higgins who was faced towards him and edged his way to the snug. It was empty. Dan, the barman slid back the wicket. "A Powers or two like a good man." Saucebottle said, thinking the wicket door of the snug slid back and forth like the slot in the confessional. He needed a drink after confession. Going to confession stirred memories. The barman slid the door open, handed the glass and the two small bottles through. Saucebottle put a half crown on the ledge and took one long drink. He lit a cigarette, stretched out his legs, let his head rest on the back of the seat and listened to this conversation from outside.

"What I want to say is this," but Mrs. Byrne's voice was drowned by drunken singing.

"I say that Roger Casement did what he had to… do.

He died upon the gallows… but that is nothing…new." The voice faded off.

"Ah give us the rest of it, Mol "

"Sure I forget it now. I've a drop too much taken."

"None of that singing," the barman's voice said. "People want to talk." And he slid back the wicket and gave Saucebottle his change.

"The worst poem Yeats ever wrote," said the schoolmaster.

"You've a great knowledge of them literary crowd," Keating complimented the schoolmaster. "And what do you think of O'Casey?"

"Banned that fellow should be. Letting down the Irish, filth!" Mrs. Byrne interjected.

"Sometimes them writers is queer fellows," Keating agreed. "Oscar Wilde, now he was a quare hand."

"A nancy boy! A proper disgrace."

"But poor Casement." Keating's voice was mournful. "I had me doubts about him 'til I read Maloney's book."

"Ah, do you have that book? Would you lend it to me?" Mrs. Byrne pleaded.

"Well I didn't exactly read it, I just read the bit about it in *The Irish Press.*"

"It'd fit Dev better to see he got a decent burial," Mrs. Byrne pronounced.

"He did. Didn't he have the priest at the last?"

"Them diaries, all a fraud. Bloody English had him for a pervert. If it wasn't for that they'd never have hung him, they couldn't have. "

"God help us," Mrs. Byrne prayed.

The drunken singing began again "*Afraid they might be… beaten …*"

"Ah, give him a drink," a voice said, then the creak of the cork being drawn.

Saucebottle slid the wicket back and put a florin on the ledge. "Another small one."

He sat morosely looking at his feet till the barman passed the glass through. He longed to sleep, to nod off there in the snug with the murmur of drinkers' voices and the slosh of porter from the tap. To sleep without nightmares, never to again hear McConnell's screams when the bullet ripped his guts. At Clover House, the Tans had been waiting for them. That night had been dark as pitch and the bullets missed except for McConnell. They turned and ran, left him bleeding, and dying, calling out for God to help him. Shots fired round them, they zigzagged, raced across the fields, leaping over ditches, leaving the pursuers confused, not knowing their way in the country. Saucebottle ran like never before until he reached their bicycles behind the school. Bent from a crippling cramp in his side, he hunkered down, back to the wall heart hammering like a sledge, trying not to think of McConnell screaming, hoping and praying he'd die before he told the Tans who they were. Slasher arrived next. He stood leaning against the wall trying to catch his breath. When Moore rounded the corner at the back of the building Slasher grabbed him by the throat. "Tipped them off at the barracks, so you did."

Moore wrenched Slasher's hands off his neck and gave him a fierce shove. "You're mad, Slasher, get off me." He stooped to pick up his bicycle. Saucebottle saw the shadow of Slasher jump on his back, heard the long sickening groan when Moore's throat was cut. Moore sank silently to his knees, fell over and Saucebottle heard the blood gurgle in his throat. Slasher wiped the knife on the stiff grass.

"Come on, sonny."

Somehow Saucebottle mounted his bicycle and bent over the handlebars, rode after Slasher his head nodding like a puppet on his neck. No moon, only the stars for light. When they got to the crossroads Slasher dismounted and Saucebottle did too and stood gripping the saddle of his bike. Slasher laid his bike on the triangle of grass in the centre. He put his arm round Saucebottle's shoulders. "You're a Trojan, sonny! The heart of a lion. Go on home now and not a word, not a single word. Don't breathe a word. We'll have more than the Tans on our tail."

Slasher stooped and picked up his bike and this time turned on the lamp and rode off very fast. Saucebottle watched his light disappearing in the dark. Then his own bike slipped from his hands and clattered on the road. He sat down trembling. After a while he saw in the distance the lights of a lorry. Soldiers! He took the bike and hid behind the hedge terrified, shivering in the cold. Even now with the alcohol softening his muscles and muddling his brain he can't stop thinking of that night. McConnell, always the talker, boasted about orders from the hard men, Mick Fitzgerald and Moss Twomey. And Slasher never said much. But who else knew? And was Slasher fleeing the IRA? On the run from a republican court marshal for Moore's murder? Rick Mulally told him when the IRA had a trial, the judge heard the evidence and then signalled the verdict by grinding his cigarette in the ash tray on the table in front of him. Then the prisoner was taken to say his last Act of Contrition on his knees before a bullet blew the back of his head off. Every time Saucebottle saw a man grind out a cigarette he thought of the IRA court marshal and was afraid and wished with all his heart that Slasher had not entrusted him with the secret. Had Slasher got away or had someone got him? Had Moore tipped off the police? Or was it just the Slasher's temper? At Middlebrook he was sure it was the bang of the Mills grenade that awakened the house. No lives lost; it was said old Waterson never got over it, was never the same again, took off for England with all their traps and the Land Commission took over the land. The only dead men? McConnell and Moore. And McConnell's mother's house and the houses of her neighbours burned to the ground by the Tans the very next day.

After all that, the shambles the country is in. Most of the old IRA comrades turned Free Staters and Broy's Harriers, spying on those that hadn't, and the Military Tribunal handing down death sentences. The IRA reduced to holding useless protest marches and drilling in the mountains on Sundays. Drilling without arms. But he could tell them where the Vicker's machine gun is, and Mills grenades and explosives, the best kind, Irish Cheddar and Paxo. The map of the world still red, British red, and up at Beechwood House Andy Wynne lords it over the country. Slasher's sister still worked there, with the old woman lamenting for old glories when Beechwood had four hundred acres. Now they had another mouth to feed, a girl from the city to watch old Mrs. Wynne, the mad woman. Saucebottle knew about that too. That was no skivvy. She was beautiful! And strange! Something mysterious about her. In the pub talk was that she had her eye on Andrew Wynne, that it was a made match.

Jimmy Henry, the butcher's boy said, "There'll be white blackbirds flying the day that fellow marries."

Rich O'Hare added, "Wynne's waitin' on the right woman." And the pub erupted in rough laughter. "Lots of stable secrets in them Protestant houses," Rick said, "And I don't mean about the horses either."

"Ah, the girl's a deserted wife, so she is. He can't marry her," Jimmy insisted.

But, Saucebottle brooded, thinking of Dominic. A Catholic lad led astray in that house. Playing jazz on the gramophone half the night! The priest at the mission said jazz was the devil's music. A mistake had been made in '20. They should have fired Beechwood, and be shot of the lot of them. And they would have if it weren't for Slasher. If things had gone differently they would have. It was a war they were fighting and a little matter of Slasher's sister working there should have made no difference. But it wasn't too late yet. All that's needed is one good man that knows the lie of the land and where the explosives are.

Two nights after Moore's murder he'd heard gravel thrown against his window and he looked out. At first he couldn't see a thing, then a figure popped up in the moonlight, signed to him. Slasher! Too frightened to disobey the summons Saucebottle tiptoed out through the kitchen, careful not to wake his mother. Slasher gripped his arm. "I'm doing a bunk, sonny, they're after me. I have to get out."

Saucebottle stared at him. "You're the only man now sonny. I'm leaving the secret with you. Behind Crew's Rock, that's where the dump is. You're the one now. Not a word till the time's right."

Saucebottle' shivered in the night cold. "When will that be?"

"You'll know when the time comes," and he gave Saucebottle a valedictory thump on the back, turned and disappeared in the dark.

Well, the time was getting on, Saucebottle thought, as he rose and groped his way unsteadily out of the pub, nodding respectfully in the direction of Keating and the other drinkers as he passed.

"Three sheets to the wind," Higgins said when he left.

"Well, he'll be at his work early enough on Monday," Keating retorted.

"Ah sure, the poor lad has neither chick nor child since his mother died and he never misses mass on a Sunday," Mrs. Byrne reminded them.

"Well he'd need to be saying his prayers," said the schoolmaster, "the way he rides that bike home in the dark, blind drunk."

"Sure his poor father, God rest his soul, came home dead from the pub one Fair Day," Mrs. Byrne related.

"I heard that story. A terrible way to go."

"Well he hadn't the worst of it, it was poor Julia heard the cart coming into the yard and opened the door and there was her husband sitting dead in the cart. The auld horse knew the way home. She never was the better of it. Saucebottle was only a lad, ten, I think he was."

'His heart that killed him," Keating declared. "Drink never killed anyone."

9

Country Woman

*B*y the end of her second week, Victoria knew the routines and rhythms of Beechwood and savoured her freedom to come and go. Most days she induced Mrs. Wynne to walk after lunch so that she would be too tired to embark on her frantic nightfall searching for revolutionaries lurking in the shadows. When she insisted on going over the grounds, Victoria took her arm. If there was no moonlight, she took a lantern and walked with her reassuring her that no one was hiding behind hedges or walls or in the outbuildings. Sometimes Mrs. Wynne would stand in the scullery door calling out instructions while Victoria searched the outbuildings, "Search the stable, Victoria. Look in the hothouse." Victoria believed she was making progress. "You are doing wonders, Victoria," Andrew said one evening.

She saw little of Andrew. Although as a cattle farmer, he did not till his land, he and Dominic worked helping George Mac Adam harvest his grain.

Her third Sunday in Beechwood, Victoria accompanied Mrs. Wynne and Andrew to their church. Andrew sat in the front seat and Dominic drove, Victoria sat in the back with Josie and Mrs. Wynne. As they neared Killcore she saw that The Church of The Redeemer was the old grey stone building they had passed on her first day. Dominic left them at their church and drove on with Josie to mass at the much larger Catholic church, Our Lady Of Victories, at the opposite end of the town.

Victoria had hesitated about church, wanting to avoid curious glances. The only time she was alone was when the family was at church, and she relished the freedom of having the place to herself. But she couldn't hide forever. Church attendance for Victoria had been part of a well-ordered life; for her family, it had centred them in their social circle. She now questioned her father's claim to be an upright man of faith, in light of his cruelty to her, but Mrs. Wynne expected her to go to church. "The numbers are dwindling, Victoria."

The church was gloomy and damp, the sanctuary small and shallow. A narrow balcony ran around three sides of the interior. Andrew led his mother and Victoria up the side aisle to a pew halfway up the nave. The family name was inscribed on a brass nameplate at the end of the pew. Kneeling cushions hung on brass hooks under the seat in front. Less than a quarter of the pews were occupied. It seemed to Victoria that she had stepped back a hundred years. A brass lamp was suspended from a roof beam; memorial plates on the walls remembered the dead of the parish. As the service progressed, she looked around discreetly. Just a handful of young people, and a few children in Sunday best: most of the worshippers were middle-aged, grey haired. She read a tablet on the wall above where they sat.

Sacred to the memory of Philip Wynne, Captain Thirty-Sixth Ulster Division.

Wounded at The Battle of the Somme. November 18th 1916.

Died at Etaples January 24th 1917

This tablet was erected in his memory by the people of this parish."

I have glorified you on the earth: I have finished the work thou gavest me to do.

John 17:4

Was this the young man in the photographs in the abandoned room on the third floor? The boy posed with the girls with the white hair bands? Andrew's brother, Mrs. Wynne's son? How sad! Victoria was an infant when the War started. It was something her parents endured, though she remembered Ypres and Somme spoken of with a grim shake of the head. It was estimated that thirty thousand Irish had been killed in the War, but the sheer size of that number diminished the individuality of the dead. The executions after the Easter Rising in 1916 had more resonance with people, the executed were so few and their names were kept before the world as martyrs. Her father considered them traitors, none more reprehensible than the homosexual Sir Rodger Casement who was said to have betrayed his King, his country and his class. Aunt Nicola mourned her husband but her grief elicited impatience from her family. People were tired of the War. She stole a glance at Mrs. Wynne. Her eyes were on her prayer book. They came here every Sunday and sat beside this plaque? Heartbreaking! There were two rows of plaques on the far wall. Would it not be better if they did not come to church at all? What good did it accomplish? People still struggled between life and death in what appeared to be a span fixed for each, no matter how often they attended church. How random life was. The tiny human she carried inside her was an accidental creature that almost missed being born.

The sun came from behind the clouds and light broke through the stained glass windows. The Minister's voice gained resonance as the service drew to an end, "*Now to God the Father, God the Son and God the Holy Ghost.*" The congregation stood for the final hymn.

Outdoors the sunlight streamed down through the trees and glinted on the lichen mottled headstones that leaned toward one another in the graveyard. The Reverend Johnson, grey haired and ruddy faced, stood at the door shaking hands with the departing congregation. Andrew introduced her, "Victoria Mulholland, she's staying with us for a while."

The Minister took her hand. "You're welcome Victoria. Glad to see you today."

Andrew had not said Miss Mulholland. Was he implying that she was Mrs? She suspected a discerning or a spiteful eye could see that she was pregnant, and she knew the minister of her church in Blackrock had arranged her stay at Beechwood through the Reverend Johnson.

"You're keeping well?" the Minister turned to Mrs. Wynne.

"Very well, thank you" and she went to speak to two middle-aged women who had moved on after having received the Reverend's greeting and were waiting at the bottom of the steps. Mrs. Wynne introduced Victoria to Mrs. Delia Mac Adam, a tall frosty looking woman, and her sister Miss Minnie Moore, small and stout. Andrew had been talking with an older man and he brought him over and introduced him as George Mac Adam. "George has the next farm to us, the one just past ours on the Killcore road."

"We haven't seen you for a while, Mrs. Wynne," Minnie said.

"I go out a bit more now that Victoria has come to stay. One of these days we'll walk over to see you," Mrs. Wynne said. "Goodbye now."

A stocky leathery looking man and a blonde woman came over. "Mrs. Wynne, how are you?" the woman asked.

"Very well, thank you, Lottie. This is Victoria Mulholland. Victoria, Lottie and Sandy Patterson."

Victoria shook hands with each. "How do you do?"

She could see them eye her figure and was relieved to see Dominic had arrived with the car to pick them up.

77

"It's nice to see you out, Mrs. Wynne," Lottie said.

"Well, the weather is so nice."

Andrew, who was still talking to George Mac Adam, moved toward the car.

"Goodbye now," Mrs. Wynne said and she and Victoria went over to where Dominic was standing at the car.

"There'll be another Mission," Dominic announced as they headed towards home. "The priest said it would be the last Friday and Saturday of the month."

"Well, if you and Josie want to drive there you may use the motor."

"Thank you, sir," said Josie.

The afternoon was radiant with mellow sunshine. After lunch, Victoria wondered if she should suggest a walk or if the old woman was tired after church services. "Would you like to take a walk, Mrs. Wynne?"

"Do go, Mother," Andrew urged. "Tomorrow we might have rain."

"I think I will. I would like to walk along by the stream."

"It's a mild autumn," Andrew said. "The mildest I recall." He checked the barometer he had mounted at the side of the window in the conservatory and tapped it with his finger. "It's fifty degrees. Not bad for the middle of October."

Andrew threw himself into one of the old armchairs and picked up Saturday's *Irish Times*. Victoria followed Mrs. Wynne out to the cloakroom off the hall and helped her into her coat and heavy shoes. Victoria wore a cardigan over her green dress which was now quite tight, and tied a scarf over her hair. Mrs. Wynne led the way down the steps, past the lawn and the garden a few fallen leaves crisp under their feet. A flock of starlings rose from the trees, wheeled into the air and, thick as a shaken cloth, turned into the sunlight; the shadow of the flock moved across the grass. Victoria thought she had never seen anything so marvellous. They passed the vegetable garden and turned into a path that ran between the meadows and a wide stream.

"Are there fish in the river, Mrs. Wynne?"

"There are. Sometimes Dominic will fish when he has the time. This little stream flows south till it joins a tributary of The Boyne. When I take this path I have my husband in mind," Mrs. Wynne said as they went along. "We often walked this way together."

Victoria did not answer, concerned that the old woman's memories would over excite her. "What a lovely season autumn is."

"Beechwood is lovely in any season," Mrs. Wynne said. "I've thought that ever since I came here a bride of twenty, in 1881."

So she was-seventy six. How vigorous she was.

"Where did you come from, Mrs. Wynne?"

"From a village in Hampshire. My husband was in the army and he was stationed nearby. And we met. When I came here I almost died of loneliness, but the next year when Andrew came I was content. A baby takes one's whole heart."

Victoria stole a sidelong glance at her. Although her pregnancy was now quite obvious, she was never sure how much of her story Mrs. Wynne knew. Was the old woman saying something to her or was she just telling her own memories? Then Mrs. Wynne said, "Over half a century ago since I came here. My people, my generation, have had nothing but trouble these later years."

She took Victoria's arm, whether for comfort or because the path was rough, Victoria did not know. They walked in silence and now the path widened and bent to the right and sloped upward away from the stream toward the base of a rock that rose thirty feet from a mossy base. Another fork led on west.

"This path goes to Callaghan's lane and the other lanes branch off to scattered farm cottages," Mrs. Wynne said.

The stream became wider here and in the distance was the glimmer of the lake. Victoria held the old woman's arm and noted how thin she was.

"Perhaps we should go back, Mrs. Wynne."

"Let's go on a little. There's a spot further on at the foot of the rock where I like to sit and rest."

They walked on past the rock and for a while the lake was hidden by high hedges. Then, round a bend in the path there it was: a big rushy pond. Mrs. Wynne stopped. "Let's sit here and rest."

Victoria removed her cardigan and spread it on the mossy bank and they sat there in silence looking at the sunlight on the water, the rock rising behind them. The breeze bent the rushes and a flock of ducks drifted about. A few feet from the base, a barbed wire fence surrounded the rock and Victoria thought its purpose was to deter sheep from climbing too high up the rock face, although there were no sheep in sight. When she looked back she noticed a tiny island a short distance from the edge of the lake. A wet face was looking back at her: a face with curved ears and long whiskers like a cat, but larger than any cat she's ever seen. The animal looked back at her through eyes black as coal and the sun glinted on the drops of water clinging to the creature's fur and long curved whiskers.

"Oh, the otter," Mrs. Wynne cried and clapped her hands. Quite unhurried the animal slipped into the water and vanished, leaving a necklace of bubbles on the surface of the lake.

"Was that an otter?"

"Yes, it was."

"I've never seen one before but I loved Otter in *The Wind in The Willows*. He was such a practical type, guided the others home."

"We've always had otters here. But it's rare to see one that close. No one comes this far now, rocky land, no use really. When I was younger I used to climb that rock. It's called Crew's Rock. I have no idea why." She turned and looked up at the face of the rock silhouetted against the sky. "When Philip and Andrew were children we would come here and they would fish in the stream, and climb on the rock. It's a dangerous drop on the other side."

It was the first time Mrs. Wynne had mentioned her younger son.

"I think we will go back now," she said and Victoria stood and held out a hand to help her up, took her cardigan and they turned back for Beechwood. Victoria was so enthralled with the otter she had to share her wonder with someone, its solemn stare, her feeling she had intruded on something rare. "Imagine seeing an otter."

"Few people see them. They keep mostly to themselves but I love to see them. They seem such self possessed creatures. I remember Charles told me once that when the female is in heat she whistles for the male and when they have mated she tells him to be off with himself and has nothing more to do with him. "

"I like that story, Mrs. Wynne."

"I do too."

As they went toward the bend in the path, Victoria looked back at the looming rock and saw a man hold down the barbed wire, step over it and climb up the rock. She wondered who he was but did not draw the matter to Mrs. Wynne's attention nor did she look back again. Even if she had she would not have recognized Saucebottle Moran.

It was getting colder and they went a little faster and as they neared home they heard hammering. When they came closer they saw it was

Dominic fastening pieces of wood into the orchard wall. Mrs. Wynne stopped to watch. Dominic grasped the edge of the wooden bird table he had just built and tried to move it. "That's going no place," he said with obvious satisfaction.

"Contravening the Sabbath, Dominic?" Mrs. Wynne asked.

"Yes Ma'am," and he hung the hammer in a cleft in the stone wall, took a pack of Wills cigarettes from the pocket of his overalls and tapped one out. "The robins, the poor things, and the thrushes, sure they stay with us the winter."

"Ah yes Dominic, faithful creatures."

"And the blackbirds too, Ma'am."

"Come along, Victoria. Let's see what Josie is doing about tea."

They walked along round by the back of the house into the yard. Out of earshot of Dominic, Mrs. Wynne said, "he'll beg stale bread and bits of suet or bacon from Josie for his bird table. And put dry oats on the ground for the blackbirds. I never like him putting food for the ground feeders. I think it brings rats. But I haven't the heart to stop him."

As they passed the clump of mint by the back door, now flowered and purple, Mrs. Wynne broke off a handful and rubbed it between her palms then held her open hands to her face inhaling the fragrance. Victoria did the same and was flooded by a sense of the rich autumn landscape. In fact Victoria, soothed by the routine of the house, often thought she would stay there forever and then remembered she was there on sufferance and her baby was due in February. Sometimes in her bedroom thinking about her uncertain future, she raged against her parents and Donny Maguire. But now there were chores to distract her. Mondays, after he had finished his creamery run, Dominic would gather the lamps and candle sticks and leave them in the scullery. Mrs. Wynne trimmed the wicks with a scissors and Victoria filled the lamps carefully pouring the paraffin oil from the green oil drum into the funnel. Then she would clean the candleholders and replace the candles.

"I shall never see electric light," Mrs. Wynne said the first Monday as she spread old newspapers on the scullery table. "Not in my lifetime. It would be such a boon to us in the country."

Darkness fell earlier now. It was colder and dust from the fires settled on the floors. Peggy, the tall ungainly black-haired girl who came on Mondays and Tuesdays to help with the laundry, now came on Fridays to scrub the floors. "I'd make more headway with a mop," she told Josie.

81

"There'll be no mops here. A dirty habit, so they are. Just for moving the dirt about, that's all they're good for."

Victoria would wake at dawn and listen to the morning sounds of the farm, the lowing of the cattle and, after rain, the cupping sound of their hooves in the muddy lane as Dominic or Matt drove them to pasture after they were milked, and the rattle of milk cans when Dominic set off for the creamery. In the night she often woke from a tangled sleep and heard distant music. She listened. *"You're the top. You're the Empire state…"* and another time *"it had to be you, wonderful you."* She knew it was the gramophone in Andrew's study. Dominic and Andrew were listening to music. Mrs. Wynne slept late and Victoria had time to walk in the orchard, noting the year advancing and wondering what long dead eye planned that orchard where equal weight had been given to practicality and beauty. The stone wall to the east that bordered the garden was fronted by laurel trees and rhododendron that grew so thick it formed an impenetrable hedge. At the south west corner two tall silver birches stretched into the sky. Some of their leaf had fallen now but what was left gleamed like shillings in the low October sun. At the opposite corner a chestnut and an oak, their leaves crinkled yellow and orange and on the ground the fallen acorns like tiny brown eggs in their cups and chestnuts gleaming like mahogany. The apple trees were thinned of their leaf and windfalls underfoot, half eaten by rabbits, were blown spongy and brown with rot. There was still some fruit on the top of the trees that had been too high for the pickers.

Always at the back of Victoria's mind was the growing child within her and how she would provide for it. She thought she would ask Andrew to rent her the empty room on the top floor and when she was ready to work she would leave her baby with some respectable woman and find work. But where would she find work? The library in Killcore? But she was a shamed woman. No one would hire her. Maybe the Minister would help. Or some respectable family? And so one autumn day flowed into another. She looked out over the terrace. Dominic was planting bulbs in the lawn under the willow trees. When those bulbs bloomed her baby would be about seven or eight weeks old. She felt they were one universe, she and the infant. It would surely be a girl and she would call her Elizabeth after her favourite Jane Austen character, and swore she would take care of her, protect her.

One morning she lay in bed, looked down at her belly and saw a sharp elevation in the skin where it bulged under her ribs. There one minute and then gone, a fist or an elbow, or a heel. Marvellous. She waited to see it again but it did not appear. Did she imagine it? And there was the matter of her confinement. She would have to make arrangements, but there was plenty of time.

There was no delaying getting maternity clothes. Everything she owned was too tight. The first Friday in November she went with Dominic on his creamery run to Killcore to arrange for new clothes. She was slow getting ready, searching through her wardrobe for something that fitted her and she kept Dominic waiting.

"I'm sorry Dominic," she said as she clumsily eased herself into the front seat. He was studying the list of provisions Josie had given him. Victoria was anticipating a free day, the first she had since her arrival. Mrs. Wynne had been gracious, "Of course you should go with Dominic and do some shopping. Maddens should have what you want, and the Misses Clark are good dressmakers. Josie is here if I need anything."

Dominic went faster than usual through the winding roads, the round capped milk cans rattling in the flat trailer behind. He drove down the main street and left her at a shop with a green façade, "There's the post office Miss. I'll wait for you up there at Shaw's when I'm done at the creamery."

Inside the post office was a long counter backed by half empty shelves and a green telephone box in the corner. The Postmistress' face was pressed close to the wicket talking to a customer. Victoria stood waiting her turn. On her right announcements pinned to the wall, yellow auctioneer's notices, hours of opening for the post office and a police poster: *Wanted For Sodomy.* Victoria looked at the photograph. A solemn faced dark haired man. She turned away suddenly, unaccountably sad, and stood looking at the grey head of the customer in front of her. Then she looked back at the poster. "Yes, Miss?"

The woman had moved off and the Postmistress was staring at her. She stepped up to the wicket and as she handed over the money and her letters she saw the woman look at the ring on her left hand and then at her belly. Victoria blushed under the searching eyes and was furious with herself for doing so.

"Here you are, Miss." The woman handed her the change.

"Thank you." Victoria left her face flaming. She crossed the street to Madden's Drapery. The bell tinkled as she opened the door and clumsily she tripped over the step but regained her footing. Behind the counter a thin bald man in a buff shop coat said, "You need to watch that step."

Flustered she went over to the bolts of cloth and without really examining the selection asked for three yards of a dark red georgette material and three of a blue wool, one yard of pongee and four yards of lining. The man unravelled the bolts thumping them on the counter then measured the material off, thumb to thumb, on a steel ruler fastened to the edge of the counter. His wife stood at the far end of the shop watching. He wrapped the material in brown paper and tied it with string. She felt their eyes on her as she left for the dressmaker three doors down. There she was shown three separate styles in a Butterick Pattern Book. How stodgy they were, as if for much older women, staid mid-calf skirts with a pleat at the back and loose jackets designed to cover her changing figure. But in reality the garments would draw attention to it. She picked a design for a flared loose top and a straight skirt with a window of pongee that fitted over her belly. There would be two maternity outfits, one in red and one in blue. She had no hope that they could be anything but the most basic garments, but at least she would not be bursting out of them.

The dressmaker, a gaunt woman with tired blue eyes, had a red velvet pincushion shaped like a heart suspended from her neck on a black grosgrain ribbon. When she had taken the measurements and pencilled them in a black notebook she slowly rolled up her tape measure into a tight yellow wheel and put it in her pocket. "I'll be ready for a fitting on Friday," she said, not meeting Victoria's eye.

"I'll come at nine then, Miss Clark."

"I charge three and six for each outfit and then the price of the buttons and thread."

"I'll come on Friday. Thank you."

A figure rose from behind a Singer sewing machine at the back of the room, a humped backed woman in black. Victoria had not noticed her previously. She followed Victoria and stood in the door looking after her as she retraced her steps up the street of low shops. At the lower end was the railway station and at the other end four substantial buildings, the Bank of Ireland, Shaw's Bar and Grocery, Hourigan's Public House and at the very end, well back from the street, Jackson's Family Hotel.

She went into Green's Newsagents and Stationery. There were three customers, two middle-aged men and a young woman. All conversation stopped when she entered. She bought *The Irish Independent* as Dominic had asked her to do, a bottle of Stephen's ink and three sheets of blotting paper. The shop assistant put the items in a brown paper bag and handed her the change. As she closed the door she heard the talk begin again. In the street two women gossiping outside the hardware shop turned away as she approached, showing her their backs, and when she had passed she knew they turned again to look after her. She saw the Morris with its trailer of now empty milk cans outside Shaw's, Dominic at the wheel. A man leaning his shoulder against the shop door followed her with his eyes and a woman passing stared at her belly. Victoria opened the front door of the car sat in. "Let's go Dominic. Please! Quick."

He started the car and she sat in silence as he drove out into the country. She felt the whole village had pronounced a crushing verdict on her and on her morals. And she had been thinking of working here and raising her child alone. Preposterous! She wrenched the ring off her finger and threw it out the window. Dominic stopped and backed up the car and stopped again and began to cough so hard Victoria stared at him. "Are you alright?"

He nodded, unable to speak, stepped out of the car and bent over on the margin of the road clearing his throat. After a few minutes he straightened up, wiped his face with a red check handkerchief and walked back along the road. She knew he was looking for the ring. She saw him search back and forth again and again and at last stoop and pick it up and come back to the car. Victoria looked out at the hedges and wept in frustration. When he got back in the car she was sobbing her face in her hands He put the ring on the floor at her feet. He touched her arm gently. "Don't be crying now, Miss."

She dabbed at her eyes and stared straight ahead. "That crowd in the town, Miss. Don't mind them. Let it all go by you, Miss. That's what you have to do around here. Just let it all go by you."

She turned a tearful face toward him. "Oh Dominic, that's a dreadful cough you have."

"I know. The boss blames it on the fags. He says I have to go to the doctor."

"You must Dominic," she urged, wiping her eyes.

"Oh I'll go over to the dispensary and see if the doctor will give me a bottle of some kind of medicine for it."

"Dominic, how do you work so hard with that cough?"

"Ah Miss, sure there's no work, not like there was all year saving the hay, and now we have Matt to help me, and the boss, he works hard."

"Dominic, why is Josie so hard on me?"

"Ah she's not a bad sort Miss, it's just that Mrs. Wynne's her whole life. She minded her, did everything for her till you came. I was helping more and more in the kitchen and she was happy with that. Then one Sunday the boss came home from the church and told her you were coming to stay with Mrs. Wynne and she was raging. She thinks no one can do for Mrs. Wynne but herself."

"I find it so hard to work with her."

"Oh, she'll come round. She's on her own you know. There's only her mother and she's in the County Home. She had a brother but he took off with himself someplace. I heard tell he was very wild, a mad man."

He started up the car and Victoria picked up the ring off the floor and put it on her finger thinking how strange, I am confiding in a servant. Dominic drove on through the white winding road between the hedges. Suddenly he pulled into the side of the road and stopped and a black Ford flashed past in a cloud of white dust.

"Dr Curran," said Dominic, shaking his head. "He's a fierce driver altogether."

Victoria looked after the speeding car, travelling very fast for the narrow roads.

"Drives up to a crossroads at forty miles an hour then stands on the clutch and the brake," Dominic said indulgently, as he manoeuvred the car back on the road. "Must be on a sick call."

They drove on in silence. When the road wound round the low mountain and Victoria saw Beechwood below, rising from its nest of trees, she had for the first time a sense that it was a refuge. It was home.

Some days after lunch the old woman dozed in her chair and Victoria read. Today she let her sleep. She planned to take her for a walk when she woke. She walked to the window. Andrew and Dominic sat in identical poses on the bench in front of the orchard wall. Turned toward each other each gripping the bench, their hands beside their thighs. Dominic leaned forward as if to make a point. She wondered what they were talking about. Two men taking a break in the autumn sunshine. Andrew laughed, changed his position, put one leg over the other, took a cigarette pack from his pocket and offered one to the other man. Her heart turned over with envy. What would she not have given for someone to whom she could talk like that? To sit in the sun and honestly talk! Servant and master those two, but how companionable they were, how at ease. They seemed equals, collaborators. The sun moved behind a cloud. She watched them talking, their figures foreshortened when looked at from above, wreathes of smoke from the cigarettes rising and then saw Andrew reach over and slap Dominic's knee as if to say let's go, let's get on with it, and they both rose and walked away. She turned back to the room. Mrs. Wynne was still sleeping. Quietly, Victoria tiptoed to her own room and lay on her bed. She was tired. A sudden burst of light as the sun emerged from behind a cloud changed the room, set the mirrors gleaming, slanted the window panes in parallel lines on the wooden floor. She felt the baby move. Tomorrow the District Nurse was coming. Yesterday Dr. Curran had been to see Mrs. Wynne: a big man with a bald bullet head, a plump childish face and very sharp eyes. He'd sat beside Mrs. Wynne, felt for her pulse, "How are you today?"

Mrs. Wynne looked up at him, an amused expression on her face. "I'm fine, thank you," and then she said, "Victoria, can you get Dr. Curran something to drink?"

Curran stood up quickly. "The very thing, a small drop of whiskey," and he followed Victoria downstairs and she poured him a glass from the decanter on the dining room sideboard. "That'll do. No soda."

"Would you like to sit down, Doctor?" she offered, but he tossed the drink off standing and said, "Mrs. Wynne seems well. Does she still make the rounds at night?"

"Not every night. Sometimes we walk so far in the afternoon that she's tired, and goes to bed after dinner."

"Excellent. Is Andrew about?"

"I think he is out in the fields, but I could ask Josie to call him."

"No. No need. Just tell him I was here. I'll send Nurse Fay to see yourself on Friday, and not before time by the looks of you."

Victoria was about to object to his assumption that she needed the nurse but thought better of it. Time was moving along and she knew that sooner or later she had to see the District Nurse.

10

District Nursing

Nuala Fay put her nurses' bag on top of the pile of magazines, *Nursing Mirror* and *Woman's Own,* on the passenger seat of her little black Ford. At the weekend, she promised herself, she would read *The Mirror.* Not that there was anything in it that helped her in the mundane work she did as the district nurse in Killcore. She looked through the misty rain at the low terraced houses leading back from the main street. She told herself, on to the next thing, Nuala. You're dealing with a regular rosary of troubles. Ring around a rosy. She had just left a house where three of the seven children were sick, all of them red eyed, coughing, feverish. She'd checked their mouths. Two had *Koptex* spots on their gums and a rash speckled their little thin chests. Measles! She'd have to report that at the Dispensary. Curran might need to close the school.

"How long have they been sick?"

The tired mother thought for a minute. "Frank and Peter, they're sick a week. Mary just got sick three days ago."

"They have measles. Keep them warm and boil the milk. Where do you get your milk?"

"From Flynn's."

"Be sure to boil it."

"I thought their milk was good."

"It's safer to boil it."

She'd left a small round box of aspirin, instructed the woman to crush half a tablet between two spoons and give it to each child mixed in a little milk and sugar. She hoped all would be well, although pneumonia was a risk. At least that family had a decent house. Her long face settled into its usual mournful cast. Next thing was old Mrs. Larkin bent almost double with rheumatism, living in a cottage with a leaking roof over near the school and fast losing weight because she had no energy to feed herself. Doctor Curran's orders were that she move to the County Home, but the old stigma of the workhouse still attached to the Home. It would be a fight to get her to move. And after that was the pregnant Protestant girl over at Beechwood. That was a surprise. The Protestants usually managed things better, used more discretion. She hadn't been at Beechwood for months. Curran called there himself. No charity patients there. A strange household, the mother a bit touched, the Protestant girl from God knows where, maybe some relation, and Josie, the walking *Good Housekeeping Institute.*

Peggy answered the door, left her sitting in the hall under the ticking clock and went upstairs. Then a young woman in a blue maternity suit came down. She held out her hand. "I'm Victoria Mulholland."

Nuala saw that she wore a wedding ring. One would expect that. The sight of a pregnant woman without one would be certain cause for scandal.

Coming downstairs, Victoria had seen a sturdy woman of about fifty in a tweed suit and flat sensible shoes, her brown hair in a short bob. "Nuala Fay, the District Nurse. Dr. Curran thought I should come and see you."

"Yes, he told me that when he came to see Mrs. Wynne. Won't you come into the drawing room?" And she led the way and they sat in the shabby chairs beside the cold fireplace and looked at each other.

Tactfully, Nuala ventured, "Are you feeling quite well, Mrs. Mulholland?"

"Please call me Victoria. I'm well but I'm a little tired in the afternoons because I don't sleep well."

"And how far on in your pregnancy are you? When was your last period."

"I'll be six months pregnant on the twenty- first."

Nuala face retained its habitual calm as she took her notebook from her bag and began to create a record. So, she knew her dates to the day! In Nuala's experience this could mean only one thing: the pregnancy was the result of a single indiscretion, or a rape, and the date would be forever burned into the girl's memory. Those girls were usually the most depressed, but Victoria did not seem so. She had likely resigned herself to the inevitable and was anticipating getting on with her life when this was over.

"So you believe your due date is in February, around the last week. We have a little time yet before we need to book a bed in St. Mary's Maternity, although it is better to book early, especially in your case, where the child will have to either be placed for adoption or in the orphanage."

"I'm keeping my baby."

The nurse's face did not betray surprise. A nice kettle of fish! Could the girl be serious? Had she any idea what she was saying, of the outrageous impossibility of the suggestion? Unless of course the woman's family had some plan, a childless married sister that would take the baby to bring up as her own, or some other such arrangement. But no matter what plans were made, having an illegitimate child was a sad business, sad for the mother, sadder for the child.

"Have you thought about this? Has your family made some arrangements?"

"I've made up my own mind and I'm strictly on my own. My family has turned me out."

"That's a hard road you're taking. It's almost impossible to bring up a baby on your own, without the help of your family. It would be better for the child if you gave it up."

"And hand the baby to some orphanage? Not on your life."

So this was it. The girl was on a mission. "How will you manage?"

Victoria told her she had a little money that would see her through most of the first year, and then she would get someone to care for the baby and she would go to work. Nuala said no more. The girl was dreaming if she thought she could get work around here. She would report the conversation to Dr Curran. The girl might change her mind when the time came. However, once a mother became attached to the child it was heartbreaking if she was forced to give it up. Much better that the child be taken away from the mother immediately so that she never saw it, and then she had some chance of resuming her life.

"Well, Victoria I should examine you. I need you to be lying down."

"Come upstairs to my bedroom."

Nuala followed her up the stairs noting that her ankles were slightly swollen. She would examine her, measure her abdomen, check her blood pressure and talk to her a little more.

That night Nuala sat at her sitting room fire in, what during conversations with herself, she called her Friday night costume: a pink satin nightgown with a fluted hem and a matching robe. She was waiting for Sam Burkinshaw's tap at the window, his step at the back door. Her pebble dashed house was the last in a row of six attached houses, two up and two down, on Church Road. Uncharacteristically, she looked back at her day. The exhausted woman in the Terraces, with more children than anyone could manage, future flotsam for the emigrant tide. The pregnant girl at Beechwood, who hadn't the foggiest notion of what was before her, the shunning, the gossip. Fortunately, Beechwood was out in the country and the Wynnes were decent people.

She'd been in love with Sam since the winter's night four years ago when he'd knocked on her door at nine o'clock startling her out of her concentration on an Annie M P Smithson novel. He'd asked to come in and she thought it was to discuss his widowed mother whom Nuala had been visiting daily. She'd been sent home from the county hospital with crutches after nine weeks in traction for a fractured femur. Sam had sat at the kitchen table and she'd made him a cup of tea.

"Would you have a drop of whiskey? I like a spot in me tea."

When she produced the bottle of Powers he said, "I'll miss you coming about the place when my mother can manage the crutches herself."

"What I'm trying to do Sam, is to get rid of the crutches, get her using a walking stick."

She'd noticed how considerate Sam was of his mother, he a big shambling farmer.

"Sure you're doing great with her Nuala, altogether."

Nuala seldom got praise from her patients or their families. They sat there and enjoyed their tea and he told her his life story, how he'd hardly ever left the fifty acre farm over beyond Meagherduff Cross. She shared her memories of a farm in Offally, three sisters and a brother, of the Presentation Convent in Mountmellick and nurses' training at the Mater Hospital and the Rotunda. Near midnight she threw a shovel of coal in the stove and when she sat down Sam said, "You know I've wanted to kiss you since the first time I saw you."

"And when was that?" Nuala wasn't altogether surprised, but Sam was a Protestant.

"About ten years ago, one Fair Day."

So of course she kissed him. And when he left at two o'clock in the morning, he asked if he could come the following Friday. Their lives took on a pattern, a secret ritual. Friday and Sunday nights, after eleven o'clock he'd come, hide his bike behind the coal shed and tap on her back window. Sam had promised to marry her when his mother, who was eighty-one died. He'd explained that if he married a Catholic girl she'd disinherit him, leave the farm to a nephew. So Nuala went about her work, grateful for her job and her house, played whist with nurse friends at the county hospital, went to the occasional social at the church hall, or to a film, and not a soul in Killcore knew about her and Sam. Now she sat waiting, thinking of that pregnant girl at Beechwood, the whiskey bottle and glasses behind her on the table, the clock ticking, the turf fire murmuring in its fierce red veins and settling on itself. At midnight, she heard his tap on the window and went to open the back door. "Cold as charity out there," he said and kissed her cheek. She put her arms around him and kissed him earnestly, passionately.

"Wait, now, till I get my coat off," he protested. She helped him off with his coat, took his hand and led him through the darkened kitchen into the firelit sitting room.

11

Shooting Season

*I*n Mrs. Wynne's sitting room the first Saturday evening in November, Victoria drank in long shadows on the orchard. The willows in the garden had their fronds yellow now, although there were few leaves down. Without knowing it, Victoria was becoming a countrywoman.

A week before when she sucked the bitter juice from a sloe Mrs. Wynne, amused at Victoria's puckered face, said, "When we were young we made sloe gin. It was such a lark to make it for Christmas."

The rowan berries now lighted the misty lanes and in the mornings when she walked in the garden, she discovered holly berries glowing, their glistening spiked leaves jutting out between the rhododendron. She was amazed that she had never noticed the holly growing there before. How little she had really looked. She could see a few red apples left on the top of the trees glowing in the last of the sun and flocks of birds wheeling from the roof into the fading light of the sky. Three weeks earlier, watching from this window, Victoria had seen Dominic stand under an apple tree and raise his arms like Solomon in the temple, and shake the last of the apples from the top branches and gather them up in a tin basin for Josie. They had been enjoying apple tart with Bird's Custard for a sweet at dinner, and apple and blackberry crisp another evening. The autumn smell of cooking apples, cloves and cinnamon floated up from the kitchen. Mrs. Wynne had been dozing in her chair by the fire since teatime and a deep weekend silence filled the house. "Where is Josie?" she asked.

"Gone to see her mother," Victoria answered, the old lady nodded and Victoria went back to her book. A few minutes later she asked again, and Victoria answered as before.

Andrew and Dominic had gone very early in the morning with the dogs to the woods west of Killcore to shoot pheasants, but Victoria thought they must be back since it was past milking time. Mrs. Wynne had dozed off. Victoria knelt and built up the fire, careful not to wake her. After lunch Josie had left on her bicycle for her monthly visit to her mother in the County Home, an apple cake in a battered biscuit tin in the basket of her bicycle. Before she'd set off, she'd prepared dinner: salad with pickled beets and sliced hard boiled eggs, and apple tart with clotted cream. She covered the tray with a tea cloth and left it. "Just make a fresh pot of tea," she instructed Victoria. "Dominic and Mr. Wynne can look after themselves. They're shooting today."

Soon Victoria would go down to the kitchen, build up the coal fire in the range, open the damper and put the kettle on. She fell half asleep in the warmth and quiet, then an agonizing cramp in her left calf woke her. It was so painful she almost cried out. She bent forward and massaged her leg vigorously for several minutes, stretched her toes and then her heels as Nuala Fay had instructed her. Gradually the cramp eased. It was now almost dark in the room and she lit the lamp. Mrs. Wynne opened her eyes. "I'm going down to fetch our dinner tray, Mrs. Wynne."

"Do, dear."

She lit one of the candles on the mantel piece and started downstairs to put the kettle on to boil. As she came down the passage toward the kitchen she caught the pungent smell of roasting fowl. She came through the baize door and paused in the shadows at the kitchen entrance. Andrew sat with his back to her and Dominic with his back to the glowing stove, before them heaped plates and open bottles of Guinness. The humps of small roast birds glittered with grease on an iron pan in the centre of the table. Beneath the table the dogs gnawed noisily on bones gripped in their paws. As she watched, Dominic sucked the last meat from a drumstick and tossed it and one of the dogs snapped it in his jaws in mid air. The other gave a low growl. Dominic speared a potato with his fork. Victoria tiptoed back and waited, uneasy, in the hall. There was something strange about the scene: the twilit kitchen, the red glow from the stove, and the lamp, the pungent smell of roasted game and of porter, the men eating without restraint. She waited, for she felt like an intruder. She heard Andrew say, "That was the best day's shooting we've had in years, Dominic."

Dominic answered, "Oh, no shortage of birds this year," and she went forward into the kitchen.

"I've just come to fetch a tray Josie left for us in the pantry."

Andrew stood up when she entered. "Please go on with your meal," she urged and went to fill the kettle at the sink. The air in the kitchen shifted.

"When the kettle boils, Dominic will bring up the tray," Andrew said decisively, standing behind his chair. Dominic wiped his mouth with a napkin and stared at her, and she put the kettle on the range but felt dismissed from the kitchen. She went back upstairs and the image of the two men eating and the dogs growling and grinding at their feet stayed with her.

"Dominic is bringing up the tray Josie left for us, Mrs. Wynne."

Mrs. Wynne yawned behind her dry spotted hand and stood up. "I'll go along and wash my hands."

Victoria took the candle along to the bathroom and placed it on the side table. She went back to the sitting room and stood looking at the black mirror of the window until she heard the lavatory flush and then she went and took the candle from Mrs. Wynne and walked back with her to her sitting room. The baby kicked sharply in her side and she saw again the savage snap of the dog's jaw on the bones.

The pace of activity at Beechwood slowed as the days grew shorter; it was dark at five o'clock. Victoria worried about the future, and about how she would provide for the child. She raged against Donny Maguire and against her family and in the same day would long for the baby to be born. Late one afternoon she stood outside the back door and watched a man drive into the yard with a load of turf piled high in a crate on the top of a cart. Peggy crossed the yard on her way to the ash pit at the back of the stables with two buckets of ashes, remnants of fires that were now necessary in every room. The man stared after her and Josie came from the kitchen and said, "I hope that turf is dry. The last load we got was no great bargain."

"They're as dry as snuff so they are, Ma'am."

The horse sneezed, the harness jingled and Dominic and Matt came from the cow byres. "We'll give you a hand to stack them," Dominic said. "One of these days it'll be winter." He took the horse's rein and they all walked out of her sight around by the back of the old disused dairy. She could hear Dominic coughing as he went. Yes, it would soon be winter. Would she at last receive a letter from her parents? She had sent them the Beechwood address her first week here but they had never answered. Maybe at Christmas? She doubted it.

Mrs. Wynne walked less in the afternoons and her circuit of the grounds occurred rarely. Mrs. Wynne trusted Victoria to check the outbuildings, which she did, to placate the old woman. So one day flowed into another. She was sleeping badly; the baby disturbed her rest, with a tiny foot kicking or a fist pushing against her side. Lying there in the dark, she worried about how much money she would need to live on when the baby came. She had saved the six pounds Andrew had paid her so far and still had the money she had taken from the bank the day she had gone to see the abortionist, as well as a little money in the bank in Blackrock. She had spent nothing except for her maternity clothes. Sometimes she lay awake for hours listening to the wind blow and the papery sound as it drove the dry leaves along the gutters above her window, homesick, if one could be homesick when one no longer had a home to return to. Sometimes she wept before sleep overwhelmed with loneliness. Not one word from her parents!

The only visitors to the house she had ever seen were the doctor and Nuala Fay. Of course there were the Mac Adams and the Pattersons whom they saw at church services. But they never visited nor had Mrs. Wynne ever suggested they walk over there. Victoria remembered how grudgingly Mrs. Mac Adam had nodded and looked at Victoria's belly when Mrs. Wynne had invited them to visit, standing at the church steps that first day.

She woke early and sometimes was content, for everything in her life to this moment seemed then a prelude to these mornings when she stood at her window watching the trees come up out of the dark while the eastern sky lightened. Nuala Fay had said she must get more exercise so if the weather was dry she would get up and walk in the garden. One morning she debated with herself if she should go out because it had rained in the night, but she so relished this time on her own she got dressed and went out. Everything was soft and moist, a dying three-quarter moon hung in a misty sky. She went round by the hothouse and stopped short. A man was standing in the yard looking at the blazing sunrise low on the horizon behind the trunks of the leafless trees. It was Dominic. Paused in his work, as if acknowledging its wonder, looking at the perfection of this one particular sunrise, already fading, that they would never see again. She stopped and watched him, and for some reason she wept. He stood for some minutes then moved off. She heard his boots on the gravel and then his coughing, saw Matt cross the yard and Dominic follow him, still coughing, toward the milking parlour. She wiped her tears away. Those damn cigarettes. She headed for the kitchen and an early cup of tea. Josie had softened a little of late, seemed almost to accept Victoria. As she spooned tea from the canister into the pot Victoria thought about that figure just standing there, facing the perfection of the rising sun. So at home, as if he had grown out of the earth, so much a part he was of the soil, so close he was to the country and the land. In contrast Matt was just the casual day labourer with his cap rakish on one side of his head, his dark wiry hair standing up on the other side and his unceasing talk about dances and horse betting and The Hospital Sweepstakes.

Late on a cold wet Tuesday afternoon Victoria came downstairs to get the tea tray and found Dominic sitting by the kitchen range, a steaming enamelled basin of water at his bare feet. Josie shook a tablespoon of Coleman's mustard powder in the water and stirred it with her hand. "Soak your feet in that, I'll make you a drink of punch and then to bed with you."

Sweat ran down Dominic's flushed face. He coughed uncontrollably, blood spotted spit stained his check handkerchief.

"You're sick, Dominic. You need to take care."

"Sick, of course he's sick, just look at the cut of him," Josie stormed, as if it were Victoria's fault. "Got wet to the skin, unloading the creamery cans."

She handed Dominic a steaming glass of hot whiskey punch. "Get that into you and get to bed."

"It's just my chest, Miss."

Dominic's face was gaunt, his red rimmed eyes unnaturally bright. "The boss is gone for the doctor."

The kettle was boiling on the range and the tea tray ready on the kitchen table.

"I'll make the tea," Victoria ventured.

"Leave it, leave it. I'll bring it up."

Seeing Josie's agitation Victoria went back upstairs. "Josie is bringing our tea, Mrs. Wynne."

"That will be nice."

"Dominic is unwell."

"Oh, I hope it's nothing serious. Andrew depends on him so much. I don't think that other lad we have is much help."

"Oh, but Matt's improving. He's a great help."

"That's a comfort to know."

Dr. Curran ordered Dominic to stay in bed. No one, but Josie and Andrew, was to go in his room. A gloomy quiet descended on the house. Only Matt seemed content, now that he was deputized to do the creamery run. He could place his bets with the Turf Accountant instead of depending on Dominic to do it. Andrew looked exhausted, silent at meals, leaving the table immediately after he had eaten, going to see to matters on the farm or in the dairy or to check on Dominic. Josie bustled about importantly, bossing

Peggy, who now came every day. Late at night Victoria heard the gramophone, and she knew Andrew was sitting up with Dominic and keeping him company. Victoria and Mrs. Wynne sat together in the drawing room after dinner. At first Victoria fiddled with the knobs of the wireless until it became clear to Victoria that Mrs. Wynne preferred to be read to than listen to the uncertain voices from the radio.

All Saturday mist lay on the orchard and the garden, wrapping the sundial, the dry pampas grass and the willows. In spite of this, so convinced were Victoria and Andrew of the benefit of a walk for Mrs. Wynne's nerves that after lunch, when a light wind began to disperse the fog, Victoria suggested they go out. She and Mrs. Wynne put on their galoshes and coats and took their walk down through the garden past the meadows almost as far as the river. Returning, Mrs. Wynne said "I'm tired of Miss Austen's perfect sentences, and her young women manoeuvring for husbands."

"And what about her young men?"

"Well they're manoeuvring too, for fortunes mostly."

"What would you like to read then?" Victoria asked, thinking the person who is tired of Jane Austen is tired of reading.

"Why don't you choose, Victoria?"

"I see we have *The Time Machine*. I've wanted to read that."

"That would be lovely. I've read it before but I'd like to hear you read it."

As they came by the orchard wall they saw that robins were feeding on crumbs Josie had spread on Dominic's table.

"Let's have our tea in the Square Room, Victoria. Then you can read and I can watch the birds."

They went in and removed their coats. Victoria saw that Mrs. Wynne's hair was jewelled with mist. She settled her in the chair, put a match to the fire and fetched a towel to dry her hair. Mrs. Wynne sat looking at the birds fluttering down in the fast fading light to peck at the bird table. They were both ready for tea and Victoria fetched the tray from the kitchen. By then it was almost dark so she lit the lamp and put it on the table beside her and poured out their tea. Today Josie had made apple cake mostly to tempt Dominic. He had been ill a week. The doctor came every second day to see him and Andrew reported that he was still very sick, but holding his own.

Mrs. Wynne sipped her tea and Victoria began to read the tale of *The Time Machine*. Mrs. Wynne listened intently and then interrupted. "I can see those five men enjoying their pipes and listening to the Time Traveller."

Victoria continued reading, *"It is simply this. That space, as our mathematicians have it, is spoken of as having three dimensions."*

"I've always understood the idea of duration as The Fourth Dimension," Mrs. Wynne interrupted again. "I think it's because I'm an old woman and I've seen people close to me go on ahead into their futures."

"Where do you think they've gone, Mrs. Wynne?"

"I don't know, but I feel they are somewhere, and that's a comfort. But if I had a time machine I'd go back in time, not forward. I'd go back to when my sons were boys, before wars and revolutions. I'd go back to when they rode their ponies around the place."

Mrs. Wynne put her cup down and pulled her shawl around herself. Victoria hoped the story wouldn't make Mrs. Wynne sad. She picked up the tea tray. "I'll take the tray back to the kitchen. I'll just be a second."

Saucebottle, standing in the shadow of the orchard wall, had been watching. He'd spent the afternoon at Hourigans drinking and brooding. Now he saw beyond the glass conservatory into a room, and could distinguish the old woman in a cane chair beside a lamp on a white table and the younger woman reading. He listened hard and thought he could hear her voice as she read. This was the closest he had ever dared to come. There were no curtains to catch fire, but there were rugs, and those cushions. And it would be easy to get in, easy to jimmy the lock on the conservatory with a screwdriver. He leaned back against the wall faint at the thought and woozy from the alcohol. He closed his eyes for a minute. The conservatory door opened.

"Is that you, Andrew? Is everything alright?"

Saucebottle ran, stumbling and falling against the bushes and Mrs. Wynne screamed, "There's someone there. Outside, over there."

Her screams followed him as he hared it across the terrace and down the avenue. Victoria, coming back from the kitchen, saw nothing but Mrs. Wynne standing at the open door screaming, and the sound of something crashing through the garden. The dogs barked in the kitchen. Andrew and Josie rushed into the room, the dogs racing ahead of them sniffing the rugs. Victoria held Mrs. Wynne in her arms, trying to calm her. "It's alright Mrs. Wynne. Andrew is here and Josie."

But Mrs. Wynne sobbed, "I knew it. I always knew it."

"Now calm down Mother. It's okay."

"There were men outside, I saw them Andrew."

"Did you see anything, Victoria?"

"I heard something running in the garden."

"Probably a deer Mother," Andrew said and walked over and stood in the conservatory doorway. The dogs rushed out past him barking.

Mrs. Wynne sat down again, her face in her hands. "There haven't been deer here for years, Andrew."

"It must have been an animal Mother, one of Mac Adam's or Callaghan's cattle."

"The gun men, Andrew."

"I doubt that Mother. There's no gun men any more. They haven't been about for years. The IRA was banned last year. You're imagining it."

"I'm not Andrew. There was a man there."

"Probably a tinker, looking to steal chickens. There's gypsies camped over near Meagherduff crossroads. I'll go in to the barracks in the morning and make a complaint. There's nothing to be done this evening. Why don't you go upstairs now with Victoria."

Like a child Mrs. Wynne allowed herself to be led upstairs. She sat at the fire in her sitting room. In a few minutes Andrew brought up a tray with a whiskey bottle, a siphon of soda and three glasses. He poured a drink for his mother. "Take a drink Mother. It will help you."

She refused, and sat silent and stared into the fire.

"Would you like a drink Victoria?"

"No thanks."

"I'll leave it here in case you feel like one later."

After he left, Victoria resumed reading. "I wish I had a time machine," the old woman wept, "to take me away from here. I wish I were dead. I wonder how long I have left on this earth?"

Dismayed by this confession Victoria said, "Mrs. Wynne, don't think like that. Think how Andrew needs you."

"No one needs me. I'm useless, an encumbrance. Read on Victoria. I like the sound of you reading."

At dinner time, Andrew and Josie brought trays up to her sitting room but she did not eat. Victoria ate a little boiled ham and potatoes. Mrs. Wynne refused even a cup of tea.

At nine o'clock, thoroughly alarmed, Andrew set off to fetch Doctor Curran. While they waited Victoria attempted to distract Mrs. Wynne by reading to her, but she wasn't listening. She suggested cards, but the old woman just sat there looking in the fire. After a while she said, "We're doomed here. And I'm an old woman. I can do nothing. If only Charles were still alive."

When the doctor arrived she was still staring at the fire. Victoria escaped and waited in her bedroom, sad to see Mrs. Wynne so low. It likely had been a tinker. She thought she had heard someone running. The previous day, Matt had mentioned a tinker who had come in the yard enquiring if they needed pots or pails mended. "Looking for what he could lift out of the place," Josie had said.

She had left her door ajar and could hear the doctor talking and Mrs. Wynne's querulous voice, and then Andrew knocked on her door. "Victoria, Doctor Curran has given my mother something to help her sleep. I think she would like to go to bed now."

"I'll help her get settled."

"Thanks Victoria. I don't know how we would manage without you."

Dr. Curran was still sitting with Mrs. Wynne and when Victoria entered he stood up. "Now Mrs. Wynne that injection I gave you will help you sleep and by tomorrow you will be alright again. I'll leave a prescription to be filled at the Medical Hall and now I'm going to talk to Andrew."

Victoria helped Mrs. Wynne undress and wash and sat beside her bed until she was asleep. There was a faint knock and the door opened and Josie crept in. "Ah she looks content, the poor soul," she whispered, looking down on the sleeping woman. Victoria was surprised to see that her eyes were moist. So the kitchen ogre had a heart.

"She'll sleep well,' Victoria said. "The doctor gave her an injection."

They tiptoed out of the room. On the landing, Josie lamented, "And poor Dominic on the broad of his back."

"Is Dominic getting better?"

"Mr. Wynne mostly sees to him. But," she said doubtfully, "he's very sick. Thin like a whippet poor lad. Now Mrs. Wynne, she's strong as a salmon. She'll be alright, please God."

Victoria had little time to think of Dominic because Mrs. Wynne's care took all her time but again one night she heard snatches of a song float up from the gramophone in Andrew's study.

"We have been gay,

Going our way"

Then the sound faded and her mind filled in the lines.

"After you've gone,

Life will go on, like an old song."

That seemed so sad. Then she told herself to stop being morbid and to think about her baby.

But Mrs. Wynne had begun a slow decline. Doctor Curran prescribed paraldehyde to be taken at breakfast, at four in the afternoon and at bedtime. She quickly appeared to be dependent on the medication and would ask for it before it was due. Although Victoria persuaded her to adhere to the prescribed times, she noticed Mrs. Wynne often fell asleep in her chair by the fire and settled to bed earlier and earlier as the days shortened. She needed help to dress, and when they went out she walked slowly, hanging on to Victoria's arm. Their walks were much shorter now. Mrs. Wynne was too tired to go far.

Victoria was sleeping, dreaming of Donny Maguire, so that when she opened her eyes for a second imagined she saw his face in the dark. She heard a commotion downstairs and instinctively she thought of Mrs. Wynne. It was dark and rain hammered on the windows. She turned clumsily on her side, felt for the matches and lit the candle on her bedside table. Ten past five. She sat out on the side of the bed, took the candle and went across to Mrs. Wynne's room, softly opened her door and heard the old woman's snoring. She shut the door gently, heard the sound of a car engine, saw lights sweep the landing, and when she crossed to the window she saw the headlights of a car disappear down the avenue. She pushed her feet into her slippers, dragged her dressing gown round her bulging belly, took the candle and went downstairs. She found Josie sitting at the kitchen table, her head in her hands.

"My God Josie, what happened?"

"Dominic took bad, a terrible turn, so he did. Spitting blood so he is. God help us."

She got up and her shadow moved, enormous on the wall, with the candle behind her on the table. She turned and leaned her back against the sink. "He's finished, so he is. Finished! Mr. Wynne took him to the doctor."

Victoria stared at her, "I didn't think he was that sick."

"He's gone to skin and bone this past week. It's the night sweats does it. Peggy's worn out washing his night shirts."

She ran the water and began washing dishes in the sink. Then ever practical she turned back, wiped her hands in her apron and declared, "I'll light the lamp. Matt's not here yet. He'll have to do the creamery run with the horse and cart today."

"I'll get dressed, Josie."

When she came back Matt was standing in the kitchen. Josie was lighting a lantern. "That Peggy's not here yet. I told her to be on time but you might as well talk to the wall."

"Can I help?"

"Well, you could make the porridge. Three times the water to the oatmeal." She handed Matt the lantern, took her coat from the back of the door and followed him out. Victoria put two measures of oatmeal and six of water in a saucepan and stood stirring it on the range, thinking of Dominic. How hard he worked, how dependent they were on him. Since Dominic's illness, Andrew appeared rushed, distracted. She'd never heard Dominic raise his voice. He was a gentle soul, always placating Josie when she was bad tempered. She wondered about his family. Had he parents, or brothers and sisters? She remembered his terrible cough. Could he be so sick as to die? What was happening in this house, Mrs. Wynne sinking into lethargy, now Dominic ill? If Mrs. Wynne became so ill as to be admitted to hospital, where would she be? She calculated how much money she had in the bank. Where could she rent a room? Maybe the Minister would help. Outside Josie was shouting at Matt, hurrying him on.

Two mornings later when Victoria came down to the kitchen Josie announced, "The bloody milk inspectors are coming. I have to scrub out the dairy and the milking parlour. Could you start the breakfast, Miss?

"How often do the milk inspectors come, Josie?"

"Never! It's because the Doctor, God blast him, said Dominic has consumption. God help us all. The damn TB is what he has. "

Tuberculosis, the awful pronouncement resonated in the steamy kitchen like a death sentence. Josie tipped a pot of boiling water into a pail. "That Matt," she complained, "a proper slacker if you don't watch him. Very careless about washing the milk churns, good job I have a strong hand over him," and she left carrying the steaming pail. Victoria heard her scolding Matt in the yard.

Victoria filled the kettle and put it on the stove. Poor Dominic! His coughing was something she noticed from the start. Why hadn't someone done something about it? Maybe she should have spoken to Andrew about it. But it was not her place. In a sense she was a servant too. She went to the pantry and brought some eggs to cook for breakfast. But who was there to eat it? Mrs. Wynne wouldn't wake for another two hours at least. Andrew was likely busy in the milking parlour. She loaded the dishes on a tray to take to the dining room, then changed her mind and laid the table for Matt and Josie and Peggy in the kitchen.

That evening Josie and Matt stripped Dominic's bed and washed his furniture with Jeyes Fluid. After dark they burned the mattress in the field behind the byres, the smoke rising like a sacrificial offering in the winter night.

12

Death in the Country

*D*ominic died at Newcastle Sanatorium in Wicklow, the last Tuesday in November. Andrew, pale, but calm and businesslike, decided his mother was not to be told. The funeral was delayed until Friday to allow Dominic's brothers to travel from England and the old cottage, which Dominic had left to live at Beechwood, was cleaned up and the fire lighted, to provide lodging for them. Matt, who attended the wake in the cottage on Wednesday, could not go to the funeral because of the creamery run. Victoria stayed with the old woman while Andrew, Josie and Peggy attended the funeral. To her amazement, Mrs. Wynne talked all morning about Dominic. It seemed as if despite their efforts to keep his death from her, she sensed something had happened. She told Victoria Dominic's father had been her husband's tenant and in the Land Reform of 1909 had been able to buy his smallholding. The house was still there, a thatched farm labourer's cottage. Dominic was the eldest of five all of whom except Dominic had emigrated, two brothers to England and two sisters to America. Dominic had chosen to live and work at Beechwood from 1914 on and let his eight acres to neighbouring farmers for grazing. Victoria knew he could not have gotten much revenue from letting the land. De Valera's decision to cease annuity payments to England had adversely affected the export of beef cattle as the British, in retaliation, placed tariffs on Irish cattle entering England, although the more recent Cattle/Coal Pacts had eased the situation. Dominic had a self possession that, she decided, was the result of his owning property.

Because of the rain they did not walk that day and the house was unnaturally quiet. Outside there was the sad drip from the eaves. When Victoria went to the kitchen to prepare their afternoon tea, Josie had returned. She was baking, frantically slapping dough on the board, her face like stone. "We have to eat no matter who dies or goes overboard," she muttered. A jar of cherries glittered darkly on the table and a slab of yellow butter was softening in the warmth of the kitchen.

"I came to get our tea tray, Josie."

"It's there, in front of you," she said crossly, "and the kettle's boiling. You just have to make the tea."

Victoria ignored her brusqueness. This frenzy of cooking was probably Josie's way of handling her grief at Dominic's death.

"Oh Carr's Table Water Biscuits, lovely, and cheese too," Mrs. Wynne exclaimed when Victoria put the tray on the table. At four o'clock she gave Mrs. Wynne her medicine. There was no sign of Andrew. When it was almost dark she heard the rattle of the creamery cans and the horse's feet clop in the lane, Matt back from the creamery. Mrs. Wynne dosed in her chair. Victoria mended her stockings. By dinnertime, Andrew had not yet returned and when Victoria went down to the kitchen Matt and Peggy were eating at the table and Josie sat opposite her eyes mournful through the steam of the tea mug she held in her cupped hands. Victoria saw that she had interrupted their conversation. A pan of cherry slab cake was cooling on the dresser. Two dinner trays had been prepared. Victoria took one tray and Josie the other and carried them up to Mrs. Wynne's sitting room. "Terrible rain Ma'am," Josie said as she put the tray down.

"Cold too, Josie."

Josie knelt to build up the fire.

"How are you, Josie?"

"Busy Ma'am. And that Peggy! I'm scalded with her. I have to be after her all the time."

Mrs. Wynne picked up her knife and fork, not interested in Josie's story. Josie stood up from the fire. "I'll get that fire going in your room Ma'am."

While they ate, Victoria tried to make conversation but Mrs. Wynne was tired from all they had talked that day. "I'd like my sleeping draught now," she said when she had finished her pudding.

"Isn't it a little early?"

"Dark rainy evenings like these, Victoria, I just want to sleep. I'm very tired. Tomorrow, if it's fine, I'll take a walk."

Victoria lit the lamp in the old woman's room, and helped her get ready for sleep. Mog sat on the hearth waiting for her chance to jump on the bed. Victoria gave her the bedtime medicine and said goodnight. Back in Mrs. Wynne's sitting room she stacked the dishes on one tray, put that tray on top of the other and carried it downstairs. The hall and kitchen lamps had been turned down low but there was no sign of Josie. She had obviously gone to bed and Peggy and Matt had left for the day. How deathly quiet and empty the kitchen was. Dominic was gone and as she piled the dishes in the sink, tears Victoria had held in check all day overflowed and she wiped them impatiently away with the back of her hand. She could not afford to weep, and she was weeping for a servant: but without Dominic, one of the props that held the household together was lost. Victoria, however, was growing beyond the naïve girl of the previous spring, and the depressed, pregnant, young woman locked in her room in Blackrock. Wiping her tears away in the empty kitchen she was a woman slowly achieving her destiny

Strange that Andrew had not returned to help Matt with the evening milking. She concluded he was with Dominic's relations and suspected Josie had seen to it that Matt did everything properly. Wearily, Victoria left the dishes in the sink for Peggy in the morning and went back upstairs. When she checked, Mrs. Wynne was asleep. She turned down the lamp, went to her own room, put a match to her lamp and the fire, sat in her chair and took up *The Time Machine*. She marvelled at how absorbing the tale of the man from the nineteenth century and the girl from the future was, despite its fantastic premise. The bleak landscape of the future seemed written for this night, the night of Dominic's funeral. She was deciding that it was the love story that made the novel credible, although it was a love story with neither passion nor sex. When car lights circled the room, she knew Andrew was home.

Victoria took her candle, went downstairs and waited for him to come in from the yard. He came slowly through the scullery into the kitchen. His face was ashen. Rain had plastered his hair to his skull. The two dogs got up from in front of the range and stood in front of him. He didn't seem to notice.

"Andrew, are you alright?"

"I hardly know how I am Victoria," he sighed, took off his soaked raincoat and threw it on a chair. She was startled to see a black diamond was sewn on the sleeve of his suit jacket. This symbol of mourning was usually worn only for family.

"Can I get you something to eat?"

"Maybe a drink."

She took the candle and went to the dining room for the whiskey and soda. When she returned, he was sitting at the table with his head in his hands. She poured him a stiff drink. "Have this, Andrew. It will help you."

"Nothing will help me, Victoria."But he took the glass and drank. She sat down in the chair opposite him. He seemed somehow broken. She knew he thought the world of Dominic, but his ravished face shocked her.

"It was awful Victoria. Pagan, primitive."

"What was, Andrew?"

"That funeral Victoria; it broke my heart! So perfunctory, so mercenary."

"Mercenary?"

"Yes mercenary! They put a table beside the coffin in front of the altar and people paraded up the aisle and put money on the table. To my shame I went up and did the same. Then the amounts were read out."

"My God."

"I wanted to overturn that table, throw it over like Jesus did in the temple, but it was not my place. His brothers were there and they didn't interfere."

"What was the money for, Andrew?"

"How should I know what it was for? Funeral offerings of some sort. Then when they carried out his coffin, and put it in the hearse to take it to the graveyard, I left! I could not make myself go. Josie went. I expect she got a lift home with the Callaghans. I've been walking the fields since."

She was appalled to see tears overflow his eyes.

"Poor fellow, Victoria. Life you know, was something he had just one of and now it's over. And when he was sick he'd just lie there. He never stirred in the bed. I thought he was afraid to move in case he shortened his time, but he never complained."

Andrew sat with his hands clasped on the table, staring into space. Victoria felt profoundly uneasy. This was an Andrew she didn't recognise, this man grieving for a servant. He said, "He was nature's own gentleman, Victoria; the best, the most honest man I've ever met."

"I know that Andrew. I know. I envied your friendship."

"Friendship?" His voice rose as he spoke, his grey eyes blazed at her. "Friendship? Victoria, we loved each other. We were lovers. Did you not know? We loved each other. Do you understand? We were lovers." He was shouting now, "The love that dare not speak its name. We spoke it! We lived it!"

His face was so altered, so angry, so defiant, his grey eyes so wounded, she just sat staring at him.

"Don't you see how it was Victoria? We were everything to each other. Everything!"

She nodded slowly, floored by his admission, but beginning to understand. So much made sense now, so many things that had puzzled her, the closeness of the two men, how at ease they had been with each other. But she was appalled, shocked into silence. The risks they'd taken. If they'd been discovered, the public disgrace, arrest, imprisonment.

Then, to her horror, he began to sob, violent heaves shaking his shoulders. She thought of calling Josie, but what could Josie do? His bowed head showed his hair thinned and streaked with grey. He looked up at her through his tears. "You don't know fear till you know you're queer in this country, Victoria. This country of Rome rule! I will never, never get over losing him. Never! He loved this place, and I had it willed to him. I thought I'd go first. I don't know how I'll manage without him. And my mother, fading away!" He bowed his head on his hands and sobbed.

She moved to the chair beside him, sat there and let him weep. It was the longest speech she had ever heard from him. Moved by pity, she took his hand in hers, "Andrew, please! Please don't cry. People get over these things."

He sat up defiant. "Get over it? Don't say that. Don't say it. You don't believe me, do you? No one understands. No one does! You can't get over being queer! Till Wilde's trial I never knew what I was. I was thirteen then, at Ranelagh School. I had no name for it, no way to think about it. And then I knew. Look what happened to Oscar, and to Casement. And poor Dominic, he was queer too. He was my lover and my friend and I've lost him." He sat with bowed head, weeping.

At the mention of Oscar Wilde, Victoria began to get some sense of Andrew's desolation, of the isolation of his existence, and she was flooded with compassion. With her free hand she stroked his head as if he were a child. "Don't cry Andrew. Please. Don't take it so hard. Look at me, Andrew, how I live. Kicked out of my home like a dog! And all because I was foolish and loved someone. And every hour of every day I worry about what to do in February when my child will be born."

He lifted up his head and nodded slowly. "We're outcasts, Victoria, both of us."

He continued to look at her his face also full of sympathy. Then he put his hand over hers. "Victoria, why don't we marry? It's the answer for us both. The world has no use for us. If we marry, your child has a name. You have a home. My mother has a companion. There are worse marriages."

She was shocked to silence by the suggestion. Andrew poured more whiskey in his glass. "I'd never be a proper husband, but you could have your own life, such as it would be in this out of the way place. And the child would be safe. What were you going to do, Victoria? Are you putting the child in an institution?"

"I am determined never to do that. I have a little money and I was hoping to leave her with some woman and go to work."

He looked sceptical. "Where would you find work, Victoria?"

"I don't know. I suppose I've been unrealistic."

"I assumed you would place the child in an orphanage and go back home."

"I'll never go home again. Never. I'm decided on that. Never!"

"If we marry, you won't have to."

"Andrew, can I think about this some more?"

"Of course."

Minutes passed as they sat there in silence for what felt to Victoria, a very long time. Andrew took a Wills pack from his pocket, and lit a cigarette from the candle. Wills was Dominic's brand. She had rarely seen Andrew smoking. Victoria wanted to get out of the kitchen, to be alone. There were things to consider. "I think I'd like to go upstairs now, Andrew."

"Of course. I won't sleep. I'll drink myself into oblivion."

Upstairs Victoria sat in the armchair at her fire thinking about Andrew's proposal. The rain bucketed down off the gutters. November dark enveloped the silent house. She took the eiderdown off her bed and pulled it round herself. She hugged her belly and wished the child would move. She listened for Andrew coming upstairs but heard nothing. His declaration had stunned her. When he wept, she was shocked and, at the same time, filled with pity that such a dignified man should weep. Now it seemed to her that since September she had lived in a dream. Her constant planning and speculating on how she would live had an unreal quality: it was impossible to keep her baby unless someone helped her. Her family certainly wouldn't, they had demonstrated that. She'd be an outcast, her baby illegitimate, a bastard. That horrid, shameful label would follow her child forever and make life unbearable for them both. Why had she not thought about that? Marrying Andrew was their only chance for a decent life. She'd be stuck here in the country, but she'd have security. And she had grown to love Beechwood. She'd never work at her profession again, of course. Married women didn't work. They retired when they married. Her career as a librarian was finished, her days at Trinity a waste. The ancient air of Trinity

College, the sun shadows on the cobbled yard, the Georgian portico, the familiar mass of Brugh's library, rose like frames in her imagination and she was filled with a degrading sense of failure. She wept for her own mistakes, for Dominic's short life, for the vulnerability of her baby, the awful severity of living. Her career was over the day she decided to keep the baby. But Andrew's offer brought a man to take care of her. Lately, she had just wanted someone to take charge and look after everything, although she knew that was unrealistic. In the end, the baby was her responsibility. She must try to be wise. She could not have predicted that she would be offered marriage, but now her marrying Andrew seemed as if it was her destiny. She understood now that her decision was long made in the dawn of that Sunday morning two months earlier when she had first felt life within her and determined to keep the child. In some sense, had she not been seeking someone to rescue her? Had she not glanced around the church many Sundays looking for a prospective husband? How ridiculous that had been! She began to weep and then, having cried her heart out, wiped her tears. Carrying the candle, she went along to the bathroom, washed her face and went down to the kitchen.

Andrew sat jammed against the chair back, staring straight ahead, one leg bent with the calf resting on the opposite knee. The two dogs were asleep under the table. The whiskey level in the bottle had dropped an inch.

"Victoria, I thought you'd gone to bed."

She sat down beside him. "No. I've been thinking about what you've said. For us to marry would make things easier for me."

"For me too."

He got up, removed the top of the stove and tipped in a shovel of coal, crouched down and poked the fire through the bars. "It's cold Victoria. We'll be in Josie's black books if we let the fire go out."

"How will we arrange to marry, Andrew?"

"Oh nothing easier! Austin Johnston will be only too happy to oblige. The Reverend believes the more good Protestant unions the better." He said this a little bitterly. "And this one is guaranteed to increase his congregation by at least one."

Victoria pictured taking her child to church. The image was reassuring. She would be joining the world again.

"I'll go over and talk to him tomorrow evening. He's not a bad sort. He'll need a few weeks to read the Bans, unless it's possible to get some sort of dispensation."

He lit another cigarette, leaned his head back, blew a mouthful of smoke and watched it rise past the clothes rack and lose itself in the beams of the ceiling. "I don't have much experience of the marriage business, Victoria."

"Neither have I."

"Before I speak to the Minister we must tell my mother. She will be pleased. To see me married will be the fulfilment of all her hopes. It's a good job I can make someone happy."

He twisted the cork out of the whiskey bottle to refill his glass.

"Please don't drink any more tonight, Andrew. You'll have such a hangover."

He replaced the cork, and came and put his hands on either side of her head and kissed her forehead. "Goodnight Victoria, You should get some sleep," and he walked through the baize door. She followed him with the candle through his study and found him standing in the room that had been Dominic's, looking at the bare iron bed frame. Then he made his way back into the hall and went unsteadily up the stairs. She heard him strike a match at his bedroom door to light his way.

In the morning when she awoke, she immediately remembered the previous night's conversation. Had Andrew Wynne asked her to marry him and had she agreed? Well, she decided, she was not being taken in marrying Andrew; she knew the worst of him. So, content with her decision and alive with a new energy, she got dressed and went downstairs. The kitchen was empty. In the dining room, Andrew's used breakfast dishes had not been cleared away. She lifted the lid, and saw the porridge was still hot so she served herself and poured out the last of the coffee.

All day she sat with Mrs. Wynne, while rain ran down the windows and the cat slept in the old woman's lap. Just as they finished tea Andrew came in. He kissed his mother. "How are you today, Mother?"

Victoria put the teacups on the tray. "I'll take these down," she announced, not wanting to be present for a conversation about Andrew's proposal of marriage.

Andrew sat in the chair Victoria had vacated and looked at his mother. She was pale and thinner than ever, but she smiled, as always, at her son. "Mother," he began, "I've something to tell you. I've proposed marriage to Victoria. I hope you will approve."

His mother's smile faded into a solemn stare.

"She's a fine person, Mother."

"I know that, Andrew. It's just that I'm surprised."

"Have you some objection, Mother?"

"Not if it's what you wish to do Andrew. If it's for your happiness."

"I believe we will be content. You know she is expecting a child and she intends to keep the baby and I have no objections."

Mrs. Wynne took a handkerchief from the pocket of her cardigan and blew her nose. Mog jumped off her lap. "It's well you marry so, Andrew."

"Thank you, Mother."

Victoria delayed in the kitchen. She put the dishes in the sink, folded the tray cloth and put the tray in the slot beside the dresser. On the landing she passed Andrew. He turned on the stairs and looked up at her. "We have her blessing, Victoria."

She nodded and went in the sitting room. The old woman did not open her eyes. Victoria sat and looked out through the dusk on the drenched garden, the drooping willows, glistening gravel. Estranged from her family, she had relinquished all her former acquaintance but soon she would be respectable again. She had however no thought of taking up her former circle of friends, or her family. She decided she was content to sit here in this isolated house with this gentle old woman, and await the birth of her baby.

Although Mrs. Wynne's eyes were closed, she wasn't asleep. She was thinking about her son, and his lonely life as an Anglo Irish rural bachelor shut off from the larger Catholic society. She had wished him to marry some Protestant girl. The Shepherd girls had seemed to have their eye on him. Later, she concluded he wished to remain unmarried, but never understood why. She knew his independent mind. She remembered when he had refused to join the local hunt. He'd announced when he was fourteen that the odds were too uneven. He would always be on the side of the fox. Charles had not been pleased.

As Andrew had hoped, the reading of the Bans was dispensed with, and they were married, by a beaming Reverend Johnson, in the vestry of the Church of the Redeemer at eleven o'clock on Friday December 17th. Victoria, who now seemed always to be too warm, wore her blue maternity suit and left her navy blue coat in the car. The church sexton and the Minister's wife were the witnesses. The Minister was so unhurried, so gracious, and Andrew so calm, she did not feel at all awkward, although this was not the wedding she'd dreamed of. She stood, an observer at her own wedding, and thought, this is the right thing to do. I'll have my own bedroom. I'll go on as before. It will be no different except that now I am no longer a hired companion. I will be secure. The searing anxiety was already gone.

Andrew dutifully put on her finger the ring her mother had presented her with that September morning three months ago as she was leaving home for the last time. She would never go back, although she sometimes thought if Beechwood had a telephone she would ring her father and say, "Remember me? I'm the daughter you rubbished, threw in the bin." Of course, he'd ring off immediately.

There was a slight sprinkling of frost glinting in the early afternoon sun when they emerged from the church. "I feel like I used to when I was a boy and got away with something clandestine," Andrew declared as he waved to the minister and started up the car for the drive to Dublin. Conversations with Andrew since his proposal had been rushed and perfunctory. He seemed to be dashing from one thing to another. He spoke no more to her than he had in the three months since she had arrived at Beechwood, except to tell her he'd spoken to Josie about their planned marriage and it was his expectation that Josie would accept Victoria as being in complete charge at Beechwood, and that Peggy would do the same. Now Andrew was in high spirits at the prospect of getting away to the city. Josie had assured him, "I'll see things are up to the mark."

Victoria had no doubt she would. Since she had been informed by Andrew that Victoria was to be mistress of Beechwood, Josie was respectful and cooperative.

They planned to go straight from the church to Dublin, for the weekend. Peggy was to stay till eight o'clock each evening to help Josie. They talked about whether his mother would attend the marriage ceremony but she herself decided not to. "I'm very pleased you are to be married," she said "but it's too cold. I'll stay here and Josie will look after me." In the end there was just the two of them and their witnesses.

Andrew believed they should call to her parents in Blackrock but Victoria was determined not to. She had not written to tell them she was getting married. Why should she? They had never written to her.

"Maybe I should go, Victoria. You could go to the shops or something."

She stared at him, wondering why Andrew, who had transgressed society's boundaries in his relations with Dominic and was, in fact, a sinner in the eyes of Christians, should be so determined to obey every convention, every precept of society. She didn't think he was a sinner, she knew him to be a good man.

"Andrew, go if you must, but I'm not going."

13

Planning Fire

*B*ecause Andrew had taken the Morris, Matt used the horse and cart for the creamery run. Waiting in line at the loading dock he regaled the farmers with news of the marriage. "They're gone to Dublin for the weekend, the honeymoon."

"Cold weather for a honeymoon," the farmer in front of him in the line said.

"A man's never cold on his honeymoon," Matt told him.

"It's long ago that woman had her honeymoon. Sure isn't she expecting," the farmer maintained.

"Ah sure God bless the mark. Sure she'll be alright now," said the man behind, invoking the Irish blessing on the unfortunate, not wishing to hear an expectant woman maligned, even if she was a Protestant.

Saucebottle, helping to heft milk cans up on the platform, listened. So Andrew Wynne and his new wife were gone to Dublin for the weekend. And poor Dominic dead! Saucebottle believed Andrew Wynne had killed him with hard work. No luck at Beechwood, the Protestant farmers were slave drivers. But this was a heaven sent chance. Lately he had begun to believe he would never carry out his plan, but now he could hardly wait till the workday was over. He needed to plan because this opportunity wouldn't come again. When Matt and Peggy went home in the evening the old woman and Josie would be alone. The old woman was mad as a March hare. He remembered her screaming when he had hidden and watched the house. That had been a near thing. He'd been frightened, but this time would be different. Josie would save herself. If she didn't, wouldn't she be another martyr for Ireland? Her brother Slasher would be proud.

At five o'clock Saucebottle collected his week's wages and headed for Hourigan's. He wanted a drink and a smoke and he wanted to think. It was early and the pub was empty. The barman polishing glasses nodded at Saucebottle. "A Powers, Alfie, like a good man." Saucebottle headed for the snug. He sat back, lit a cigarette and stretched his legs. The thing to do was to go early in the morning and dig up the dump and get the guns. Then, tomorrow night he'd cycle to Beechwood, knock on the door and when Josie answered he'd stick the gun in her ear, tell her to get to hell out of there and then fire the place. He imagined her shocked face. He'd say he was there to do the job her brother didn't finish. Let her put that in her pipe and smoke it. But she had a bicycle and could go for help even if it was dark. And she'd turn him in to the Gardai. Maybe he'd shoot her. Dead women didn't talk, nor did they ride bicycles.

The barman slid open the wicket and passed in the drink. In his excitement, Saucebottle downed it in two gulps and asked for another. Almost immediately he felt relaxed, confident. If he was careful and took his time, what could go wrong? Nothing! His muscles softened and his racing thoughts slowed; he lit another cigarette and imagined Beechwood burning. He'd cycle away and when he got clear of the grounds he'd climb a tree and watch the flames lighting the dark. His heart thumped wildly thinking about that blaze. He dozed off for a few minutes and woke when he heard noise, voices, customers coming in the pub. What had he been thinking about? That he'd go to Crew's Rock and dig up the arms' dump for a gun. What if someone caught him? There was never anyone out there, certainly not in this cold weather. Still it was a risk. And he didn't know how to load a gun, although he thought he could work that out. He tapped on the wicket and when it slid over, "A Guinness, Alfie."

He crossed one knee over the other, lit another cigarette and waited for his drink. What did he need with a gun? Sneak up there at two in the morning, break a few windows and fire the place. Look how it had worked at Middlebrook. Of course the bastard Wynne had dogs. But they'd be inside these cold nights, coddled whelps. They could yelp and bark all they liked but by the time Josie was awake he'd be long gone and by the time she'd gathered her wits about her, the fire would be well started. And she had the old woman to look to and no one but herself. So the cursed place would burn, like Middlebrook burned. And Wynne and his new wife would come home to a ruin. And he'd be home in his bed listening to the wireless, waves of sound, voices out there in the void, in the dreamed of countries he remembered the schoolmaster indicating with his pointer on the green oilskin map. Europe, the continent beyond the hated England, the vast space where the strong man was rising. But he had to be quick. Wynne and his new wife would be back on Sunday. Matt said they were gone for just two nights. They would be back for milking on Sunday. So it had to be tomorrow night. The Slasher had said guns were dicey. Fire was the thing. Tomorrow he'd buy a can of paraffin, tear an old shirt into rags, soak the rags in the oil and he was away to the races. He knew where to put those rags. He'd break a window in that room where he'd seen the old woman and the girl sitting, and in the scullery at the back, and maybe at the front door. The dogs could yelp all they liked. By the time Josie got the old lady out, the place would be in flames. Just like Middlebrook had been. And the country would be shot of Wynne.

14

After The Wedding

*A*ndrew had booked to stay at the Wicklow Hotel and intended to drive to Blackrock on Saturday afternoon and break the news to Victoria's parents. They had never met Andrew and he believed he should meet them, even if Victoria was very angry with them. She gave him directions to find the house. "Well Victoria, I hope I can find it. I know the city quite well but not Blackrock."

"Oh, I'll go with you and show you the house but I'll stay in the car. They had their chance to help me but they didn't even want me in the house."

"Don't be bitter, Victoria."

"I am bitter. I've been waiting for one word from them, or from my sisters, one word, and it hasn't come, and Christmas is just a week away."

"But it's not just them Victoria. It's everyone. It's the way it is."

They stopped for lunch at a country pub outside Clonsilla and it was dusk when they reached the outskirts of the city. Andrew decided to leave the car on the Quays because Victoria said she needed to walk. He carried her bag and she linked her arm in his for the first time and they set off along the river, the lighted buildings reflected like a dream city in the dark water. They crossed O'Connell Bridge and went up toward Westmoreland Street and, when they reached their hotel on Wicklow Street, Victoria felt she had completed an enchanted walk through those streets she knew so well.

Their room had two beds with ornate headboards against a yellow plaster wall. Victoria sat at the window and thought about how she missed Dublin, its green domed buildings, its wide streets, Dublin Bay and the encircling hills older than memory: *Sally Gap, The Feather Bed, The Silver Spears*... How had she ever endured the loss of this city? She would insist on Andrew taking her back here often. Her clothes were rumpled so she changed into her red maternity suit in the bathroom. In the looking glass she thought she looked like a fat Santa Claus. When she came out Andrew was sitting at the table. "Dinner Victoria? What about Jammet's?"

"I'm hungry. It's a bit of a distance."

"We'll take a cab. It's Friday. Jammet's will have fish, delicious."

"I'm not very well dressed."

"You look fine. That colour is very pretty on you."

It was the only time he had remarked on her appearance.

Despite her discomfort with her clothes, she agreed to go. Her coat no longer buttoned over her belly. Saturday morning, she decided, she would buy herself a new coat. She could afford it now that she was married. She, Victoria Mulholland, married to a man she had not known existed three months previously. It was extraordinary, yet she felt quite comfortable in Andrew's company. He seemed like the brother she'd never had. Apart from her parents example, she had no experience of marriage but her favourite writer, Jane Austen, had lots to say about its necessary accommodations, from the bickering Bennets to the indifferent Bertrams. But nowhere did she describe a union such as hers. Still, Victoria felt the ghost of Jane Austen would approve, since Victoria had done the sensible thing. So for the moment she was happy. Their room had two beds, she would undress in the bathroom and she was certain there would be no sexual overtures from Andrew, not after his confession of his love for Dominic, although now he seemed to be carrying on as if that part of his life had never happened.

Andrew had told her he had loved to come to Dublin when he was younger so she was not surprised that he dealt effectively with cabbies and waiters. Sitting in the low light of the restaurant sipping C and C Ginger Ale, surveying the lively crowd, she thought what pleasure dinner in a good restaurant could bring.

"This South African Sherry is not half bad," Andrew said. "We must get used to it. No hope of any Spanish sherry till the war there is over."

"Do you think it will last much longer, Andrew?"

"Everyone has taken sides in that war, Victoria: Germany, Italy, England. I see nothing but trouble in Europe, maybe in Ireland too. Neville Chamberlain puts me in mind of a fussy nanny, always tidying up."

"I wonder, Andrew, that you stayed in Ireland after they signed the Treaty, that you didn't move to England, or the North."

"Why should I? We've had our foot in every square mile of this country for almost two centuries. My great grandfather's father was given land near Cork, but there was some sort of trouble with the people and he sold up and went back to England. But my grandfather came back and bought six hundred acres from an Edgar Walton who had cleared out the tenants in the mid forties. Those were terrible times. Walton was almost bankrupt, behind in the rates, and taxes. My grandfather made a fresh start at Beechwood, but in the depression from '79 on, he acquired a lot of debt. Then, the English insurance companies wouldn't lend on Irish land and my father borrowed heavily from The Church of Ireland. The old mole wanted me to marry. He would be happy to see me married to you, Victoria. My mother liked to keep up a stylish front, hunted and that sort of thing but in the end that style wasn't possible financially."

He paused to take a sip of his sherry. "At the end of the last century we were forced by the Land League War, and the Land Courts and all that land hungry business to sell about 300 acres. My father was paid in Land Bonds and my mother still gets some income from that."

She'd never understood this history. At school she'd learned English History. She was quite familiar with The Wars of the Roses but what Andrew was saying was news to her. "How many acres in Beechwood, now, Andrew?"

"Just a hundred. In '26 I sold two hundred acres through the Land Commission to clear up debt. So now I have a hundred left. That's enough for me to manage. In a way, it's well my father sold. We didn't get the attention of the IRA when they took to burning the big houses from '19 to '22. We were never a big house."

"Your mother still worries we will be burned out."

"Not like she did before you came. You've been wonderful for her Victoria."

Andrew paused for another sip and then continued. "We're the first of the colonies to go our own way and we're just feeling our way. Look what happened when Edward abdicated to marry that American divorcee. De Valera took the opportunity, when the crisis was at its worst, to remove every trace of the Crown from the Irish constitution. Astounding what divorced women can do, Victoria." He was teasing her. "You had better not take it into your head to divorce me."

"It's a little early for that, Andrew. Anyway there's no divorce in Ireland."

120

"But seriously, I often think women don't know the power they have. Kitty O'Shea's divorce ended Parnell's career and the chance for Home Rule in Ireland. If he'd succeeded, how different things would be: no 1916 Rising, Casement would still be alive, no Civil War."

Victoria was surprised Andrew talked so much but felt he now viewed her as an equal, no longer an employee. Exchanging Beechwood for Dublin had enlivened him. She wasn't sure if Andrew was in earnest in his musings but it was fascinating to listen, so starved she had been for conversation now that Mrs. Wynne spent her days in a medication induced lassitude.

"I wonder how your mother is doing, Andrew?"

"Oh she will be fine with Josie, and Josie likes nothing better than to fuss over her. Josie has been with us for a very long time."

"She sleeps well now with the medicine the doctor ordered."

"Yes, but she's frail, Victoria. I just want her to be at peace."

Victoria was sleepy in the cab on the way back to the hotel and could hardly stay awake to wash. When she emerged from the bathroom Andrew was reading *The Irish Times,* with his shoes off, his feet on the bed nearest the window. "De Valera is talking to Malcolm Macdonald, Victoria. Now there's a pair. Macdonald's so young Dev will talk rings around him."

"What do you think about De Valera, Andrew?"

"A strange one, romantic talk about country life, and his childhood in Bruree. But I notice he doesn't live in the country. He lives in Blackrock, where you lived Victoria."

"I don't live there anymore."

He looked at her over the newspaper, amused. "I know. You're mistress of Beechwood now. You'll have to start reading *Model Housekeeping* and writing to Nora in *Women's Mirror* about any little problem you have." He was teasing her again and she loved it.

"Seriously," he continued, "I think De Valera has a good chance of getting the Treaty Ports returned. Chamberlain wants a friendly Ireland at his back when this trouble with Hitler comes to a head."

"Andrew, you don't mean we might have a war?"

"Looks more like it every day. The Disarmament Conferences were a flop."

"I can hardly bear it," she said thinking about her baby.

"Well we can do nothing about it. If it comes it may not last long. Don't worry about it Victoria." He folded the paper over. "I see this new lot, The Irish Farmers Federation, are launching a no rates campaign. I'm certainly in favour of that."

"I expect you are," she said. She slipped out of her dressing gown, slid under the cool sheets, turned on her side and tucked a pillow on a slant to support her head. "Good night, Andrew."

"Good night, Victoria."

Her last thought before sleep was, what a strange wedding night.

When he knew from her breathing that she was sound asleep, Andrew put on his coat, took his shoes in his hand, stepped out into the corridor and softly closed the door. He left the key at the front desk and stood on the steps of the hotel. Across the street was the silhouette of a man in a cycling cap. Andrew signalled to him. The man walked toward Grafton Street and the shadows of St. Stephen's Green. Andrew followed.

A leg cramp woke Victoria an hour later. Quietly, so as not to wake Andrew, she stretched her leg, pointed her toe and then her heel as Nuala Fay said she must. Then she saw his bed was empty. Where on earth was he? The leg cramps eased and she sat up on her bed thinking. Suspicion, like a stealthy predator, crawled the bottom of her consciousness. She thought of Dominic, not quite four weeks dead, and anger coursed through her and then subsided leaving her helplessly dejected. Just what had she expected when she had made this Faustian bargain? How terrible life was, a few moments of joy and then reality walloped once again. She lay awake for a long time listening for his returning steps. This strange man who wept for Dominic, who chatted to her, teased her. Where had he gone? Part of her wanted to get up, dress and leave and then she almost smiled at herself. Where would she go? Tired from all that had happened that day, she eventually slept.

In Killcore Nuala Fay added a little whiskey to Sam Burkinshaw's tea. "Do you know who got married this morning, love?'

"No. Who?"

"Andy Wynne."

Nuala stood with the whiskey bottle in her hand. "Are you serious? To who?"

"The girl that looks after his mother. The one that's expecting."

She put down the whiskey bottle. "Unbelievable! Everyone is marrying but me."

"Come here to me pet, till I give you a kiss."

She sat beside him and he put his arms round her. "You know, Nuala, if my mother wasn't in my way I'd marry you tomorrow. And I will as soon as I can."

"I know Sam, and I'm content enough with that."

And she was. She had her house and her salary and a man to love her and she had no great desire to marry. The married women she knew were mostly drudges. She had Sam where she wanted him, in her bed, and in the daytime out of her hair, and no one in Killcore was anything the wiser.

Saturday morning at the Wicklow Hotel when Victoria woke Andrew was back, snoring in his bed by the window. She was reassured to see him. It was half past eight by her watch. And she was in Dublin! As always these days she was ravenously hungry when she woke. She longed for a cup of Bewley's steamy coffee and a sticky bun. She dressed in the bathroom, took her purse and key and went downstairs. She left her key at the desk and went out into the cold December morning. The store fronts of Grafton Street glittered like diamonds in the frost. She walked down the muffled pavement. In Westmoreland Street she bought *The Irish Times* from a newsboy and hurried on toward the welcome aroma of coffee.

Victoria was leafing through the newspaper and waiting for her coffee when she sensed a figure at her shoulder. She turned her head and Donny Maguire was standing staring at her belly and the wedding ring on her finger.

He had not seen her come in, but looked up from his newspaper and saw at the far wall that head of fair curling hair that was like no other. Wildly elated he threaded his way through the tables and as he reached her he saw her belly and the wedding ring. He stood paralysed with shock. "My God Victoria, you're married. How could you, Victoria?"

She was stunned. She stared at his livid face and pulled her coat protectively around herself.

"Donny!"

"You promised you'd come back. Did you forget that?"

The prim waitress stood behind him eyes downcast, white cap quivering in anticipation of a scene. Other customers stared.

"I did write."

"You never wrote. You never meant to write."

She became conscious of her ill fitting coat and hastily combed hair.

"I wrote twice and you never answered," she shot back, stood up suddenly, slamming her chair against one at the table behind and rushed out on Westmoreland Street.

"Ma'am your coffee," pleaded the waitress after her. Donny fumbled in his pocket, threw a coin on the table and rushed after Victoria. She was well ahead, he ran to catch up and caught the edge of her coat. "Victoria wait. Listen."

She broke away and ran along Grafton Street, the few early morning walkers standing aside and staring after her. She turned on Wicklow Street and he watched her enter the hotel. He followed and paused at the door, saw her collect her key and rush on. He entered and pocketbook in hand spoke quietly to the desk clerk .The clerk nodded and for half a crown turned the opened guest register round and pointed to the name and address of the agitated woman who, a few minutes earlier, had so imperiously demanded her key: Mr. and Mrs. Andrew Wynne, Beechwood House, Killcore, County Meath.

Donny walked back the way they had come, leaned against the railing of Trinity College and tried to control his anger. So while they had what he thought was their sweet spring of passion she had another, was in love with someone else, engaged to someone else. Beechwood House? So she married into the big house. Small chance he had, a struggling vet without an acre to his name. Damn fool she made of him. Took off for Dublin and left him to face the music, the shocking beating he had endured for daring to walk out with a Protestant girl. Momentarily the terror of that night came back, but he dismissed it, no sense in thinking about that. He walked on across Fleet Street but the Pearl Bar was not yet open, so he wandered back through Westmoreland Street and made his way to Abbey Street and his room at Wynn's Hotel. Strange the hotel had the same name as the fellow Victoria married. Old Anglo Irish name. How beautiful she looked this morning, her face fuller than he remembered. She couldn't wait to get away from him, rushed off as if she couldn't stand the sight of him. He thought of her expecting Wynne's child and was filled with flaming jealousy. She must have married immediately after she had left Obanbeg. So he was her last fling before she settled into marriage, must have been engaged when he met her. He felt utterly betrayed and alone, regretted coming away for Christmas. Tonight he was expected at his sister Una's place in Rathmines.

She'd have invited a girl or two for him to meet. How could he endure the jollity of the season? He just wanted to be left alone.

Victoria's hands shook and she couldn't fit the key into the lock. The door opened and Andrew said. "Victoria, what's wrong?"

She swept past him and threw herself on the bed, her heart pounding and lay curled up, her arms protectively around her belly. Andrew sat on the bed beside her. "My God Victoria, what's the matter?"

She sat up and he saw the tears overflowing her eyes. "Oh Andrew, I had such a shock."

"What happened to you?"

"I ran into the man whose baby I'm expecting."

"And he upset you?"

"He was furious, said I walked out on him."

"And did you?"

"I wrote to him, twice. He said he didn't get my letters. He's a blackguard."

She sat up and held her head in her hands. "Have you a headache, Victoria. Should I go out to the chemists and get you some Aspro?"

"No. No, I'm all right, just upset. And I'm so hungry."

"Why don't we go up to the Shelbourne and have our breakfast?"

"I have nothing to wear," she wailed and began to weep. He put his arms around her and held her as if she were a child. "Victoria, what is this? We're a hundred yards from the finest shops in Ireland and you're crying because you have nothing to wear to breakfast. Why didn't you say you needed to buy clothes?"

"I was going to go to Clery's later. I didn't want to spend too much money."

"Clery's? I thought they sold nothing but ladies' corsets. Isn't that what William Martin Murphy made his millions on?"

He was teasing again, to distract her. "Why not go to Brown Thomas or Switzers? That's where my mother shopped when she was able."

"Brown Thomas is so expensive and anything I buy will be too big after the baby comes."

"Victoria, I'm going down to the desk to order some tea and toast brought up for you. Then we'll go out to Brown Thomas and get you anything you want."

"Andrew, you are very kind."

"Nonsense! I'll go down now and I'll get some Aspro too if you need it."

Brown Thomas was aglow in Christmas lights and had a surprising number of shoppers for such an early hour. Two men were ensconced in chairs on the landing at the top of the stairs leading to the ladies' salon. Andrew sat there too and read *The Irish Times* while Victoria shopped. Shopping! This was what she needed. She hadn't shopped for months. The headache was gone. And such brilliant colours and the styles! Shop assistants showed her to a dressing room, and presented suits and coats for her to try on. She chose a loose flared navy wool dress with white trim and gold coloured buttons collar to hem and a kick of pleats at the back. And to wear with it, a three-quarter length red swagger coat that swung from the shoulders in a flare that almost obscured the bump of her pregnancy. Finally she bought a small matching hat with an upturned brim and jubilantly told the shop assistant to bin her old navy coat. She felt marvellous! Andrew filled out the cheque, signed it, relieved her of the bag that held her blue suit, arranged for it to be delivered to the Wicklow Hotel, took her arm and they descended the stairs. When they reached the street she turned to him, "I hope I didn't spend too much, Andrew."

"It's Christmas and you do look wonderful. A different woman."

"What clothes can do."

"The apparel oft proclaims the man."

"In this case it's the woman, Andrew."

"And a real looker too. I'm sure people think I'm your father. Now why don't we swank it up to the Shelbourne and have our lunch and then we'll brave the citadel in Blackrock."

Victoria sat on a banquette in the dining room of the Shelbourne Hotel and surveyed the Saturday luncheon crowd. Clearly the women had adopted the neat wool dresses that fell below the knee with long matching belted cardigan jackets that Norman Hartnell was making for the new queen. And the queen's hats with upturned brims were the rage. When she got her figure back, first thing she'd come to Dublin and shop on Grafton Street. She deserved it. The comfort of money! She thought about all that had happened since morning, how she had met Donny Maguire. She hadn't thought about him since Andrew's proposal. His anger, making a scene in Bewleys, running after her in the street. What was he doing in Dublin? The bastard blaming her, saying she didn't write. She swore to herself never ever to think of him again. He would have no part in her thoughts, or her life, ever.

126

Andrew ordered a chop and a bottle of Guinness. Victoria had plaice.

"Had you gone out this morning for a walk, Victoria, when you met that fellow?"

"No. I woke early and decided to slip down to Bewleys for coffee. He either must have been there when I went in, or came in and saw me."

"Victoria was he a married man? I've always wondered."

"No. He was RC. The usual. I was visiting my aunt in Obanbeg in the summer and I met this man, we began walking out and before I knew it I was head over heels. And of course my heart was broken."

"Well Victoria, you know the sweets of love are mixed with tears."

"It was impossible anyway. I was so stupid, Andrew. I had this dreadful row with my aunt and uncle about it. I left and about six weeks later I realized I was pregnant. I wrote to him twice. He never answered and of course I had to tell my parents. You know the rest."

"You're better off without him. Those mixed marriages are risky. The *Ne Temere* rule that the children must be brought up Catholic causes nothing but grief."

"I was very unwise, Andrew."

He smiled at her ruefully. "My dear, as they say, wisdom is sold in a desolate market. So you were foolish, but who hasn't been in their lives?" He took a sip of his porter.

His previous night's absence came to her mind. It already seemed a long time ago. Perhaps he had just gone for a walk, for some fresh air, or perhaps not. It was more likely that he had left his bed for some sort of assignation, which she didn't want to spoil the happy afternoon thinking about. He had come back and he was so kind and generous, and everything was so pleasant. Sitting there among the lights and the Christmas holly she decided that she would not mention the matter, that she would put it out of her mind, and in that decision she set the grammar of their lives together.

"Victoria, I wish you would change your mind about your family and come with me to tell them we're married. I really don't see how I can go alone."

"I'll think about it, Andrew."

He had been so reasonable and generous she felt she had to relent, but she had no stomach for what she knew would be an unbearably awkward meeting.

While they had been eating, the skies over Dublin darkened and they

127

hurried back to their hotel. They just reached the entrance when a cold drenching shower broke over the city. Victoria was tired with the sudden exhaustion that sometimes overcame her, which Nuala Fay had explained was the baby stealing her energy.

"I'd like to lie down for a bit before we go to Blackrock."

"Do, Victoria. When do you want me to wake you?"

"Oh, I'll wake. I never sleep long in the daytime."

Andrew went across to the apothecaries on Grafton Street and then to fetch the car. When he came back he sat in the lobby reception area and read the paper. The baby's movements woke Victoria after an hour. She felt quite refreshed. Outside the sky had lightened again. It was ten minutes to three. She dressed in her blue dress, put on some lipstick, went down to the lobby and found Andrew waiting. There were packages on the floor beside him. He stood when she approached. "Andrew, I've had a nap and I am ready to go with you to see the parents."

He leaned over and planted a kiss on her cheek. "Terrific. Thank you, Victoria. I hated to go on my own. It wouldn't be right."

"We should go now while we still have daylight. We'll take an umbrella. You know how the Dublin weather changes. It may start to rain again."

They went upstairs and Andrew put the packages in his bag. "What's in the parcels?"

"Oh just a little something for my mother."

It began to rain and the scant December light was fading when they reached Blackrock. Andrew parked the car down the street from Victoria's house, took her arm and held the umbrella. When they got to the door he stood a little to the side and Victoria pushed the bell. She shivered as the December wind chilled her legs and billowed the striped canvas blind on the door. She was doing this for Andrew. She wanted more than anything to run back to the car. Victoria heard footsteps, the door opened and her father stood in the entrance. In the dim light his face turned livid with anger. "Victoria! What are you doing here? How dare you! How dare you come here like this? You know better than that."

Andrew stepped forward his hand held out. "Andrew Wynne, Mr. Mulholland. Victoria is my wife."

The sight of her father's jaw dropping sent Victoria into a fit of nervous giggling. She leaned against the doorjamb weak with the effort not to laugh.

Andrew put his arm around her. "Victoria," he reproached.

But her father recovered his assistant bank manager's composure, "Delighted to meet you, Mr. Wynne, delighted! Come in, come in."

"Call me Andrew, please," said his son-in-law as they followed him into the sitting room. The fire had been lighted against the December chill and the mantelpiece decorated with holly. Victoria saw the dining room table laid for tea. It was as if she had never been away. Nothing had changed. Their youngest daughter had been banished and tea was served every afternoon as usual. Did they ever mention her? Ever think of her? Ever talk about her? There was no sign of her mother, Nicola or Kathleen. Her father said, "It's almost teatime, Andrew, or would you like something stronger?

"A small whiskey if you have it, Mr. Mulholland."

He opened the cabinet, took a glass from the sideboard and poured a whiskey for Andrew. "Would you like something to drink, Victoria?"

"No, thanks."

"Sit up to the fire and I'll get your mother."

He left, closing the door after him. Victoria tried but couldn't imagine the conversation between her parents upstairs. Andrew asked, "Victoria, are you alright?"

"If I can keep a straight face, Andrew."

"Victoria! Think what a shock it is for them."

But she wanted to triumph over them. She was married now and didn't need them. They'd kicked her out and now, because she had a wedding ring, did her father think she could just forget all that had happened? How could she forget his cruelty? Andrew, with his regard for appearances, was all for playing happy family but he hadn't been around in September to see how she had been treated.

They heard her father returning with her mother. Margaret entered holding out her hands. "Victoria darling, what a wonderful surprise. How well you look."

Victoria took her mother's outstretched hands thinking how much older she had become, then took a deep breath, reached forward and put her lips to the flushed proffered cheek. Andrew had stood when she entered. He held out his hand. "Andrew Wynne, Mrs. Mulholland."

They shook hands and Margaret said, "I'm so pleased to meet you, Andrew. You must be cold after your journey. Would you like some tea?"

"I would, Mother," Victoria said.

"I'll speak to Kathleen." And she left them and Nicola sashayed into the room holding Queenie to her chest like a feather boa. Victoria introduced Andrew and she saw Nicola look him over with a calculating eye and felt a proprietary protectiveness towards her new husband.

"Would you like a drink, Nicola?" her father asked, keeping up appearances before his new son-in-law.

"Maybe after tea."

Victoria had never heard her father offer her aunt a drink or Nicola refuse one. This show was staged for Andrew's benefit. She got up from her chair, "I'll see if I can help with the tea."

In the kitchen Kathleen was slicing Christmas cake while Margaret arranged sandwiches on a plate. "You're home for Christmas, Ma'am. "

"Oh I can't stay that long Kathleen, we have to get back."

"Sure you have your own place now Ma'am and you'll be wanting to be with your husband."

Her mother pursed her lips. "Kathleen, the kettle is boiling."

Nicola came in, picked a piece of cake of the plate and nibbled it. "If you don't look burgeoning, kiddo."

"Thank you, Aunt Nicola."

"Nice scoop, Victoria."

"Oh dry up, Nicola."

"It's tea time now," Margaret interjected and carried the laden tray herself.

Margaret poured the tea and Nicola passed the sandwiches. Victoria was hungry. She had forgotten how good Kathleen's cooking was. Her father was regaling Andrew with his dire predictions for the future of the country under De Valera. Andrew did not disagree with him but said, "Well the governments after Independence had to be cautious, but De Valera hasn't been the wild revolutionary I thought he'd be. For one thing he's not the front for the IRA that people accuse him of. He's cracking down on them. Cancelling the Land Annuities backfired but he's trying to make up for that. I must say as a dairy farmer, I've done alright."

"Cosgrove was our man. We'd never have this public debt with him," his father-in-law grumbled. "We'll see what the Banking Commission has to say about that."

"You should have told us you were planning a wedding," Margaret said, afraid talk of politics would agitate her husband. "We would have come up to the country."

"We wanted a quiet wedding," Victoria told her, incredulous that her mother was ignoring the circumstances of her departure from home.

"I think we must have an announcement in the *Social and Personal*," Margaret continued.

The bemused look on Andrew's face at this proposal almost sent Victoria into another fit of laughing. First they hid her in her room, then kicked her out and now they wanted an announcement. How had they explained her sudden absence in September? "Mother, there will be no announcement."

"That's right," her father interjected, "there's no call for that."

"But what will our friends think, and the neighbours."

"When you see them just tell them the truth - that I got married."

"Victoria, when you're finished your tea can we talk upstairs."

"If I can be excused, I'll go now."

Her mother led the way up to Victoria's old bedroom. She switched on the light, then sat on the bed. Victoria sat in the chair by the table and thought about when she had last been in this room. She would never forgive that imprisonment. "Victoria," her mother began anxiously, "I wanted to ask what arrangements you made for your lying in?"

"Oh, the local maternity hospital I think."

"That won't do, Victoria, you must have a nursing home. What about Holles Street Private?"

Victoria struggled to keep her temper. "Mother, you had your chance to make those suggestions before I was shunted off to the country."

Her mother looked down at her hands and then up at Victoria, "Victoria, you know your father…"

"It's over, Mother. I'm fine. I'll arrange with the district nurse about my delivery."

"Victoria."

"No, Mother. We should go back downstairs."

"You could have stayed with us," her mother told Andrew when they were back in the sitting room. "We would have been pleased to have you."

Kathleen, having removed the tea things, was clearing the crumbs with her brush and pan. "That's fine now, Kathleen," Margaret said from the sitting room. Victoria took her purse and followed the maid to the kitchen and closed the door. Kathleen began washing the dishes. Victoria put some money on the window ledge above the sink. "A little Christmas present for you, Kathleen."

"Ah no Ma'am, sure that's too good of you altogether."

"Please, Kathleen. Take it and buy yourself something."

"Myself and Theresa will go to the panto."

"Do."

"The mistress told me when I was getting the tea ready that you got married. You're going to have that baby Ma'am. That'll fill your heart."

It was rather like what Mrs. Wynne had said when they walked to Crew Lake and had seen the otter. A baby takes one's whole heart. That day now seemed a long time ago. Kathleen wiped her hands on her apron and shook Victoria's hand. "Happy Christmas, Ma'am."

"Happy Christmas, Kathleen."

They left early. Andrew explained that he was worried if they stayed longer that evening frost following the rain would make the road slippery. Nicola and Victoria's parents stood on the step to see them off. It seemed to Victoria that her father had an aggrieved look on his face, as if he were not at all pleased. Well, she was done pleasing him.

"Don't wait in the cold," said Andrew as he shook hands. Stiffly, Victoria accepted her mother's kiss on her cheek, shook hands with her father and Nicola, took Andrew's arm and walked away. In the car Andrew said, "Victoria, I never intend to do that again."

"Do what? Visit my family?"

"No, go tell some man I've married his daughter. We're a pair you know Victoria, we two."

"I suppose we are but I'm glad that's over. At times it was so stiff, such awkwardness, but now I'm not sorry I went. I'm very angry with them all but especially with my father, but I could see he thinks you were a good choice."

"Well, your father would. He's employed by a bank. He'd have had to pay quite a fee to be taken on there. You must understand he's of his time and class."

"What about you, Andrew?"

"Me? I've no class. You know I'm a bit beyond the Pale, Victoria."

She shifted round in her seat. She didn't want to think about that. Her back ached and she wanted to lie down for a while. It was dark now. She thought about Donny, his angry face. She'd never seen him angry before. Well he was a blackguard, a complete rotter. Then she thought about the baby. It was just two months till the child would be born. On balance she decided she was content. She had secured the child's future. That was the important point. Andrew broke into her thoughts. "If you like you could look around the book barrows and I could have a glass in *The Bodega* and wait for you."

"No thanks, Andrew. I'd like to go back to the hotel and lie down."

"Right. Have a sleep and I'll wake you for supper. Now that you have your new rig out, we could try *The Red Bank*. Excellent roast beef, Victoria"

Andrew wanted to get all the pleasure possible from this visit to Dublin.

15

Fire

*I*t was his last chance and Saucebottle knew it. Petrol was the stuff but it was too risky. They might ask at the garage what he needed it for since he didn't have a car. Paraffin oil was as good, he told himself, fastening the paraffin can on the carrier of his bike. He'd been too drunk last night to try his little Galena and this morning he tried to connect the wires again but got nothing but muffled crackling that made his headache worse. He'd have a go at it again after he'd done the job at Wynne's. Beechwood going up would be the news tomorrow.

"You don't want to be running out of paraffin these dark nights," the wizened little shop boy at Shaw's said, as he put the funnel in the mouth of the can, and began to fill it from the steel drum.

"I nearly did run out," Saucebottle lied, to make conversation.

"Well I don't know what we did to have such a winter," the shop boy sighed and passed over the change. A farmer waiting to be served predicted snow.

"I'd say we'd have snow alright," Saucebottle agreed.

He bought four Baby Power in the pub and cycled home, the paraffin can secured with twine to the basket of his bike, the little whiskey bottles in his pockets. He cycled slowly now that the can was full of oil. It was almost dark and he switched on his bicycle lamp. He'd have to wait till at least eleven to be sure Josie and the old woman were asleep. He'd break the glass in the door in that room where he'd seen the girl reading to the auld one. A stone wrapped in a rag would do the job, then reach in, open the latch and splash the paraffin on the rugs and chairs, a few lighted matches as he backed out, and he'd be done. The dogs would be barking like the hounds of hell but they wouldn't attack. Spoiled articles. They'd be shut in these cold nights. By the time Josie was awake the blaze would be going well and he'd be gone. She'd run for water to douse the flames but she'd be too late. First, she'd have to get the old woman out, and she'd be hysterical. There were no near neighbours to call, just the Mac Adams and Callaghans a quarter mile away.

Over at Beechwood Josie checked the lock on front door, thankful Mrs. Wynne settled early, her medicine keeping her calm. That should have been ordered for her months ago Josie thought. She locked the Square Room door and stood looking out. She could hear Matt and Peggy talking in the kitchen, finishing their supper, getting ready to leave. When they left she would lock the back door and have a cup of tea at the fire before she said her rosary and went to bed. Outside darkness was fast seeping up from the ground enveloping the old garden seat, Dominic's bird table, the wall and the laurel hedge. She watched a few flakes of light snow swirling down. She thought she saw the snow falling on to the bench through the faint outline of a figure seated there. She blinked then stared. Now all she could make out was the bench, the bird table and her own breath on the glass. She made the Sign of the Cross. If it was a ghost it'd never hurt you. Poor wandering scrap. It was the live ones you had to worry about.

"Haven't things worked out wonderfully for Victoria," Margaret said in Blackrock, complacently spreading her dinner napkin on her lap.

"I just hope it continues that way." Her husband's tone was guarded.

"What do you mean, Henry?"

"He just didn't seem to me to be the marrying type, that's all."

"But they're married now."

"Well, let's hope it lasts."

Margaret looked to check the kitchen door was closed. Nicola, who had long ago learned to behave as if she were deaf during certain dinner table conversations, concentrated on eating her soup, her face expressionless.

"Henry, why wouldn't it work out? I can't wait to visit when she has the baby."

"I don't think you should bank on that. She's a flibbertigibbet! Set her cap at that fellow and what do we know about him? She made her own bed up there in the country, and she'll have to lie on it."

Margaret looked at her husband's sulky face. Was it Andrew's age? Certainly he was old enough to be Victoria's father. But still, in the circumstances. Of course it would have been better if Victoria had written beforehand and told them she was getting married. But Henry had risen to the occasion splendidly.

"Think how things were months ago before you talked to our minister, Henry."

"I can assure you, having to appeal to the Reverend Gordon was not an overture I relished. Victoria's a gadabout, no sense in her head. Almost disgraced the family. No shame whatsoever! And now she's married to that fellow. There'll be no adoption now, she's keeping the child, and I'm telling you Margaret if things don't go right I don't want her back here and that's that. And I don't want you up there visiting and giving her ideas about coming back either."

Nicola put down her spoon and sat very still. Margaret lifted up her spoon and the meal continued in silence.

At home, Saucebottle lit the lamp and built up the fire. He ate a wedge of shop loaf and some cold ham, sat in the heat from the hearth, drinking the whiskey straight from the bottles. He smoked a Woodbine and decided he was in top form, ready for the job. He lay on his bed relaxed, thinking about Beechwood ablaze, the glasshouse cracking, the flames lighting the dark winter sky. He dozed on and off till eleven o'clock. Then slow and clumsy from the whiskey he put on his coat, stuffed the rags, three stones, and a box of *Friendly Matches* in his pocket, and went outside. Soft snow was falling. He checked the can of paraffin was still secure. He fastened his bicycle clips, lit another cigarette, mounted the bike, and turned out of his gate towards Beechwood. The snow on his face revived him and, as he stood on the pedals going uphill and then coasted down, he held the cigarette cupped in one hand; with the other he held the centre of the handlebars. He sang an old rebel song and the spirit of the exploit filled his mind, the moist air swelled his lungs and he became invincible, a rebel on a mission to fire the Planter's house that had been missed the first time round.

"*Viva la The Old Brigade,*

Viva la the new one too

Viva la the Rose shall fade..."

He was almost there. "*And the Shamrock shine forever new.*"

He crested another rise and braked to coast down. As he took a last draw on the butt of his cigarette he felt a monster hand strike him and toss him high, he flew up free of the bike and knew he'd made some colossal error, before he plunged downward to the earth.

Dr. Curran and his wife had spent Saturday night at Callaghans playing cards. As they got in the car to drive home Nora cautioned, "Drive easy, Pat. It's snowing a bit."

"Ah it's late, we'll have the road to ourselves," and he drove carefully down the lane but picked up speed on the main road, and accelerated as he took the hill. Just over the rise a cyclist reared up out of the screen of falling snow. The doctor swore and braked, the car skidded, then a terrifying thump.

"Jesus, Mary and Joseph, help us," his wife screamed and prayed as she saw the figure fly up into the dark before the windshield, the bushes rush to meet the car and then in the window a flash of fire. The car's engine cut out. The doctor tried to open the door but it was jammed against a tree.

"Get out Nora, let me out," and he climbed out over the passenger's seat and rushed over, pulling his overcoat off as he went. He wrapped the burning figure in his coat and rolled it in the snow. The paraffin and smoke filled his nostrils. In the car lights he saw blood oozing through the matted hair but the man was alive, unconscious, but breathing.

"Nora, give me a hand here," and they carried Saucebottle and laid him on the back seat of the car. "You sit back there with him Nora and keep his head turned so he doesn't choke. We have to get him to the County."

Dr Curran climbed over into the driver's seat and succeeded in starting the engine but when he tried to back out onto the road the wheels spun spraying sand and earth. Then he ordered Nora to take the driver's seat and he pushed from the front, but again the wheels spun, the engine raced, the car did not move. "Leave it, leave it, Nora." And he stood looking at the stuck vehicle.

"Nora, I'll watch him and you run back to Callaghan's. Tell them to bring the horse."

Before he had finished speaking she was gone running, back up the hill for help which Doctor Curran suspected would be too late. He took a torch from the glove box and shone it on the man's face. Blood was trickling from his nose and his eyes were turned up motionless in their sockets. His laboured breathing stank of whiskey. "Moran, Saucebottle! Poor fellow. Drunk, went past his own gate. Going the wrong way. I should have told her to send someone from Callaghans for the priest."

In Dublin that night Victoria slept heavily, the covers over her head and in the morning when she woke a weak winter light was seeping in at the edge of the curtains. Andrew was still asleep. She did not know if he had embarked on a nocturnal escapade, and decided she would not think of such a possibility. She crossed over to the window. The street and window ledges had a light frosting of snow. She touched his shoulder, "Andrew, it snowed in the night."

He sat up tired faced, his hair bedraggled like a schoolboy's. "What time is it?"

"Half past eight."

"We must get on then. The roads may be bad. I have tire chains with me but I'd like to get on the road. I must be home to help Matt with the milking."

After breakfast they set off. Andrew did not put on the tire chains but it was a slow journey out of the city through flakes of snow drifting from a slate sky. Clonsilla was deserted as they drove through, everyone at eleven o'clock mass, and when they passed Clonee the snow ceased but the road had a covering of melting snow and Andrew drove carefully and was silent as he turned off the main road at Dunshaughlin and headed for Killcore and Beechwood. Victoria, wrapped in a rug in the passenger seat, watched his long melancholy profile and could sense a deep reserve encompass him again as he neared Beechwood. Through gates and gaps in winter thinned hedges she caught glimpses of empty snow covered fields. She knew he had to proceed slowly but wanted to be home, to begin her life, to plan for her baby. "Andrew, I need to think about things for the baby. A cradle for a start."

"McEntee, the carpenter in Killcore can make you one, or you could order one from Dublin. Nurse Fay will know."

"I wonder how your mother is, Andrew?"

"She'll be glad to see us, but Josie will have taken good care of her. I'm more worried about the cows and Matt. He's not the worker poor Dominic was."

It was the first time he'd mentioned Dominic. He didn't speak again till they were on the slope leading to Beechwood gates. "I'm hungry, are you Victoria?"

"I am. We've had no lunch and we didn't tell Josie when to expect us."

"I'm sure she'll have something ready."

They drove up the avenue and through the lane and parked the car in the yard. Andrew got out, hurried over towards the milking parlour leaving Victoria to carry her bag. She could hear the dogs barking a welcome and when she opened the scullery door they rushed out looking for Andrew. In the kitchen she smelled the aroma of cooking meat. She went up stairs and left her coat and bag in her bedroom, then went to Mrs. Wynne's sitting room and softly opened the door. Mrs. Wynne was in her chair and Josie was sitting in what was usually Victoria's chair. Josie stood up. "Hello Josie. How are you, Mrs. Wynne?"

"I'm well dear. Just a bit tired."

"Oh she's grand Ma'am. She finished all her lunch and her tea. And she took a drop of Wincarnis with her tea." Josie now clearly accepted Victoria as her boss.

Victoria left Josie on her knees building up the fire for Mrs. Wynne and went to unpack her bag. When she came back she said, "Josie, Mr. Wynne and I need something to eat. We've not had lunch."

"Yes Ma'am. I've shepherd's pie in the oven keeping warm."

When they sat down Andrew said, "I'm not fond of meat pies, but this is tasty because I'm so hungry. When I'm finished I have to see to the milking."

"How did Matt manage when you were away, Andrew?"

"Alright, but now he's anxious to get off, no doubt a dance or something."

He ate quickly and left the table and Victoria went back up to Mrs. Wynne. Josie was there.

"Cold ham and beets tonight Ma'am. Jam sponge for after."

"That's fine Josie. We will not eat till late. What about you, Mrs. Wynne?"

"I'd like to go to bed soon. I'll have mine up here on a tray."

In the kitchen Matt reported to Josie, "Awful accident. Saucebottle's a goner."

"God help us all."

"He went right past his own place. Drunk in charge of a bicycle."

Peggy washing pots in the sink said, "Dr. Curran's always driving too fast."

"Just get on with your work Peggy. It's soon time for you to go home," Josie bossed, fishing pickled beets out of a jar. How in God's earth would she tell her mother when she next went to see her in the County Home? Saucebottle dead! Poor eejit. Drunk and went right past his own gate. Was the ghost she thought she saw waiting for him? She'd heard he was part of her brother's lot. And where on earth was her brother? Maybe they were well rid of him.

Andrew and Victoria sat down to dinner at nine o'clock in the low light of candles and Victoria thought the Wynne forebears were looking down on a new reality, a new mistress at Beechwood.

"Matt tells me Dr. Curran had an accident last night. Skidded and hit a cyclist on the road this side of Callaghans."

"Oh dear. Was he badly hurt?"

"He was. He's in hospital. He's not expected to live. Nora Curran was pretty shaken up. I've always thought he drove too fast for these roads. And last night it was snowing."

"Did you know the man, Andrew?'

"I did. Poor chap! He works in the creamery. Matt said he had been drinking and went past his own house in the dark, which seems strange to me, to go past your own house, even if you're drunk."

"Andrew, I wish the winter were over. These dark evenings are depressing and your mother doesn't go out anymore. I'd like to see the garden in bloom."

"You will. All in good time Victoria."

He was quiet during the rest of the meal and when they had finished he poured two glasses of port and they went across the hall and sat at the fire. Andrew got up to turn on the wireless, but there was no response from the radio. "The battery's run down. Monday Matt can take it to be charged."

"Andrew, this day week is Christmas, What about the help? Do we do anything for them?

"I give Josie an extra week's wages on Christmas Day. I used to give the same to Dominic."

"What about Matt and Peggy?"

"Something smaller for them. For my mother I got some Eau de Cologne in Grafton Street on Saturday while you were sleeping and a Rowntree's Dairy Box."

"Andrew, I never bought a thing, or sent a Christmas card."

"You still have a week. What do you need to buy?"

"Something for your mother."

"Give her the chocolates, or the scent, whichever you wish."

"Thanks, Andrew, I'll give her the chocolates."

He finished his port and waited while Victoria finished hers. "It's bed time I think," and he handed her the lighted candle off the chimneypiece. They went out into the hall, he lowered the wick in the hall lamp and together they mounted the steps. At the turn of the stairs he took her hand, raised it to his lips in a theatrical flourish. "Good night, Victoria dear," and he turned decisively and walked up the three steps toward his bedroom.

She watched him go and then turned away to her own room, her fire and her hot water jar. She was very tired. She stood for a minute at her window. The wind had dispersed the clouds and a cold moon shone down on a silent, snow-covered world. She checked on Mrs. Wynne, extinguished her light and left her door open lest she call out. As she undressed she told herself her first evening as mistress of Beechwood had gone well, as well as she could have hoped.

16

Country Christmas

*I*f Victoria had not prepared for Christmas the same could not be said for Josie. In November, she had made a Christmas pudding and a fruit cake and stored them in crocks in the pantry. Each was so well laced with whiskey as would have preserved them till the following Christmas.

The snow of the previous week melted and a gentle intermittent misty rain fell. On Tuesday Victoria cut holly and ivy in the orchard hedges and decorated the hall, the dining room and Mrs. Wynne's sitting room. "Is it Christmas already?"

"Sunday is Christmas Day, Mrs. Wynne. Today is Tuesday."

Christmas Eve, Josie dressed the turkey ready for the oven and then Matt drove her to the County Home to visit her mother. They were back before tea. Matt came for a few hours on Christmas morning to help with the milking and Andrew gave him his Christmas money. "I'll manage this evening with Josie's help, Matt."

"Many thanks sir, and Happy Christmas."

Josie, who had gone to midnight mass the night before, stayed with Mrs. Wynne on Christmas Day, while Andrew and Victoria attended church. She wore her new red coat and hat. No one congratulated them on their marriage but some of the congregation nodded to her. Josephine Patterson and her husband Sandy came over; Josephine's shrewd blue eyes took in Victoria's clothes, her figure. "Happy Christmas, Mrs. Wynne."

Mrs. Mac Adam and Miss Minnie Moore, each in tired grey tweed and a fox fur piece around their shoulders, shook Victoria's hand and wished her Happy Christmas. Andrew was off to the side talking to George Mac Adam and the Minister.

"Drop over for tea," Victoria invited.

"Yes. We'll come tomorrow if that suits."

"Yes, tomorrow."

So, Victoria reflected, the married state made her worthy of a visit.

As Andrew turned the car for home Victoria said, "Mrs. Mac Adam and her sister are coming for tea tomorrow. Wonderful what a wedding ring will do."

"They're good people, Victoria."

"I'm sure they are. But they never mentioned visiting before we married."

"My mother will be glad to see them. St. Stephen's Day is always quiet. The Wren Boys never come to Beechwood."

"We never had them in Blackrock either."

"They're more of a country custom."

They sat with his mother in the drawing room in the fading afternoon light to hear the new king's Christmas broadcast.

"Poor chap," Andrew commented. "He did well."

"I remember the first Christmas broadcast," Mrs. Wynne said as Victoria helped her upstairs to rest. "Kipling wrote that one. He did the king proud."

Josie served Christmas dinner at half past six and Mrs. Wynne came downstairs holding on to Victoria's arm and dined with her son and new daughter-in-law. When Josie had served the coffee, tea and plum pudding, Andrew excused himself, returned with two packages, handed one to his mother and one to Victoria.

"Oh Andrew I've nothing for you," Victoria lamented.

"That's alright. I've outgrown Christmas."

When they opened the packages the presents were identical, blue and gold flagons of 4711 Eau de Cologne. Mrs. Wynne flushed with pleasure and held hers out to her son. "Open it for me, Andrew." He did and she sprinkled it on her hands and her handkerchief. "I love to splash it on my pillow. I'll go upstairs now."

Victoria helped her to bed and offered to read to her but Mrs. Wynne shook the cologne on her pillow and said she wanted to sleep. Victoria pulled the eiderdown up on her shoulders, turned down the wick of the lamp and left.

Mrs. Wynne lay back on her pillows, the steady heat from her hot water jar turning the air around her body deliciously warm. The fire threw dancing shadows on the walls. Mog purred at her feet. She breathed the scent of the cologne and remembered a favourite blue crepe de chine evening gown forty years earlier, so glamorous it had seemed. She lived again the parties they had at Beechwood when the rugs were taken up in the drawing room and they danced to the gramophone till dawn. And the Ruthledges sang duets, *"Oh why is my love so cold to me?"*

She couldn't recall the rest of the verse. All that was before everything changed, before the War that had taken her son Philip and the awful revolution. It was so long ago and she was tired. Sleep began to creep over her and she relinquished it all, memories, and dreams, the future, and gratefully yielded Beechwood and all it had meant, to Andrew and Victoria.

When Victoria came back to the dining room Andrew poured their port and they sat at the drawing room fire listening to a music program on the BBC.

"Andrew, thank you for the present. Your mother is delighted with hers too. And she liked the chocolates."

"She's content enough, but she's so frail."

"The doctor thinks she is doing alright."

"I suppose she is, for her age, but it bothers me she doesn't go out."

"The days are so short and so cold Andrew, she sleeps a lot, and lately she hasn't wanted to go out. The medicine makes her tired."

"Next time Curran comes to see her ask him if the dose should be reduced."

"I will. That's a good idea."

They finished their drinks and Andrew switched off the wireless. At the turn of the stairs he kissed her cheek. "Good night Victoria."

"Happy Christmas, Andrew."

"And the same wish for you, my dear."

She checked Mrs. Wynne and, seeing she was sleeping, put out her lamp. She settled into bed and thought, next Christmas there will be a baby in this house.

Victoria was with Mrs. Wynne in her sitting room when Peggy came to tell her the Mac Adams and Miss Moore had arrived. "Thank you Peggy. Please show them into the Square Room. Make sure the fire is built up there and tell Mr. Wynne they are here. Then, tell Josie."

Andrew and George Mac Adam stood at the glass doors looking out through the conservatory at the winter afternoon and talked politics, cattle prices, and the merits of liming land, their teacups in their hands. George declared that the discussions between Ramsay Mac Donald and Dev would end the Economic War for good. "Then beef cattle will be the thing."

The women sat at the fire in the sitting room sipping tea and praising Josie's fruit cake. Minnie Moore talked about a church tea at New Year. Mrs. Mac Adam complained about the dwindling congregation, "Young people leaving for Australia, just like my lads did."

"Next thing the school will go," Minnie predicted. Victoria found the conversation boring, and thought that they made a dull closed circle. Mrs. Wynne was trying to seem interested. "And how are you keeping, Mrs. Wynne?"

"Oh quite well Minnie. Of course it's all down to Victoria. I don't know what I'd do without her."

Victoria changed the subject. "It's mild for December, isn't it?"

"Oh the winters get milder every year. I remember when we could count on a foot of snow at Christmas," Mrs. Moore said.

"And your lake would freeze so hard you could drive a horse and cart across it," Minnie added.

At half past four Mrs. Wynne said, "I'm quite tired. If you'll excuse me I'll go upstairs now, but you please stay and visit with Victoria."

'Oh we were just leaving." Mrs. Mac Adam stood up, walked out to the hall. "Come along George, it's almost dark."

"I'll see our visitors out and then I'll help you upstairs, Mrs. Wynne," Victoria said.

Victoria helped the women with their coats. "Thank you for coming. Mrs. Wynne was so pleased to have your company."

"Ah the poor soul," Minnie whispered, "she looks very bad," and she fastened the fox's head to its paws and shrugged her ample shoulders into the fur. The fox eyes glinted in the dusk of the hall as if it were alive.

Victoria felt George's eyes on her as Andrew held his coat and handed him his hat. He opened the door and Victoria waved and went back in. Mrs. Wynne had fallen asleep. Victoria sat down by the fire. Tomorrow Nuala Fay was coming to confirm with her the details of her confinement. Andrew, having seen their guests off, came in rubbing his hands together, "Now that the good living people are gone I'd like a whiskey. What would you like Victoria? You've been accepted into society here, you know. That calls for a drink."

145

"Nothing for me Andrew," and she smiled up at her husband. Sometimes he hit exactly the right note.

Clery's catalogue is what you need," Nuala advised when she came. "I have a layette list and a list for lying in that you can use. You have just about two months to go."

"I thought six and a half weeks."

"Well the first is often late. Dr. Curran is wondering if you still mean to go to St. Mary's Maternity in Killcore. He now thinks you should be referred to a Dublin nursing home or Holles Street Private."

"I'm not going to Dublin."

Curran would not be happy. He would have collected a fee for the referral. "Of course you could have your baby at home."

"How would I arrange that?"

"Sarah Higgins is a good woman, and she'd come and stay and Dr. Curran and myself would attend the delivery."

"Do I have to decide now?"

"There's lots of time. But Mrs. Wynne's care would have to be considered."

"Maybe I should go to the hospital."

Two days later Nuala brought the list and Victoria copied it: receiving blankets, napkins, cot sheets, two shawls, bonnets and flannel baby dresses. She ordered a Moses basket which Nuala said would do for the first three months, and then she could shop in Killcore for a cot. She ordered a perambulator though Nuala said she knew where a second hand one could be had. Victoria could not wait to see the baby things. She would make out her order for Clery's on approval or return and give the letter to Matt to post.

Nuala looked over her notes, trying to calculate Victoria's delivery date. "You could go into labour any time, but I think you'll go to full term, or longer."

"Longer?"

"The first can come anytime."

"I'm nervous. What would you do if you were me, Nuala?"

"Me? I'd book my bed at St. Mary's for the due date and hope to stay home until a few hours before the delivery. A lot of women having their first go to the hospital too soon."

This will be my first and only, Victoria thought. "Why is that?"

"Some live a distance. Some are nervous when labour starts and rush in."

"Well I want to do everything right, go in when I'm ready, you know?"

"We'll book your bed for the second week of February. You don't have to go in then. You can wait till you're well on in labour. We'll manage it as it comes."

There was greater ease in Nuala's approach now that there was a husband, although the marriage was a surprise. Who would ever think Andy Wynne, that confirmed bachelor, would marry? And a disgraced girl at that. But thankfully there it was and there would be no heartrending decisions about giving up a child.

Josie's changed attitude, and the peace of mind she acquired in regard to money and her future, confirmed for Victoria that she had been right to marry Andrew. Any other disadvantages there were to the match she ignored till the following Friday night. She had stood at the landing window looking out. Heedless of the cold she threw up the window and breathed the fresh chilled air. The full moon was shining on the silent earth and in the orchard the leafless trees threw webs of shadows and a hare hopped across the frozen ground. In the garden the willows drooped their skirts of bare branches. Already the days were lengthening and in the soaring optimism of late pregnancy, she began to plan changes she'd make in the garden. She wanted planters at the entrance steps and a couple of decent garden seats. In March Dominic's daffodils would bloom and she saw herself walking with her baby under the trees. How silent it was now and how dear this old shabby house had become, how familiar the sounds of the place, the crunch of wheels on the gravel, the throb of the milking machines and the crowing of the roosters in the morning in exuberant welcoming of the day, so reminiscent of fairy tales and bible stories. She lowered the window and went to bed. She was reading before sleep with her door open lest Mrs. Wynne should call when she saw Andrew's long shadow at her door. He knocked and she sat up in bed. For one mad moment she imagined this was a romantic approach. "Victoria, may I talk to you for a minute?"

"Of course. Is there anything wrong?"

"No, nothing's wrong."

He came in and sat on the edge of her bed. "Victoria, tomorrow I'd like to go to Dublin. The roads are clear now. Matt can look after things for one night."

To the city! She was still as stone and it seemed the room and the garden and the dear silent house all joined with her in opposition, in refusal. "No

Andrew. No! Absolutely not. You can't go back there."

"Please Victoria. I must get away. It's just one night. And Matt is here."

"Andrew, the danger you could be in, the law."

"I'm not a fool, Victoria."

"This won't do, Andrew."

"It's just one night. I'll be back on Sunday afternoon."

"Just one night? There'll be another and another."

"Goodnight, Victoria."

He got up abruptly and left and she sat with clenched fists lest she run screaming after him. Her anger rose in a swell and her heart began to race. *Mr. Hyde.* She remembered the teasing, joking Andrew in Dublin, as if marrying her had released a spring of spontaneity in him. She contrasted him to the contained, earnest, work driven man he became when he returned. Now he was off for the city again. *Dr. Jekyll and Mr. Hyde.* That tale of blackmail, murder, and wills. She got up and dressed and went down stairs, put on her coat and boots, and walked up and down the avenue in the moonlight. Had Andrew changed his will? He'd said the house and farm were willed to Dominic. Where did that leave her? Women had so few rights. What would happen if Andrew died? And he could be blackmailed, or arrested and jailed. What would happen to her and her child then? She turned at the old gatehouse and walked back, then turned and strode back again, in her ears the report of her boots on the frozen gravel like an army on the march. This would have to be sorted out. She had no idea of his financial affairs. There seemed to be enough money day to day but what did that mean? She should have had this resolved before she married him. She was a fool. She had not expected he would be taking off for the city like this. So soon after Dominic's death! She had never seen him leave the farm when Dominic was alive. He and Dominic now seemed in retrospect to have been as close as any married couple, whereas she and Andrew were like a cat and dog. She hated this gulf between them. There was an unspoken agreement that they would not discuss his sexual affairs, but that didn't mean they couldn't have an agreement on everything else. But he was so tight lipped. He'd given no warning he was going back to Dublin. He couldn't have just made up his mind? Or had he?

Up and down she paced till her tired legs could walk no more. But she was calmer and she slipped back indoors and crept up to bed. In the morning she would have the matter out with him. She was always tired now, she couldn't remember when she'd had a full night's sleep, and in the mornings her fingers tingled as if she'd sat on them. She sprinkled the cologne that had been his gift on her pillow and, inhaling the scent so redolent of her mother and her childhood, she fell asleep and dreamed of a lost little girl, where somewhere in a wood the child screamed. She woke and shot up in bed. Someone was screaming. Then all was quiet again. Had she imagined it? Then she heard it again. A desolate cry. She fumbled for a match and lit her candle, pulled on her dressing gown and ran along the passage in bare feet, stumbled up the steps and burst into Andrew's room. "Andrew, there's someone screaming outside."

"It's foxes Victoria. Just foxes. Go back to bed."

"Foxes? That's all? It sounded like someone in pain."

"It's foxes mating, Victoria. You hear them in winter."

She stood in his doorway feeling like a fool. "Sorry, I woke you."

"I was awake."

"Good night, Andrew."

Again the shrieks shredded the quiet of the night. Foxes mating? My God how ignorant she was of the country. Good thing she wasn't here alone. She heaved herself into bed. Her abdomen was blown up under her diaphragm and she had a scorching heartburn. She thought of going downstairs for some Enos Salts but lay there and wished for her little Secret Sharer to move and assuage her loneliness but the baby was quiet. She was too warm and threw off her bedclothes. Still sleep eluded her and Friday night became Saturday morning. She lit her candle and checked her watch. It was ten minutes to five. Towards dawn she fell into an exhausted sleep and did not wake till she heard Mrs. Wynne call at ten to nine. Andrew had already had breakfast and she did not see him, but as she ate lunch with Mrs. Wynne she heard the car go down the avenue. He was gone. Heartless man! Leaving her here to worry. She hated him. Her thoughts now raged on disaster, on whispered stories of the Dublin docks and the brothels of the old Monto. He'd be caught and jailed, or beaten and robbed, or even killed before she made him change his will. She'd be destitute, alone with his mother.

Josie had the afternoon off and she'd gone to visit her mother in the County Home. At teatime Mrs. Wynne asked, "Where's Andrew this afternoon?"

"He had to go to Dublin. He'll be back tomorrow."

"I wish this winter were over. If it warms up we could go for a walk and you might see the otter."

"The days are getting longer. Maybe by the end of the week we can go out."

Mrs. Wynne closed her eyes and Victoria went back to worrying about Andrew. She felt a raw tiredness from the sleepless night but there was tonight and tomorrow morning before she could stop fretting. As soon as he came back she would have it out with him about his will and tonight, as soon as Mrs. Wynne was settled to sleep, she was going to bed. There was a knock on the door. Peggy was on the landing. Victoria put her finger on her lips to signal Mrs. Wynne was sleeping. "You're wanted downstairs, Ma'am," Peggy whispered.

"Who is it, Peggy?"

"Some fella in a car. I put him in the Square Room. The fire's lit in there."

"Peggy, you stay with Mrs. Wynne. You can bring the tray down later."

Victoria hesitated on the stairs. Had this something to do with Andrew? He'd left less than an hour ago. He could not be in Dublin yet.

Downstairs Donny Maguire stood looking out through the glass doors of the conservatory at the bird table attached to the orchard wall. He had not been able to get Victoria out of his mind since he'd seen her in Dublin and in the intervening time all anger against her evaporated replaced by a romantic longing to see her again, to declare that he still loved her, to explain he'd never received her letters. He argued with his best friend Charlie Lever about his plan to find her. Charlie thought he was mad. "She's a Protestant. Donny. Did you forget the thrashing you took from her relations?"

"She wrote to me twice. I believe her. Something happened to those letters. Her family maybe."

"If anyone interfered with them it was here. Even the dogs in the street knew about you and that girl. It could be the postmistress or your landlady."

"Masie wouldn't do that."

"Like hell she wouldn't! She'd burn those letters and think it was for your own good. And maybe it was."

"I'll kill her, the old rip."

"Maybe it wasn't her. It could be anyone. It's ages ago now, last year."

"All the more reason for me to go and see Victoria. She's married now. Can I not go and pay a call and see if she's home?"

"And have her husband set the dogs on you."

"I'm not afraid of dogs."

Finally Charlie stopped arguing, drank his stout and listened to Donny's plan. He would drive to Killcore, spend the night in a pub or a hotel there and on Saturday he'd get directions and drive to Beechwood.

"And what are you going to do then?"

"I'll say I was passing and decided to call in."

"The husband will throw you off his property."

"For what? Because I came to pay a perfectly ordinary visit, because I knew his wife before they were married?"

"Mind you I'm saying nothing," Charlie said in disgust. "Just watch yourself, that's all."

He set out late on Friday afternoon and, by the time he'd reached Kells, night had fallen and slowed his progress. He drove past the orange lighted windows of cottages and through the nocturnal gleam of fox and cat eyes floating in the darkness, rehearsing in his mind the coming meeting with Victoria. Now he waited looking at robins pecking on Dominic's bird table. The resentment and anger he'd harboured because she'd moved on and left him were gone, replaced by a longing to see her, to explain that he hadn't received the letters, to connect again with the woman he believed was the love of his life.

He turned when he heard a step on the hall and Victoria walked in. She stopped short, the last person she expected. In the dull afternoon light the planes of her face were shadowed, the hair he'd adored dry and bedraggled. As she came closer she looked pale as a ghost in her loose navy blue dress. His idea of her was of a joyous woman. As he looked at her, he felt all his romantic love seep away replaced by a profound sympathy, a love deeper than longing that only wanted to take care of her. He went forward and held out his hand and without knowing what she did Victoria took it.

"Victoria I had to come. I had to see you. To tell you I never had a letter from you. Never! I waited for weeks and no letter came."

"I did write." She withdrew her hand and turned away.

"Don't go, Victoria. I've thought about it ever since that morning in Bewleys and all I can say is that someone interfered with my post. I thought I'd never see you again. You have not been out of my mind for even one hour since Christmas."

She stood there with her hands loosely clasped round her belly. He looked the same yet was someone from another life, the life before her world unravelled. Why now? If only he'd shown up weeks ago, before she'd married Andrew. But that time was irretrievable and his arrival here now threatened the life she was building for herself out of the precarious hand she'd been dealt. She didn't know whether to believe him or not about the letters. It didn't matter now. Her life was here. Just then the baby kicked hard against her side and the spark of that connection was revealed in her blue eyes. Donny, watching her face, sensed a shift in her emotions just as she was deciding above all else to keep her secret.

"You have to go now."

"Victoria, I'm here because I can't forget you."

"You can't talk like that. You must leave."

"Where is your husband?"

"He's in the city but his mother is here with me."

"Can I come again?"

"What is the use of that, Donny?"

"Can I write to you?"

"No. You can't. It's better we forget about each other. You must go now Donny," she insisted walking back toward the hall. He followed her and took her in his arms and meant to kiss her but she turned her head and broke away and the hard carapace of her belly brushed against him. He recoiled, shocked. Sometimes there are moments that move the frame of consciousness and change the whole course of lives. "It's mine isn't it? The child?"

She turned. "Don't be ridiculous," she snapped and even as she denied it he knew it was true.

"Victoria?"

"Please leave now. This minute!"

He watched her go up the stairs, took his coat from the hallstand and left.

Victoria's knees shook as she went upstairs. At the turn she sat down on the step distraught that he now suspected her child was his. Above all, her baby must be shielded from sordid rumours about parentage. She heard the door open and close. He was gone. She leaned against the banister and wept. She wanted someone to hold her and assure her everything would be all right. Incredibly, she wanted Andrew. The Andrew who held her in the Wicklow hotel as if she were a child, who had teased and cheered and reassured her. The Andrew who handled her father so competently, who was capable of rising to any occasion. She wanted him back.

She heard Mrs. Wynne's door open. She had forgotten that Peggy was sitting with Mrs. Wynne. But Peggy had seen the car disappear down the avenue and was taking the tea tray down. Victoria wiped her eyes and stood up. "I put coal on the fire, Ma'am. Mrs. Wynne was cold."

"Thank you, Peggy." The maid started down the stairs. "Don't forget the ironing Peggy," she reminded her, hoping her distress was not apparent.

"No Ma'am."

Donny had stood on the steps and counted the weeks since the night he and Victoria had spent together. The last weekend in May? Then he counted three months back from the coming May to calculate the expected date of the baby's birth. The last week in February, barely five weeks away. My God, he was a fool. Why hadn't he thought of that? No wonder she'd written to him. What she must have been through. His child would be born here among strangers, brought up by another father. The face of his own father rose before him, the father he had just begun to know. The father who had left him when he was a month old to go to America. When he had returned home seven years ago Donny had difficulty accepting him as his father. He thought of his dead mother, and cursed himself for not looking for Victoria months ago. He strode to his car, started it up and went fast down the avenue and onto the main road. He drove west and north through the cold winter evening oblivious of the light draining away, the red sunset blazing through the leafless trees, driving as one in a trance. She hadn't denied the child was his. She just said it was ridiculous and it was. It was absurd, but it was fated and wonderful, heartbreaking and exciting too. Now he believed he'd known in his heart, ever since he'd seen her in Bewleys, that the child was his. That was why he followed her. She was carrying his son and his son would be born in just over a month and he tried to imagine that tiny creature, his fists and feet and his little face. So preoccupied was he with dreams of a son that he forgot time and season and where he was driving until he was snapped out of his reverie by the lights of Kells. Almost an hour had passed. He was just over an hour from home.

When Josie returned, Peggy was ironing Mrs. Wynne's skirt. Splotches of candle grease had hardened on the front of it. "Get some brown paper and put it under that iron," Josie told her crossly putting the kettle on to make herself a cup of tea after the cold ride back from Killcore. Peggy did as she was told. The brown paper soaked up the melted grease.

"The missus had a visitor," Peggy said.

"Which missus?"

"The young one."

"Who was it?"

"A fella that came in a car. A Cavan plate it had. An ID plate."

Josie pondered this for a minute. "Peggy, whatever you say about that, say nothing. Do you hear me now?"

"Ah sure, I won't as much as open my mouth."

Victoria was having lunch on Sunday with Mrs. Wynne in her sitting room when she heard the sound of Andrew's car on the gravel. She was relieved he was home and after a night's sleep she was calmer than the previous day. When Andrew came upstairs and breezed into the room he looked as he always did. And she'd spent two days worrying about him? "And how are the ladies?" he asked as he kissed his mother's cheek, and then Victoria's

"Oh we're fine," Victoria said, marvelling at how calm she was.

Mrs. Wynne smiled indulgently at her son.

"I'll go down and see what Josie can hustle up for me to eat."

Victoria didn't move, didn't offer to arrange for his lunch. This day, she promised herself, she'd confront him about his will because she believed it would be only a matter of time before he took off again for another tryst in Dublin.

17

Illness in the Family

*T*he milking was finished and Andrew was sitting in the Square Room waiting for dinner, reading Saturday's *Irish Times*. Sally lay on the floor, her chin resting on his instep. Victoria went in and closed the door.

"Andrew, I need to talk to you."

He lowered the newspaper. "Yes Victoria?"

"Andrew I'm worried about your mother, myself and the baby if something happens to you."

"What are you talking about Victoria? Nothing is going to happen to me."

"It's dangerous for you to be going to the city, as you just did, and you told me you had willed this house to Dominic."

She saw his face harden, "Oh, so let's choose executors and talk of wills. Is that it, Victoria?"

"There's no need to get dramatic about it."

"Aren't you the one that's being dramatic?"

"Well I'm worried. I couldn't sleep while you were away. The deal we have is that I'm your wife. And I'm entitled to be considered in that way."

"Any complaints so far?"

She looked at his tough unrelenting face, the air tense, hostile. The dog got up and walked away. This was not how she had imagined the conversation. "All I'm saying is that I don't want to end up destitute if this house goes to Dominic's relations, or yours for that matter."

"What's the matter with you Victoria? I have no relations except my mother and you knew what I was when we married."

"I didn't expect you to be taking off for Dublin any time you fancied."

"Victoria, do we have to talk about this now? I'm tired."

"You're tired?" she screamed at him. "You're tired! You wouldn't be tired if you weren't running off to Dublin any time you felt like it," and she ran out of the room and up the stairs fighting back tears. Josie coming down stood aside to let her pass with the imperturbability of a maid who had seen everything in her lifetime and knew her place. Victoria sat in her bedroom crying, furious with herself for losing her composure. But she vowed, as she dried her tears, she'd have the thing settled before the day ended. But Andrew left the table before Victoria and Mrs. Wynne had finished dinner and she did not see him again that evening. In fact there was no opportunity to talk to him in the following days because a flurry of activity began with the cattle as, one after another, the cows calved. Andrew seemed to spend day and night in the cow byres and Josie provided commentary on the events, rejoiced and made beestings pancakes and pudding from the thick yellow postpartum milk. The rich smell nauseated Victoria and she avoided the kitchen. Mrs. Wynne slept more than before despite Dr. Curran reducing her medications. Snow piled up under the hedges and in the lanes. The days were lengthening. Victoria's bed was booked in St. Mary's Maternity Hospital for Monday February 14 and Mrs. Wynne was slowing dying.

On the first Sunday in February when Andrew left for church services, and Josie for mass, Victoria went to check on Mrs. Wynne and found her awake. Her face was flushed, her eyes puffy. "Are you alright, Mrs. Wynne?"

"I have a dreadful headache. I don't feel well."

Victoria was alarmed. She held the woman's hand. "Would you like some tea?"

"No thank you."

Victoria felt her forehead. She was burning with fever. "I'll get you some water."

When she returned with a pitcher and glass Mrs. Wynne was lying back on her pillows, her eyes closed. "Will you take a little water?"

"Yes please."

She took a sip of the water and pushed it away.

Immediately after Andrew returned from church, he went to get Doctor Curran. He came quickly, bounding up the stairs. Victoria waited on the landing with Andrew while the doctor examined Mrs. Wynne. They could hear his hearty voice, "You'll be right as the mail in a few days, Mrs. Wynne."

But when he came out on the landing he said to Andrew, "Severe chest cold. Bronchitis, quite serious."

He ordered aspirin every four hours and plenty of fluids to drink, and discontinued her paraldehyde. Matt was dispatched to Killcore for Cantrell and Cochrane mineral waters and Victoria sat with Mrs. Wynne and tried to make her drink. Sometimes she took a few sips but more often turned her head away.

In the evening Doctor Curran returned and pronounced the patient worse. "Pneumonia," he said to Andrew in the Square Room. "It's worth trying the new drug Sulfonamide, Andy. I'll drop by the medical hall and leave a prescription. I'll have to get the chemist to open the shop."

Andrew followed him to Killcore and brought the drugs home. That night he sat up with his mother and it seemed the drug was helping her. But Monday her fever returned, her breathing became rapid and Andrew went again for the doctor.

After spending a short time with his patient, Doctor Curran came to Mrs. Wynne's sitting room where Andrew and Victoria were waiting. He looked grave. "She's worse Andy. There's not much more I can do for her. At her age you know. Pneumonia! Sometimes it's a blessing. An old person's friend."

The colour leaked from Andrew's face and Victoria watching him saw his body stiffen and he went quickly to his mother, leaving Victoria to show Dr. Curran out.

The doctor sent Nuala Fay to help and ordered Brofman's Cocktail, two teaspoons every three hours. An expectant gloom fell on the house. On Tuesday the Minister visited but Mrs. Wynne seemed unaware of his presence.

"Call on me anytime," he said to Victoria as he left. "Anytime at all."

Mrs. Wynne's breathing seemed more laboured each hour that passed. Victoria had never seen anyone so ill but courageously she sat there offering the patient water from a cup that had a spout like a teapot. But Mrs. Wynne turned her face away. The sad resignation on Andrew's face hushed the house. Josie and Peggy whispered in the kitchen and Josie crossed herself and said, "God help her. All anybody can do is pray."

18

Death Watch

*I*n the evening, when the farm work was done, Andrew took Victoria's place and she escaped to eat dinner alone in the dining room, the candle light flickering on the old portraits, the clock in the hall ticking loudly in the quiet. Andrew sat and held his mother's hand till Sarah Reilly, a stout woman in a black dress and shawl recommended by Nuala Fay, came at midnight to spend the night with her. Now Andrew and Victoria moved each in a separate sphere, he in the farm, she looking after Mrs. Wynne. She hardly saw him and had not broached the subject of his will but she worried about it. She knew a wife could be disinherited under the British Marriage Acts still in force in Ireland but to speak of it now, as his mother lay dying, was unthinkable. Wednesday after lunch she fell asleep holding Mrs. Wynne's hand. She woke with a start and for a moment stared at the sick woman. Her breathing had changed. She leaned closer. "Mrs. Wynne?"

There was no response. Victoria ran downstairs. Nuala Fay was hanging up her coat in the hall.

"Nuala, quick. I can't wake her." Nuala ran up stairs. Victoria followed.

"She's comatose," Nuala said quietly. "Can you call Andrew?"

Victoria ran downstairs, through hall and kitchen and out to the yard. Andrew came from the stable. "Andrew, come quick. She's worse."

He went immediately and stood holding his mother's hand. Her breathing was now frightening to see. She took long noisy inspirations and then stopped breathing and, when it seemed she would never breathe again she took another laboured breath. "Cheyne-Stokes breathing," Nuala whispered. "Poor thing can't last like that."

When Andrew had to leave, Victoria sat and kept what she knew was a death watch. The horror of the woman's struggle to breathe was heightened by the frozen landscape outside and the desolate stillness in the house. She had never felt so tired. Her reflection looked back at her from Mrs. Wynne's looking glass, a huge figure in a navy maternity dress. The baby no longer pushed into her ribs but had dropped into her pelvis and it was uncomfortable to sit. She got up and walked round the room and waited for Josie to bring up her afternoon tea.

Downstairs Josie halted between the kitchen and the baize door, the tea tray held firmly in her hands. "Let me by now," she demanded. "Let me pass." She waited. She could see the shadow of the ghost on the baize, could smell his cigarette. Yesterday she'd heard him cough. Someone had come for Mrs. Wynne. Now Josie thought she felt the air move in the hall. He was gone. She pushed open the baize door, went through the hall and plodded up the stairs. She put the tray in Mrs. Wynne's sitting room, tiptoed across the landing and listened to the laboured breaths. She mopped her eyes impatiently with the corner of her apron, knocked on the bedroom door and went in. Mrs. Wynne was propped on pillows, Victoria standing, holding her hand. "Your tea is in the sitting room Ma'am. I'll stay with her while you take your tea."

When Victoria left, Josie knelt, took her rosary from her pocket and began to pray. She looked at her mistress, her oatmeal face, her sagging mouth, her terrifying breathing. Not one prayer had been said in this house for the poor soul's journey. But Dominic had come for her. One of these winter nights, or in the early morning, Mrs. Wynne's soul would leave her body and before it left the room it would turn back from the window and, in the old Irish way, kiss her body goodbye. Mrs. Wynne might be a Protestant, but she was a good woman, and she wouldn't go to hell, she'd go to Limbo, to the state of rest for those who led good lives but could not enter heaven because they were not baptized Catholics. Dominic was, Josie reasoned, in Purgatory. She said a prayer for his soul, so that it would rest and stop wandering. Then she prayed for her mad brother Pat, the Slasher. Her mother boasted that he was in Spain, that Michael O'Riordian, the bastard who had given her brother his orders, was a hero in Spain. But all Josie prayed for was that her brother would stop his IRA shenanigans and go to confession. It had been so many years since she'd seen him, in her mind he was the kid with wild eyes and scraped knees, for all the whispers that he was a killer. When she heard Victoria's step on the landing, she stood up, wiped her eyes and pocketed her rosary beads. Victoria took up her vigil again, mopping Mrs. Wynne's face, swabbing her mouth with a cotton and glycerine tipped stick, watching the woman's life drain away and outside the dusk coming on.   Andrew came to relieve her; she just wanted to go to bed, but she went down to the kitchen where Peggy had ham sandwiches ready.

"Where's Josie, Peggy."

"In her room crying, Ma'am. The eyes in her head red like a ferret's."

"Did she have her dinner?"

"She doesn't want anything, Ma'am. How are you yourself, Ma'am?

Victoria was surprised at Peggy's question. Servants never enquired about the feelings of their employers. "I'm fine. Why do you ask?"

"You look dead tired, Ma'am."

"I need something to eat."

"I could make you something else, Ma'am. Warm you some soup."

"The sandwiches are fine."

When Victoria had finished eating she climbed wearily up the stairs. Andrew sat holding his mother's hand. "Andrew, you've had nothing to eat."

"I'll wait till Sarah comes."

"Shall I bring you up something?"

"No. I'll wait till she comes."

She put her hand on his shoulder, leaned down and kissed his cheek. "You try to get some rest too."

As soon as she laid her head on the pillow, she fell into a dreamless sleep. She woke when Andrew touched her shoulder at six next morning. "Your mother, Andrew?" she said hoarsely when she saw his face twisted with grief.

"She's gone, Victoria. At half ten last night, she took her last breath."

"I'm so sorry. You should have called me, Andrew."

"I couldn't. You were too tired." He sat on the edge of her bed. "I know she was dying but I still can't believe it, Victoria."

"Andrew, she was so sick."

"Yes but I didn't want her to go. I wanted her to be better, to have her for even another few days."

"But she had a good life Andrew."

"She lost my brother. That was the heartbreak of her life. And my father, she missed him terribly. I hope she's at peace now."

"I'll get dressed and come down."

"Sarah Riley is still with her. She'll stay till Nuala Fay comes."

He stood up wearily. "I have to get on. I'll go down now to tell Josie. She doesn't know yet."

Victoria's hips and back ached as she got dressed. When she went in the kitchen Peggy was slicing bread for breakfast. "Good morning, Peggy."

"Good morning, Ma'am."

"Peggy, you know Mrs. Wynne passed away last night."

"I do, Ma'am. God be good to her."

"Where's Josie?"

"In her room, fit for nothing since she heard. And there'll be people calling."

The temperature had risen in the night and fog blanketed the yard. If neighbours were expected Josie would be needed. Victoria's back ached as she climbed the stairs to the third floor. When she knocked on Josie's door there was no answer, so she went in. Josie was sitting erect in her wooden chair, fingering her rosary beads. Victoria sat on the bed. Josie began to weep. "Oh Josie don't cry."

"The missus is gone, that's all."

"I know, Josie. I know you were fond of her but we need you! Peggy just reminded me neighbours will call. We need to receive them, offer them tea."

Josie clenched her hands in her lap and lifted her shoulders. "I don't feel right cooking and she gone. Them auld ones that'll be comin', what do they know about her?" Tears rolled down her face. "She was father and mother to me Ma'am, so she was. Father and mother."

This declaration alarmed Victoria. This was not the time for Josie to quit: they couldn't manage without her. And now Victoria's backache was worse. Nuala Fay was expected and she would ask her about it when she came. Meantime, what to do about Josie? "I know you worked for Mrs. Wynne for a long time Josie but..."

"Sure it was no work. I'd work for nothing here. She was like my mother."

"Yes I know you were close to her Josie but..."

"She saved me, Ma'am, so she did. I'd have died if it wasn't for her."

"Saved you, Josie?"

"Yes Ma'am. The lot of us were dying of the fever. We all had it except me and the quarantine was on. We were shut in. Locked up. No one let come near us for fear they'd get it. She came down in the rain and talked to me mother through the back window and I was just a scrap and me mother handed me out the window. Mrs. Wynne brought me here away from the fever, so she did. Me father and me two brothers died. Lord have mercy on them." She mopped her eyes with the corner of her apron. "Me other brother, Pat, the oldest, never got sick at all. He went very wild."

Victoria imagined Mrs. Wynne standing in the rain receiving a bundle handed clandestinely through a window. Whole families were obliterated by diphtheria or scarlet fever, but this account of the gentlewoman rescuing the child of the poor touched something inside Victoria, as if it were an epic, and rendered Josie's grief noble.

"How long ago was that, Josie?"

"I was four months old. I'm nearly forty now."

"And are you here ever since, Josie?"

"No Ma'am. When the fever was over she brought me home again. Mr. Andrew and Mr. Philip, God rest him, were just lads. Then when I was fourteen and done school I came here to work. We'd a Mrs. Reynolds in the kitchen that time. She's dead in the County Home fifteen years, and now Mrs. Wynne's gone."

Contrary to all orthodoxy, Victoria took Josie's hand "Stay here Josie and I'll get Peggy to make you some tea."

"I don't want tea." Josie's wide solemn eyes streamed again with tears.

"Josie, we need you. Mrs. Wynne would want things done properly."

Josie took up her rosary again. Her lips moved in soundless prayer. Going downstairs, Victoria wondered if this praying was doing any good. She found Andrew in the milking parlour. "Andrew, Josie's crying in her room. I can't do a thing with her."

He heaved a tired sigh. "I'll see what I can do. Matt, you take over here."

She followed him to the house and in the kitchen told Peggy to make tea for Josie. The prospect of callers was daunting; Mrs. Mac Adam and Miss Moore with their fox furs and galoshes, Lottie and Sandy Patterson, Lottie acting superior. As she started upstairs, a cramp moved from her lower back through her abdomen. She held on to the banister and it passed. Was her labour starting? She went on carefully, waiting for a recurrence of the cramp but none came.

In her room, she checked the suitcase she had ready, the Moses basket on its stand, the box of napkins. She opened drawers and looked at the tiny infant shirts. All was ready. She had hoped to get rid of the old wallpaper with its design of pagodas and geishas, but in caring for Mrs. Wynne that had been forgotten.

Another cramp swept through her, more severe than the first and when it passed she went downstairs and met Nuala Fay in the hall. "So Mrs. Wynne is gone," Nuala said holding out her hand to Victoria. "The poor soul. I'll go up and help Sarah."

"Nuala, I'm so glad you're here. I think I'm in labour. I've had a few pains."

The nurse looked at her sharply. "What kind of pains?"

Victoria described them.

"How far apart are they?'

"I've had two in about an hour and a half."

"I'd say you're alright for a while, but we have to get you on the road."

"How long Nuala, how many hours?"

"Maybe ten or twelve, maybe more."

"I'd like to stay home as long as I can. I'm needed here."

"Well you can't! This is no place to be in labour. The hospital is the place for you. I'll go up and see if Sarah needs help."

Nuala went quickly upstairs and found Sarah wrapped in her shawl beside the corpse. Mrs. Wynne's mouth was held shut by a bandage from chin to forehead, she was dressed in her black dress, a copper penny on each of her eyes, a bible in her hands. Sarah had the window open to let her soul fly out. "Sarah, it's freezing," and Nuala pulled down the window.

Downstairs in the hall, Victoria was standing holding on to the wall waiting for the next contraction to pass. When it passed she trudged upstairs and called, "Nuala, can you come here?" and went and lay on her bed. Nuala came smartly from Mrs. Wynne's room.

"I think I'm really in labour now."

"Let me have a look at you."

When she had examined her she said, "We have to get you over to St. Mary's now."

Victoria got off the bed and took her purse and Nuala took the suitcase and they went downstairs. In the kitchen, a fire was roaring in the range and Josie, still red-eyed and weeping, was rolling out dough at the table.

"Josie, I must go to the hospital now."

Josie dropped the rolling pin. "My God Ma'am, and Mr. Andrew gone with the car to see the Minister."

"I'll take you," Nuala said. "Josie get Mrs. Wynne's coat."

Victoria stuck her arms in her coat. "Tell Mr. Wynne I'm gone to the hospital. Tell him Nurse Fay is with me, that I'm fine."

"When will you be back, Ma'am?" Peggy asked, gaping.

"In about a week," Nuala said impatiently. "She has to have her baby first."

"When will she have it?"

"Probably this evening," Nuala told her, hustling her patient out. As Victoria heaved herself into the car a sharp contraction pushed through her and she held on to the door. "Nuala, hurry! That was another pain."

At the scullery door Josie watched the car turn and crossed herself. "God took one and He'll give one. Come on Peggy. Get out the good delph. We'll have people coming and wantin' tea."

The morning mist had drifted off and Nuala drove in the weak winter light between the snowy fields under a cloud littered sky, Victoria holding tight to the sides of the seat. "I'm going to have a baby," she told herself.

"Relax when the contractions give you a chance. Don't think about the next one," Nuala urged. And Victoria tried to do that.

"And time them," Nuala instructed. But Victoria was so tense that when the pain started she would forget to check her watch and then belatedly tried to estimate the time. "I think that was twenty minutes."

Nuala drove fast on the wet narrow road. On the outskirts of Killcore she turned into a short drive and parked in the forecourt of a grey stone building. A sign carved above the open door proclaimed this was St. Mary's Maternity Hospital. The stooped old hall porter came down the steps and took Victoria's bag and she followed him up and collapsed in a wheelchair. Nuala pushed the wheelchair fast down the corridor, through swinging doors, past a nun standing guard with her hands hidden in her sleeves. Good morning Sister," Nuala said and pushed on through another set of doors. A nurse came forward, they wheeled Victoria into a side room, helped her on to a step stool and then up on a stretcher. Unceremoniously, they lifted her legs, stuck her feet in stirrups and, bereft of all dignity, she endured their examination.

"No time for a shave prep," the nurse exclaimed. Another nurse came crashing through the door and Victoria felt the stretcher being wheeled and turned and she was in a room under bright lights. The contractions were coming fast, she cried out and something was put over her face. She felt all consciousness fade and then return. The nurse took Victoria's hand and placed it over the mask. "Hold it there, Mrs. Wynne."

A voice said, "Call Doctor Devlin."

A wave of pain swept through her, she gulped the gas and all was darkness.

19

Country Funeral

"**D**onny," said his sister, her green eyes angry, "you're the limit. For God's sake have sense." She lifted her youngest child into his chair, tied a bib round his neck and began to spoon a mixture of mashed potatoes and parsnips into his mouth. The toddler grabbed the spoon and Nan let him have it. "Good work, Finn. There's a big boy feeding himself."

The child threw the spoon on the floor and looked at his mother. She ignored him and he took a handful of food and shoved it in his mouth. His older sister Bridget sat opposite, neatly handling her fork. "When will Daddy be home?"

"Before you go to bed," Nan told her and came from the stove with plates of chicken and vegetables for Donny and herself. "How long has this being going on, Donny?"

"Just before Christmas. I ran into her in Bewleys. I realized then she's the only one in the world for me."

"Nonsense, Donny. Don't talk such rubbish. Forget about her. She's a Protestant. There's nothing but trouble there. I thought at the time it was just a Romeo and Juliet thing with you two. You wanted her because she was a Protestant and you couldn't have her, and she had the same notion of you. It's an old story."

"It wasn't like that at all."

"Looked like it to me. More potatoes, Bridget?"

Donny said no more. Sometimes his sister could be such a hard little rip. He talked to the children, helped her clear the table and then played with Finn. They lined up animals for his Ark.

"What's this one called Finn?"

"'Affe."

"Good man. A giraffe. And this one?"

"'Effant."

"Elephant. That's a big word for you to pronounce Finn."

"He learns everything from Bridget. His father thinks he is away ahead of what you'd expect for his age."

"Of course he is. He's my nephew."

When he was leaving, she walked him to the door and stood on the outside steps. "Just forget about that girl Donny. You know as well as I do that in Ireland everything depends on where you hang your hat on a Sunday. And I don't see that change. Not in our lifetime."

"Thanks for supper, Nan."

He walked down the road toward his digs through the late winter afternoon. A neighbour greeted him, "That sky'll sow snow."

"It will indeed," Donny assured him absently, while he thought about Victoria and wondered if she'd had the baby. He hadn't told his sister that Victoria had married, or that she was pregnant and he hadn't told Charlie that he believed the child was his. Charlie would have launched into another sermon, and Donny'd had enough of sermons.

It was dark and she lay on her back pinned to the bed in tight sheets. She felt her belly. It was over. Where was her baby? She remembered a long night, pain waking her, remembered holding the mask on her face and greedily sucking the gas, the pain fading and the mask falling away as she lost consciousness and then pain again. Then everything sped up, and the nurse pushed the mask tight on her face. Someone gave an animal groan, then screamed, then darkness. Next thing voices, the light above her head unbelievably bright, and an infant cried. Someone tapped her face gently "Wake up, Mrs. Wynne. You have a girl, Mrs. Wynne."

Now she was wide awake. Her baby? Where was her baby?

"Nurse! Nurse," she called, tugged at the tight bedclothes and swung one leg out of bed. The door opened, the light came on. "You can't get out of bed yet, Mrs. Wynne," the nurse cautioned. Victoria thought she was bossy. "Where is my baby, nurse? My little girl?"

"We have her in the nursery. I'll tell them you're awake."

Victoria lay back on her pillows. Her chest was bound tight with some sort of bandage. There were two beds in the room. The other bed was empty. She heard voices outside and another nurse came and put a tiny bundle in

Victoria's arms and turned on the light over the bed. "Has all her fingers and toes, Mrs. Wynne," she declared and lifted the outer blanket off the baby's face and loosened the wrappings that swaddled the infant. "A little dote she is. I'll leave her with you for a bit. You have the bell there if you need anything."

Victoria was nervous, wanted the nurse to stay but she wanted to be alone with her baby too, the lovely soft weight of her, the cowpat of black hair over her podgy face, her tiny definite mouth, her little receding chin. She gazed at the perfection of the red fists and tiny knees. The surprise of her, so different from what she had imagined, but perfect. Yesterday she had been a weight inside of Victoria and now look at her!

All too soon the nurse came back. "I'll take her now."

"What time is it Nurse?"

"It's ten past six."

Had she been asleep that long? "Nurse what are these bandages I have around my breasts?

"Oh that's to dry up your milk. Dr. Devlin wants his patients to use the condensed milk. He thinks it's best," and she wrapped the baby in blankets, switched off the light and went out leaving Victoria helpless in the rigid routine of the hospital. Outside the dawn light crept over Killcore and Victoria slept.

When she opened her eyes it was daylight and a nun was standing motionless at the foot of her bed her clasped hands hidden in her sleeves. The white coif and wimple emphasised the austere face, the clear grey eyes and pale lips. It was the closest Victoria had ever been to a nun and she was surprised to see how young she was, no older than Victoria herself.

"Mrs. Wynne," she began. "I'm the sister in charge, Sister Philomena. You have a healthy baby, thank God. How are you feeling?"

"I'm well thank you. When will I be going home?"

"Not for at least a week. Dr. Devlin will be in to see you this morning," and she turned and went out. Victoria decided to ask the doctor to go home early. It was Saturday. Mrs. Wynne's funeral would be today. She had completely forgotten. The baby had driven everything else from her mind. Poor Andrew was burying his mother. If it had been possible, she would have got up and gone to him.

Andrew had been plodding listlessly through the morning's work. His neighbours Brendan Callaghan and George Mac Adam had come over to help. Brendan stripped the cows and helped Matt load up for the creamery and George helped clean the cow sheds and drive the cattle out to pasture.

"I'm sorry I won't be at the funeral," Brendan said shaking Andrew's hand before he left to do his own work.

Andrew helped Josie wash the milking machines and was on his way to the house to change out of his yard clothes when he heard the dogs bark and the sound of a car engine. He went round to the front and saw Nuala Fay step out of her car. She held out her hand. "You have a daughter, Andrew. Congratulations!"

Andrew hesitated a minute then took her hand. He had a daughter? "How is Victoria?"

"Tired. It took longer than I expected."

"We're burying my mother at eleven but I should run over and see Victoria first."

"She was asleep when I was there. She's fine. I'd wait if I were you till the funeral is over. I can't go to it of course, I'm sorry, Andrew."

He said he understood and went to get dressed for his mother's funeral.

Each Protestant family sent at least one representative. Jack Lundrigan, his solicitor, a few of his Catholic neighbours, forbidden by their bishop to attend Protestant services, stood bareheaded outside in the churchyard. The Minister's wife sat beside Andrew in the front of the shadowed church while her husband prayed and then spoke from the pulpit of his mother's life. This saddened Andrew. He wondered what these people really knew about his mother, the bravest and gentlest of women. They stood for Lyte's hymn:

> *I fear no foe with thee at hand to bless*
> *Ills have no weight and tears no bitterness.*
> *Death where is thy sting? Where grave thy victory?*
> *I triumph still if thou abide with me.*

As he followed the coffin out under the low door of the old church, a faint snow was falling. The slow tolling of the bell began. It told him the person who had known him the longest was gone, his last connection with his father and brother severed. At the moss lined grave he shivered, felt the breath of time, his own mortality. When the Minister finished with a few handfuls of earth shaken on the coffin, the gravediggers began, and the congregation walked to the hall for tea, the thump of the earth on the coffin lid in their ears as they went.

In the church hall people shook his hand. Frank and Mary Rutledge, a white-haired couple he had not seen at church for months, had braved the cold to attend, and he went to speak to them. Mary was sitting near the refreshment table holding a cup of tea with a Marietta biscuit balanced on the saucer.

"To think your mother is gone," she said raising sad eyes to Andrew's face.

"Ah," said her husband, "the parties at Beechwood when we were young. The day we christened you, Andrew, we had a party till dawn. The whole country was there, the Shepherds, and the Wiltons. All those people gone now, gone this seventeen years."

Andrew suddenly realised his parents had a life before he knew them, one he'd never imagined. George Mac Adam said, "She's a great loss, so she is."

His wife said, "She went so quick at the end."

Minnie shook her head sadly. He stood talking a few minutes and then moved on to Lottie and Sandy Patterson. Lottie took his hand, "We never even knew she was sick."

When it was over and he had thanked the women clearing away the dishes and everyone had gone, the Minister walked with him to the door. Andrew was startled to see it was just early afternoon. It had stopped snowing and a weak winter sun shone on the frozen ground. The Minister held out a hand red with cold in the lacy cuffs of his surplice, "I'm always here Andrew, drop by anytime." His vestments billowed in the draft and he asked, "How is Victoria?"

"She had her baby in the maternity home this morning. A little girl. I'm on my way there now. With my mother's passing, I haven't seen her."

"Well, a child is a great blessing. A great blessing indeed." He turned back inside and Andrew walked to his car, brushed the light film of snow off the windshield with his sleeve and drove slowly through empty roads to Beechwood.

At home he stood in the drive looking at the petrified garden: the willows an untidy fall of dirty yellow branches, the oak and birch cages of sticks reaching skyward. He entered by the front door and the dogs came to him, Sally nosing at his hand, Major wagging his tail furiously. They looked after him as he went upstairs the clock ticking loud behind him. In his mother's sitting room, Mog was asleep in the armchair, the kindling in the fireplace awaited the match, *Country Life Illustrated* and her *Book of Common Prayer* on the table. He went back along the landing and up to the third floor, the silence broken by his tread. In his brother's room he opened the curtains and stared at dead wasps on the window ledge, at the dusty butterfly case and the old photographs. Surprised by a trembling sorrow, he sank on a chair and sat as he had with his mother's body on Friday before the undertaker's men had carried her from Beechwood, past the weeping Josie and Peggy, lifting the coffin high over the turn in the stairs. Ghosts assailed him, the lost laughter of children in the orchard, the hollow report of struck croquet balls, the clink of glasses. He tried to remember the good times, picnics in the woods, the ponies he and Philip rode. But clouds moved in front of the sun, the room filled with shadows, a sad lethargy enveloped him and he mourned for the past. He mourned for the fractured narrative in his own life because it held the secret of his sexual desires that if disclosed would ruin him. His mother's death was so heartbreakingly final. History weighed on him too: here he was the last Wynne in the detritus of his family in a house that had escaped the flames of '20 and '21 but that some still believed was cursed because he was of the Planter class and Edgar Walton, from whom his grandfather had purchased the land, had evicted the starving tenants when the potato crop failed in '47 and they could no longer pay rent. Catastrophe creating an opportunity to clear the land for grazing cattle of which his own Friesian herd was the modern descendants.

Often he could be dismissive of his provenance believing that if one traced the inheritance of property back to the beginning someone had been dispossessed and that was the way of the world. But not today! Today it seemed to him that life was so brief that no acquisition realized by another's loss was worth it.

His father had been ambitious for Beechwood, had expected him to marry and have sons to carry the name. But his father had died young, his brother too, and he was left here with the weight of time past and the burden of ownership. He wept thinking of Dominic gone, and now his mother. He felt the gaping hole in the world left by Dominic's death could never be filled but he ached for someone who understood him, to put an arm round him and hold him. Dominic's voice came to him, "All that old history, nothing to be done about it, let it go by you now, sir. Best to keep busy. The work never lets you down. Best to keep going ahead."

Ahead was the child in St. Mary's Maternity Hospital. The prospect of being, at least in name, her father was daunting. He heard the racket of Matt coming from the creamery, the dogs barking. He left and on his way down heard Josie scolding Peggy in the kitchen. He took the newspaper from the hall table and set off to see Victoria.

While Andrew grieved, Victoria held her baby. The infant opened her blackberry eyes, closed them and yawned. It was Victoria's father's face. Then she seemed for a minute to resemble her grandmother. Victoria saw that the little mobile face with its shifting expressions resembled now one antecedent, now another. How unexpected that was, her accidental daughter so bonny, so helpless. She held the solid little bundle and promised she would never let anything hurt her: she had after all married Andrew Wynne to provide a home for her. And she decided she would have the matter of his will out with him when she got home and decently could. In his mother's last illness she had not mentioned it, but her baby was what mattered now. She was astonished by the intensity of her love for the baby so small and yet so alive and in that moment she forgave herself. She accepted that Donny Maguire, when he had taken her hand and led her to bed, and she herself, when she had followed, had been acting out of their deepest instincts. Her parents too, her mother in her cruel rejection, her father snared in his blind rage, had been driven by an inherited orthodoxy they could not escape.

It was past visiting hours. Andrew sat on a bench and read the paper while the porter went to fetch the Head Sister. He hadn't looked at a paper or listened to the wireless for three days. There was flooding on the Norfolk coast, but that was no news. There were floods there every spring. But the malevolent twerp in Berlin was now in full control of the army, ranting in the Reichstag about the drive for fertile land. The paper said Lord Halifax had declared that no war was imminent, that time was on the side of peace. Was the man blind? This time there'd be no Wynne to fight. His mother was lucky to be gone before what was surely coming.

The Head Sister came briskly down the corridor. "We're sorry for your trouble. I understand your mother was a good woman."

"Thank you."

"I'll take you to your baby first."

She led him through a frosted glass door into a brightly lit room with a nurse at a desk and a grid of twelve tiny cots.

"Nurse! Mr. Wynne to see his baby."

The nurse came forward.

"When he's finished, direct him to his wife's room."

"Yes Sister."

The nurse walked over to a cot near the desk. "Here's your baby, sir."

His eye first caught a sign tied to the top of the little white iron cot, *Girl Wynne February 19ᵗʰ 1938*. He was unprepared for how tiny she was. She lay on her stomach, her head turned to one side, her fists on either side of her head, her eyes closed. "She's a great little sleeper," the nurse said.

Looking down at her he became aware of the flame of common life alight in this morsel of humanity and the ghosts that haunted his day receded. He reached out and touched her tiny hand with his forefinger. It was warm as toast.

"I'd like to see my wife now," he told the nurse.

Victoria was lying on her side almost asleep. She turned and sat up when the door opened, "Andrew! I didn't really expect you today."

"I wanted to come. I've been to see the baby. " He lifted her hand and kissed it. "Well done, Victoria! How are you?"

"I'm fine you know. I'm ready to get up if they'd let me."

"I wish my mother were here to see the baby."

"I wish that too. I'm so sorry I couldn't be with you today, Andrew."

"I got through it. One does you know. But as Swift said, my last barrier to death is gone."

"Oh Andrew."

"It's alright Victoria."

He sat and stretched his legs. He was very tired. He looked at his wife, at the light on her dark blond hair, and wished he was a different sort of husband, one that would share fully in her life, take her to bed and make love. Still, he vowed he'd do his best. He'd married Victoria and they'd make a home for the baby, a life.

"The baby, she's so tiny."

"She weighed six pounds ten ounces. That's average, the nurse said. Andrew I want to call her Elizabeth."

"Elizabeth Wynne has a fine ring to it. It's the queen's name, and a sensible everyday name."

She smiled up at him, his quotations were always so charming.

He remembered the eerie silence in the house. "When do you come home?"

"Oh, in about a week the doctor said."

"The house is so empty with my mother gone."

"I'll be bringing another Wynne home with me. Maybe more than you bargained for."

"I'll do my best. Poor little girl is born into an unsettled world."

"So was I. Look at me now. I have Elizabeth and she has a father."

She was surprised by tears in his eyes when she said this. "Well, Monday, I'll see the solicitor and I'll instruct him to add your name to the Beechwood title."

She was deeply touched. She wanted to tell him he was a good man and very dear to her, but tears itched her cheeks and impatiently she brushed at them. "Andrew, I was just worried about the baby's future."

"There's no one else, Victoria, after my day, and I'm fifty-six."

"Thank you, Andrew."

"I'll go now. I'm hungry. I'll come tomorrow. Anything you need?"

"A packet of Lemons. I'm craving something bitter sweet."

"*Lemons Pure Sweets* it will be. Goodbye Victoria."

Andrew kissed her cheek and left. Outside the sky was the deep mottled blue of a late February evening. Soon the cattle would be out of their winter quarters and spring sowing would begin. As Dominic always said, the land was all. Victoria would be home soon and she was dear to him. He recalled Dominic had started hyacinths in the glasshouse. Josie would have taken care of them, watered them. He would bring a pot to Victoria tomorrow.

20

Homecoming

When Elizabeth was eight days old, Andrew brought her and Victoria home. He gingerly took the baby from Victoria. She stood out of the car in the dull February afternoon and saw splashes of snowdrops on the lawn. Josie came down the steps and took the bundled baby. "Such a fine child, Ma'am, thanks be to God. Peggy has a roaring fire above in your room."

Andrew watched Josie fuss over little Elizabeth and wondered if the baby would one day learn in her history books what a momentously dangerous time the first week of her life was. The world was a shambles. Anthony Eden had just resigned as Foreign Secretary after a meeting with the Italians and Lord Halifax had replaced him. Andrew was disheartened by Eden's resignation; Mussolini would consider it a personal victory that he could push the British Foreign Secretary from his post. It would be celebrated in Berlin. And British politicians were arguing about whether communism or fascism was the greatest threat and in Palestine partition was being proposed, the British solution which was still being challenged in Ireland as no solution at all. The Irish were negotiating with their old enemies for the return of the Treaty Ports. He took this as ominous too; it pointed toward war. Otherwise why was England making friendly overtures to the Irish?

Victoria gave Elizabeth her six o'clock bottle and after dinner they sat in the drawing room, Andrew with his ear to the wireless, Victoria content by the fire with the baby beside her asleep in her basket. She leafed through the *Irish Times*. Switzers was showing Viyella suits and jersey dresses for spring. By Easter the baby would be eight weeks. Tomorrow Nuala Fay would come. Victoria would ask her if it was reasonable to plan a trip to Dublin at Easter to shop. She hoped by then to have lost all the weight she had gained when she was pregnant.

By nine o'clock, Victoria was tired. Andrew carefully carried the basket with the sleeping baby upstairs and put it by Victoria's bed. The fire was glowing, the room warm. Andrew kissed her cheek. "Are you sure you're alright?"

"I'm fine. Good night, Andrew."

But by the time she was ready for bed the baby was crying. She went down to the kitchen. "Josie I need a bottle for Elizabeth."

"I'm getting it. You go back up Ma'am and I'll bring it up to you."

When she went back up the baby was screaming, her little face red and puckered. Victoria took her from her basket but she kept crying. Josie arrived with the bottle followed by Andrew. "What's wrong with her?"

"Ah sure the poor child is starved," Josie declared taking the baby from Victoria's arms and beginning to give her the bottle. The baby closed her eyes and blissfully sucked. Josie sat down at the fire. Andrew left, Victoria lay on her bed. She remembered standing outside the public ward at the hospital watching the new mothers breastfeeding their infants. Maybe she should have breast fed Elizabeth. But the nurses had said the condensed milk was better.

Josie settled the baby in her basket and Victoria slept. Just after midnight the baby's crying woke Victoria. Josie, who was still sitting by the fire, went to the kitchen to prepare a bottle. Victoria paced the landing with the baby. When Josie came back Victoria said, "You go to bed. I'll give her the bottle."

What kind of mother was she if she couldn't take care of her baby? She settled herself on her bed and fed the baby. A little later she jerked awake. She had fallen asleep. My God if she'd dropped her? But the baby was sleeping, the bottle half finished. How did women manage this?

When Nuala Fay arrived at nine the next morning she found Victoria in tears, Elizabeth sleeping angelically and Josie in full charge.

"We had such a dreadful night. She woke screaming at twelve and again at two and I had to get Josie up and it was after three when we got her settled. She was screaming again at five. And Josie has her own work to do."

"Ah you have the baby doldrums," Nuala declared. "You need help for a month or two. Sarah Reilly will come."

Sarah? That glum creature who had helped when Mrs. Wynne was dying?

"She's used to babies. She'll take over, let you get on your feet. It's constant work. In a few months you'll be yourself again."

"A few months? I want to go to Dublin at Easter."

"Well, we'll see. I call round to Sarah and tell her to come over."

In the afternoon Victoria was in the Square Room when Josie showed in a neighbour, Vera Callaghan. She had come to see the new baby. A small woman with expressive grey eyes in a pale face, the first visitor Victoria had, and she was a Catholic. Victoria had met her once in October when she and Mrs. Wynne had been walking the lanes, and Mrs. Wynne introduced her. She had not seen her since. She had a knitted yellow shawl for the baby. She cooed and marvelled at Elizabeth. "I won't stay long, Mrs. Wynne. You must be dead tired."

"But you'll have tea."

"Ah, I'll not. I have a three month old at home so I have to get back."

"You have a baby too? "

"Indeed I have, Mrs. Wynne. A little girl too, Carmel."

Victoria realized she was very lonely, needed someone her own age to talk to. "Call me Victoria," she said now as her visitor got up to leave. "And please come again, come for tea. You could bring the baby with you."

"That's a thought," said Vera.

At five o'clock Sarah arrived with her black shawl and her bundle and despite Victoria's misgivings she proved a success. On Nuala's advice Mrs. Wynne's old sitting room was converted into a nursery and Sarah slept there with the baby, having first banished Mog to the kitchen. "That cat's jealous," she declared. "I wouldn't have cats about a place where there's a baby."

Victoria had the baby during the day while Sarah washed nappies and prepared bottles. A routine developed that Sarah said would see Elizabeth sleeping through the night.

Then Minnie Moore and Mrs. Mac Adam arrived with a present, *Bible Stories for Children,* praised Elizabeth's robustness and declared they didn't know whom she resembled. "She's the image of my mother," Victoria told them firmly.

"A bible, no less," said Sarah scrubbing baby bottles in the sink.

"Well," Josie told her, "Isn't that all you'd want in the house? A bible and a bottle of whiskey."

"I'd say you wouldn't catch them auld ones with whiskey."

Josie pursed her lips. "Look at the time," she exclaimed and went out to check on Peggy who was beating carpets on the clothes line. Sometimes, she decided, that Sarah Reilly forgot herself, got too long in the tongue.

That evening Andrew said "Victoria, maybe you should write and tell them in Blackrock that the baby has arrived."

"They never wrote to enquire how I was, or even sent a Christmas card."

"Maybe they are waiting for you to write."

It was so characteristic of Andrew to make excuses for her family and to insist conventional etiquette be adhered to.

"Oh, I suppose I could write to my mother."

"And your sisters."

"Not on your life Andrew. Beatrice has never written me and anyway I don't have Georgina's address in England."

To please Andrew she wrote a few lines to her mother.

Dear Mother,

I am writing to tell you my baby arrived on February 19th. Her name is Elizabeth Wynne.

Andrew sends his regards.

Victoria.

She read it over. It was the least she could write. That neither her parents or her sisters had written at Christmas confirmed for her that they considered their relationship with her over. To them she was still in disgrace.

Three weeks later a package from Blackrock arrived, addressed to Miss Elizabeth Wynne, a pink dress from her grandmother. Enclosed was a card with a gloomy blue and grey reproduction of a painting of Eilean Donan Castle on the front. Inside it said *from Margaret Mulholland.*

For Victoria there was no post at all. She threw the card in the drawer of the writing table she had set up for herself in the Square Room and put the little dress aside to show to Andrew.

Elizabeth's first spring came early. Matt and Andrew were busy with spring work, nesting birds were busy in the bushes and eaves, the birches, willows and oaks budded. One windy day Victoria and Andrew stood on the front steps. "The daffodils are out, Victoria."

"Oh I love to see the daffs," said Peggy behind them, sweeping.

Andrew carried the baby down the steps. "Dominic's daffodils, Victoria."

"Yes. They're blooming well now, they're lovely." He crouched down to look at them. "See how he planted them, Victoria."

The yellow fluttering flowers were in straight lines that converged. "Notice anything peculiar?"

"He certainly spread them out, but they're beautiful."

"Look again Victoria. They make your initials V. M."

"Oh Andrew they do."

Tears welled up in her eyes. She was so damn weepy since she'd had the baby. He stood up and handed her the baby and she turned her face away. "Poor Dominic, Andrew."

"I know."

"Don't you miss him, Andrew?"

"More than I can say."

She was about to ask him if that were so, why he sometimes took off for Dublin on a Saturday but she did not. It occurred to her that this would be cruel, and perhaps missing Dominic was what drove him to his city escapades. She realised he had lost the two people who were nearest to him. She also now knew there was a part of him she didn't understand and she never actually wanted to know. He was distant and preoccupied these days with the news from Europe, furious that German troops had occupied Austria.

"How long more can England stand that German bully?" he had asked the previous evening, jumping up from his chair by the wireless in the sitting room. Victoria said nothing. She was reading *The Irish Times*. She needed clothes. Switzers was showing country skirts with flared front and pleated back, one pound six shillings. Clery's was advertising a Twilfit corset fitting week. She didn't seem to be able to lose the weight she had gained with Elizabeth. She was a frump and her hair came away in clumps on her brush. "Don't worry about it," Nuala Fay advised. "It'll grow back, happens all the time."

Easy for Nuala to talk. Vera Callaghan, when Victoria walked over, said her hair had thinned out too but had grown back. Carmel, Vera's baby, was sitting propped up by pillows.

At Easter, Victoria left Elizabeth with Sarah Reilly and went to Dublin to shop for new clothes. Nothing seemed to fit properly, she worried about her baby and rushed home having bought only a grey country skirt and a pink cardigan.

May came with the cuckoo and apple tree blossoms and Josie declared, "I never saw the like! We'll have a right good crop this year."

21

Memories of Spring

*E*ach day Donny Maguire had looked in *The Irish Times* for a birth announcement. Not finding one, he began to doubt his own conclusion that the child Victoria was carrying was his, and to believe that the pregnancy had been less advanced when he had seen her in January than he had thought. He was somewhat mortified at his impertinence in suggesting the baby was his. At Easter, the other veterinarian in the district retired and Donny found that he was busier than he'd ever been. He went back to reading *The Irish Press*. But he thought about Victoria when he woke each morning, wondered if she'd had her child and if it was a boy. The May wildflowers and returned swallows depressed him. In such early summer days he had fallen for her.

"There'll never be anyone else for me," he told Charlie, sitting in the corner of the pub.

"That's a load of rubbish, Donny. That girl was bad luck from the start. And you're not yourself. You're like an auld one of fifty. There's lots of girls dying to step out with you: that little teacher Jessie, for one. Have another Guinness and have sense."

Pub talk buzzed round him. "There'll be no war. Eden wasn't up to the job, that's all."

"And Churchill's in a sulk over the ports."

"They're ours now and not before time."

"It's their bloody war anyway. What do we care? Let them fight their own corner. We'll stay out of it and get top prices just like the last time."

Donny didn't care. He worked hard, served his customers, went to summer dances with Charlie, stood at the refreshment stand talking to other wallflowers and thought about Victoria.

Down at Crew Rock clouds of midges danced in the hazy summer air and sometimes, when Andrew could take time from his work, they went down past the garden and along by the meadows. "I love going a Maying with my beautiful girls," Andrew would declare as he carried the picnic things and Victoria carried Elizabeth, a muslin cloth over the infant's head to shield her from the flies and sun. Andrew spread the blanket away from the water in the cool leaf-filtered light. Victoria prepared their afternoon tea while he rested on one elbow and admired the baby. The infant pulled her little legs up and turned them to the side. "Look Victoria she almost turned over that time."

He shook the baby's rattle. "Hello little Lizzie," and was rewarded with a smile.

"Don't call her Lizzie."

"She's smiling at me"

"Nuala says that's just wind."

"Nonsense! You mean every time I talk to her, she gets wind?"

She gazed at them with her inscrutable eyes. The breeze rippled the lake. "Andrew, I only saw the otter once. I'd like to see him again."

"He likes his privacy. I respect that in an animal. A bit like myself."

"I hope he's not gone. I'd like some day to show him to Elizabeth."

"Lizzie will make her own discoveries."

She noticed her own hair was darker as it grew back and Elizabeth's grew lighter and so did her eyes. She was now almost four months and on fine mornings Victoria propped her on her pillows and wheeled the pram into the orchard. The rhododendron were a riot of purple trumpets, the blackbirds sang from the bushes, the apple trees showed tiny pale green buds of fruit. And in the joy of that first spring and summer, the weeks flew by.

The first week of August, Donny Maguire wrote to Victoria. He said he just wanted to see her. He proposed they meet in Killcore at Jackson's Family Hotel where he'd stayed when he'd come to see her in January. He said he'd be there from twelve o'clock on the last Saturday in September. Going through the post two days later she saw the handwriting and guessed the sender. Her first instinct was not to read it, but her curiosity overcame her good intentions and she read it. She then got up from her writing table, walked back to the kitchen and stood beside the stove. The dogs were stretched on the floor and as she stood there the dreaming Major twitched and thumped his tail on the floor and she remembered Donny's dog, that rambunctious Kerry Blue that romped round them when they walked together. She read the letter again, lifted the lid off the stove, threw it in the fire and went out to the yard. Elizabeth was sleeping in her pram in the shade of the house and Peggy was hanging nappies out to dry. How rosy and precious her baby was. Donny Maguire could go fly a kite.

Then it was haymaking season and extra men were hired by the day. She rarely saw Andrew except at dinner and she couldn't stop thinking about Donny Maguire. She marked September 24th on her calendar. Toward the end of August she allowed herself to day dream about meeting him while at other times telling herself she wouldn't meet him. There was plenty of time; she could make up her mind in September. Then it was the middle of September and then the last week.

"Andrew, Saturday I'd like the car in the afternoon. I want to go to Killcore to see the dressmaker about some clothes."

"Of course Victoria! Anytime you want the car take it. Matt can always take the horse. Do the horse good. In fact I've told Matt to slacken off the oats to that horse because he's doing very little work."

What to wear? Her summer dresses were a bit summery for late September. She settled on a linen dress with a matching cardigan in mauve that she had been wearing to church. A dress that called for a hat and gloves would be too much. After they had lunch and she had given Peggy instructions about the baby's bottle and nap, she set off. Early autumn, the poplar trees along the road still green. She was very late, but felt no compunction about that. Let him wait. And if he didn't wait she didn't care, she told herself, excited and driving a little too fast. She parked in the forecourt of the hotel. There were two other cars there. Neither was Donny Maguire's old Austin. Maybe he had a new car, or forgot, or had given up and gone home. She was late, but she expected him to be there. No desk, so she asked at the bar. An old man drinking a Guinness looked at her with tired eyes.

"Just round the corner Missus, round at the back," the barman told her, wiping off the counter top. She went round past the bar and Donny was sitting in an alcove where there were two tables. He watched her come toward him, how she'd changed, her hair darker, turned under framing her tanned face, her walk determined. He stood up and came toward her, "Victoria, I was beginning to despair of you coming."

"I had to see to your daughter." She stood stock still and her face flushed scarlet. How had she blurted that out? She had been determined that he should never know the child was his. He led her to the table and pulled out a chair for her. She found herself trembling as she sat down. She should not have come. How could she retract that statement? "Would you like a drink, Victoria?"

"Yes, I would. A shandy."

He went to the bar and she tried to regain her composure. She'd deny it. She'd say she had been teasing him. But she couldn't summon the necessary frivolity. He came back, put the drink before her and sat in the chair next to hers.

"So, I have a daughter?"

"No you haven't. I don't know how I said that. That was a slip of my tongue. I'd been thinking how you said last time I saw you that you thought you were my baby's father."

He felt she was lying, could see how distressed she was, her eyes huge, staring like a trapped animal, deathly serious in her insistence that the baby was not his. She took out her handkerchief and wiped the sweat off her upper lip and when she looked up at him he saw a defiant pleading in her eyes and with a rush of tenderness for her he lifted his glass. "Let's drink to your daughter then. What's her name?

"Elizabeth."

"Elizabeth! Well long life to her."

They drank and sat for a minute in silence.

"How old is Elizabeth now?"

She wasn't going to be caught on that one. "She's five months," she lied, "and sleeps all night."

He did the arithmetic and decided the child was probably not his after all, unless of course she was lying.

"You look well, Victoria."

"I am well. I'm getting used to being a farmer's wife."

A shadow crossed Donny's face at the idea that she was someone's wife.

"When did you get here, Donny?"

"At half ten. I was awake before dawn. I walked around your town, bought the paper. Then I came here and waited in case you came early."

His right arm was stretched along the back of her chair. He watched the curve of her arm in the mauve sleeve, the dress falling over her crossed knee. "Would you like to take a walk, Victoria?"

"No, Donny."

If she had looked up and smiled at him or touched his hand he would have taken her in his arms. It seemed a cruel fate that he could not do so. He still loved her and with wry resignation accepted that he had lost her. She had changed beyond what he had expected, her face fuller, her eyes seemed brighter. No longer the blonde good looker of the previous year, or the tired woman he had seen in January, but a more mature, and to him more beautiful, Victoria.

Victoria was silent, preoccupied, thinking about her baby, about Andrew and how she would lie to him about her afternoon in Killcore.

"Would you like another drink?"

"No, Donny, I must go. I have to get back."

"The little girl? You're thinking of her!"

"Yes. She'll be awake." She rose to go.

"Goodbye Donny."

He walked her to the car and held the door for her. She sat in and as she drove off, the last sight she had of him was in the rear view mirror standing looking after her. She stepped hard on the accelerator and small stones scattered as she turned into the road. His last sight of her was the blur of her mauve cardigan. Then he walked to his car and sat with his head in his hands and a surge of rage and frustration at losing her swept through him.

It was after four when she got home. She parked the car and rushed in the house, feeling guilty at having left the baby so long. Elizabeth was propped up in her pram in the kitchen being entertained watching Josie's thumbs and fingers rubbing butter into flour. "How has she been, Josie?"

"Just grand Ma'am. Took her bottle and all and had a great sleep. You'll take your tea in the Square Room I expect."

Sitting in the nursery giving the baby her bedtime bottle, she thought about their meeting, went over each word they had spoken, and knew that at the end if he'd taken her in his arms she would have gone with him wherever he wanted. That realization terrified her. At dinner, she had an uneasy feeling that Andrew knew she had done something clandestine that afternoon, although from his conversation it was clear that he was preoccupied with the new Anglo Irish Agreement on Defence. "It's the last thing England had to do before she goes to war: settle with Ireland."

As soon as he had eaten he said, "I'd like to go across to listen to the wireless, Victoria. Please ask Josie to give me my coffee there. Will you join me?"

Victoria told Josie to serve the coffee and apple cake on a tray in the drawing room and went there and dutifully poured the coffee while Andrew sat with his ear bent to the radio. She supposed she and Andrew got on as well as most. In any case, this was her life. She would not meet with Donny Maguire again, ever. She must have been crazy to meet him. She was not going to think of him again. He unnerved her so completely, that discussion of Elizabeth's age, the way she blurted out that she was his daughter. She would never see him again, and she'd get over this crazy fantasy she had that they might again be lovers. Andrew was a good man and he provided a home for them. They would never be lovers, she understood that, but she must never let herself forget that if she hadn't married Andrew, Elizabeth might be in some brutal orphanage. She could not bear to think of it, her beautiful baby with that red tint in her hair and her solemn eyes.

Anyone looking at them would have concluded that they were a settled couple with shared experiences and a much loved child. They were devoted to Beechwood, to their mutual comfort and the dwindling Church of Ireland society around them. Her only model was her parents' marriage and her memory of that was of accommodations made by her mother and tacit agreements that certain matters were not spoken of, such as her Aunt Nicola's drinking or her sister Georgina's disappointing marriage to a mere clerk. She remembered how her parents had banded together in their heartless decision to throw her out. She would never treat Elizabeth in such a cruel way. That still hurt deeply.

She joined with the other women in planning church functions, in catering Saturday suppers. She and Andrew attended the church socials. When she'd waltzed with Sandy Patterson, Lottie stared at her censoriously as they circled the room. But there were what she privately thought of as Andrew's Mr. Hyde moods when he became restless, his face with a hard closed look that told the world, "I can't stand this place another day." Then he'd announce on a Saturday that he was going to Dublin and she'd say nothing. What could she say? He was going no matter what she said. She worried when he was gone, raged at his desertion of her and Elizabeth and sometimes walked over to talk to Vera Callaghan. They sat at Vera's kitchen table and had tea and scones, Elizabeth on her knee, Vera's baby Carmel in a playpen. The Callaghans had three other children: the oldest was ten. Vera put them out to play and they romped with the dog and made mud pies on the dairy steps with clay from the garden and water from the pump. Victoria wanted to talk to Vera about Andrew's trips to Dublin, but she couldn't, so they talked mostly about their children. An hour later Victoria would be pushing Elizabeth's pram up the avenue and rehearsing in her mind the row she would have with Andrew when he came home. But when he came home there were just tense silences and his face told her, "Ask me no questions and I'll tell you no lies." So she asked no questions and invariably the routine of the farm and their love for Elizabeth drew them together into their future. That he was besotted with Elizabeth never ceased to amaze her. He would come from the dairy, having seen Matt off to the creamery, and play with her in the Square Room. Peggy brought their mid morning tea there and the baby rolled around on the floor, grasping the paws of the tiger rug trying to propel herself forward.

"Don't you think Lizzie is much smarter than other babies her age? Look how she can roll over already."

"Don't call her Lizzie. I don't know other children her age, Andrew."

"Well you know Callaghan's little one."

"She's three months older. Nuala Fay says Elizabeth is about average."

"About average? With due respect to Nurse Fay I think Lizzie is brilliant."

"Andrew, you know I've asked Vera Callaghan to tea a hundred times and she always has an excuse, never comes over."

"It's not The Done Thing around here, to visit with Protestants. Protestants and Catholics, it's like Shylock I always think, they'll buy and sell and talk and walk, but they won't eat or drink or pray together."

"I hated that play when we learned it, full of awful hatred of Shylock."

"I liked it. It was about love and money."

"Love and money? I don't believe we studied the same play, Andrew."

"No? We could debate that Victoria. What about Antonio and Bassanio? Were they not lovers? And the attraction of Portia is that she is a lady richly left."

She stared at him not really having an answer and then said, "It's about how terribly Jews were despised."

"That's the plot, but it's not what it's about."

She'd never win a debate with him. Antonio and Bassanio lovers? It just reminded her of his running off to Dublin.

"The Callaghans came when your mother died."

"That was Brendan coming to help me out. Not the same as coming for tea."

"Will this country ever get over that Catholic-Protestant hatred?"

"Not I expect in my time, Victoria. It's history. It depends on which English king one's ancestors supported, James the Second or William of Orange."

"That's centuries ago."

"It's very real Victoria. When the Black and Tans committed atrocities in the name of the English my mother's generation were ashamed. Their sense of right and wrong was offended. And the English have lots to answer for."

"And what about the IRA and all they slaughtered?"

"That's true. Including many of their own, Victoria. "

"What's the answer Andrew?"

"Each side must think differently. Imagine your father doing that."

"I can't."

"It's dangerous ground you're on Victoria, Catholics and Protestants in Ireland."

"But that's just in the North."

"Here too, if things get stirred up."

"But we all worship the same God, or claim we do, if there is a God."

"Oh there's a God, Victoria, but not always as the church tells it. My mother had great comfort from her bible and I do too. There's often comfort in religion, but there can be comfort in illusions too. Still the Church holds us all together."

"One time I saw a couple praying their beads in a train and it seemed like a conversation they were having, just the two of them."

"Maybe that's it. We feel better if we pray."

"Then shouldn't we all pray together, Catholics and Protestants?"

"No chance of that. I think you're on a crusade Victoria." He was teasing her again.

"I am not."

"Oh, I think you are."

"Oh, dry up, Andrew."

Over in Callaghans', Brendan said, "Vera, that wife of Wynne's comes over a lot, the two of you kettling and drinking tea."

"She's lonely. She's from Dublin and he's old, could be her father."

"Well, just so long as you don't take to going over there and having the whole country talking that you're getting close with the Protestants."

She rolled her eyes and poured his tea, "Mighty Christian altogether, Brendan."

"You know yourself how they talk." He went back to the paper. "I swear to God we're going to have another war. Then try to get men to help about the place. They'll all be joining up, like the last time."

22

Dancehall Dreams

At the Halloween dance in Mountnugent, Donny stood inside the door with the other partnerless men and watched the dancers. He couldn't stop thinking about Victoria and their brief meeting. She'd been in such a rush to get away. He hoped her coming to meet him hadn't caused her husband to be suspicious. He envied him, imagined him a tough, no nonsense, Protestant landowner. If he thought too much about them together he'd go mad, especially if he thought about her in Wynne's arms, or his bed. The dance was almost over. He thought he'd slip away. Then the band leader announced that the next dance was Ladies' Choice and suddenly everyone was watching to see whom the ladies would favour. He watched a tall sharp featured nurse from the County Hospital approach Charlie. Then someone said, "May I have this dance, Donny?"

He turned and saw it was Jessie O'Toole, the pretty dark haired teacher from the vocational school.

"I'd be honoured Jessie, he said gallantly, took her hand and stepped out with her onto the floor.

"We don't see much of you at the dances, Donny?"

"Well I've been busy. I'm helping my brother-in-law work on his house."

"It's great you came out tonight."

His excuse wasn't strictly true. He'd spent exactly one Saturday helping Declan work on the cottage he and Nan owned. Now he felt he was on display, all the farmers watching. Donny Maguire the vet, no better man with a lame horse or a cow with the staggers, fox-trotting with that fine girl Jessie, whom everyone knew had been mad keen on him for two years at least, Jessie with her black curls and teasing eyes. He liked Jessie, and maybe he should try to forget Victoria. Jessie's dark head came to his shoulder, he could smell her perfume. "Are you enjoying the dance, Jessie? "

"Very much, the band is great." She moved in close to him, her head just under his chin. The music wound down, it was over. Other couples separated but Jessie stood close to him. "That was nice, Donny" she said and then the band leader announced the last dance. He looked in her brown expectant eyes and said, "May I have this one?" and she stepped into his waiting arms and they circled the floor other couples, surrounding them in the smooth slow waltz ......' *flow on lovely river, flow gently along...*'

Then the lights were being lowered and Jessie clung to him, light as a shadow in the sea of swaying couples and they danced close and in silence and the singer gave it his best:

`'By thy waters so sweet, Sang the larks' merry song .... '

Charlie danced past with the nurse and over her shoulder he nodded approvingly at Donny. Jessie said, "This is a favourite of mine. I have the record at home."

Then the song was ending, ' *And you lovely Molly, The Rose of Mooncoin.'*

The lights came up, the dance was over. "I'll see you home, Jessie?"

She nodded, "I'll get my coat."

In the car, she leaned her head on his shoulder and they drove slowly through the dark. The headlights picked out couples from the dance, arms round each other, walking home. At her digs, he left the engine running, went around and opened her door and when she stepped out she reached up her arms to kiss him. He kissed her cheek, put his arm around her shoulders, walked her up the path and stood on the step. He took both her hands in his. "Jessie, you're a lovely girl. You know that yourself, and I'm not going to ruin your life."

He had to take the key from her trembling hands to fit it in the lock. "Good night Jessie."

A month later, Charlie told him Jessie was walking out with the manager of the creamery. "And bully for her. Sick waiting on you to make up your mind."

"Charlie, shut up!"

"Alright lad. What are you drinking?"

"I'll have a Bass if you're buying. Then I have to go."

"And I have as well," Charlie said.

It hadn't taken long for Jessie to find someone else. Walking up from the pub to his digs he decided he had to see Victoria again. Of course Charlie was dead right, he should forget Victoria. But Charlie wasn't tormented thinking about her day and night, wondering what she was doing, what her life was like, dreaming of taking her in his arms. Charlie wasn't in love with her. Donny's wasn't much of a family if numbers meant anything. His two sisters, Nan and Una. Una he thought was more like his aunt. She'd been gone out of the house before he started school. She lived in Rathmines, a suburb of Dublin, and was always writing asking him to visit and then, when he did, trying to set him up with some girl. There was Aunt Emer and his Uncle Joseph who raised them after his mother died. And of course his father, a reserved quiet man who had had little part in his life because he had quit farming and emigrated when Donny was born and had returned in 1930 when Donny had already left their little village for school in the city. Lately he was trying to know him better. His father had lost a love too, when Donny's mother died. But he hadn't lost her to another man, and wasn't eaten alive with jealousy as Donny was of Andrew Wynne. Then there was his Uncle Patrick, who had emigrated more than forty years ago to America. Aunt Emer usually had a card from him at Christmas, no news, just a card. Another Irish bachelor! That was his clan, and maybe little Elizabeth, Victoria's baby. He couldn't get it out of his head that she might be his daughter. He and Nan had always been close, she was a good egg. Of course she was like the rest where Victoria was concerned, uncompromisingly against his having anything to do with her because she was a Protestant. The cold autumn night sky was full of stars and he picked out Orion and the Plough as he walked through dry leaves that had been swept into the gutter by the wind. It was only a quarter after ten. He was wretchedly lonely. A Friday night, Nan and Declan would still be up. He walked past his digs and on up the road. Nan opened the door. "Donny, you're out late. Come on in."

She took his coat and hung it up and went before him into the sitting room. Donny sat in an armchair at the fire. It was a fierce glowing lump of coal.

"Declan is upstairs. He'll be down shortly. Would you like a cup of tea or anything Donny?"

"No I just came from the pub and I just didn't feel like going home."

She turned up the wick on the table lamp. "Donny I hope you're not drinking too much."

"Ah for heaven's sake Nan, can't a man have a few drinks?"

"Is there anything wrong Donny?"

He closed his eyes and stretched his chin up toward the ceiling, then lowered his head and looked straight at her. "Wrong? Well nothing's right.

It's Victoria Mulholland. I can't get her out of my head." He could see her expression harden. "She's married now."

Her face cleared. "Well, that's that Donny. I didn't know she was married. When did this happen, not that it matters?"

"When I met her last Christmas she was married. And she has a baby."

"A child?"

"Yes."

"Donny, for heaven's sake why are you pining for a woman who is married? And has a child. I had no idea."

She got up and stood with her back to the table.

"Nan, I think the child is mine."

She stared at him incredulous. "What? My God Donny, how could you? How did that happen?" She turned her back and he could see her in the mirror her arms folded across her chest.

"Nan I don't know."

"What about her husband?"

"Nan what happened was that she left here last May, I never heard from her again and I met her in Dublin at Christmas and she was already married and the child was born sometime before Easter. I feel sure I'm the father."

"And what does she say?'

"I haven't been really able to talk to her about it. It's just I'm sure the child is mine."

"But she never said that? Never reproached you about it? Never made any claim on you?"

"No."

"Well Donny, count your lucky stars she didn't."

"She'd make no claim on me. She's married."

"Correct! She's married. You think the baby is yours and you've never talked to the mother about it and she's married to someone else. I think you're stark raving mad."

"It's just I feel it's my only chance at a life."

Nan threw up her hands and walked away, then turned. "Donny, you've taken leave of your senses."

"It's all well for you and Declan, you have your two great youngsters and each other."

"Donny, you haven't got the ghost of an idea about what it's like for us. Not the foggiest notion. We're resented in this town especially since we've started to put the addition on the house. The expression is the Houlihans, with her brother the vet at one end of the village, the school principal at the other, they've the town sewn up. Nothing left for anyone else. They're a begrudging lot in this town. The opinion is everything we have came through Uncle Joseph being a County Councillor. As if we never did anything for ourselves. And the parish priest, managing the schools, has complete control. Think of the disgrace if that were known, that you fathered a Protestant child. It'll be read out from the altar. I can just hear it 'There's a Catholic man in this parish that's sinning with a Protestant girl.' And the begrudgers in this village would have a field day."

She saw that Donny sat with a hard, unrelenting face. Footsteps sounded on the stairs. "Here's Declan," she whispered. "Say nothing about what we were talking about."

"How are you Donny? Great to see you," and Declan held out his hand. He was a thin slightly stooped man with thinning black hair and a harassed look in his grey eyes.

"Did you get Finn back to sleep?"

"I think he's settled now. How about a cup of tea Nan? Donny you'll have one too?"

Donny left at midnight. He hoped she wouldn't blather about himself and Victoria to Declan. But at heart he knew that she would eventually tell him, although not right away because, as everyone knew, Declan Houlihan was a worrier.

The summer Victoria had left Ballynamon, he had thought to borrow money from the bank and buy a farm and looked around at what land was for auction, but his energy failed him. After he had met her at Christmas, he thought why bother if she was not there to share his life. He believed his feelings for Victoria were the best part of him so resigned himself to bachelorhood. He worked hard at his business and to his sister's dismay he stayed on in his confined lodgings and seemed to be just another Irish country bachelor. He joined the new golf club in Obanbeg and became a frustrating enigma to the matchmaking women who played there.

23

Motherhood

*S*eldom had Victoria felt so alive as in Elizabeth's first year. Each stage of the baby's development was a wonder. Taking on the running of the household at Beechwood was satisfying, never more than when she went over the household accounts, consulted with Josie on what meals to prepare or filled in a cheque for Matt to take to the grocer in Killcore. She was aware of the threat of war because by the end of March 1939, when the German Army had occupied the whole of Czechoslovakia, Andrew was spending his evenings alternately listening to the radio and studying a map of Europe he had attached with drawing pins to the wall in the Square Room. At nine o'clock he would switch on the wireless and the sound of Big Ben would drift out into the hall. After the news, he would go to the map and move the drawing pins according to the BBC news. Sometimes, seeing him there, Victoria would go to him and put her arm round him and he would also hold her and she was strangely comforted. One evening in late March she asked, "What are you worried about, Andrew?'

"I'm not so much worried as saddened Victoria. With France and England pledging to protect Poland you know the Germans will go after Poland. There's no stopping the war now."

She felt he was thinking of his dead brother. Elizabeth was sitting on the floor chewing her teething ring. Victoria lifted her in her arms, wrapped her in her blanket and walked with her out into the cool foggy air. The orchard was full of the smell of rain and growing things, and a blackbird calling to another. Around mossy stones near the fence bluebells were growing and over in an open space Dominic's daffodils were budding. She couldn't think of war, not today when the whole earth was alive with renewed growth. The baby turned her solemn little face up to the budding branches. "What are you thinking Elizabeth? What's in that little curly head? You're more than a year old now. You know nothing about this war your father talks about. It will never happen and if it does it'll be over before you know it."

She was so content with her baby that although it was a spring and summer filled with rumours of war and debates about Irish neutrality, she couldn't take the talk of war seriously. Andrew wasn't surprised about neutrality. "It has been the policy for years, fifteen at least. But if war comes the Irish boys will join up like they did the last time."

By July, Elizabeth was toddling after Peggy to the henhouse and pulling the pots and pans from the cupboards in the kitchen and Victoria spent her mornings in the Square Room playing with her. The child showed a marked preference for the box of old toys Andrew brought down from the third floor, Lotts bricks and toy soldiers. One Sunday evening in the middle of August, after he'd spent a Saturday in Dublin, he told her, "Victoria we have to lay in supplies, tea, coffee and the like and you need to think about what needs to be got for Lizzie."

"Her name is Elizabeth, Andrew."

She was angry that he had spent the previous night in Dublin. So he came back after a Dublin escapade full of plans for what she should do. But she held her tongue because on that subject there could be no rational conversation with him. "Are you worried prices will rise?"

"They're rising already. We're getting an extra penny a gallon for milk. No. I'm worried there'll be shortages. Anything imported, you know. And the last time some foods were bulked up disgracefully."

"How do you mean?"

"Well coffee for instance, ground acorns were added to stretch it. It was impossible to get good coffee. Make a list and we'll go to Dublin. Sarah could come back and take care of Lizzie for a few days, or she could stay with Josie."

She was suspicious of his desire to go to Dublin. He'd just come back from there. She was not convinced about the need for hoarding supplies.

"You should go to Blackrock to see your family. The times are uncertain."

"My family? They don't care a damn about me, Andrew. They never came when Elizabeth was born, never wrote to me."

"Victoria, I don't want you to be sorry you didn't at least try to visit them."

She walked away from him and out to the kitchen to check on what Josie, who had the evening off, had left ready for dinner.

But on Monday afternoon Josie said, "Ma'am the shops are running out. Shaw's are out of tea and candles and there's no paraffin to be had."

At tea time Victoria said, "Andrew, Josie says the shops in Killcore are out of paraffin and tea."

"I don't believe that. They're hoarding for a higher price. I'll lay in paraffin and petrol if you'll see to what foods are needed. Ask Josie."

"Well Ma'am" said Josie, "sugar and tea and coffee, and cocoa, that Rowntree's Elect, and flour."

"You're not suggesting we need to lay in a supply of flour?"

"I don't know Ma'am but you know the Christmas baking, we need that good Boland's white flour and some of that Royal Baking Powder and we'll need fruit and peel for the cakes. We need to order a chest of tea."

Would things get that bad? Josie and Peggy cleared space in the pantry and scrubbed some apple barrels for storage.

"I think we should go Friday morning. That gives you Friday afternoon and Saturday morning to shop. You might want to visit your parents and I'll stay in the city."

He had it all planned. Kill two birds with one stone. She had never been invited to visit her parents. They had never even come to see the baby. Why did Andrew think it was up to her to approach her parents? His plan was that she'd visit her parents and he'd find some diversion in the bars or on the docks. She felt herself getting more agitated with him so she put Elizabeth in the pram and went over to talk to Vera Callaghan.

Elizabeth and Carmel played with empty boxes on the floor. Carmel climbed into a box. "Vera, sometimes I find being married so hard," Victoria ventured.

"I know. Brendan is no stroll by the river either. Men, they're like children. If he didn't need me in bed, I'd never manage him. The Irish women should bloody well go on strike, lock the bedroom door."

Victoria thought she didn't even have Lysistrata's card to play. Vera got up to put two chairs in front of the range as a barrier to the children who were playing on the floor. "Now Carmel and Lizzie, they'll have it different. They'll be their own women."

Then because the weather was fine, Andrew decided he could not go to Dublin. It was the haying season and he couldn't lose a day. "If we put our shoulders into it we should have the hay in by Saturday evening."

In the end she left Elizabeth with Josie and on Saturday morning at seven o'clock set out. "Drive carefully Victoria," Andrew called as she drove away. In the rear view she saw that he waved his white handkerchief.

Elated at the prospect of a day in the city she drove fast down the avenue, the morning sun glinting on the metal of the car, through Killcore and on past Dunshaughlin. She found parking at Eden Quay. The shops were busy, the streets full of anxious crowds abuzz with speculation and rumours of shortages and higher prices. She headed for Clery's. In the children's department she got a pink coat, hat and leggings for Elizabeth for the coming winter, a green wool dress for herself, and material to keep on hand to have made up by the dressmaker in Killcore. She spent more than she intended and on impulse bought a dollhouse for Elizabeth in Talbot Street. She was hungry and stopped for lunch at a café. Two men at the next table were talking about the war, declaring that the Nazi advance could not be reversed either by persuasion or threats. The older man said heatedly that the declarations by the politicians in the Dail that the country would stay neutral were rubbish. Victoria realised that it was not just Andrew who was anxious about events in Europe. She got up quickly, gathered up her packages and rushed to Findlater's for raisins and spices, Lawlor's candles, and a case of Frank Coopers Strawberry Preserve which was Andrew's favourite. Outside Findlater's she gratefully accepted a young lad's offer to carry her packages for sixpence. Together they made their way to the car, and when everything was loaded into the boot, flustered, she gave him a shilling, and he disappeared like a shot into the crowded Dublin street.

When she got clear of the city traffic she drove recklessly fast on the country roads anxious to get home. It was after five when Andrew heard the approaching car and was waiting with Elizabeth at the foot of the steps. "We missed you Victoria. Didn't we Lizzie? Now we can have tea."

"Didn't you have tea yet?"

She stepped out and took the baby. Andrew leaned over and kissed her cheek. "We were waiting for you." And he began to unload the car.

"I got everything on the list," she said.

"We'll need it all."

He was as interested in the dollhouse as the child was. He sat with her on the floor in the Square Room, "This is the front door. And look at the chimney where Santa Claus comes down, Lizzie."

Josie came in and set the tea tray on the table. "Andrew, don't call her Lizzie. Thanks Josie."

Josie tied on Elizabeth's bib. "Soldiers of toast ducky, and mashed eggy."

Elizabeth sat on Andrew's knee at the table and Victoria poured their tea.

"We've a splendid crop of apples this year," Andrew announced. "We're lucky to have our own produce. At least we won't be hungry if things go bad."

"I wish everyone would just dry up about this war," Victoria told him. "It's all they talk about in Dublin. Everyone shopping and hoarding."

"You can't blame people for that."

"I don't want to hear another word about it Andrew. Think of Elizabeth."

"I am thinking of her."

There was no escaping it. Andrew stayed up late in the night listening to the wireless. On Tuesday morning when she came down to breakfast he said, "Victoria the wireless said the British navy are hunting German warships in the North Sea."

"What does that mean?"

"It probably means war, Victoria." He was smoking again, always a sign he was agitated.

It was golden late summer and every morning she took Elizabeth out in her pram for a walk. Sometimes she visited Vera and sometimes she just walked. On Friday the first day of September, when she came down for breakfast, Andrew had already left to help Matt, and at ten o'clock she wheeled Elizabeth down the avenue and along the road to Killcore. She taught her the names of the animals they passed in the fields. "A sheep Elizabeth. What does the sheep say?"

"Ba ba."

"Good girl. Look at the cows."

"Moo."

When they reached the school at Crossbawn, she sat on a mossy rock and gave Elizabeth a bottle of milk which she sucked blissfully and closed her eyes. Before they reached Beechwood, Elizabeth was sound asleep. Victoria parked the pram at the clump of mint by the kitchen door.

"Just leave her there, I'll watch her," Josie said. She shooed Mog away with a flap of her apron and looked significantly at Victoria. "Something's up. On the wireless, Ma'am."

Victoria could hear the announcer's voice as she went into the front hall. Andrew came from the drawing room. "Andrew, what's wrong?"

"The Germans are in Poland. They invaded this morning, at dawn."

"Just like that?"

"Well, they say the Poles invaded first. It's war, Victoria. Just like the last time, but probably worse, more widespread."

"Oh Andrew! Will Ireland be in it?"

"Not if Dev can help it. Neutrality is his policy, has been for years. It's so disheartening to listen to it," he sighed and turned back to switch off the wireless.

"Let's eat our lunch anyway Andrew."

"Where's little Lizzie?"

"Asleep in the pram. Josie's watching her."

They ate looking out at the afternoon sun shining on the garden and afterwards went together to look at the baby who was now wide awake waving her arms joyously at the washing that fluttered on the clotheslines like bunting hung out for a festival.

On Sunday morning, the Reverend Johnson led the congregation in prayers for peace. After service Andrew hurried to the car and Victoria followed, greeting knots of anxious people on the church steps as she went. At home Andrew went straight to the radio in the drawing room. The BBC was playing over and over again Chamberlain's address warning people to stay off the streets and to attach labels to their children.

"He's afraid of an invasion," Andrew said.

"My God! Can it be that bad?"

Then the King's speech came on, asking for calm. There was no doubt England and France were at war with Germany. A fatalistic inertia settled on the room. Victoria thought something would surely be done, something would happen to forestall the conflict. She went out to the kitchen and picked up Elizabeth from her playpen. Josie had the evening off and had cycled over to the County Home to visit her mother. Victoria fed the baby her supper, settled her in her cot and went looking for Andrew. She found him still as a stone leaning against a tree in the shadow haunted orchard. "Andrew, it's dinner time," she reminded him and was suddenly aware of how quiet he was, how deep in thought. "Try not to think about it Andrew. It does no good."

"I can't help myself, Victoria. I keep thinking about those lads saying goodbye. All over England they're drinking their last pint, saying goodbye to friends, putting a brave show on for their mothers, never admitting it's journey's end for most of them."

"Last time you came home safe."

"I did but we lost my brother."

"You never talk about it, Andrew."

"About what?"

"About what you did in the war."

"I wasn't in it long. I didn't join till March 1916."

She wanted to keep him talking. She was worried seeing him brood. "Why didn't you go earlier?"

"When my brother left, there was just me to run the place. My father was getting frail. But then they were calling for volunteers."

"So you went."

"I did. I enlisted in 1916 and after a bit of training we were sent over to Calais in June. It was June, the 16th I remember. I think it was a Tuesday. By October I was home. I was badly wounded by shrapnel in my right shoulder. I was sent to hospital in Le Touquent but it was trench fever that almost killed me."

"But it got you home."

"Yes. And glad I was to be home. I hated most the confusion of it. We didn't know what we were doing, what the plan was. At the Etaples camp they were just boys. I was a junior but the oldest except for the senior officers, old fogies from the Boer War. Eventually we were sent by train to the Front. We walked from Amiens station and the men slept in barns along the way. Everywhere villages were in ruins. It was dreadful. They billeted us officers in the farmhouses. It was a shambles."

"But from what I've read, war always is, Andrew."

"The incompetence! The communications system was water logged, full of mud and we were reduced to relaying in flag signals. And then my brother, poor chap, died in January. He had been wounded too, he died of his wounds. There was just me then, so it was not expected that I would go back. My father never got over losing Philip."

"We should go in, Andrew."

They walked back through the dusk and into the house. In the dining room when he struck a match, already thinking of the scarcity of war, lit just two candles. After dinner he again sat listening to the wireless. Victoria cleared the table and carried their dishes to the kitchen. Late that night she heard Major barking and Sally whimpering outside and the distant call of an owl as if all the lonely countryside was disturbed by the tramping feet of troops. She lit a candle to check on Elizabeth but she was sleeping sweetly. From the window she could see the full moon begin its slow decline. In bed she lay thinking of the actors, the parade that peopled her life: her older sisters, her aunt and her parents and Kathleen in Blackrock. Maybe she should have swallowed her resentment and gone out to Blackrock. She should have listened to Andrew. He was older, and despite his faults, wiser than she was. She thought about Andrew and little Elizabeth, and Josie who worked so hard to maintain their household. Then Donny Maguire. She imagined these people, like herself, invaded by a dread of a war that was now beginning in earnest and wished all of them safe.

When Donny Maguire was a child, he'd left a space beside himself everywhere he walked, for his guardian angel who, his aunt had assured him, walked with him always. Now, he reflected ruefully, it was Victoria who filled that space beside him and came to him in his dreams. For some reason his longing for her was greater when the seasons were changing. It seemed a lifetime since he'd seen her, though it was only a year. After the meeting at Jackson's Hotel in Killcore, he promised himself he'd forget her but now he knew he never could. In his head he composed letters to her, passionate hopeful letters, which were never written. But now there was such uncertainty in the very air people were doing things they'd put off for years, settling differences, writing wills, marrying hastily, making last sentimental journeys. He had to see her. He wouldn't write or plan anything, he'd just go like he'd done the first time, just arrive. He set off very early on a Saturday morning, had his lunch in Kells in a pub looking out at the old stone cross. When he started out again he began to think that it mightn't be a good idea, maybe her husband would take offence. What excuse had he for the visit? He could say that he'd been in Dublin and decided to make a little detour to see Victoria. But why, the husband might ask? And this might embarrass Victoria. The last time they'd met it had been so perfunctory. She'd had to go back to see to her baby. That idea he had that the child was his? Was that lunacy? He should have written before he came. As he came down the slope towards Beechwood past the farmhouses and cottages he became more uncertain. When he geared down to turn in the avenue a man cutting the grass at the gatehouse rested the scythe against a tree and went over to the car. Donny sensed something hostile in the man's demeanour. He wound down the car window.

"Could you tell me the way to Dublin?"

"Which way did you come?"

Donny recognised this question for what it was, a not too friendly enquiry about who he was, where he was from, and what was his business here.

"I came from Kells."

"You're a ways out of your road.'

"Can you help me get back on the road?"

Matt considered for a minute, "Go back the way you came and when you get to the first crossroads take the turn for Killcore, round the foot of the hill. Go right through the town, you'll see the Dublin road. Just stick to the tar."

Donny waved his thanks and backed up the car. He was a complete fool to have come. Was that rough looking man her husband? He looked very young. Or was he a hired man? He looked more like the hired man.

"Some eejit came in a car when I was mowing there at the gate," Matt reported to Josie.

"He said he was lost. Looking for the Dublin Road. An ID number plate."

"With all that has cars now you wouldn't know who you'd see," Josie told him.

Angry with himself Donny drove fast through the turning fall leaves. He was going to put this madness behind him and never attempt to see Victoria again. He was going to forget about her completely.

It turned out to be the loveliest autumn in memory. The apple trees fulfilling their vernal promise yielded a rich crop, rowan berries glowed in the lanes and blackberries and sloes weighed down the bushes. Josie squirreled away sugar to make sloe gin when the first frost would have sweetened the berries. Autumn advanced toward winter, the evenings shortened, the light faded the edges of the trees blurring in the dusk and fewer lamps were lit to conserve paraffin. As war descended on the continent, in Ireland there was rumour and speculation and endless talk. It was called the Emergency in Ireland after the Emergency Powers Act passed in 1939. Northern Ireland resisted conscription, though on both sides of the border young men lined up to join the army. In the South, alarmed that the flood of young men and women migrating to England would leave the farms without workers, the government passed regulations restricting workers under thirty-three years or from farm areas from leaving. But emigrants found ways around these obstacles. In the pub, the talkers argued endlessly about emigration and prices, and declared neutrality was the only policy for Ireland. Still smarting from the battles of their youth, they declared that they did not exactly want England beaten, but if England was half beaten that would be no bad thing.

24

Wartime

Victoria was keenly aware of the war because Andrew followed it assiduously, never failing to listen to the BBC nightly news and, later, the Home and Forces Program. The censorship of news and information in Ireland meant that the real conditions in Europe were not at first known. He was less disturbed by evacuation from Dunkirk at the end of May 1940 than she would have expected, insisting it was a rescue not a retreat and saying the Chiefs of Staff were at that very time submitting plans for victory. In July and August of 1940, the Battle of Britain raged and sometimes the drone of a plane that had gone off course was heard in the night. Was it a lost bomber that had been headed for London or Kent or a RAF fighter lost? She lit no candle when she got up to check on Elizabeth but felt her way to her cot and stood listening to her breathing. As August gave way to September, Andrew was glued to the wireless: Germany had now overrun all of Europe, where should Ireland stand? It had no army or navy to speak of, but the government resisted England's request to use the Irish ports as bases to service ships. Ironically the partition of Ireland, which was such a thorn in the sides of the Irish, saved the country from more severe pressure since Britain could use the ports of Northern Ireland. The Germans, having the advantage of operating from the French Atlantic ports, were now believed to be planning invasion for the seventh of September 1940. Nervously, anxiously, Ireland considered its position and its neutrality, but tide and moon gave so short an interval for action that the German's opportunity for invasion was lost and the great air battles of the second week in September showed that in the air the British had the superior force.

Slowly at first, but relentlessly like smoke drifting from the conflagration in Europe, war affected Ireland and Beechwood. There was rationing of tea and sugar and control of wages and prices. In England, wages were allowed to rise and prices were fixed so more Irish than ever sailed for England although the Dail claimed this was conscription by other means. In August 1941 when Peggy, like thousands of other Irish girls attracted by the better wages, gave notice and went to England, Josie said waspishly, "God grant us no greater loss than that."

But the household was unable to get a replacement. Talking after church Mrs. Mac Adam said there was no help to be had, especially in the country. Minnie Moore nodded solemnly in agreement, "Now if you were in Dublin, it'd be a different story."

Victoria worked hard to help Josie. Elizabeth now walking, followed her as she struggled with the Acme mangle and the box iron. One day she realized that she had not read a book in months and decided she had become a drudge. There was so much work keeping the house in order, it was too big to keep clean or to keep fires going when the weather got colder. The stockpile of coal Andrew had laid in the previous summer was dwindling and new supplies unattainable. Turf made a pleasant fire but fell short in the kitchen stove and in heating the water in the cistern. "I hear in England they're cookin' with hay, God help us all," Josie said to Matt in the kitchen, "Hay Box Cookery they call it."

"That's not what Peggy was expecting when she headed for England."

"England isn't all it's cracked up to be. There's more gone over there than is doing well, Matt."

When Victoria talked to Andrew after church the third Sunday in September, he agreed with her on the difficulty of heating the house in the coming winter. He suggested parts of the house be closed off for the duration of the Emergency. "Just beating that turkey carpet in the drawing room takes hours. I'd close that place up, and the dining room. We can use the Square Room. It gets the evening sun and stays warm till late in the year. And I'll move to Dominic's old bedroom. It backs on the kitchen so the range keeps it warm."

He said he was glad to move downstairs, because his legs felt heavy and ached sometimes and he found the stairs difficult.

Late Monday afternoon Josie and Matt moved Dominic's old bed frame outside and stored it in the garage. Then they helped Andrew move his bed to the vacated space, then Josie's bed to Andrew's room, and the third floor of Beechwood was closed off, the door locked.

Coming down the stairs after Josie, Elizabeth cried, "Mine Teddy."

"Wait now ducky, when I'm finished here we'll look for Teddy."

Andrew went outside to check the milking machines and get away from

Josie and Victoria's reorganizing of the house and Elizabeth, ignored in all the fuss, ran after him through the yard and into the dark cold milking parlour. Andrew was checking the batteries. "Papa, Teddy gone," she wept.

He turned and picked her up and dried her tears with his handkerchief. "We'll find Teddy. I think I know where you left him." He carried her out to the yard and across to where the bear lay on a pile of sand beside the stables. "There's Teddy."

He set her down and she ran to pick up the bear. The furry toy was deliciously warm from the sun. Andrew lifted her up and she buried her face in the bear's fur. "Lizzie, let's go and see how the apples are ripening."

And they went. Elizabeth wonderfully safe and warm between her soft furry bear and her father's chest. Meanwhile, Victoria and Josie tackled The Square Room while Matt stood awkwardly waiting their instructions. The old wicker table, if put in front of the doors to the conservatory, would be fine for dining but to make room for it and two extra chairs, Victoria's writing table would have to be moved aside. Josie picked up the inkwells and pens and Matt lifted the table. The drawer fell open and a sheaf of papers slid onto the floor. "Sorry Ma'am."

Victoria stooped and gathered up the papers. Matt put the table on the other side of the room, and turned for Victoria's approval. He saw her standing staring at a paper in her hand dismay frozen on her face. After a minute he said, "Is that where you want it, Ma'am?"

She stuffed the paper in the pocket of her skirt. "That's fine Matt," she said and walked out to the hall and up the stairs.

Matt looked enquiringly at Josie.

"We're done here now," she told him cutting off any discussion and walked out to the kitchen.

In her bedroom Victoria took the card her mother had sent her more than three years earlier, with the pink dress for baby Elizabeth, from her pocket. When she had picked it up off the Square Room floor she had seen it was a thin double folded card and that in the inner fold was writing she had not noticed when she had thrown it in the drawer. She sat on the chair beside her bed and read that writing now.

Dear Victoria, I am very happy that the baby arrived safely. I have not been well of late and your father is much opposed to my travelling up to the country to see you.

We do not live that far apart and if you should visit Dublin I would be glad to see you.

Your loving Mother.

She reread the words her mother had written and something inside her drained away, into despair. Her mother not well? Why had she not seen the writing the first time? She had hastily thrown the card in the writing table drawer and if the table had not been moved she might never have found it. If she could just retrieve that time. Her family in Blackrock and her sisters in England never crossed her mind these days, so resolutely had she suppressed any thought of them. But now her mother might be ill. Andrew had always thought she should have tried to fully reconcile with her mother. She ran downstairs and out the front door calling for him. He came with Elizabeth from the orchard. "What's wrong, Victoria.?

She handed him the note to read. "When did this come?"

She explained how it had laid in the drawer of her writing table since Elizabeth was an infant. "I feel terrible Andrew. My mother wrote that she had not been well. I wish I'd gone to see her."

"Mummy's sad," Elizabeth said and buried her face in Andrew's shoulder.

"Victoria, I'm surprised she didn't write again."

"It's clear from her note that my father would not allow her to see me. And of course I never saw her note, never answered it."

"You should go to see her now. I have enough petrol coupons for that trip although I believe they're the last we'll see."

"I wish we had a telephone."

"No chance of that. I'd be satisfied with electricity. No hope of that either. But you could write your mother and tell her we're coming to see her and we could go on Friday."

"Thank you Andrew, I will."

On Friday little Elizabeth stood behind her mother's seat and watched the hills which seemed huge in the distance grow smaller as the car came near them. Then she knelt up on the back seat to see the road stretch out behind the car and the hills become high again. There were no other cars on the road. As they neared the city Andrew said, "You can drop me off at Ryan's pub there by Dalymount Park and on Sunday I'll wait for you there at lunch time.

"Aren't you coming out to Blackrock with us?"

"Victoria, it wouldn't do for me to spend the night in Blackrock."

She saw he was right. The reality of their lives was that they had separate bedrooms and their lack of a sexual relationship was a fact accepted but never spoken of. When they reached the pub he kissed her cheek and then Elizabeth. "I hope you find everyone well," he said. "Tell them I had to go to the cattle sales."

"Oh Ma'am. You came to see your mother." Kathleen said when she opened the door to Victoria's knock. "And who's this you have with you?"

"This is Elizabeth. Say hello to Kathleen, Elizabeth."

Elizabeth shook hands. "Such a lovely child Ma'am. Your mother will be glad to see you."

Victoria found her mother aged in ways she did not expect. Her hair was almost completely grey now, she was very thin and seemed to seldom go out. She appeared happy to see them and dug out old copies of *Girls' Own Annual* for Elizabeth, but the child preferred to look at the pictures in the magazines Kathleen found for her. Margaret said sadly that both Beatrice and Georgina had husbands in the army now, and the last time she had seen Beatrice and her granddaughter Stella, was almost five years ago. Now with the awful nightly bombing in England would she ever see them again?

"Mother don't dwell on it. Andrew says England will survive. He's been saying that since Dunkirk."

"That's what I always tell her," said her aunt Nicola, who had not aged at all, but who appeared to have taken over the running of the house. "We should go into town tomorrow and shop," she suggested, "and we could have lunch."

Her father, when he came home, was his usual blunt self shaking hands coldly chucking Elizabeth under her chin. "And how are you, young lady?"

Elizabeth buried her face in her mother's skirt.

"And where's that husband of yours?"

On being told that he was at *Goffs Livestock Sales* he stuck out his lower lip and nodded. Victoria decided she hated him. She lay a long time awake that night thinking about the changes in her life since she had last slept in her old room. She had her own home, her wonderful child and if she was alone in her bed at night, and still longed for Donny Maguire's arms, she would accept all that for the security marriage had brought.

She left Elizabeth with Kathleen and her mother and went with Nicola in to the city. The streets were quieter, fewer cars, but there were waves of cyclists and trams and buses were full, Dubliners determined to carry on enjoying their city. Victoria bought a blue velvet dress for Elizabeth. She could find nothing that she thought Andrew would like. When she tried to buy stockings the shop assistant said, "It's only one pair per customer Ma'am."

Over lunch Nicola said, "You know your mother's such a handful. She doesn't rest as she should, or try to eat."

To Victoria, her mother seemed dominated by Nicola and she thought, I hope my mother is a handful. I hope she gives as much trouble as she can.

She slept badly Saturday night, thinking about Andrew, of what risks he might be taking. Elizabeth slept in a cot beside her, a reminder of what was precious in her life. Sunday morning her parents said goodbye and left for church. Nicola again talked about Margaret, the doctor had said she was anaemic and must eat a richer diet, liver three times a week for a start. But Margaret ignored the advice. Nicola's dog was nowhere in evidence and Victoria decided Nicola had Margaret to boss about now, so of course she wouldn't need the dog. She was glad to leave. When she got to Ryan's pub, Elizabeth was asleep in the back seat and Andrew was waiting, his eyes bloodshot behind the rimless spectacles he now wore, as if he had been drinking, but she was very glad to see him. "Let's not stop for lunch, Andrew. I don't want to wake Elizabeth."

He looked in the back. "Little Lizzie. She's so precious."

"You know Andrew, I prefer you to call her Elizabeth.."

"When she goes to school she'll be Lizzie."

And Lizzie she became.

He asked how the visit went. "My mother doesn't look well. Nothing specific, she just looks worn out."

"She's probably worrying about your sisters in England, over there with the air raids."

He cheerfully took the wheel and she relaxed in the passenger seat feeling a strange satisfaction that she was not under her father's roof, that in a way she had triumphed over him, she journeying to her own home with her child asleep in the back seat of the car, past fields of contented cows cropping clover and swishing flies with their tufted tails, the sun of a September Sunday afternoon shining on fields of ripening oats and wheat.

Of course her mother's frailty was worrying, but she agreed with Andrew that it was probably worry about her family. She, Victoria, had presented her with a wonderful grandchild in Elizabeth and every indication of her own contentment, and she felt that she at least would not cause her mother worry.

Isolated on the edge of Europe, Ireland kept going its own way. Slowly at first, then suddenly things began to change and every change was said to be just for the duration. By spring private cars were banned and Beechwood was dependent on a pony trap Andrew acquired and on the horse and cart, not only for the creamery run but to get supplies from Killcore and to take the heavy milking machine batteries to be charged. The pony and trap was a novelty for Victoria, but soon she was mostly riding her bicycle. Now with the Morris stored on blocks in the garage till petrol again became available she was sure Andrew would not be going to Dublin but on the first Saturday in April, as they were finishing lunch, he said, "I'm going to cycle into Killcore and take the half past four train to Dublin."

Bleakness settled on her like snow. She wanted to scream, but Lizzie, now four, became upset if her parents quarrelled so she just said, "I wish you wouldn't, Andrew."

"Oh Matt will look after things. I've talked to him."

As if that made everything all right! He stood up and kissed Lizzie. "I'll bring you barley sugar sticks from Dublin, Lizzie. Peggy's Legs."

He came round the table and kissed Victoria's cheek. "Don't worry dear. I'll be back tomorrow about five."

And he was gone.

She plodded through the afternoon anxiety eating at her but after Lizzie had her bath and had gone to bed her anxiety turned to anger. It had been one thing to discreetly drive to Dublin on a Saturday afternoon and return on a Sunday, but cycling to Killcore and taking the train was quite another matter. There might be ugly gossip which would affect them all, including Lizzie. And the risks he took in Dublin. For a man of sixty it was outrageous. She slept badly, and Sunday did not go to church but read to Lizzie from her book of bible stories. Lizzie's favourite was the account of the baby Moses being saved from the water so Victoria read it twice, all the while rehearsing in her mind the argument she would have with him when he came home. His sexual excursions had from the start been the glass wall between them, never scaled, rarely mentioned. Well she'd remind him that they were sinful, abhorred by all the churches, and criminal to boot. Lizzie was growing up and it was time to clear this up.

Her mood lightened in the early evening as she imagined him cycling up hill and downhill in the blustery wind on his way home. But when he hadn't returned by seven she was frantic although she hid that from Lizzie. As she served dinner Josie said, "The trains are slow. No proper coal. That anthracite is no good you know. And they mix it with wood, damp wood sometimes."

She read Lizzie a bedtime story. "Where is Papa?"

"He'll be home when you wake up tomorrow."

If she had a car she would have gone to look for him. Then she remembered that all signposts had been removed from crossroads and side roads in fear of an invasion, and thought he might have taken a wrong turn in the dark like the man who had been hit by Doctor Curran's car the Christmas she and Andrew were married. But that couldn't happen because he knew the country so well. But in the dark, country roads could be confusing. She sat thinking about Andrew, remembering his kind gentle nature, his concern for her and Lizzie, the life they had built together. She realised she loved him, and prayed he would be safe.

"I left Mr. Andrew's dinner in the oven, Ma'am," Josie said before she went up to her room at half past eight. Then Victoria was completely alone, sitting at the fire worrying, praying and waiting. Almost an hour later she heard the dogs bark and he walked in windblown and tired, but he was home safe. She stood up from her chair and went to him. "Andrew where on earth were you? I thought you'd met with an accident."

"The train was late and I had to walk. Someone stole my bike. Lifted it out of the station store room."

"Oh Andrew! Did you report it lost?"

"No. I don't trust the gardai."

She went to get his dinner from the oven. Of course he wouldn't report the theft. The gardai would ask questions. She put his dinner tray on the table and said, "Andrew, these meetings. This meeting men in Dublin, it's sinful. What would Reverend Johnson think?"

He began buttering a slice of bread. "No it's not sinful and it's none of the Reverend's business either."

"But Andrew the bible says...."

"The bible was edited by men to suit themselves. God looks at what's in our hearts, looks at our spirit, not our body!"

Well that was one way of squaring it with his conscience. She was stunned by the defiance in his voice, but went to the kitchen to put the kettle on for his tea.

"Corner boys! They'd steal the cross off a donkey's back," Josie told Matt the next morning loading the milk cans for the creamery. But in the afternoon

Matt came home with Andrew's bike in the back of the dray behind the empty milk cans. The station master had sent it over to the creamery.

That evening when Andrew turned off the wireless after the nine o'clock news Victoria said, "Well you've got your bicycle back, Andrew. That's a relief."

"It is and it isn't. Someone moved it, hid it."

"For a joke?"

He looked grave. "No joke! A warning, maybe."

"My God, Andrew. You can't mean that."

"I'm afraid that's what I do mean. You'll be glad to know I won't be going to Dublin again. Not on the train anyway."

She reached for his hand. He looked at her pleadingly. "I'm doing my best, Victoria."

"I know you are."

Although Victoria knew it was ungracious to complain about rationing and shortages when they had escaped the war itself, she longed for what peace would bring, good white flour, proper coffee for Andrew who groused about the chicory laced Camp Coffee, all that was available. But the war drew people closer. At church Lottie Patterson organised the women to knit socks and scarves for the soldiers and collected the silver papers that lined the cigarette packs for the war effort. Supper parties continued. Delia Mac Adam and Lottie Patterson vied with each other in entertaining and when it was Andrew and Victoria's turn, Josie always seemed to have saved enough sugar to produce a plum cake or an apple tart. And there were social evenings in the church hall when they danced to the gramophone. She was surprised Andrew danced so well. George Mac Adam, when he danced with her, held her too tight and Sandy Patterson stepped on her feet. Sam Burkinshaw just sat and watched the dancers, changed the records and wound the gramophone. Nights after a social, Victoria, despite her determination to forget Donny Maguire, found herself awake for hours thinking about him, building what she knew were foolish dreams, inflating the memory of every caress. They had never danced, but she longed more than anything else to be in his arms. When morning came she dismissed these feelings and tried to forget him.

But in Ballynamon, Donny Maguire had become to all appearances a dry country bachelor. He was allowed a car to carry on his practise as a veterinarian but it could not be used for any other purpose. He gave up his membership in the Obanbeg Golf Club and when the Local Security Force was formed, in expectation of an invasion, he joined it. He was a fixture at dances in the local hall, rarely dancing, just standing around at the refreshment stand. He went to football matches and to the pub. His sister Nan was sure he drank too much and blamed all his shortcomings on the Protestant girl he'd made a fool of himself with years ago. She was relieved he still went to mass on Sundays even if he stayed in the back porch of the chapel among the stragglers who impatiently knelt on their caps on the stone floor and snuck out before mass was finished.

25

Return

At her mother's austere wartime funeral in August 1943, Victoria wept as much for herself as for her mother. She had known from the visit two years previous that her mother was a frail worried woman but she never expected her to die. She would have come again to see her despite the difficulty of wartime travel and her father's coldness if she had thought she was really ill. Two days earlier Victoria had been sitting in the Square Room watching Andrew rest a ruler on Lizzie's head, mark her height on the wall and then measure the space with the ruler.

"Lizzie Wynne, you've grown half an inch, so you have."

Lizzie studied the ladder of her height on the wall. "I'm taller than Carmel, Papa."

Josie walked in and handed Andrew a telegram, and said to Lizzie, "Come with me duckie and help me make a cake."

Andrew crouched down beside Victoria's chair. "It's not good news dear."

She felt herself grow cold, "From England?"

"No dear. It's your mother."

"Oh Andrew. It can't be. She's only sixty-four."

Andrew couldn't go, couldn't take time away but as she was packing for the trip he said, "Victoria, I know things have been strained with the family, you have grievances, but try to overlook them, for your own peace of mind."

Now she remembered that conversation and struggled to let go of her resentment of her father sitting beside her. Nicola had black rimmed bloodshot eyes, whether from drinking or weeping Victoria did not know. Neither the relatives from Clones, or Enniskillen or her two sisters in England had been able to attend. Neighbours came back to the house where

Kathleen managed, despite rationing, to serve a decent afternoon tea. When everyone had gone, to Victoria's surprise her father opened the cabinet, and poured a restorative glass of whiskey for Nicola and Victoria, as well as for himself.

"Poor Margaret," he said and sipped his whiskey. Then, "I retire in five months. I'm not sure what I'll do."

"Don't upset yourself, Henry," Nicola said. "You've plenty of time to think of that."

Victoria hated them. Nicola talking about going to England "to find something to do there," sounding like the war was a career opportunity. In the morning her father shook her hand. "Goodbye Victoria."

Then he left for work and it seemed to Victoria that her mother's death had not touched him at all.

"Ma'am I'm going to England," Kathleen informed Victoria after breakfast. "You know Theresa my pal that worked up the Vico Road? She's over there in London this six months. Now, with your mother, God be good to her, gone, I'll go too."

"I hope everything works out well for you Kathleen," Victoria said, saddened but not surprised that the maid who had kept house for her mother for so long was leaving for higher wages in England.

Sitting by the window in the crowded carriage on the slow journey home, time, for Victoria, ran backwards, like the track behind the train, weighted with memories: her seven year old self collecting shells on Sandymount strand with her sisters, and her mother, when the tide was out. She saw again the dark shadow the houses on Strand Road cast on the sand, and her mother's blue veined feet, her mother fussing about Victoria's hair before her first grown up party, and the awful rift when she left home pregnant and in disgrace and took this very train. This morning when she was leaving, Nicola had shaken her hand. "I think your father will go back up to the North. I'll go to England myself. "

Then time seemed to run ahead, to jump forward and she saw herself older and Andrew too nearer the end of his life. And her father? Contemplating that one day in the future another telegram would come with news of his death, she could no longer withhold her sympathy from him. Then she remembered Andrew's age and it occurred to her that maybe he wouldn't be there to meet her when she arrived and for a few minutes she was paralysed with dread. She told herself she was just exhausted, inventing possibilities that were ridiculous but she pulled her scarf up around her head and turned her face away to obscure the tears like the August rain that ran down the window obscuring the passing landscape. When at last she stepped down from the carriage at Killcore Andrew and Lizzie were waiting in the trap under an umbrella. Lizzie jumped down and ran to her. Andrew followed, took her bag, and kissed her cheek. "You must be tired Victoria."

"I'm just very glad to be home. To be with my family."

That evening after he had switched off the wireless she told him about the funeral and he said, "All the same your father will miss Margaret. He'll miss her company."

"My mother always acquiesced to anything he wanted. Anything! As if she had no wishes of her own."

"Well they had each other. Not everyone is that lucky."

That to Victoria seemed a shabby sort of existence. "But Andrew my mother suppressed every aspiration, every interest of her own because he was so domineering."

"Maybe she loved him."

"Maybe, but he was very hard to live with."

"Now that I'm an old man I see that the only love that survives is the one that overlooks all faults, accepts everything."

"Oh Andrew, you're not an old man."

"I'm not young. And at best it's a brief candle. But you've stuck with me Victoria, and I'm grateful for that."

She saw in his face the beginning of the frost and resignation of age and it pierced her heart. "Andrew, where would I have been without you? I wouldn't have Elizabeth."

"Our lovely little Lizzie. And I have your company. That's all I want."

26

School Days

*I*n August, when Sam Burkinshaw's mother died of pneumonia in the county hospital, Nuala Fay, not for the first time, told herself that some of the rules of the church made no sense. She'd have liked to go to the funeral, to be with Sam who, she knew, was profoundly sad even though the death was expected. However as a Catholic she couldn't. But Sam understood that. The evening of the funeral he came to her house at seven in broad daylight. "I don't care a tinker's curse, Nuala, who sees me or what the people say. Life's too short to be hiding. We hid long enough."

His mother had outlived all her family except himself. He stayed the night and when he was leaving in the morning he said, "I'll have to spruce up my place in Meagherduff my love. Or maybe we should wait and we can do it up to your taste."

"There's lots of time for that," she said and kissed him goodbye.

As she washed up the breakfast dishes Nuala considered if she really wanted to marry Sam. Even though she knew the old woman was dying, she hadn't thought of her own life changing. There wouldn't be any difficulty with her marrying a Protestant, because at her age there would be no children. Sam would have a few hours instruction, a chat with the priest who would perform the ceremony in the vestry some morning and Sam would promise to be a faithful servant of Rome or whatever he had to. But moving out there to the back of beyond, giving up her job, her salary, selling her little house? But she couldn't let Sam down now, not after all this time. And if she said no she might lose him. Why couldn't things have gone on as they were?

Victoria had been teaching Lizzie her letters and numbers and that September when she was five and a half she started in First Class at the National School at Crossbawn. Victoria walked with her over to the end of

Callaghans' Lane and Lizzie walked to school with the Callaghan children carrying her school bag, her bottle of milk with a paper cork and her sandwich wrapped in muslin. The previous year the teacher at the Church of Ireland School had resigned and gone to England and having accepted that there were too few pupils to keep it open, the Board closed the school and arrangements were made for the Protestant children to attend the National School. The house seemed empty without Lizzie. Josie watched the clock and every day had her milk and hot buttered scones on the table when she arrived home.

Lizzie barely remembered the trip to Blackrock and her mother said because her grandmother had gone to heaven and there was no petrol for cars, they would not go there any more so she often asked her mother to tell her about Blackrock. She remembered sleeping in a cot beside her mother's bed in the room Mummy told her had been hers when she was a girl. They had electricity in Blackrock. The blackout was a big wooden frame with black cloth nailed on it that fastened over the window. Her Great Aunt Nicola said it was because they lived on the coast. In Blackrock she was allowed to stay awake till Mummy came to bed and to look at pictures of film stars in *Photo Bits* and of the Queen and the princesses in *The Irish Tattler and Sketch*. When her mother went into town with Great Aunt Nicola Kathleen gave her real Rowntree's Cocoa with lots of sugar and told her that her mother had worked in the library.

"Why did she stop working in the library?"

"Sure hadn't she you to mind?"

Another memory was when she watched at the door of the garage as her father and Matt jacked up the green Morris, twisted off the wheels, first the back ones and then the front, and shoved wooden blocks under the car. The very next afternoon when she was sitting with her teddy on the top front step her father drove up the avenue in a black shiny trap. There was a brown pony with a white spot on his right foreleg between the shafts.

He stopped in the circle of the drive. "Come and meet the new pony Lizzie."

She ran down the steps and her father lifted her up to pat the pony's neck. "What's his name Papa?'

"It's a lady. She doesn't have a name. You can name her."

"Can I ride her?"

"We'll see. We have to ask your mother. Where is she?"

"She's in the kitchen."

"You call her for me. Tell her I'm back."

Then Lizzie sat on the step and watched her father and mother disappear into the avenue and then appear again, her mother holding the reins, her father walking at the pony's head. "Hold them lightly Victoria, but keep control," her father urged. Up and down they went and Elizabeth got tired watching and began to skip again. And after a while her Mummy called, "Elizabeth, come for a ride in the trap" and she and Teddy climbed up and sat beside her mother and her father stood watching as they progressed down the avenue and her mother pulled the right rein to move the pony to the right and then the left to turn him and he walked back and her father clapped and said, "Well done ladies. It's tea time."

After tea when Papa opened the gramophone Lizzie waited to see the white wide awake dog on the record on the inside of the gramophone lid. "Papa what is His Master's Voice?"

"The dog thinks his master is singing *The Teddy Bears' Picnic*."

"That's silly."

"Well he's just a dog."

When she started school Josie said, "It's hard on the poor child all that learning."

Carmel Callaghan waited for her at her gate and together they walked the half mile along the dusty road to the big yellow two storey building in Crossbawn. At school she was special but that was not a comfortable feeling. With the other Protestant children she was released for lunch at half past eleven while the rest of the pupils had to stay for a class called Catechism and then for the Angelus. There were four Protestant children in school as well as Lizzie but they were older and boys and didn't play with her. They played football or handball or marched in a circle and chanted what Miss Rooney called, "very nasty rhymes." So Lizzie sat on the steps at the girls' entrance and waited for Carmel. They were best friends and they scratched the back of their hands with a pin till they bled and rubbed them together to mix their blood to prove their undying friendship, then sucked their hands to stop the bleeding. Lizzie told Carmel about the books her mother read with her, *Swallows and Amazons* and *We Didn't Mean To Go To Sea*. Carmel said when they were older they would go to Laytown and sail away like the kids in the books. When she went to play at Carmel's house she felt it was cosy, you'd never be lonely there. Carmel slept in a big bed with her older sister Patricia in a room at the back of the house and her two brothers, Dessie and John, slept in the middle room; Mr. and Mrs. Callaghan slept in the front of the house in a big old iron bed and Seamus the baby had his cot

217

there too, over near the window. At home everyone had their own bedroom and Carmel said that was because they were Protestants. Carmel said she worried about Lizzie because she might go to hell. Lizzie asked her father about that and he said "There's no hell. Hell is here."

"Here Papa? Where?"

"In Europe, child."

"Am I going there?"

'Certainly not. You're staying here with me."

The best fun at school was skipping if Carmel and Sheila would take turns with the rope, but sometimes they were barefoot and preferred Blind Man's Bluff. Lizzie was the fastest skipper. She chanted as loud as she could:

Edward Carson had a cat

And he slept by the fender

And every time he caught a rat.

He shouted no surrender.

When she sang that at home her father laughed and danced her round the Square Room, "*Edward Carson had a cat..*

Her mother came to the door and said, "Andrew please! Don't encourage her."

Sometimes the Catholic girls skipped and rhymed and the boys stamped their feet and joined in:

On St. Patrick's Day

We'll be merry and gay

We'll kick the prod goats

Out of the way

If that doesn't do

We'll cut them in two

And send them to hell

With the red white and blue.

But Carmel never joined in that game.

Then the Protestant boys ran to the edge of the playground, stamped their feet and yelled:

Slaughter slaughter holy water

Slaughter the Papists one by one

Tear them asunder

And make them lie under
The Protestant lads
That bang on the drum.

That brought Master Green, who always stood at the open window at recess, running out with his cane and he slashed at the boys' bare legs and boxed their ears and Miss Rooney came too and went after the girls with her ruler, her hair flying wild and everyone had to go back inside and sit at their desks in silence for the rest of recess.

That evening Lizzie sang the slaughter song and her mother said. "Elizabeth, if I hear you say that again you will go to bed without your supper. It's very naughty to sing sectarian songs." Her father winked at her but he said, "Better listen to Mum, Lizzie."

Sectarian songs? She wondered was that like what Peggy and Matt got up to when Josie caught them in the hayshed before Peggy went to England. She knew there was a row, Peggy had left, and Josie said, "Good riddance."

Her mother got Mrs. Beeton's Book of Household Management from the bookshelf and began to help Josie with the cooking. Everybody talked about when the Electricity Supply Board might bring electricity out to the country.

At bedtime her father always came to kiss her good night. He fastened the heavy curtains tight round the window. "Is that for the blackout Papa? Are German bombers coming?"

"We don't have to worry about the blackout. That's just in Belfast."

When she got into bed he held her hands and sang the hymn from evening prayer with her:

Keep me, oh keep me
King of Kings
Beneath thine own
Almighty wings

Then he kissed her and tucked the bedclothes round her and Baba, her woolly stuffed sheep.

Matt was restless that October. "I'm sick of this country, Josie. Maybe I'll go to England, maybe join Mc Alpine's lot."

"That's construction, heavy work."

"Or I might join the army."

"That'd put manners on you. You wouldn't be giving back answers the way you do here, or betting your few bob with that turf accountant."

Josie thought it was all just talk but two weeks later he gave his notice and Andrew did not try to dissuade him. He talked to Victoria about selling the herd. "I can't manage without Matt," he said.

"What if I helped?"

"Victoria it's too hard, early morning and evening milking, the creamery run. And a couple of cows are due to calve."

"Can we afford to lose the creamery cheque?"

"Well, we'll have the cash from the cattle sale, and of course with the compulsory tillage, I'll have to let the land to someone who'll till it, so we'll have that."

When Rafferty and Woods, Auctioneers, advertised the sale at Beechwood of horned stock, the property of Andrew Wynne, it was the talk of the town lands. Some said he was a bankrupt and others that he had so much money he could afford to be a gentleman. Then Sam Burkinshaw, whose mother had died in August, let it be known that he was going to marry that Catholic woman Nuala Fay, and the talk turned to who would get Nuala's nursing position. The begrudgers said he was just marrying her to have a nurse to look after him in his old age and the gossips forgot about Andrew and the selling of his herd. But Andrew lost more than cattle when the herd was sold. His way of life was severed because, for Andrew, keeping cattle was an inheritance going back not only to his grandfather but to Deuteronomy: the round of the seasons, the lowing of calves, the contented cows chewing their cud in summer shade, the warm smell of milk. He would miss all that. He hired a young lad by the day to dig the flower and vegetable gardens and he drove the two cows they kept for milk to pasture and foddered them in the evening, and Josie milked them. His face had a slight lopsided droop from what Doctor Curran called a chill. He was always tired and slept late. "I'm a proper slug-a-bed," he told Victoria.

But she attributed that to his listening to the Home and Forces Program late into the night. He marked on the maps on the Square Room wall the ferocious advance of the Soviet army as it pushed back the Germans from Russia, and the battles of the British and Americans in the Pacific. When he recounted these events to Victoria at mealtimes she listened with only half an ear. What she knew was the tide of the war had turned, the Allies were prevailing and it was the place names that stuck with her, the incongruity of such names for places where men were slaughtered, *The Coral Sea*, *The Solomon Islands*. Besides Victoria had decided with Josie's help to get into egg production. The Poultry Instructress from Killcore came to give advice on extending the hen houses and in April 1944 she had purchased four dozen day old chicks from the hatchery. Lizzie was enthralled with the tiny white fluffy mites but when they began to grow and change into awkward pullets she lost interest. Andrew teased Victoria, "What a mother hen you're turning into."

"Just wait till I start making money, Andrew."

"Actually you are doing a brilliant job, Victoria."

She was anticipating when the fowl would begin to be profitable and paid little attention to Andrew's talk of an impending move in the European front. It rained so heavily on the first Sunday in June that they did not go to church. It rained on Monday as well but early Tuesday morning, when Victoria was in the poultry yard feeding her fowl, she felt the earth tremble and thought she heard the rumble of aircraft. She went quickly into the house to tell Andrew. He came and stood with her at the door but could hear nothing. On the one o'clock news they heard the Allies had landed in Normandy and Andrew said, "It'll soon be over, Victoria." At night he remained glued to the wireless. But from January 1945 onwards the name of one place remained with Victoria forever as it did with millions of others, Auschwitz! The ghostly pictures of the prisoners in the papers were all the more shocking because they revealed the extent of wartime censorship of papers and radio.

At teatime the first Monday in February Andrew pointed out a photograph in the *Irish Independent*. "Lizzie, that's who's in charge of your world," and Victoria looked over Lizzie's shoulder at Churchill smiling, Roosevelt haggard, and the self satisfied face of Stalin, at Yalta. But by the second Tuesday in May the war in Europe was over. There would be a United Nations and there was an end to rationing and shortages. Cars were back on the road and Lizzie agreed that they sell the pony and trap. She seldom rode that plodding pony now because she had a spanking new bicycle.

Despite high expectations, peace did not bring prosperity to Ireland. Wages had been frozen for six years and prices were rising. Continued rationing in England kept prices for Irish farm produce low, there was unemployment and labour unrest and the flood of emigrants continued. But the Shannon Scheme of Rural Electrification was said to be coming to Killcore in six month's time.

27

Electric Light

"**I**f you don't buy the poles I'll buy them myself," Vera Callaghan stormed at her husband. "I'll go out scrubbing in Killcore for the money and you'll be the laughing stock of the country."

Brendan continued reading the paper. The grid of poles to carry the electricity stopped at the school at Crossbawn. If the Callaghans or Wynnes or anyone else north or west of there wanted service, they were required to pay for the grid. Andrew said, "We pay the same rates as people in Crossbawn or Killcore."

"One way or another we're getting the electricity," Victoria vowed. "Just to have light, and a proper washing machine."

After church on Sunday George Mac Adam said it was a bloody disgrace people having to pay for the poles. In the end Andrew, Brendan Callaghan and George Mac Adam arranged to share the cost of the poles Brendan Callaghan borrowing his share from the Ulster Bank.

Each person at Beechwood valued electricity for different reasons. For Lizzie and Andrew it was the new electric radio which Andrew listened to lying on the Square Room sofa. Josie praised the electric iron and the clothes washing machine, but refused to drink tea made from water boiled in the new electric kettle. "You wouldn't know what'd be in it," she claimed. For Victoria it was the electric heater which could be carried from room to room and plugged in as needed especially so when the winter of 1946/47 turned out to be the coldest in more than a hundred years. Each morning Josie walked around checking the property because Andrew now slept late. When she looked into the orchard the tree trunks were growing out of the ground mist and a shadow walked among the trees. She crossed herself and went to have her tea. When the old dog Major was discovered dead in the kitchen one morning Andrew said it was the cold that killed him. Lizzie cried and

Andrew told her that Major was old and hadn't wanted to live any more. Before Christmas 1946, Victoria had the dining room painted a sunny yellow and replaced the old pictures with landscapes from Waddingtons. Now the little family dined there again and she plugged in the electric fire for the duration of their meal.

Today it was very cold, even for the end of February, and she warmed up the room before she called Andrew for lunch. She had her back to him apportioning the liver and bacon on their plates at the sideboard. "Victoria, I've been thinking," he said and stopped and she looked up and saw in the mirror his face working strangely. He was leaning over the edge of his chair. She ran to him. "Josie! Josie come quick."

Then he seemed to recover himself and she and Josie helped him to the Square Room sofa. "I'm alright," he said.

"Josie, run to Callaghans and get Brendan to go for the doctor."

Victoria put a pillow under his head, and covered him with a blanket. "Rest Andrew! The doctor won't be long."

She removed his shoes and began to rub his icy feet. Then she quickly brought the fire from the dining room and plugged it in. His pale face with its threads of blue veins had a slightly amused expression as if her distress and her attentions were an unnecessary but endearing whim. "Victoria dear, it's okay."

She sat and held his hand and he closed his eyes. She could hear the hall clock tick. She calculated how long it would take Brendan to cycle over to Curran's dispensary, debated in her head whether, when Josie returned, to get Andrew out to the car and drive him over to the doctor. But the doctor might be on his way. If only he would come. Andrew opened his eyes, "I'm all right with this, Victoria. It's okay. If it's my time…" and his voice faded, his eyes closed. She felt the air dense, thick; she held his hand tightly and waited, scarcely able to breathe.

He died half an hour after his arrival at the county hospital and Victoria sat beside his corpse and wept till the nun came and led her away.

After school Lizzie Wynne walked from Callaghans' lane toward her house thinking about chilblains. She did not have chilblains, nor did Carmel, but many children in school had. Now she'd lost her gloves and Mummy would be cross. But yesterday Papa said once March came it had to warm up. She smashed the ice puddle in the lane with the heel of her boot. Papa had promised to play the gramophone for her after school. She smashed another sheet of ice and then saw Josie hurrying to meet her and knew

223

something was wrong because Josie was not wearing her coat.

"Lizzie, your mother wants you to go back and stay at Callaghans." Josie's breath came in clouds of vapour in the cold.

"Why Josie?"

"Because your Papa is sick."

"I want to go home."

"Well you can't, duckie."

"Why?"

Josie took her shoulders and turned her round. "Your Mammy said you have to stay at Carmel's house for a little while."

Josie walked her back and Mrs. Callaghan met them at the door. "Look who's here," she said in a voice that sounded much too high.

Lizzie tried playing Snakes and Ladders with Carmel but all the time she was thinking of Papa. She remembered how wrinkled and puffy his eyes always were now when he took off his glasses and lay on the sofa. She knew he was older than Carmel's father, or than Mr. Mac Adam or Mr. Patterson. She had supper with the Callaghans and Carmel was allowed to stay up past her bedtime. Then at ten o'clock Mummy came and the adults were whispering in the hall and then her Mum put her arms around her and said, "Papa got very sick. The doctor couldn't make him better."

"Is he dead?"

"Yes dear. He's in heaven. You know he is Lizzie, don't you?"

Lizzie didn't answer. They went home and it was strange that the wireless was still there, and the gramophone, and Sally lying in front of the range, and Papa was dead. She sat at the kitchen table and Josie gave her a hot drink that was very sweet and smelled of whiskey. When Josie and Mummy went with her up to her bedroom she was so sleepy she could hardly climb the stairs. She thought her Mummy kissed her but she was not sure.

Donny Maguire was working his way through *The Irish Independent* when Andrew Wynne's obituary caught his eye. He read it twice. The notice gave no cause of death but said he had died in hospital. His first thought was to get in his car and drive to Beechwood to be with Victoria. Then he thought that would be intrusive, crass. The Wynnes would see it as offensive even impertinent. And so would Victoria's family from Blackrock who would be gathered at Beechwood. They certainly had no time for him. Ten years ago he had been kicked and beaten for the crime of walking out with a

Protestant. He didn't want a repeat of that. It was definitely Victoria's husband. The paper said he was survived by his wife Victoria and his daughter Elizabeth. Victoria would now be in that in between universe of grief, reminded of him by every mundane item in her world, trying to get used to her loss, to go on with her life. He himself was well acquainted with bereavement. Two months ago his father had died of pneumonia, and a year earlier in June his Aunt Emer had died just short of her sixty-ninth birthday, falling down at her rose hedge, the clippers dropping from her hands. At her wake he left, went outside, leaned on the gable wall of the house where she had raised him and wept. Three months later her husband, whom Donny believed could not live without Emer, was diagnosed with lung cancer. When he was dying in the hospital he said, "Donny lad, I know I won't go home out of here, but I have a great curiosity to know what's on the other side."

Donny was stunned with grief. Aunt Emer had always said "life's just a ceilidh, that's all."

He wouldn't attempt to go to Beechwood now, although Victoria was the only woman he'd ever loved. He'd think about it, then decide. He wasn't going to take that road before he took time to consider it. Maybe she'd refuse to see him. He put the paper aside and went down to the pub which was now offering potato cakes and bacon for its evening customers.

"Nuala, I don't think I can ever eat a meal in that dining room again" Victoria wept. "I'd see him again, trying to speak, to reassure me."

"That's only natural. It takes time to get over these things."

It was three days after Andrew's funeral and Nuala Fay, who was now Nuala Burkinshaw, had come to see Victoria. They had tea in the Square Room and Victoria told her how Andrew had taken ill at lunch and was dead before dinner time. Nuala was a friend and someone she could confide in.

"You know Victoria," Nuala said, before she left, "you have your little girl, something I'll never have, and as she gets older she'll be company for you. So don't let losing your husband make you depressed. He was older, and older people dying is natural. Now if you died, God forbid, that would be tragic."

"Andrew was not that old."

"Well we've come through a terrible winter, Victoria. The worst they say for over a hundred years and the cold is hard on people."

She got up to leave. "Come over and see me when you feel like a chat."

Victoria was shaken by gusts of grief. She couldn't eat, she had loved him like a brother. He was dead. And yet his absence filled the house, the days lost their shape, and she felt as if Beechwood had lost its heart. She was unbearably lonely. At Andrew's burial the Minister had read from The Book of Common Prayer, "Of whom may we seek for succour, but of thee, O Lord, who for our sins art justly displeased." Resentfully she thought, "What sins? Andrew was a good man." Had the Minister known of Andrew's homosexuality? She thought not. Beside her Lizzie wept and held her hand tightly. She knew she had to keep going for Lizzie's sake. Lizzie cried herself to sleep the night of Andrew's funeral but the following Wednesday she was back in school. Josie said she was too quiet in herself. Lizzie still walked from school with Carmel Callaghan and she often retired early after supper to lie on her bed and read. Victoria was reassured by that, remembering the hours she herself had spent reading. She had little time now for reading. There was farm business to attend to, letting the land, hiring someone to plant the garden. One day she realised that Andrew's death had driven Donny Maguire from her mind, and with that she began to think about him again in the round of solitary tasks that filled her days. Where was he now? Had he married? Maybe he even had children. If he had Lizzie would have step sisters, or brothers.

One April afternoon Josie carried in the tea tray, "Ma'am, the cows?" She put the tray on the table and stood with her hands on her hips her long face earnest. "We need to be thinking of taking the younger one to the bull." Victoria stared at her. "Over to Baxter's bull Ma'am. That's where the boss always took them."

"Josie I hadn't considered that. Let me think about it."

What a green fool she was. She knew nothing about farming. She sat looking out at the orchard wall and the old garden seat. There were infant buds on the rhododendron. Oh Andrew why did you die and leave me with all this. The two cows were so much work. She'd sell them and buy milk for their needs from a neighbour. She'd concentrate on her poultry. It made her money and the dealer came every week to buy her eggs.

Her anxiety about the letting of the land had come to nothing as the two farmers who had been renting it from Andrew for grassland and hay asked to continue the lease for two years. She refused because some instinct told her not commit for more than a year. Then they asked for a reduction in the rent and she gave it to them and when they had left she thought herself a fool. They had obviously colluded in asking for a reduction in price. She hired back the young lad who had dug the vegetable garden for Andrew.

"Just dig up and turn over the ground," Josie bossed him. "That'll do."

Then to Lizzie she said, "We'll sow the vegetables ourselves."

They seeded the garden with carrots, cabbage, beets and seed potatoes and had satisfaction to see the tiny shoots start up.

After service on the first Sunday in June, Reverend Johnson said at the church door, "Victoria, I was hoping to drop by for a visit."

"Please do, I would be happy to see you anytime."

"And how are you, Elizabeth?"

"I'm fine sir," Lizzie answered primly.

"Tomorrow afternoon then, Victoria," he confirmed and turned to speak to other congregants.

"I've wanted to come and see how you were getting along," he told Victoria the next day, spreading blackberry jam on his scone, "but I didn't wish to intrude."

"I seem to be managing much better than I was in the beginning and I know I'm lucky that Josie is such a good housekeeper."

He nodded in agreement and then said what she realised later was the declaration he had come to make, "Victoria, my dear, of course you will not continue alone indefinitely. In time there will be someone to take Andrew's place."

She was quite taken aback and he appeared to take her silence for acquiescence. "Well Victoria, Myles Dignan, you know, they have the quarry over by Meagherduff, Would you consider him as a future companion?"

Stunned, Victoria answered more sharply than she had intended. "I'm not thinking of taking up with another man. I am fine on my own."

He nodded sagely, "Of course you're not. Of course! Maybe later."

When he was leaving he said, "Thank you for tea, Victoria. Anytime you wish to talk just come over to the rectory. Anytime! Anytime at all."

She walked out with him, and stood on the steps while he turned the car and drove away. She remembered Andrew saying something about Reverend Johnson promoting good Protestant unions. Miles Dignan? He lived with his widowed old father. Once after church when they had stopped to speak to them the old man asked Andrew, "Are we still under British rule?" In the car Andrew had said, "Old Dignan, not the full shilling any more I'm afraid." What could the pastor be thinking about?

By the end of June she realised that neither Lottie Patterson nor Delia Mac Adam now invited her to supper parties, although if the women got together for tea on a Tuesday afternoon when the men were at work she was included. Twice George Mac Adam dropped by to enquire if she was getting along alright. The visits were hurried and he did not accept her invitation to sit down, just stood sheepishly leaning on the door jamb. She saw that it was a world of couples and without Andrew she did not fit into that world. She thought of selling the farm and moving to Dublin. But she had no one there. She never heard from her sisters. Her father had written to her in December 1946 to tell her Georgina and Richard were emigrating to Canada and that he had moved back to Enniskillen, and was to be married to a Mrs. Penelope Murray, a widow he had met in church. Victoria did not answer the letter although Andrew had said she should. She was alone. Just herself and Lizzie, and of course Josie. She couldn't run the farm herself but Andrew had left her a small annuity and the poultry and letting the land brought cash. Food was cheap in the country and she had few expenses except the rates, which had risen, and Josie's wages of thirty shillings a month. In the coming September she would be thirty-six years old and have been ten years at Beechwood, so this was her life.

28

Constancy and Change

When Donny Maguire's father's will was read Donny hid his resentment. His Aunt Emer's land and house had passed to her husband and when he died, to Donny's father. He in turn left it and his own small farm to his three children, so the Maguire land was sold and the proceeds divided. Donny was deeply hurt, though he knew he was being unreasonable. Still he was the only son and the Irish way was for the son to inherit the land. Of course he might have bought out his sisters, but the Land Commission had had its sights on the land. There was other land he could have bought, but except what he got when the land was sold, Donny had little cash. And he was bitter about the whole business. He'd loved that land. He wondered what had happened to Beechwood. It was possible that some Wynne nephew or brother had it now. Such was the labyrinth of succession and ownership of Irish land. It was possible that Victoria was no longer at Beechwood. He had envisioned her and her little girl in that shadowed house at the end of that beech lined avenue but maybe not. And if she was there and did own Beechwood, the matchmakers round Killcore would be eyeing her. And with that thought, jealousy seized him.

Despite her calm exterior Lizzie missed her father terribly. Carmel said he was in Limbo, at rest, at peace. Mummy said he was in heaven. All Lizzie knew was that he was gone. They had buried him just as they had buried Major. Instinctively she hid her tears because she was afraid if her mother saw her crying she would cry too and that would be awful. But sometimes if she couldn't sleep or woke in the middle of the night and thought, "Papa's dead," she crept along the landing to Josie's room and climbed in bed beside her.

In late August Donny wrote and asked Victoria to meet him at Jackson's Hotel. He said he'd be there the first Saturday in September at noon and he'd wait till six o'clock. Driving about his work past mown hayfields and ripening corn he thought about her constantly, imagining her in his arms, in his bed. Then he thought that she might never get the letter. She could be gone from Beechwood. Or maybe she wanted nothing to do with him.

As if in compensation for the freezing winter the summer was warmer than usual and every afternoon when Carmel had finished washing the dinner dishes for her mother and her baby brother was napping, she and Lizzie went to the lake. They splashed in the shallow water near the edge and watched for the otter family but never saw them. Today Lizzie lay face down on the bank looking at the stones in the river. Carmel was trying to catch pinkeens in a jam jar. It was hot. Carmel gave up and they lay in the shade and read books from the library. Carmel was reading *National Velvet* because they had seen the film in the cinema in Killcore. Lizzie thought the ending silly, Velvet Brown turning down a chance to go to America? That made no sense.

"Mum said she had to go to Killcore, that she might be late. I can go to your house after or you could come to mine and we'll play on the swing."

When she took turns with Carmel on the swing or read, she forgot that Papa would not be there to play the gramophone with her when she got home.

While Donny waited for Victoria he ate his lunch in the same alcove where he'd waited nine years earlier. He wondered if she would come, if she had changed, told himself he was a fool to have driven all this way when she hadn't answered his letter. He tried to read the paper. The barman watched him occasionally get up from the table and walk to the door and back. But barmen are used to customers' idiosyncratic behaviour. At a quarter to two he was standing on the hotel steps when she came in the drive and over to the opposite end of the forecourt. He went forward to meet her. He watched her park, step out of the car. She turned and saw him and walked into his open arms.

Lizzie and Carmel hung around at the lake until Carmel said, "I'm hungry. It must be late, Lizzie." and they raced each other along the path. When Lizzie got home Josie had dinner on the table, but her mother had not come back. "When will Mum be back?"

"Oh she can't be too long now. Still you should have your dinner, it's almost six. And it's Saturday. I have the immersion heater on for your bath."

Lizzie read her book and ate her supper. Her Mum wouldn't let her read at the table, but Josie didn't mind.

It was so natural to sit at the old deal table around from the bar, her hand in his. Donny said he was sorry about her loss, that he knew it was painful to lose someone so close to her, so final. He went to the bar and fetched her a shandy, and then asked her how she was managing on her own at Beechwood.

"I'm doing better than I was. In the beginning I was a bit overwhelmed, you know. But then I decided to make some changes. I sold our cows. I buy milk now, and of course the land is let."

He wanted to ask her about Andrew's will but that would be intrusive, impertinent. Instead he told her about his own life, and how he'd lost his Aunt Emer and his uncle who had brought him up, and his father. How he resented the land being sold.

"And you never married, Donny?"

"No," he reached and stroked her hair, fixed a stray curl behind her ear, and with his voice thickening from a decade of longing said. "You were the only girl I ever loved, Victoria. And you broke my heart."

She looked down at her hands, at the old wedding ring her mother had given her. "I've had a hard time too, Donny."

Was memory betraying her now or was it her loneliness? She was longing for him to hold her, to feel his body close to hers. Could he hear the riotous pounding of her heart?

"I can only imagine my darling, how you've suffered."

She got up and walked away from him out and down the steps and he followed her.

Lizzie stayed in her bath till the water began to get cold, then wrapped herself dry in a towel, put on her nightdress and looked out the landing window. It was still light. There was a pale moon in the sky above the willows. "Pale moon, rain soon," Papa always said. She ran downstairs through Papa's old study and into his bedroom where his everyday clothes still hung in the wardrobe. She rubbed her face in his jacket. It had a faint smell of tobacco. "I love you Papa," she whispered and ran back upstairs.

Then she heard the car coming up the avenue. When her mother looked in she pretended to be asleep.

Victoria had walked away from Donny in Jackson's Hotel with her feelings in such turmoil it seemed the only thing to do. He caught up with her, took her arm. "Victoria, don't leave now. Please! You can't go like this."

She let him lead her around by the side of the building to where the ground sloped away into some trees. He took her in his arms and kissed her. "I can't let you go. Please stay with me darling, stay the night, let's see what's left of our love."

She shook her head. Her face was turned away now.

"You're thinking of your little girl."

"Yes. Yes I am. I must go."

"But come back later, after she's asleep. I can take a room here. We'll spend the night together. Don't you want that, darling?"

"I do. I do. But not here Donny! Not in Killcore. We've probably given cause for talk already."

He saw that. She was a respectable Protestant widow in a small country town. "Then let's meet somewhere else. In Dublin if you like. Will you, Victoria?"

"Yes."

He walked her to the car. "Next Saturday then. At The Central. You know it, off Great George Street. Near Dame Street. Or I'll pick you up. We could go anywhere. To Laytown, Navan, Dublin. Anywhere you like."

"No Donny. You can't come to Beechwood." Lizzie would see him and she hadn't told her.

"What then?"

"I'll meet you behind the creamery in Killcore on Friday. There's a place there to park my car. I'll be there at two o'clock."

She had to get back. "Two o'clock on Friday then." And they held each other and passionately kissed before he walked with her to the car.

At breakfast Friday morning Lizzie's mother said she was going to meet a friend in Dublin. She would bring her back a present. Who was that friend? Oh just an old friend. Nuala was her Mum's friend, and in a way so was Carmel's mother. Actually she was more a neighbour than a friend. In

232

fairy tales no one had friends, Cinderella had no friends, nor Snow White, unless you counted the dwarfs, but in *Swallows and Amazons* friends were everything. But none of these examples fitted exactly. Then Josie came in and said blackberries were the best crop in years and they would go picking and eat supper down by the blackberry briars.

"Can Carmel come?"

"Certainly, and you can help me make jam."

She grabbed her schoolbag, shouted, "Bye Mum, Bye Josie," and ran to meet Carmel.

Late in the night in a summer boarding house up from the beach at Laytown Victoria told Donny her story: her lonely life, how she and Andrew lived, he a gentle honourable man, a homosexual who had often gone to Dublin and left her to worry and later she suspected had an occasional liaison with someone nearer home and in the last years had hardly left Beechwood. She wept of course, and he comforted her and they made love again and she made him swear that he would keep secret that he was Lizzie's father. "It is too much for her to rake up that old stuff. She loved Andrew so much, and he was the best of fathers to her till the day he died."

"Poor chap," Donny said and meant it and promised not to reveal that Lizzie was his daughter.

After breakfast they walked the beach in the cool autumn morning, went into Drogheda for lunch and Victoria bought a music box that played *Over The Waves,* with a dancer in a full skirt on the lid. In the afternoon they sat in the dunes and planned the future. They would marry as soon as they could.

"It will be in a registry office in Dublin, Victoria. I've no use for churches. Look what religion did to us. I believe in God but not in the crowd that say they represent him."

She agreed, although for her religion had not been quite as harsh an orthodoxy as it had been for him. She would go and explain matters to her minister. He would of course want her to marry in church but Donny was insisting he was done with churches. They stayed another night, the only customers, summer being over, and felt safe, registered at the guest house as Mr. and Mrs. Donagh Maguire. Donny wanted to stay till Monday morning but Victoria needed to get home. They left on Sunday after breakfast.

Donny was burning his boats and he knew it. He went first to Rathmines to tell his oldest sister, Una. She was ten years older, more like his aunt really. She wept and said, "Connor will never speak to you again, Donny. You're turning your back on the family."

"I know that, but this is the person I want to live my life with."

She made him tea and showed him her garden but he could sense she wanted him gone before her husband came from work. She wept again when she kissed him goodbye. "Connor may come down to talk to you about this"

"Tell him not to bother. He'll be wasting his time."

Connor with his lovely wife, his civil service job and his sailboat at Portmarnock. To hell with him.

Nan was a tougher proposition. First she tried to reason with him, talked about the priest being the school manager, her and her husband's boss. When he did not relent she got very angry and screamed. "You can't. You can't do this. I thought you were done with that bitch."

"I'm done with you Nan, that's what I am. And don't you dare call her a bitch." He left and slammed the door hard.

In the evening she sent her husband to talk to him but when Donny answered the door he said, "Declan, I know why you're here and I'm not talking about it."

"Can I come in Donny?"

"Not if that's what you want to talk about. I'm nearly forty years old and I'll make my own decisions."

"Donny, don't be so pig headed."

"I just had a lecture from Nan and I'm in no humour to take one from you."

He left and Donny went down to the pub. He was on his second beer when Declan pushed himself into the stool beside him. "Donny, I want to talk to you."

"I'm listening."

"I don't think you've really considered this."

"I've only thought about it for ten years, Declan. Ten long years!"

"Nan's totally against it."

"Nan?" Donny's voice rose. "I don't care what she thinks." The hum of talk in the pub ceased, drinkers, all ears not to miss a word. The barman studied the glass he was drying.

"Hush," Declan whispered. "Come outside, Donny."

Donny got up and followed his brother-in-law, and in the street said, "I'm done with Ballynamon. I'm done with you and I'm done with Nan and Una too. Priest ridden this place is. I can't wait to get the hell out of it." He pushed past Declan and went up the road.

He expected they would send the priest to talk to him. But they didn't. They decided to act as if they had not known of his plans and had no idea where he had gone and as far as they were concerned he had left the family as surely as if he had died.

Lizzie loved the music box and when Victoria had given it to her she said, "Lizzie I have something very important to tell you."

"Is it a secret?"

"It is for a week. Then you can talk about it."

Lizzie began to wind up her music box. "What is it?"

"I'm going to get married again."

Lizzie stopped winding. "Are you not married to Papa?"

"Papa is in heaven."

"Why?"

"It's to an old friend. His name is Donny." The child stared at her. "He'll be able to help Josie and me here. There is so much work to be done."

"Can I tell Carmel?"

"Not till next Sunday. I want to tell Josie, and our minister and Nuala first."

"Can I run over and show Carmel my present?"

"Of course."

Two days before the marriage Donny paid his landlady a month's rent, packed up his gear and arranged to have his books, his desk and a few mementoes from his old childhood home shipped to Killcore by rail. He took his dog, Bouncer, and drove to Beechwood to meet Josie and Lizzie. Lizzie shook his hand politely.

"Do you like school, Elizabeth?" he asked.

Lizzie stuck out her lower lip. "She likes to be called Lizzie," Victoria said.

"Oh I'm sorry. Do you like school, Lizzie?"

She nodded and sat down at the kitchen table for her after school milk and plum cake. Donny and Victoria said goodbye, left his dog with Josie and set out for Dublin.

"I don't like that dog, Josie."

"Ah you will. The thing is if he gets along with old Sally. That poor creature has the rheumatics."

They stayed at the Central Hotel, were married next morning the last Friday in October. They had a celebratory dinner at the Gresham, shopped for books at Easons, saw Laurence Olivier as the brooding Hamlet at the Metropole and arrived in high spirits at Beechwood at five on Sunday. Lizzie was over at Callaghans playing and when Carmel and her mother walked her home, Vera politely shook Donny's hand. Victoria sensed a coldness in Vera.

Lizzie lay awake for a long time hoping to hear her mother and this new man come up to bed. The big front bedroom that Josie said had been her grandmother's, old Mrs. Wynne's, was painted and her mother's bed had been moved in there. Carmel said that her mother and her new husband would probably sleep together in that room. But she fell asleep before they came up and in the morning her new stepfather was out in the yard when she woke up. "He's weird," she told Carmel as they walked to school. "He keeps looking at me."

"It's too bad altogether," the Station Master said to Donny on Monday afternoon. "But sure you'll have the insurance."

Donny looked at the broken packing cases, his books stained and soaked with water, his desk smashed in three pieces. Nothing salvageable!

"Just scrap it," he told the man. "Nothing worth saving," and walked away to his car and drove home to tell Victoria his belongings had been vandalised.

"Why Donny?"

"Oh some bigot, some mad eejit who can't stand that I married a Protestant and not even in church."

"What are you going to do?"

"Nothing! I don't want you or Lizzie involved in any way so I'll lie low, say nothing. Keep quiet. Not react at all."

It worried her but she thought he was probably right. She too had left her family or rather they had left her.

Soon she was sensing definite coldness when she went to Killcore to shop. Nothing overt, of course. The shopkeepers could not afford to lose customers. But it was there. She and Donny settled into a quiet rural life, occasionally taking a weekend away. Seeing them in a Dublin restaurant, or walking on the pier in Dunlaoghaire one might be struck by how intimately they talked, how conscious of each other they were as if together they had endured much, had passed through events that had made them a couple with a mutual past, a shared life story, indifferent to the rest of the world. Victoria and Lizzie occasionally went to church services but it was not a significant part of their lives and neither the Mac Adams or Pattersons made any move to socialise with them. Donny put his profession as a veterinarian aside and worked all autumn on the neglected lawns and gardens and greenhouse. In the Spring of 1948 they did not let the land and Donny began with his small inheritance to buy beef cattle to fatten for the cattle markets and two milk cows for the household. Again cattle grazed on Beechwood land.

29

New Beginnings

"**N**uala, I wouldn't be surprised if I'm starting that change of life business," Victoria said. "And I'm gaining weight.".

"Well, what age are you now?"

"I was born in 1913."

"You're too young for menopause."

"Well I'm tired all the time. And my periods are irregular, which is a sign, isn't it. I missed altogether last month."

Nuala started to laugh, put down her cup, and bent forward in fits of mirth. "What's so funny, Nuala?"

"Ever think you might be pregnant?"

"What?"

"Sounds like it to me."

"Uh no! I don't think so I'm not sick in the mornings or anything."

"Well I'll have a look at you when we're finished our tea."

She certainly was, Nuala confirmed, and estimated she was due in October give or take a few weeks. As was the custom, Victoria did not tell Lizzie. That evening as they sat in the Square Room, she told Donny, and was surprised by the tears standing in his eyes when he rose from his chair to come to her.

It was an uneventful pregnancy, but Donny seemed unduly anxious about her welfare, hovering over her, always enquiring how she felt. Sunny afternoons she walked down to the lake with him and did not consult the district nurse till June. This time she wanted to have her baby at home and Nuala supported her in this. "To give birth in your own bed with your family around you is wonderful, especially if you have the right support." Nuala told her.

Victoria, resting in the afternoons, watching the clouds drift past the turning leaves, parsed her life, its confounding randomness, the unexpected road she had been forced to take, her brief impulsive affair with Donny eleven years earlier, her banishment to the country, Andrew's proposal and their marriage. Lizzie's birth, meeting Donny again, and the baby that was growing inside her. The accidental and sometimes harsh realities of her life had somehow culminated in the amazing contentment she now enjoyed.

At the beginning of September, Sally, the last of Andrew's dogs, stopped eating. Donny said she should be put down. "Lizzie's heart will break, Donny. Is there not some medicine that would help?"

"The dog can hardly walk, Victoria. It's cruel to keep her alive. Can you talk to Lizzie about it and I'll see that the dog is put out of her misery?"

"Lizzie dear," her mother said next morning at breakfast, "you know Sally's a very old dog. She doesn't want to live any more."

"Why? Does she not like us?"

"She's too sick to think about us. She just wants to go to sleep."

"Like Papa did?"

"A bit like that."

Lizzie grabbed her school bag and ran to tell Carmel. "And Mum, she's so fat now."

Carmel whispered in Lizzie's ear "She's going to have a baby."

"No?"

"Mammy said she was. I heard her say it to Daddy."

"I don't believe it. It's disgusting."

The following Friday when Lizzie came home from school Sally was not lying in front of the range. "Where's Sally?"

"Sally went to sleep, Lizzie."

Why did they say things like that? They had put her down. Lizzie ran to the swing and wept and swung till Josie came calling her. "I've plum cake, Lizzie, especially for you."

She jumped down and ran to the house after Josie who was the most reliable person in the world. When she ran through the scullery the two dead chickens thumped the door where they hung by their feet curing for Sunday dinner.

Donny Maguire cleaned the byre then walked around to the side of the house. Dr. Curran's car was still parked in the drive, beside the district nurse's. After he had summoned the doctor and the nurse, Victoria had sent him to tell Nuala. "I'll come home with you, Donny. Another pair of hands you know."

Now he went back, put straw in the cows' stalls, hay in the cribs, and stood leaning on the pitchfork and he prayed, recited the prayers of his childhood, the Our Father, the Hail Mary. Though Donny had seen hundreds of animals give birth and knew giving birth was natural, he felt for Victoria to be in labour was inhuman. And he wept and pleaded with the Almighty to spare Victoria the fate of his own mother who had died giving birth to him. He washed his hands at the pump and drank the cold water, then got the wheelbarrow and went to the orchard to clean up the windfalls that were rotting in the grass.

Lizzie said goodbye to Carmel at the lane and raced home. The days were colder now. The kitchen was hot and steamy and smelt of Dettol. Nuala Burkinshaw was giving Josie instructions. "All right Ma'am."

Josie turned to Lizzie, "I've got apple pie especially for you."

Lizzie wolfed down the pie and her milk. "Where's Mummy?"

"Upstairs."

Mum was always lying down these days.

"Oh she has a big surprise for you," Nuala said. "I'll take you up to see her."

Her mother was propped up on pillows in bed. She looked pale. Lizzie went over to the bed. "Are you sick, Mummy?"

"No dear. I'm fine and you have a little brother."

She turned and saw in a cot by the fire a white shawl, a tiny red face framed by two clenched fists. She stared at the baby for a minute. "Can I run over and tell Carmel?"

"It's starting to rain, dear."

"I'll take an umbrella."

As she went down the path under the dripping trees she saw her stepfather get out of the car with packages from the chemist. She ran on to give Carmel the news. Carmel's Daddy said that Donny Maguire had thrown his cap in the air and kicked it about when Dr. Curran came downstairs and outside to tell him he had a son. Lizzie hung her head in embarrassment at the recounting of such a ridiculous performance, then ran home for another piece of Josie's pie.

For Victoria the golden autumn days slipped by as she cradled her son. He seemed even more precious because she herself had come from a family of girls. And she felt doubly blessed to have Elizabeth whom each day seemed to her to grow more beautiful. Dreamily she planned the future, Christmas with a baby, spring when she could walk with him to the lake. And when he would be a little over a year and Elizabeth would be twelve, it would be a new decade, it would be the Fifties. She thought of her sisters, Georgina somewhere in Canada, Beatrice probably still in England, her father remarried in Enniskillen, her mother dead. She had long ago forgiven them. In truth her Blackrock days were distant shadows thrown across a pre-war world. And there was Andrew, who in memory was so dear to her. She and Donny would, she promised herself, have a household ruled only by love.

A week later an agitated Josie came hurrying to the orchard where Donny was gathering the very last of the apples. "The priest, sir, Father Cahill. He wants to see you."

Donny stepped down carefully off the ladder and laid down the apple bag from his shoulders. "Where's Mrs. Maguire?"

"Resting sir, above in her room."

"And the priest?"

"I put him in the sitting room, sir."

"Bring us some whiskey and brandy, Josie."

She hurried ahead and Donny followed her to the house. Father Cahill was standing looking out the window at the trees. He offered his hand and Donny took it.

"Father Cahill, Mr. Maguire. The curate."

"Won't you sit down, Father."

A knock and Josie came in and put the drinks tray on the table.

"Thanks Josie. Whiskey or brandy Father?"

"Ah whatever you're having yourself. Just a wee drop now."

Donny poured two substantial glasses of Hennessey's and they looked at each other over the rim of their glasses.

"What can I do for you, Father."

"Well, I came about your boy, the new baby. We'll have to get that child baptised. You know I said nothing about the marriage, but now it's a different matter altogether."

Donny sat for a full minute and had another sip of brandy. The priest had another sip too, crossed one leg over the other and then reversed the posture.

"Well Father," Donny said evenly. "I kept quiet when your hooligans vandalised the few belongings I had at the railway station a year ago."

The priest's face flushed with annoyance. "I knew nothing about that. That was not a performance I approved of. It was a matter for the guards."

"I believe you, Father."

The priest took a satisfied sip.

"But the people that did it did it in your name."

"Now that's hardly fair, Mr. Maguire."

Donny had another sip. "Father Cahill, I will see to it that my son is baptised, in due course, in the vestry. I will let you know when I have his mother's consent. But neither she nor I will be attending church."

"Well now, I can't agree to that."

Donny cut him off. "In due course he'll go to school and follow the religious program there, and if all goes well to the college I attended."

Father Cahill finished his drink, put down his glass. He was withdrawing from the battle. "I'll be off, so."

In the hall Donny handed him his hat, wished him good day and saw him out the door before going up to tell Victoria about it, his stomping steps on the stairs the only evidence of his anger.

Victoria sat with her baby in Mrs. Wynne's chair and listened to Donny's account of his row with the priest. When he had finished she passed the baby to him. "Go to Daddy, Peter."

He held his son and watched for his wife's reaction. It came quickly.

"I understand how you feel, Donny. But we can't be fighting with people. Just think about us. I've no family connection now, neither have you. We just have our children. We have to think of them. We must get along with people, you know. Lizzie goes to school with Catholics, and so will Peter."

He was shocked at how earnest she was. She had clearly thought about these things. "So what do you want me to do, Victoria?"

"When things settle down I want you to talk to the priest."

Donny's expression hardened. "I'm not doing that."

"Donny, for our sake, just go and see him. Tell him your wife wanted to be married in a registry office. Or tell him I'm the boss. That it's up to me. Tell him I'm a staunch Protestant."

"I haven't seen much evidence of that."

"Well religion is mostly a social and political thing."

"Is that what you really believe, Victoria?"

"Yes. I believe that. We have to find God ourselves, study our bible, pray. But religion forms a community and we've isolated ourselves here. We have no real friends, Donny, except Nuala, and maybe Vera."

He saw how very earnest she was. Religion had hurt them, kept them apart but it seemed she wanted to embrace it again.

"So I go and make peace with the priest and blame you for everything?"

"Sure. Why not? Just don't be fighting with people. Whatever we have to do we'll do. If I have to marry you again in church I'll do it."

"You would do that, marry in the Catholic Church?"

"Why not? Whatever's required to facilitate Peter's education, his happiness, I'll do it. It doesn't matter about churches, what matters Donny is that our children are happy, and get a chance in life. We want them to grow up to be good people, not harnessed to one religion or another. And that we have a good life, that we love each other."

He went to her and held her and the baby in his arms, "You'll never know how much I love you, Victoria. You're far wiser than me. All I really care about is you and our children."

"I know that, Donny."

He told her he was the luckiest man in Ireland. Then he carried his son and together they went downstairs to meet their daughter who was running up the avenue through the autumn leaves, home from school.

LaVergne, TN USA
10 March 2011
219486LV00001B/11/P